S.J. MARTIN

The Papal Assassin's Nemesis

Resurrection. Regicide. Reprisal.

First published by Moonstorm Books 2023

Copyright © 2023 by S.J. Martin

All rights reserved. No part of this publication may be reproduced, stored or transmitted in any form or by any means, electronic, mechanical, photocopying, recording, scanning, or otherwise without written permission from the publisher. It is illegal to copy this book, post it to a website, or distribute it by any other means without permission.

This novel is entirely a work of fiction. The names, characters and incidents portrayed in it are the work of the author's imagination. Any resemblance to actual persons, living or dead, events or localities is entirely coincidental.

S.J. Martin asserts the moral right to be identified as the author of this work.

First edition

This book was professionally typeset on Reedsy. Find out more at reedsy.com

Contents

The Papal Assassin Series	1
Chapter One	2
Chapter Two	7
Chapter Three	18
Chapter Four	27
Chapter Five	42
Chapter Six	56
Chapter Seven	67
Chapter Eight	79
Chapter Nine	95
Chapter Ten	103
Chapter Eleven	113
Chapter Twelve	125
Chapter Thirteen	140
Chapter Fourteen	153
Chapter Fifteen	162
Chapter Sixteen	175
Chapter Seventeen	185
Chapter Eighteen	196
Chapter Nineteen	213
Chapter Twenty	223
Chapter Twenty-one	232
Chapter Twenty-two	245
Chapter Twenty-three	256

Chapter Twenty-four	269
Chapter Twenty-five	278
Chapter Twenty-six	287
Chapter Twenty-seven	302
Read more	312
The Tattooed Horse Warrior Series	313
Author note	321
List of Characters	324
Glossary	328
Maps	332
About the author	336
Also by S.J. Martin	338

The Papal Assassin Series

The Papal Assassin
The Papal Assassin's Wife
The Papal Assassin's Curse
The Papal Assassin's Wrath
The Papal Assassin's Nemesis

Moonstorm Books

Chapter One

October 1099 – Marseilles

The Abbot of the Abbaye de St. Victor in Marseilles stood looking down on the pitiful wreck of a man the fishermen had brought to his door nearly two weeks before. In some ways, the man had been lucky that he had been immersed in seawater for three or four days before they found him, for it had prevented any infection from taking hold. This could not last, however, the extent of the open wounds was too widely spread, which usually killed victims of such horrendous burns.

The man had been screaming when they arrived with him, and the Abbot, seeing the extent of the burns on his left side, didn't know how he was still alive. They had poured a heady potion of Theriac down his throat twice a day since then. This had kept him sedated, although he still groaned and thrashed with pain each time the effects began to wear off.

The Abbot now decided they could do no more for him at the Abbaye, but he knew a man who might be able to help.

Friar Francis was a Benedictine monk and famed physician who had experience with men who had been burnt in battle by Greek Fire, a hellish substance that burnt and stuck to the skin. If anyone could help this poor wretch, it would be the Friar.

The Abbot ordered a cart to be made ready to transfer their patient to the Monastere de Saint Benoit. Whether the man would survive the full day's journey in the back of the cart was another question; he would be in God's hands.

He decided to pen a missive to Friar Francis, relating what he knew and asking for his help.

Friar Francis

I am sending a poor soul to you who may be even beyond your skills, but perhaps you may be able to save him. I believe he was on a ship that went up in flames on the isle of Cabrera. At first, I assumed he was one of the crew or even one of the galley slaves, but I noticed the glitter of a gold ring in the charred flesh of his left hand. He may be a senior guard or even one of the Sheikh's captains.

We have done all we can here using the usual mixture of frankincense, wine, tallow and wax to seal the burns against infection. Now, if he has survived the journey to reach you, the wretch is in your and God's hands.

May the Holy Spirit be with you and guide you in this task.
Abbot Joffre

Two days later, as the sun was beginning to set, the cart rumbled through the stone gates of the St Benoit Monastery. By this time, the victim's jaws were clamped shut, only occasionally opening to issue strangled screams. His burnt body writhed agony whenever they encountered a bump, or hole, in the track up to the monastery. The Prior, who led the party, made his way to Friar Francis, who, as usual, was mixing unguents in a large room attached to the infirmary. He greeted the young Prior and broke the seal on the vellum.

'Well, what do we have here, Prior?' he asked, scanning the missive.

'A poor soul covered in burns; we have him in the cart outside. The Abbot did not expect him to survive the journey, but he has, and he's screaming to wake the dead out there as the Theriac wears off.'

Friar Francis nodded and came around the tall table. 'Sometimes screaming is good; when they are too quiet, we worry. Take me to him,' he ordered.

As he followed the Prior, he motioned to two other monks in the infirmary to follow, and they made their way to the cart. One of the young monks gasped when he saw the man in the cart.

'He cannot possibly live! Surely it was a waste of time bringing him here, Prior.'

'Brother Tomas, as you know, we never turn away any of God's souls. He needs heavily sedating before we lift him from the cart. See to that, Brother Tomas. We will remove the bindings and assess the scale and depth of these burns. Then, we will try our proven remedies that promote the healing of burns. I will ensure he has a bed in one of the isolated cells outside the infirmary or he will disturb all our patients.

'Prior, you are, as usual, welcome to join our table this evening. You can bring us the news from the outside world that we rarely get up here in our more remote location.'

As he returned inside, Friar Francis admitted to himself that he was equally concerned by what little he had seen. The man looked as badly burned as any he had previously dealt with, and none of those had survived.

CHAPTER ONE

An hour later, they carried the groaning man into the Friar's room and laid him on the long table. He had already requested the unguents and linen strips to bind the wounds. He had found in the past that he had a modicum of success with a mixture of butter, sweet woodruff, lily root and brooklime. They gradually peeled the puss-soaked dressings from the groaning man and lay underneath was as bad as he was expecting.

'Do we know what he was burnt with?' he asked the young Prior, for although he could see no trace of Greek Fire, the wounds looked similar.

'The fishermen said the water was covered in a film of oil.'

The left side of the man's body had been presented to the blaze, and the left side of his head looked as though it had melted. The mouth was pulled down, and the skin was covered in huge open blisters. Friar Francis nodded; flaming oil could indeed result in such burns. The shoulder, arm, thigh and upper calf were the same. Fortunately, his manhood was intact.

'Small mercies,' muttered the Friar. Lifting the left arm to a loud groan from the patient, he thought it odd, as the underarm had survived, but the left hand was drawn into a claw. Bone was showing on two of the fingers—they would need to be amputated. A gold ring did indeed show on one of them, but the swollen and blistered flesh covered the design.

'Give him more Theriac, as I intend to wash his wounds with vinegar and wine mixed with mercury chloride. You must hold him down, as the pain will be intense, but the mixture will clean the wounds and may save his life.'

The screams could be heard all over the monastery as they worked on him. At last, it was over, and the young, white-faced Prior from Marseilles was shaking.

'If he survives that, it will be a miracle indeed,' he whispered.

'That is what we need, Prior, a miracle,' answered the Friar, whose forehead was covered in a light sheen of sweat from the exertion.

The man on the table heard the words through waves of pain and swore he *would* survive. Then, when they had carried him to a bed and propped him on his right-hand side, he offered a prayer of thanks for the soul of the guard who had pushed him into the sea.

Chapter Two

October 1099 – Paris

Piers De Chatillon had been back in Paris for nearly six weeks.

Burning the candle at both ends, he was determined to do everything he could to put out of his mind the events of Cabrera and the refusal of his stolen wife, Isabella, to return home. Overall, he was succeeding with the help of several beautiful married women.

At that moment, he knelt between the legs of one of the prettiest, Lucette De Salvais.

Three years before, Lucette had been forced into a marriage with Lord Pierre De Salvais, a member of the French aristocracy who desperately needed funds. Lucette's family were wealthy merchants and could provide a very large dowry. In exchange, she received a title, and her father received the patronage, favour and influence of one of the King's cronies. It had been a very advantageous deal for the wealthy merchant— not so much for the daughter, who at only twenty-one years was married to a fifty-seven-year-old man, almost in his dotage, who had great problems maintaining an erection for any length of time.

Coming from a large, loud, lively, close family, Lucette had been desperately bored and looking for love or affection. She had carried on several discrete affairs with the young bucks at court, however, these young men were tedious in other ways, full of themselves and their accomplishments. She'd found they had little interest in her as a person.

Then, six months ago, Piers De Chatillon had appeared at the French court.

In a delightfully forward, no-nonsense way, he had whispered in her ear that he intended to bed her that night. She had assumed the usual shocked expression and told him she was married, casting her eyes down in a demure way. To her astonishment, he'd simply laughed at her and walked away.

She had watched him working his way around the chamber, noticing not only how the women's eyes followed the handsome French lord, but also the apprehension displayed by some of the men, as he approached them. She didn't know who he was, but he was certainly influential, she thought, as he stood laughing with Gervais de la Ferte, the King's Seneschal. As she covertly watched him, he looked directly at her with an amused smile as if he knew exactly what she was thinking.

Within an hour of talking to various ladies in the room, she had discovered exactly who he was.

"He's the most dangerous and influential man in France, an envoy of the Pope, but unusually he's not a priest.'

'He's from an old aristocratic French family and is very wealthy, with houses and estates all over Europe.'

More importantly, 'He's probably the most exciting man you will ever take to your bed. But, don't fall in love with him, for it is purely about the thrill of the chase and the pleasure in the bedchamber with him,' They had whispered to her and warned her.

CHAPTER TWO

Lucette did not consider herself naïve, but had been shocked to find that he'd bedded them all.

She'd watched as he made his farewell bow to the King, who stood and embraced him as a brother. And then he was striding down the chamber for the doors, stopping fleetingly at her side and raising her hand. She'd expected him to kiss it, but instead, he gently bit the ends of her fingers. Excitement had raced through her body as she met his almost black eyes.

'Make sure your window is unlocked and unshuttered,' he'd whispered.

'But, you don't know—' she began, and heard him laugh again as he exited the audience chamber.

Several hours later, she had lain on her bed wide awake with apprehension as he had stepped through the window into her room. Without saying a word, he'd slowly removed his clothes. Then he'd walked to the bed, his eyes never leaving hers, and lifted the hem of her gown to pull it over her head. He'd made love to her for the next two hours in ways she'd never imagined. Then he was gone.

That had been the beginning of a week-long affair before he'd disappeared back to his family estate.

Now he was back in Paris again and frequenting her bed several nights a week. She knew he had several other lovers, but somehow he'd taught her not to care. With Chatillon, it was never about ownership; it was all about enjoying intoxicating pleasure with the chosen person.

However, the Piers De Chatillon who had arrived back in Paris at the end of September was different to the one who had left six months earlier; he now had a brittleness, a hardness about him. And yet, his attitude towards her seemed to have softened.

When he'd swived her in that first week, it was as if he was trying to exorcise some demon as he'd plunged into her. Tonight had been different, for after they had walked arm in arm along the riverbank, he had taken her to a friend's house and introduced her as his mistress. She had glowed with pride and had to admit that this had made her somewhat reckless as they returned to the De Salis residence in the city. Usually, he came up the servant's staircase, but tonight, she had carelessly taken him into the hall where they had laughed, ordered wine from the Steward and ascended the dimly lit staircase to the second floor. She knew that her husband, Lord Salis, would have been in bed for hours, but she did not notice the earnest, frowning young man who suddenly appeared in the doorway below. Chatillon did, as he was on constant alert, but he recognised the young man and dismissed him from his mind.

And now, they were naked and laughing on Lucette's bed. He had already brought her to the heights of pleasure, and she was begging him to now enter her.

Kneeling between her legs, he appreciated her charms in the firelight; she had a perfect hourglass figure with a small waist and ample bosom. She was also a delight to be with, light-hearted, and fun, and she adored making love, throwing herself into it with enthusiasm.

He deftly tied the silk sheath onto his erect manhood; no matter how much wine he had imbibed, Piers never forgot, and to date, he had avoided pox and other maladies.

He positioned himself to enter her and slid the tip inside to tease her, moving it gently back and forth while she squirmed and begged him for the whole of him. He grinned, ready to oblige, when the bedroom door burst open just at that moment.

CHAPTER TWO

'What is this? How dare you, Sir?' an angry voice yelled behind him.

Chatillon didn't move a muscle as he looked down at her surprised expression.

'Husband?' he asked softly.

She shook her head. 'Stepson,' she whispered back, but couldn't resist a giggle. This infuriated the young Chevalier even more.

'I ask you, how dare you, Sir? Unhand my father's wife at once.'

Chatillon turned his head slightly to glance at the young man's face, which was lit by a small candle he was carrying.

'By your leave, Chevalier, I'll be with you shortly, but I have my reputation to consider, and I can't leave a lady's demands unsatisfied.' So saying, he thrust into Lucette, ordering her to wrap her legs around him.

The young man's mouth opened in astonishment. Who was this devil, this blaggard who ignored him with such disdain? He had the greatest desire to run him through, but every ounce of knightly chivalry in him prevented him from doing so. Therefore, he turned away to stare into the fire while hearing every moan and squeal from behind him.

Finally, it was over, and Chatillon, extracting himself, walked naked over to the chair where he had thrown his clothes. He dressed with his back to the young man, and finally, turned and suggested that they leave the lady in peace. He led the young man into the hall, closing the door firmly behind them.

'I challenge you, Sir. Whoever you are, I will fight you tomorrow, for you have impugned my father's honour,' he exclaimed.

'Don't be so ridiculous; fight over something as petty as this? I'm sure, Chevalier de Salvais, that your father is delighted that I'm meeting his wife's needs, for we both know he cannot do so,' responded Chatillon.

Piers could see that the young man was almost apoplectic with rage, so he stepped into the full torchlight in the passageway. Now, the young man could see who he was challenging. It was dark in his stepmother's room, and the young man had not recognised her lover. Now, he realised who it was and gave a sharp intake of breath.

Two things went through the young knight's mind: the first was that he had just challenged the best swordsman in France; the second was that he had paid court to Marietta Di Monsi for several months during her sojourn in Paris. He loved her and intended to ask her guardian for her hand. Now he had found her guardian, Lord Piers De Chatillon, in bed with his stepmother, but his family pride and honour wouldn't let him back down even if it meant losing Marietta.

Chatillon watched the emotions chase across the young man's face; he already knew about the young man's pursuit of Marietta. He put a hand on the young man's arm and tried the voice of reason.

'Salvais, I do not accept your challenge and will not fight you. You are very young, twenty-four years old, with your whole life ahead of you. Anger and wounded pride can be admirable, and they may inspire you at the moment, but they will not keep you alive when faced with cold steel. I refuse to fight you.'

'Then you are a coward, Sir, and not worthy of my blade!'

Chatillon ran his hand over his eyes and through his thick, still predominantly black hair.

CHAPTER TWO

'For your father's sake, as you are his only son and heir, I'll pretend I didn't hear those words,' he said, turning to go, but the young man gripped his upper arm tightly.

'Then I will repeat them in the court tomorrow if you are in attendance on the King. We hold honour most dear in the Salvais family. We do not grind it beneath our heel as some do!'

Chatillon laughed harshly. 'Do that tomorrow, and I may well run you through where you stand, while your sword isn't even a handspan out of its scabbard. For, as you may already have heard, I don't always obey the rules and niceties of the court. I tell you truly, Salvais, that if I do kill you on the spot, no one will naysay me, for they will turn their heads away and pretend they did not see aught, like the cowards they are. The women and men will sweep their gowns and cloaks aside as your blood-spattered body is dragged heels first from the chamber. If you are very lucky, King Philip may wake up in his chair and say, 'What's to do?''

Chatillon narrowed his eyes at the young man as he tried to scare him off; in truth, he really didn't want to fight him. The Chevalier let go of his arm, and without another word, Piers went down the main staircase and out of the Salvais' residence.

The next morning, Piers spent an hour with his sword in the pell yard as usual, with Daniel and his men. He had dismissed the incident of the previous night from his mind. He decided to give Lucette a wide berth for a week or so with the chance of the Chevalier still stalking the corridors, sword drawn.

At noon, he had business with Gervais and King Philip. Pope Paschal wanted to hear the King's views on the return of Duke Robert to Normandy from the Crusades. Rumour had it that the manipulating Chancellor Ranulf Flambard was not prepared to let King William Rufus give up his overlordship of Normandy without a fight.

To his surprise, Prince Louis, the Dauphin, the heir to the throne, was also there. Chatillon had not seen him in such meetings at his father's side before. He was aware that the young prince had fought against, and repulsed, the forces of William Rufus in the French half of the Vexin province. Louis had earned himself the nickname *Le Batailleur*, The Battler, because he always led the charge from the front.

When they left the inner chamber several hours later, Gervais noticed that Piers looked thoughtful.

'What is it?' he asked.

'Oh, nothing of great import, but Prince Louis has become a very forceful and opinionated young man. I can certainly see him as a much-needed warrior-King of France, but he needs guidance, and I believe that one of his main aims will be to claim Normandy and absorb it into France.'

'I think you are right, Piers, but his father, King Philip, is still alive. If the King's mistress, Bertrade de Montfort, has her way, she may persuade him to disinherit Louis and put their illegitimate son, Philip, the Count of Mantes, on the throne.'

They passed into the large audience chamber, which seemed unusually crowded, and Gervais noticed the buzz of conversation as they entered.

'Is something amiss?' he asked Piers, as many eyes seemed to be on them.

Chatillon glanced around the chamber and noticed the young Chevalier De Salvais approaching them with a group of friends, who seemed to be encouraging the young man while

CHAPTER TWO

failing to meet Chatillon's eyes. He groaned softly; he had hoped that the Chevalier would come to his senses overnight.

'Tell me, Gervais, do you ever feel what they call *déjà vu*? A similar event occurred here in this very room when I was sixteen, except it was I that was challenging an older cadet son.' Gervais initially shook his head in amusement, but then his eyes widened in astonishment as the events unfolded before him.

'I issued you a challenge, Piers De Chatillon, and you refused! I called you a coward, yet you still refused.' The large crowd of courtiers who had got wind of this challenge gasped at this accusation.

'So, in front of my friends and yours, I issue the challenge again. I challenge you to a dual, to defend my father's honour, as you have seduced and despoiled my stepmother.'

That was too much for Chatillon, who burst out laughing. Several people joined in, as he pretended to wipe a tear of laughter from his eye.

'You have missed your vocation, young Salvais, for the King desperately needs a new jester.'

The young man's face became thunderous; he glowered at Chatillon, and his hand went to his sword hilt. Chatillon smiled as he hoped the young fool would draw, and then he could disarm him in minutes and claim honour settled. Unfortunately, De Salvais' friends calmed him, telling him this was not the way, and certainly not in the King's audience chamber. Gervais noticed that the King and Prince Louis had emerged and mounted the dais behind them.

'Have a care, Piers; the King is now present,' he warned. But Piers ignored conventions at the best of times, and since events at Cabrera, he had thrown caution to the winds.

'So I seduced and despoiled the very pretty Lucette De Salvais, did I? Shall I ask you how many of your friends had your stepmother before me? If you wish, I could name them for you. She named and laughingly gave me the prowess of each of them. Who was too quick, who was too slow, and who sent her to sleep while he was still inside her.'

Piers was playing to the audience now, and the chamber was with him apart from the red-faced young men. Many might fear him, but they envied his prowess in the bed chamber and respected and admired him.

'And let us look at whose honour you are defending. Your father married a young girl, thirty-five years younger than himself, younger than his only son, for the money that her family brought. Money to save the broken finances and estates of the De Salvais family, which was on its knees because of his gambling, whoring and poor management. What of her family, I hear you ask?' he said, turning and holding his hands out to the rapt audience.

'They're chicken farmers—the great De Salvais family name now aligned with a family that plucks chickens.'

The chamber roared with laughter while Gervais approached the dais to explain this challenge to the King and Prince Louis, who was also laughing.

This insult was too much for Salvais. With his fists raised, he rushed at Chatillon who knocked him down with one punch.

'Pick yourself up and go home, boy; there's nothing for you to defend here; your family reputation is already in tatters,' said Chatillon as he turned away, but young Salvais was not done as he got to his knees and implored the King.

'Majesty, I am one of your loyal knights. I am not a boy; I am four and twenty, and I demand the right to satisfaction. I say this man is an adulterous coward, and I'll meet him tomorrow morning.'

Watching the exchange, Chatillon sighed again; he had done his best, but now his reputation was at stake. He noticed the excitement on the face of Prince Louis as he conferred with his father. He noticed that Gervais was shaking his head in doubt.

Prince Louis stepped forward. 'Why not here and now, Salvais? This chamber is of ample size. Anyone of faint heart or a nervous disposition may leave; everyone staying can move to the sides. Chatillon, as we know, is a notable master swordsman and has no doubt fought in rooms a quarter of this size.'

Chatillon raised a cynical eyebrow. Was that supposed to reassure his young opponent, he wondered. The Chevalier de Salvais looked uncertain for the first time, but his friends egged him on, and he reluctantly agreed. Chatillon also inclined his head, in acceptance, and pulled the heavy velvet papal tunic over his head to reveal a fine cambric linen shirt beneath.

'Are you mad?' whispered Gervais.

Chatillon smiled reassuringly at him. 'I'll disarm him, and I assure you it will be over in no time.'

Looking at the tall, white-faced, tight-lipped, determined young Chevalier, Gervais wasn't so sure.

Chapter Three

The excitement was palpable in the large chamber, and not one person had left. No one wanted to miss this duel. The two opponents faced off, having agreed on first blood, and began to circle each other warily once the King nodded his permission to begin. There was an audible gasp as the loud sound of clashing blades echoed around the chamber.

To give him his due, the Chevalier was not a bad swordsman, just inexperienced, thought Piers as he purposefully clashed the blades several times to give the audience a show and to get the measure of his opponent. He gave them a few rounds of slash, parry and thrusts just slow enough for Salvais to respond in time before he whisked the sword out of the young man's hand. It was very deftly caught by a courtier who received a round of applause from the King, who was enjoying the break in the daily routine of the audience chamber.

'Do you concede?' asked Chatillon.

Salvais did not reply as he stomped to the courtier and demanded that his sword be returned.

This happened twice again his sword spinning across the floor, yet young Salvais returned for more. Chatillon knew he must draw blood to finish this, so he deftly nicked the young man's upper arm. The shirt blossomed red, and the audience gasped again.

'I have drawn first blood, so now you must concede,' demanded Chatillon.

The Chevalier knew he was seriously outmatched; he could not reach Chatillon to touch him with a blade. The master swordsman just danced away with that same taunting half-smile. The fight having gone on far longer than he'd expected, Salvais also found his arm tiring. He might be twenty years younger, but Piers spent at least an hour daily in the pell yard, honing his muscles.

However, Salvais wouldn't concede, even though blood was now dripping from his fingers. Instead, he decided to try to anger his opponent.

'So why do you steal other people's wives, Chatillon? Is it because yours refuses to return to you?'

Again, there was a sharp intake of breath. Everyone knew some aspect of the story of the blood feud with Sheikh Ishmael and the kidnapping of his wife, but few ever mentioned it in Chatillon's hearing.

Piers, seeing it for what it was, just laughed the comment off, again playing to the crowd.

'No, it is purely because I love bedding women; such beautiful creatures deserve to receive pleasure from the men they bed. If any of you charming ladies would like a visit, please give your name to my servant, and I'll try to oblige.'

The crowd roared with laughter, but Chatillon had given Salvais the ultimate insult, for as he'd played and bowed to the crowd, he had turned his back on his opponent, showing that he considered him no threat. It was the last straw for the Chevalier, who burst into a run at the back of Chatillon, his sword raised to slash down at his head.

Gervais shouted a warning, and Piers whirled around, dropping to one knee to strike upwards with his sword in defence. The blade went up under the young man's rib cage and into his heart. Salvais' sword clattered to the ground with an awful finality as he collapsed into Piers' arms.

'You foolish, foolish young man. I was trying not to kill you,' he whispered as the Chevalier's head fell back. He closed the young man's eyes.

Gervais appeared beside him with two courtiers, who lifted the young man's body off Piers' sword and carried him out, leaving a trail of blood. As Piers had foretold, the courtiers simply pulled their gowns and cloaks to one side, an expression of distaste on their lips. Such fickle creatures, he thought as Gervais pulled him to his feet.

'You did your best, Piers,' he said softly and then announced to the chamber, 'A challenge was issued, honour was questioned, and it was met fairly and openly in front of their majesties. Piers De Chatillon is the victor.' A small cheer and a smattering of applause rose, but most courtiers began to leave.

Chatillon bowed to his old friend, King Philip, and a stunned Prince Louis who never expected either man to die in front of him in the chamber. Gervais led Piers away along the corridors to his large, sumptuous rooms worthy of the Seneschal of France.

'That was unavoidable, Piers, but the whole matter was not well done. The King's audience chamber isn't a Roman arena where men fight to the death.'

Piers shook his head. 'I turned him down several times, Gervais. I disarmed him three times, but he still returned for more. By God, I need a drink,' he said, dropping into a chair.

CHAPTER THREE

They sank several goblets of wine, and then Gervais called for Daniel, Chatillon's captain, and instructed him to see his master to his home.

'I now go to the King, Piers, to hear his mind on the matter, as Lord Salvais is one of his friends, and he won't be happy that you have killed his only son and dragged the family name through the mud. The King may now have misgivings about allowing the duel to go forward today, and I will try and allay those. I'll come and see you at your house this evening.'

Piers walked with Daniel and two of his men back to the large house. It was an old fortified manor house with large gardens down to the southern banks of the Seine. It had stood apart, but as the city grew and spread, it was infringing now not far from its high walls. Chatillon felt at home in this house because it reminded him of his mother, Annecy, and his very happy childhood here. Her tapestries still adorned the walls, as did the carved chairs she commissioned, that sat by the fire. He sank into one of them, and Daniel brought him some food. As he devoured it, he realised his captain had not eaten all day and offered him some.

'Stay and pour yourself a drink, Daniel; I don't want my own company yet.'

The Captain happily agreed and joined him. 'It will not be long before Edvard is back at your side on these visits, Sire.'

'Yes, he's almost back to his old self, but Ahmed thought that six weeks in Paris with the attractions of the better quality fleshpots would be too much for him. You are right, though, I do miss his council. He would have talked me out of that ridiculous duel!'

Daniel had stood with the other servants at the doors of the audience chamber and watched the drama unfold.

21

'You gave him every chance, Sire. You were honourable in how you tried to dissuade him from going on, and everyone said that. He was the one who introduced the foul play at the end, so you have nothing to regret.'

Chatillon gave a bark of laughter. 'How long have you known me, Daniel? You have been the Captain of my men for over ten years. Have you ever known me to regret anything? I do not regret killing him; if I may say so, my final thrust was perfect. There's only one thing that I regret, and that is not locking the bed chamber door as I usually do. That way, he wouldn't have had to stand and watch me cuckolding his father while I enjoyed his stepmother.'

Daniel grinned, thinking how incorrigible Chatillon was, but then he rose to his feet, hand on his sword hilt at the sounds of arrival at the doors. They were all still on alert, for it was suspected that several assassins were still out there despite the death of their master, Sheikh Ishmael.

'It will be the Seneschal; show him in,' ordered Piers.

A very wet Gervais de la Ferte strolled into the hall, shaking the water from his tunic and hair. 'The skies have opened out there,' he announced, wiping the rain from his face and hair with a cloth proffered by Daniel.

'I have just come from the King, and he found the spectacle you put on for him very entertaining.'

Chatillon laughed. 'That is so like Philip of France; he probably thinks that I purposefully set that up for him to relieve his boredom.'

Gervais nodded. 'However, it is likely that Lord de Salvais will not let this lie.'

'Let me guess, King Philip wishes me to leave Paris for a few months to let the gossip die down.'

CHAPTER THREE

Gervais smiled and nodded. 'There's no blame attached to you for the killing, for the young man brought it on himself, but I'm sure that it will become a more salacious tale in the telling. The young wife of a French Vicomte is wickedly seduced by the Papal Envoy, who then kills the stepson in a duel before the King. It will spread like wildfire, Piers; it will go around the cities of Europe and undoubtedly enhance your already fearsome reputation. However, now that he is fat, indolent and older, the King worries about his soul more than he did, and he is concerned about how the new Pope, Paschal, will view the tale. Will it give his court a licentious reputation where adultery and duels are tolerated, or even encouraged?'

Now Chatillon did burst into laughter while guiding Gervais to the dinner table.

'Do you honestly think Paschal will give this a second thought, Gervais? I already have a list upstairs with four names that the Pope wants me to silence one way or the other. The King is fawning to the Pope because my uncle, Pope Urban, excommunicated him for his ongoing adultery with his mistress, Bertrade De Montford. Philip wants the new Pope to lift that excommunication order, and I don't think Paschal is inclined to do that anytime soon.'

Gervais knew Chatillon was right but, as the Seneschal of France, he was loyal to his king.

'You are possibly right, Piers, but go back to your estates or, better still, take the boys to see their mother in Genoa and begin your campaign to get Isabella back. She should be by your side.'

Piers, looking away, did not reply to this, and they talked of more pleasant things until Gervais stood to leave.

'I must go, for we are hunting at dawn tomorrow; the Prince has seen a huge tusker in the forest that he must immediately track and kill.'

'Listen to the heavy rain out there, Gervais; the scent will be gone for the hounds, and the ground too wet underfoot to hunt. Spend the night here instead, my friend,' Piers suggested.

But Gervais was not to be deterred. Piers reluctantly escorted him to the doors.

'At the very least, take a cloak!' he demanded, waving at Daniel, who brought one with a hood from the pegs.

Gervais swung it over his shoulders. 'I feel just like a cardinal, Piers. I will be resplendent in deep purple with this gold papal badge of office emblazoned on the side,' he said, laughing as he put the large hood up.

'I'll send a servant back with it tomorrow, but think about what I said, Piers. Go to Genoa and talk to her; you are one of the most persuasive men I know. You can win her back,' he announced, as he lifted a hand in farewell and went out into the dark, wet night.

The rain bounced high as Gervais headed back to his rooms in the palace of King Philip on the Ile de la Cite; he was eager to get home and peel off his damp clothes. He strode out and soon approached the long wooden Grand Pont. An ancient wooden bridge, it had been rebuilt many times, and now Prince Louis wanted to rebuild it in stone. Gervais agreed with him. His foot was on the first planks of the bridge, and the palace gates could just be seen in the murk ahead when they attacked him.

The sound of drumming rain and the large hood had prevented him from hearing their approach. He was unsure

CHAPTER THREE

what made him turn, but he spotted the man lurking at the side of the bridge with a sword in his hand, who was now moving towards him. He drew his sword, thinking that this was probably some of the scum of the Paris streets out to take his purse. He threw back his hood; he was a confident swordsman, and as the blades engaged, he held his own and began to drive the man back until a sound behind made him turn to see another behind him.

This man was an Arab in Berber robes armed with a vicious, long, curved dagger. Gervais moved swiftly to try and get his back against the wooden sides of the bridge, but he was too late. Still fending off the attack from the man at the front, he could not prevent the second from jumping on his back and bringing the blade to his throat, where it pressed against his skin.

'My name is Ishmael. You and yours deserve to die for killing our Sheikh and his son,' the man hissed loudly at him.

For a second, Gervais thought of shouting, *No, I am not Chatillon; I do not need to die.* But he knew they would kill him anyway, and if he did shout, they would know that Piers was still alive. So he gave a smile at fate as he sacrificed himself. His fingers loosened on his sword, it dropped to the ground, and he began muttering a prayer as the blade sliced across the vein in his neck.

He dropped to his knees, and his hand pressed against the gash to no avail, as the blood flowed down through his fingers onto Chatillon's Papal cloak. *Of course—it was the cloak*, he thought, as he toppled sideways to the ground. He saw the curved dagger the assassin had dropped beside him, the rain splashing off the vicious blade. He repeatedly blinked as everything began to grow darker, but reaching out, he curled his blood-covered fingers around the blade and clutched the dagger in his hand. At least Piers would know who killed him; that thought was comforting as he let out a shuddering breath. The last thing he felt was the rain drumming on his face as his lifeblood ebbed away to flow across the bridge and drip into the river.

Chapter Four

December 1099 – Genoa

Chatillon rode down into the prosperous city of Genoa with his two sons, Gironde and Gabriel. Edvard, his old friend and Vavasseur was back riding at his side, which was a consolation, as he felt a small amount of apprehension at seeing his wife, Isabella, again.

It had been nearly two months since the death of his friend Gervais de la Ferte, and he blamed himself in some ways for letting him walk abroad in a Papal cloak with no escort. Edvard, however, although saddened by the event, was more sanguine about the sad death.

'Every one of us knows the danger of being at your side, for as we thought, the blood feud continues, so we're all a target. But, we willingly take the risk, Piers, for none of us expect to die in our beds.'

Although Chatillon had nodded in agreement, he still felt the pain and loss of a close and dear friend. Gervais had been there since he had first entered the French court as a callow, naïve sixteen-year-old, guiding him through the pitfalls of court life. Gervais had also been his main conduit to King Philip, who listened to the sage advice of his Seneschal when he would listen to no one else. And now he was gone.

Chatillon had sent a bird immediately to the Malvais Chateau at Morlaix, in Brittany, as Minette, Morvan's wife, was the Seneschal's youngest daughter. They had left Morlaix immediately, risking a rough sea journey up the coast and along the Seine. Fortunately, they had arrived in time for the funeral, which had been a grand affair. Gervais had been the Seneschal of France for several decades; he was also the friend, companion and confidant of the King. As such, he had been one of the most powerful men in France. The Cathedral of St. Etienne on the Ile de Cite had been packed with the great and good from many courts in Europe, for he had been well respected and well liked.

Afterwards, Piers spent some time with Morvan and Ette. Morvan had certainly not been as accepting of events as Edvard.

'Who would have thought that Gervais would be the victim of a Saracen knife? As we have said before, it never ends, does it, Piers? So we all have to be ever watchful. The Sheikh may be dead, but the blood feud lives on. There must be a way to stop this. Have you considered approaching the head of the Ibn Hud family, his older brother, Abu Ja'far?' he suggested.

Chatillon had shaken his head. 'We killed his brother and his nephew and burnt his family palaces to the ground. I can't imagine him being willing to listen to me. I intend to leave for Genoa as the boys have not yet seen their mother. I want her back, but the blood feud was one of her reasons for not returning. I fear this news about the murder of Gervais will harden her resolve and convince her she has made the right decision to stay away from me.'

Morvan hadn't replied, as they both knew there were

several other reasons for her absence, and he could see that the death of his friend Gervais had deeply saddened Piers. Instead, Morvan had tried a different tack.

'Go to Genoa, Piers, for she fell in love with you for who you are: handsome, charismatic, confident but with that dangerous edge. Don't crowd her, but spend time in her father's palace with the boys so she can see the family you once were.'

'And Coralie? Do I just accept that she bore the Sheikh's child?' Chatillon had asked.

'Get to know the child; she is not her father, so don't taint her with his evil. She's a little girl as your daughter Annecy was, and as I remember, Annecy adored you.'

Morvan had given Piers food for thought, and he mulled it over again as they rode down through the narrow, crowded streets to the bustling port. From there, they would climb the winding track up the steep slope that led to their house, a marble-floored villa built on the cliffs that had been left to him by Bianca. He had always loved the house because the windows and balconies facing the sea were large and flooded the rooms with light. It was a house where they had always been happy.

Once inside, the boys raced around, as it had been nearly four years since they had last been here in Genoa to visit their grandparents. Chatillon sat on the balcony and gazed out across the port. Genoa was in a sheltered position, nestling at the foot of the Apennine Mountains in the Gulf of Genoa. There seemed to be over a hundred ships anchored below them in the bay, most with their sails taken down, or close-wrapped for the winter, while others had been pulled out of the water to be scraped, repaired and sealed, ready for the new trading season.

Gironde stood with his hands on the stone balustrade entranced by the scene, so different from home. The twins were now twelve years old but looked older, especially Gironde, a tall, handsome boy very like his father in looks with his dark eyes and hair. He also spent an hour daily with Finian and the men in the pell yard, especially since the attack on the Chateau. This practice had built up the muscles in his shoulders and arms. He was beginning to look like a young warrior.

Gabriel, however, had more of his mother's colouring and nature; his hair was a deep dark auburn, and he had his mother's amber eyes. He was a scholar, an artist and a musician; yes, he trained a few times a week in the pell yard and was becoming a good swordsman, but not with his brother's energy and obvious enthusiasm. He stood and leaned against his father's shoulder and listened to Gironde's commentary on what was happening in the port below.

'When do we see Mother?' he asked his father softly.

'I'm sending a message to the Embriaco Palace to say that we have arrived and will call on them at noon tomorrow. She'll be delighted to see you, as your mother loves you dearly and has missed you both.'

Piers heard the snort of disgust from Gironde. 'She is our mother; if she's missing us, then she should have come home where she belongs, not stayed away.'

Piers didn't reply. Gironde had not taken the news well that they had found and rescued Isabella from Ishmael, but she was not returning home. All Gironde saw was her rejection of them; his mother had a new child and a new life, and he assumed that she didn't want them anymore. Piers had told

Gironde most of the truth. He'd watered it down much more for Gabriel, who was still affected by the dark events at the Chateau.

'Can we go down to the port?' asked Gironde, who was ready to explore. Piers glanced up at Edvard, who was standing quietly behind them as usual, and Edvard grinned at Gironde and nodded.

'There are several hours of sunshine left. I'll send two of the men with you.' Gironde whooped and, pulling his brother with him, followed Edvard to the stairs.

Chatillon remained, sitting in the sunshine. It was an unusually warm December day, and the mellow stone walls of the villa were warm to the touch. He closed his eyes for a few moments and admitted to himself that he was excited at the thought of seeing his wife, but concerned at what Gironde's reaction might be. Gironde was young and impetuous and often spoke without thinking of the impact of his words—no doubt he would learn. He vowed to have a quiet word with his eldest son before they left the next day.

They walked up to the Embriaco Palace with its incredibly tall tower at noon the next day. Piers stood for a second and gazed up at its square crenellated top.

'I first met your mother up there on the very top, and I persuaded her that throwing herself off it would not be the romantic gesture she envisaged, as her body would slam onto the cobbles below.' Both boys looked at him wide-eyed in surprise.

'Why would she ever want to do something like that?' asked Gironde.

'She told me she was being forced into a marriage with a man old enough to be her father, a dry old stick only into politics and the Church.'

'Did you save her, Father?' cried Gabriel.

'Yes, of course, but I was the old man! She just hadn't realised that,' he said, laughing at the expression on his boys' faces.

'But that description isn't you, and you are only twelve years older than her!' exclaimed Gironde.

'Ah, but when you think a bad thing will happen to you, your imagination makes it ten times worse, so in her mind, she saw a doddering old greybeard with a stick. Now, enough of that. Let's go in, greet your grandparents and your mother and meet your new little sister, Coralie.'

As they entered the palace and made their way to the impressive family chamber upstairs, Piers noticed the hard-set line of Gironde's mouth. He took his son's arm.

'Try to envisage what your mother has endured, Gironde, and remember she loves you dearly.'

They went into what seemed a crowded room with family and servants as they made their bow to the Signori, Guglielmo Embriaco, who was delighted to see Piers and his grandsons.

'You have doubled in size since I last saw you,' he shouted, hugging them both, as did their grandmother, still a stately beauty in her mid-fifties. Gabriel's eyes, however, were on his mother, who now opened her arms to him. He ran into them and tried to hold back the sobs but failed, and her tears fell freely as she held him tight and kissed his cheek. She looked across at Gironde, who was standing apart, but he held himself aloof. She could see the hurt and anger on his face as he gave her a curt bow. Seeing his response to her, she felt an immense sadness.

Standing beside Embriaco, Piers watched all this; Isabella

looked different but just as beautiful. Her hair was now shoulder length and curly, as she had cut out the black dye they'd used on her. She had regained some of her lost weight and looked well.

He waited until Gabriel let her go and then went to greet her. He took her by the shoulders, smiled and kissed her on both cheeks as if she was a distant cousin. He then went to sit in a chair while refreshments were served. Gironde came and stood behind him, beside Edvard.

Isabella could feel the pain of loss as she stood looking at them. Piers was still so handsome; no wonder women still fell at his feet, and Gironde had become the image of him. Embriaco, aware of the tension, asked Chatillon what his plans were.

'I intend to stay in Genoa, with the boys, for Yuletide, and we are, with your permission, hoping to spend it here at the palace with you, if we may?'

Embriaco nodded. 'This is your family as well, Piers; you and the boys are welcome here at any time,' he said, staring at his daughter in displeasure, for he did not pretend to understand her position, or why she hadn't returned to her husband.

Chatillon continued. 'Then I must go to Rome as Pope Paschal has need of me. I intend to leave the boys here with you, and their mother, and pick them up a month or so later to return to the Chateau.'

Gironde stepped forward and touched his father's shoulder. 'I want to come to Rome with you, Father. I don't want to stay with her, for she no longer wants us.'

Isabella gasped. 'That is not true, Gironde; of course, I want you. I just can't return to the Chateau yet as there are so many bad memories there and so much danger.'

Gironde was unconvinced. 'We had happy memories there for nine or ten years before the attack. Annecy is there as well, and you have not even bothered to come and see her grave, and the beautiful stone Father had them carve for her tomb in the chapel. She was your daughter as well!'

Isabella had no possible answer to that as her stomach clenched in pain and sorrow.

'Father buried her little spaniel with her, for Pierre broke its neck as well as hers and left them both on the altar steps,' added Gabriel, in a sad voice.

There were gasps from his mother and grandparents, for no one had heard of this yet, and his grandmother dissolved into tears. At that point, Chatillon clapped his hands together as this was becoming maudlin, which he did not want.

'I'm sure your mother will visit Annecy and us soon, but now I can imagine that you are keen to meet your new sister, are you not, Gabriel?'

Isabella looked uncertainly at her parents, but her father gave her a stern nod. He was only prepared to face her reluctance to return to her husband for a short time. Piers had spent years risking his life searching for her, and Embriaco had not minced his words, calling his daughter a coward when she mentioned the danger of the blood feud.

Now she waved at the nurse who went to fetch the child and bring her into them. Chatillon saw at once that the child had changed; the curly blond hair was longer, and her eyes had rounded and opened so that she now looked more like Isabella than her father, Ishmael. Isabella stood the little girl beside Gabriel, who smiled and held his hands out.

'Coralie, meet your brother, Gabriel,' said Isabella, not

CHAPTER FOUR

daring yet to look at Piers or Gironde. The child held out a hand and clutched at Gabriel's fingers.

'How old is she?' he asked.

'She is two years old now and running everywhere,' said Isabella, smiling at her son.

Gironde did not move, his face set in a frown as he stared at the child. He had overheard his father's conversations, and he knew this child resulted from the Sheikh raping his mother.

'Gironde, do you want to say hello to your sister?' asked Isabella, hoping to win him around. He shook his head and clamped his lips shut to stop himself from saying what he thought. He could not understand why his mother was keeping her. The child shyly approached them, and Gironde stepped back into Edvard, who clamped a hand firmly onto his shoulder to keep him in place.

However, the child made her way to Piers; there was something familiar about him, the black hair, beard and dark eyes. He held out a hand and smiled while Isabella held her breath. Piers waved his other hand at Edvard, who held a box.

'I have a present for you, Coralie,' said Piers as Edvard opened the box and handed him a doll. It was a padded, wooden cross doll, but Rollo, the carpenter at the Chateau, had beautifully carved the head to look like a child with curly hair.

'This doll is from your adopted sister Marietta, who has dressed it in a velvet over-gown with a little cap to match,' he said, handing the child the doll. Isabella watched in astonishment as she had expected him to shun her again.

Coralie had opened her eyes wide at the doll, and she reached out to stroke at the velvet before pulling it into her arms and running back to her mother to show her. Once there, she turned and smiled at Chatillon. *Morvan is right; we can mould her into one of the family,* Piers thought, as he watched her.

They spent the afternoon and evening at the Embriaco Palace. Piers had long and interesting conversations with Guglielmo about the expansion plans of the new Maritime Republic of Genoa. Piers was happy to invest in a vast, extended merchant fleet, knowing the returns would be good. Gironde stayed near his father and Edvard, while Gabriel never left his mother's side. Before dinner, Piers took the boys to the top of the tower, and they stood looking over the city in the dusk.

'Gironde, I'm proud of you. You have developed into a fine young man and warrior. Now you need to work on those other skills that will help you to survive in this dangerous world; you have not mastered them yet. You need to be able to mix and communicate with people from all levels of society, no matter their background; otherwise, they will label you a boor and begin avoiding your company. I want you to study and develop an understanding of people and why they do what they do, because those skills may save your life one day. Edvard will help you in this.'

Gironde looked at him in surprise; his father delivered the odd blow or slap when he deserved it, but he rarely outlined his failings or criticised him.

'How you treated and spoke to your mother today was unacceptable, and you showed no understanding of her plight. You will not do that again, or I swear I'll leave you alone with the servants at the Castello, while we enjoy all of the Yuletide festivities here with the family. Do you understand? I don't want you to become another reason why your mother doesn't want to return home.'

Gironde nodded and hung his head.

'Puppets!' said Gabriel, and they both looked across at him in surprise.

'Grandfather says he has arranged a giant puppet show, and they are life-size, almost bigger than a man. They even have a horse that two men operate.' This quip brought a smile to both of their faces as they followed Gabriel to the winding staircase, to return to the family downstairs.

Piers met Isabella's eyes as they entered the Great Hall. She smiled, and for the first time, he felt a glimmer of hope that he may get her back.

However, that hope was diminished by his conversation with her the day before he left for Rome. He found her alone in the small walled garden, in a patch of winter sunshine, and she invited him to sit. It didn't start well.

'I have just overheard Edvard telling my father that you fought a duel in Paris over the beautiful Madame De Salvais, and you killed her young stepson, who was trying to defend her honour.'

'That was not exactly how it happened; he insisted on fighting and wasn't supposed to die.'

Isabella gave a bitter laugh in response to this. 'These last week's watching you with the boys and Coralie, you almost convinced me to return, but everyone around you dies, Piers. Even our loyal friend Gervais was killed because they thought he was you. I shed several tears over that, for he was still a dear, much-loved friend even though I had some suspicions about his involvement in the French Queen's death.'

Unusually, Piers found himself wrong-footed and unsure what to say to her, and he stared at the trickling water of the old fountain for a while. This garden had been an old Roman courtyard, and his eyes followed the shapes of dolphins on a small mosaic, still intact, on the wall opposite while he found the right words.

'Circumstances, Isabella, but you know that they are often beyond my control. You are not thinking logically about this, and your emotions are inevitably close to the surface after what you have endured. It was not my fault that the Sheikh attacked our ship, and I certainly had to kill his son to stop him from taking you captive. However, I have doubled our men and protection at the Chateau, and I am exploring pathways to end this blood feud. I believe I have found a solution, and then you can return to us.'

She did not reply at first but stared away from him. 'You have not asked me the question I expected from you,' she said.

Surprised, he raised an eyebrow, then realised what she meant and knew it had been at the forefront of his mind for several months.

'I presumed you would tell me, or at least send a message to warn me, if you were carrying the Sheikh's child again,' he said softly, as she shook her head to assure him that was not the case. He saw her eyes fill with tears, and he mentally cursed the man who had done this to them.

He pulled her into his arms, but although she sobbed on his shoulder, she was stiff and unbending. 'Come home, Isabella; you know you belong with us. I love you, as do the boys, and Coralie will thrive there in a proper family.'

She pulled away from him and wiped her eyes. 'I cannot do that yet, Piers, for I only feel safe here away from you and the cloud of death and disaster that follows you at the moment.'

With those words, she stood and left him sitting alone,

confused, but with a wave of building anger at both fate and her stubbornness.

January 1100 – Leon

Henry Beauclerc, the youngest son of King William I, was in Leon, the capital city of the northern province of Leon and Castile in Spain. From here, King Alphonso VI planned, and set out on, the Reconquista wars against the Moors, to drive them out and reclaim the land they had taken. Leon had been an important Roman city with a large Roman garrison, and as Henry walked around the city walls in the early evening, he could see many remaining signs of Roman buildings and walls throughout the city.

He had been there for nearly three months, having spent some time in London, in the court of his brother, King William Rufus, where he had ensured that his relationship with his sibling was on an even keel. When William took the Normandy overlordship from Robert, Henry stayed out of his brother's way, retreating into his fortress at Domfront. To give William Rufus his due, he had left his younger brother alone in Normandy.

Henry had appeared at the King's court in London, paid the usual niceties, and regularly went hunting with his brother, while quietly building his contacts and allies. He had aimed to gather support amongst those Norman and English nobles, who were acutely aware that King William Rufus had never married, and never would. Therefore, his only possible heirs would be Duke Robert of Normandy or Henry Beauclerc, Count of the Cotentin. He had hoped and prayed that Robert wouldn't survive the years of the Crusades; he had even considered sending someone to kill him in battle, but he'd decided that was beneath him, and he would leave it to God and fate. However, Robert had survived and was now returning as the triumphant taker of the Holy City of Jerusalem, also bringing a wealthy wife who may be with child, a legitimate heir to both Normandy and England.

Tonight, however, he hoped that everything might change for the better, for after long conversations with his cousin, King Alphonse, the King had finally agreed to summon Abu Ja'far, the head of the Ibn Hud Dynasty, to Leon. Alphonse had agreed to Henry's request to pressure Abu Ja'far to stop the blood feud against Piers De Chatillon. King Alphonse would threaten to withdraw the protective alliance he was providing for the Ibn Hud Taifa unless Abu Ja'far agreed. He would tell the Berber Emir that Leon and Castile could not condone a continuing link with a family that tried to murder a Senior Papal Envoy and his family. Especially now, for they had discovered that the Ibn Hud Dynasty was behind the murder of the Seneschal of France, outside King Philip's palace gates. He would tell the Emir that France and the Holy See would ask why King Alphonse was continuing to protect this murdering Berber family.

Later that evening, Henry left the palace highly satisfied with the result. Abu Ja'far had agreed with their request; he'd told them he desperately needed their protection against the Almoravid forces in Spain, and his brother Yusuf, known as Sheikh Ishmael, was now dead. Therefore, the feud must and would end. Abu had admitted that it may take until the end of the summer for the order to reach the assassins who were sent out by the Sheikh. Henry insisted that Abu Ja'far sign the charter in the summer, agreeing to this, which he would ensure that the Pope and King Alphonse would countersign. If he broke this agreement, the Ibn Hud dynasty and their Taifa would be seen as a hostile enemy and open to attack.

The shaken Emir had agreed. He had little choice, and in his heart, he was truly relieved that his brother, Yusuf, was dead, for he had become more and more difficult to control.

Prince Henry was pleased that his plans had come to fruition; he would ride north back to Domfront in a few days and make plans to meet with Piers De Chatillon, possibly in Paris. He believed he now truly had the means to persuade the Papal Assassin to carry out the ultimate, and daring, plan he had in mind.

Chapter Five

January 1100 – Rome

It was lashing with rain as Chatillon and Edvard made their way across the Lateran Square to the Papal Palace. Once inside, they shook the water from their cloaks and made their way to Chatillon's chambers, in a corridor, not far from the top of the impressive staircase. It had not been a bitterly cold winter as in previous years, but it seemed to have rained nonstop since they left Genoa. Once changed into his velvet Papal tunic with the gold insignia, Chatillon made his way to the Pope's rooms. The young Papal Secretary at the desk in the antechamber greeted him with relief.

'I'm pleased you are finally here, for his holiness has been agitated for days.' Chatillon smiled at the young man whom he had chosen and trained. He placed a reassuring hand on his shoulder as they knocked, and entered the large oak-carved wooden doors into the Pope's inner sanctum.

Pope Paschal was both delighted and relieved to see them as he had several pressing matters he needed Chatillon to deal with.

'I hear that the anti-pope, Clement III, is very ill again. Is it wrong that I hope he does not recover, Piers?' whispered

CHAPTER FIVE

Paschal, waving Piers to a chair by the fire while Edvard stood near the window.

Chatillon, looking at the concerned face of the Holy Father, shook his head in mock dismay and smiled.

'The anti-pope, Clement, is a stick that Henry, the Holy Roman Emperor, has used to beat us with for the last twenty years Paschal. No one could have believed that the Emperor would set up an alternative Pope to the one chosen by God.'

'As you know, Piers, he has nearly all of the German princes behind him and several allies in northern Italy. I hear Emperor Henry has also reconciled with your old enemy, Duke Welf of Bavaria.'

'Yes, I was disappointed to hear that Duke Welf survived the crusades despite my best efforts to have him killed,' he said, laughing. Paschal raised an eyebrow, never quite sure when his Papal Envoy was being serious. However, Chatillon sat forward and lowered his voice.

'I have several men in the household of the anti-pope, Clement. Apparently, his sickness comes and goes, but he's approaching seventy years now, and as an annoying thorn in our sides, we both know that he has lived for far too long.'

Paschal's eyes widened. 'Poison,' he muttered to himself, then looking up, he met Chatillon's eyes.

'Are you poisoning him, Piers?' he asked, in a low voice.

Chatillon gave a thin smile. 'The arrangement I have always had with the previous popes was that they never wanted to know the details when rivals and enemies were removed. I have only ensured for the last few years that Clement has been too ill to cause us much trouble. We forced him to retreat away from Rome, and as you know, he's now ensconced to the north of Rome at Civita Castellana. I promise you, Eminence, he will not leave there alive.'

'How soon?' murmured Paschal, his hands gripping the arms of the carved chair.

'He will be gone before the end of summer—unless you want me to expedite it?' asked Chatillon, with a raised eyebrow.

The Pope stood and paced the large chamber. 'Ah, Piers, the Devil is always at my shoulder with temptations. My conscience wouldn't agree with what you suggest, no matter how much I wish it was true. Also, the problem remains: when he dies, who will Emperor Henry replace him with, Piers?'

'I have been told on good authority that it will be Theodoric, the Cardinal and previously supposed legate of anti-pope Clement. However, he is a shadow of a man compared to the proactive and vociferous Clement III, and he will be easily managed and threatened.'

Chatillon could see the dismay and distress on his new master's face. Paschal was a gentle soul, but Piers knew he could really not afford to be that way in his position. He needed to develop a ruthless streak, or he would never survive as Pope.

'Would it help if I just let Clement's illness take its course, dosing him as we're doing at the moment? That way, it will look natural that the anti-pope succumbed after a long illness,' he suggested.

Paschal met his stare and held it, but before he closed his eyes and nodded, the temptation to end it now had been there to see on his face. Chatillon smiled; he would guide Paschal on the right pathway and increase the dosage.

'Chatillon, I want you to arrange to seize the town of Civita Castellana as soon as Clement is in the ground. I believe we still have sufficient French and Norman troops in our entourage to achieve that. I do not want Henry, the Holy Roman Emperor, to be able to place another anti-pope this close to Rome again.'

'I assure you, Eminence, that Henry has enough on his plate at the moment dealing with rebellions at home. As you know, his second, very young, wife, Eupraxia, accused him of deviant sexual practices, said he had forced her to participate in orgies and even offered her to his son. When she became pregnant, she was even unsure who the father of her child was. Emperor Henry had already been excommunicated. Pope Urban could, therefore, do little more except condemn these practices and offer Empress Eupraxia sanctuary and shelter in Hungary, away from the Emperor. However, now she has returned to her homeland in Kyiv to seek the protection of her royal family. Emperor Henry's son, Conrad, stood with his stepmother, rebelled against his father and backed up her stories. I think Henry may be too preoccupied now to worry about his anti-pope's death.'

Paschal nodded in satisfaction.

'How are things in your life, Piers? I know Gervais was a close friend, and although you must blame yourself for his death, you should not do so.'

Chatillon shrugged. 'He was wearing my cloak, so yes, I should have sent a servant with him. However, I made some progress in Genoa, and the boys are there with their mother. But the threat and fear of the blood feud mean that none of us sleeps easily in our beds.'

'I may have some news, for our friend Prince Henry Beauclerc has been in Leon. He has requested my permission to put the seal of the Holy See on a document he is preparing with King Alphonse. This concerns your blood feud, as they discussed bringing the Ibn Hud Dynasty to the table. Did you know of this?'

Chatillon looked thoughtful and cast his mind back to his last conversation with Henry.

'He mentioned the possibility to me, but for some time now, Henry has tried to persuade me to undertake an assassination of import, that of his brother, King William Rufus. My uncle, Pope Urban, was aware of this and asked me to stall the Prince while appearing to offer our support to him. Henry is a clever and ambitious young man, and I believe he may become very dangerous.'

Paschal sat back in his chair and reached for his goblet of wine. He took a long draft and then dabbed at his lips with a kerchief while he gathered his thoughts at this news.

'King William Rufus is certainly no friend to the Church, but if we agree to support Henry in this way, we will need to extract written promises from him to support and protect the Church in England, if he becomes King.'

Chatillon inclined his head in agreement.

'But what of Duke Robert? Is he not the heir of King William Rufus? The King is now in his mid-forties, unmarried, with no other heirs. Would it not suit us more to have Robert in his rightful place as King of Normandy and England?' asked Paschal.

'Probably, but I don't believe that would stop Henry Beauclerc. He is determined to have England and wants to make his move before Robert returns from the crusades in late summer.'

Paschal stood and paced again. Watching him, Chatillon smiled. How many Popes had he watched pace the floor as they held the future of princes and countries in their hands? Finally, Paschal paused and turned to Chatillon.

'I will pray on this, so let fate take a hand for a while. Meanwhile, I need you to go south to Conversano, Piers; Duke Robert is getting married there in a week or so to his wealthy heiress. You shall be my envoy and sound him out on his plans simultaneously. Warn him about his brother Henry and know his mind on the matter. However, don't mention the assassination, for that word never goes down well with kings and princes.'

He took his leave of Pope Paschal, and with Edvard at his side, Chatillon returned to his chambers.

'We leave for Conversano tomorrow, Edvard; please make arrangements. Once there, I will recommend that Duke Robert does not tarry on his way home to Normandy, but I will not mention the possible death of William Rufus, for that could only inflame the situation,' he said, moving to stand at the window.

'I believe King Philip of France and his heir, Louis, would support the death of King William Rufus, but if you tell Robert, then Paschal is right, for he was always closer to William than Henry, and he may even warn his brother or join forces with him to attack Henry again,' added Edvard.

That last night in Rome, Edvard and Chatillon sat in one of the better hostelries. The innkeeper gave them his best table near the fire as the rain still hammered down outside. After a quick glance of recognition, none of the locals came near. One or two of Chatillon's informers came and went, but it was peaceful as the two men stretched their wet, booted legs to the fire.

'So we go south early tomorrow; let us hope the rain does

not follow us,' murmured Edvard.

'Yes, we go to the court of Geoffrey of Brindisi to attend the wedding of Duke Robert to Sibylla of Conversano. However, they tell me the sun always shines down there, Edvard.'

His friend laughed and then assumed a more serious expression.

'Before we left Genoa, Isabella approached me. She asked for a boon, a favour.'

Chatillon raised an eyebrow in surprise that Edvard had not mentioned this before, but he knew that Edvard always thought things through before burdening him, so he waited for him to continue.

'It appears she had a dear friend named Mishnah in the Castel of Alaro; she was one of the Sheikh's concubines. This woman risked her life to help Coralie escape, and Isabella did not doubt that Mishna would be punished for her actions and may even be dead. However, she wishes me to try and find her. I was unsure about the wisdom of this, so I waited before mentioning it.'

Piers stared into the fire for a while as he mulled over the implications. Would finding and bringing the woman back serve to remind Isabella of what she suffered at Alaro? Finally, he sighed and nodded.

'We still have a few informers on the island of Mallorca; find out if she's alive. If so, where is she, and how easy would it be to get her out? Since the Sheikh's death, we have had little need to know what was happening at the fortress of Alaro.'

Edvard nodded. 'I will send a bird tomorrow before we leave; it may endear Isabella to you more if we find and rescue her,' he suggested.

CHAPTER FIVE

Chatillon shrugged. He was not so sure, for Mishnah was an unknown quantity.

Three days later, they rode into Brindisi to Count Geoffrey's palace. Their welcome was overwhelming despite being surrounded by several other guests of high nobility. The Count was delighted that the Pope had chosen to send his Senior Papal Envoy to his daughter's wedding. It had been beyond the Count's expectations that Duke Robert had chosen Sybilla to be his bride. To say that the feasts and entertainment that followed over the next few days were lavish was an understatement, as the Count demonstrated his immense wealth.

Two days later, they all stood in the Basilica of St. Nicholas, in the town of Bari, to see Duke Robert marry his wealthy heiress. Chatillon had been here once before with his uncle, Pope Urban, as he had consecrated the Basilica. It was a place of pilgrimage, with beautiful mosaic pavements in the crypt below, that housed the tomb of St Nicholas.

Chatillon thought Robert was the fittest he had ever seen him; tanned and lean, he looked every inch a returning hero warrior from the Crusades. The crowds greeted him ecstatically wherever they went, for this was the man who had taken the Holy City of Jerusalem back. However, when he finally got time alone with his friend, he found Robert to be very self-effacing about his success.

'It was no more than any other of the Crusade leaders would

have done. I was just lucky on that day,' he insisted, but Chatillon knew that his organisation and courage had won the day, so he slapped him on the shoulder while snorting with disbelief.

'What are your plans, Robert? I hope you plan to return and reclaim your inheritance in Normandy from your brother William Rufus.'

The Duke nodded. 'We intend to set off home in the spring, but there are several places we mean to visit on the way, and then I intend to take Sibylla on a *Progress* around Normandy so my people can see us.'

They could talk no further as others claimed his attention, but Chatillon indicated clearly that he still needed to talk to him alone.

It was to be two days before he could extract him again from the ongoing celebrations of his new father-in-law. Piers suggested they ride out to the coast so they wouldn't be interrupted.

They dismounted on the cliffs and, hobbling the horses, sat on the rocks looking out over the sea in the direction of Asia Minor. Robert shaded his eyes, but the land was too far away and the sea too hazy. He turned to his friend.

'Soon, it will be nearly four years since we risked our lives crossing these treacherous waters to reach Constantinople.'

'I heard that you lost nearly a hundred men and supplies in these waters, but I also did warn you, Robert, that this Crusade would be dangerous and take years to accomplish,' murmured Chatillon.

'Ah, but we were full of zeal and excitement then; it was almost like a fever that consumed us in those first six months. The excitement soon wore off with the heat, the dust, starvation and disease that seemed to accompany every hard-won battle and siege. Thousands died. However, the zeal was still there to save the Holy City in those final months, no matter the odds. Now two great cities have been restored to us; Behemond rules as King of Antioch, and my dear friend Geoffrey of Bouillon is ruling Jerusalem. But you are right, Chatillon, it has been at a great cost, and no doubt people in the future will decide if that cost in lives was worth it.'

Chatillon could see that these four years had changed Robert; he was less impulsive and more philosophical, which wasn't a bad thing.

'I'm not sure if you heard, Robert, but unfortunately, my uncle, the Pope, died before he was aware that Jerusalem had fallen. He waited every week for that news, but his faith in you never wavered, and he was so impressed by what you had achieved. He kept your letters by him at all times.'

'The news of Pope Urban's death saddened me, Piers, as he was the inspiring figurehead of our Crusade and a great man.'

'So now, you finally return to your capital of Rouen, Robert. Tell me, do you expect William Rufus just to hand Normandy back when you repay the loan?'

'I expect and need you to be by my side when that happens, Chatillon, as the original Vifgage document was witnessed by the Church and countersigned by Pope Urban. In that document, my brother pledged, with his right hand on the holy relics, to return my country to me when I repaid the loan,' proclaimed Robert.

'I will be there, Sire, but I don't expect him to do so willingly, so I will ensure that all of the senior Anglo-Norman nobles are also present.'

Robert put a hand on his friend's arm and clasped it in

thanks.

'Do you hear much from your brother, Henry?' Piers asked the Duke.

'Nothing! As far as I know, he is keeping his head down in his fortress at Domfront. William has not mentioned him either, and if he continues in this way, then I'm minded to leave him there.'

'He is very ambitious, Robert. I would advise you to watch his movements as he seems to be gathering supporters.'

Robert shrugged and was dismissive of Chatillon's warnings.'William Rufus and I put him in his place when we chased him out of his refuge, in Mont Saint-Michel, and put him into exile in Castile.'

'Well, he then crept back to his fortress at Domfront and spent far more time building bridges with William in the English court. Now he's back in Castile, reinforcing his alliance with King Alphonse. Before that, he was in the French court, becoming friendly with the Dauphin, Prince Louis. This is not a younger brother who is keeping his head down. Just be wary of him, Robert, for I believe he has designs on England or Normandy. Don't linger too long to make your return.'

Robert met Chatillon's eyes and saw the concern there. Piers never issued warnings lightly, so he grasped his friend's arm.

'I promise I will heed what you say, but I think you worry unduly. Henry isn't a problem.'

Chatillon had to settle for that, but as he listened to Robert and his new wife discussing their plans over the next few days, he prayed that Robert *would* heed his words, and soon—Henry Beauclerc was impatient and would certainly act.

CHAPTER FIVE

Chatillon felt guilty that he may be about to facilitate this assassination against his friend Robert's interests. Still, at the same time, if he decided to accept the assignment, he would get Henry's word to leave Normandy alone and not attack Duke Robert.

The news of Robert's marriage to a wealthy wife was not received well in the English court by two invested but completely different parties....

Ranulf Flambard, the King's Chancellor and friend, was annoyed that William Rufus was taking the news of Robert's success so stoically when they had worked so hard to acquire Normandy. The money they had expended on men and bribes was immense.

'Not only is your brother returning as the conquering hero of Jerusalem, feted by the kings and nobility of Europe and glorified by the Holy See, but he's returning with a wife, Sibylla of Conversano, the wealthiest heiress in Italy. You do realise, William, that he will pay off the vifgage, take back the dukedom, and none will naysay him with his restored reputation as a warrior and leader of the Crusades,' Ranulf spat, as he paced back and forth in the King's private chamber.

William reclined on one of the divans near a window; a young man plucked at a citole at the King's feet, which annoyed Flambard so much he ejected the young musician from the room, to a raised eyebrow from the King.

'Will you listen and take this seriously, William,' he said, pulling up a chair alongside him. But William shrugged and delved again into the bowl of nuts in his lap, while his advisor blew air through his teeth in exasperation.

'Your humour and phlegm are too high today, Ranulf. It can't be good for your health to be that red-faced. I promise you we will keep troops on the border with the Vexin. Ostensibly with the excuse that they are protecting Normandy from King Philip of France. You forget that I know my brother, Robert; he will soon lose interest in managing the dukedom. He is also, as we know, profligate with his money, and Sibylla's dowry will run through his fingers like water.'

Flambard was not convinced. 'I wish I had your confidence, Sire, but my informers tell me that, while Sibylla may be much younger than her new husband, she has been managing her father's many homes and properties for years. You may remember that your mother, Queen Matilda, was a far more efficient and respected ruler of Normandy than your father. We may find that Sibylla becomes the guiding hand for Robert.' Flambard, for the first time, had William's full attention, and he was satisfied that he had given him food for thought.

Meanwhile, northwest of London, in their large sprawling manor in Buckingham, one highly influential Countess was incandescent with rage at the news of Robert's marriage to a wealthy and beautiful Italian heiress. Agness de Ribemont had been the mistress of Robert Curthose for over twenty years. Keeping him at her side had been no mean achievement, but she had many charms and was still considered a beauty. They had a son, William, a notable soldier born years before, in 1079, who was now the Lord of Tortosa.

Despite their ongoing arrangement, Agness had married Walter Giffard, the Earl of Buckingham and Justiciar to the

King, in 1095. The Earl knew of the affair and reluctantly looked the other way, especially as Agness kept her side of the bargain and presented him with a son and heir, young Walter. She was now furious that Robert had married a much younger beauty without giving her any warning, but communications had been far and few between them while he was away crusading. She discovered that the happy couple would return to Normandy in late summer or early autumn, and she intended to be in the court in Rouen waiting for them when they arrived. She had plans for her son, William of Tortosa, to inherit Normandy, and she would do everything she could to stop Robert from having any legitimate children, as she made plans for some of her own ladies to be around the new Duchess. If Agness had her way, Robert's new wife, Sibylla, would not carry a child to term or hopefully even survive childbed.

Chapter Six

March 1100 – The Monastere de St Benoit

Against all odds, the man from the boat was still alive, but he certainly wasn't out of the woods yet, as Friar Frances battled infection in several of the deeper burns. This meant a rewashing and rebinding of the wounds every three or four days. In the past, he had succeeded in keeping gangrene at bay by using Sulema, a mix of mercuric chloride and vinegar. But he knew from experience that it could only be used for a short time. They were nearing that limit now, and after that, fate would take its course as he was left with a mixture of salt, vinegar, honey and wine. Their patient had somehow learned to become stoic about his constant and often excruciating pain, and Friar Francis admired his courage and resilience as they still tried to alleviate that pain with regular doses of opioids.

The man said little; he was not a prepossessing sight and would frighten people or have them recoil in revulsion when they saw him slowly being helped to the treatment room. He only had hair left on the right-hand side of his head, and they had cut this very short so it did not look too incongruous. The left-hand side of his head and lower face was badly scarred, the skin pulled down around the mouth as if it had melted. They had amputated two fingers on his claw-like left hand, but there was little movement in the remaining fingers as the tendons in the hand were damaged and shortened; however, he did have movement in his thumb.

Friar Francis walked into his room, sat beside his bed, and pulled up a stool.

'I thought you and I might take a short walk into the herb garden, as it is a pleasant day out there. If you are ever going to walk any distance or ride a horse again, you need to get movement into your left leg, no matter how painful it may be. Fortunately, it is nowhere near as badly burned as your arm and shoulder, for the flames shot upwards. Given time, your leg may return to as near normal as possible, with only a slight limp.' The man nodded and slowly swung his legs to the floor. He knew he was fortunate that his leather boots had protected the lower part of his calf and foot.

He had hardly left this room, except for painful treatment, since he entered the monastery, so he felt somewhat apprehensive about going out into the open air. The Friar reassured him, and led him, by his good right arm, out through the sprawling monastery buildings until they finally came through an arch into a very large, well-tended kitchen garden. The man saw the horror on the faces of the younger monks as they moved out of his way—he had expected that. However, the pity and sympathy on the faces of others almost cracked the hard shell he had taken care to build around himself and his emotions.

The Friar led him to a bench in the shade of the high wall, and they sat and watched the monks tending the gardens in the spring sunshine.

'I want you to do this walk every day to this bench come rain or shine. Can you do that?' he asked the man, who nodded. It occurred to Friar Francis that he had rarely heard the man utter a word apart from the groans, moans and the screaming of "No!" while they were cleaning and washing the wounds out again. However, the old monk who tended to him daily had assured the Friar that he had spoken to him.

'Your healing process is only part of the way through. It will take many more months before the deeper wounds heal—that is, if they don't become infected—but you are in the prayers of the brothers every day. It may not be to your God, or we don't know it may be the same God that we call by a different name, for you are a Berber, which means that you will be Muslim unless you are a Mozarab?' The Friar spoke to him in Latin and the man replied in the same language.

'Yes, I am Berber and Muslim, but I will pray to any God to help me heal and recover.'

The Friar gazed thoughtfully at the man beside him; he sounded well-educated, which could prove useful to them. However, first, he needed to find out more about their patient. He opened the leather pouch at his belt and brought out the gold ring he had taken off the finger he had amputated.

'This is yours, I believe. I saved it for you, but I don't recognise the crest. It seems to be some type of bird with its wings spread.'

'It is the family crest of the House of Al Cazar. The bird is a lammergeier; you might know it as an ossifrage. It is a huge bearded vulture that dominated the skies over the deserts during our childhood. It was never frightened of any animal and would swoop to see off hyenas and even desert lions. This ring belonged to my brother and was returned to the family

CHAPTER SIX

recently after his death; I now wear it in his memory.'

The monastery might be remote up in the hills above Marseilles, but pedlars and visitors called on a monthly basis, and the Friar certainly knew the name of Al Cazar, the ruthless right-hand man of Sheikh Ishmael.

'You are the brother of Al Cazar?' he asked in surprise.

'Yes, he was three years older than me.'

'So you served the Sheikh as well?' he asked.

The man nodded, narrowed his eyes and stared across the gardens.

'I was one of his Captains. We were in the tents on the island of Cabrera, but then I was called to take three men to the Sheikh's galley for guard duty. I was on the galley, fighting for my life, trying to protect the Sheikh as the Horse Warriors attacked and then burnt the ship.'

'You are very lucky to be alive and may be one of the only survivors. I hear that a few crew members managed to jump overboard but perished in the flaming water,' added the Friar.

'It all happened so quickly, Friar, they seemed to come silently out of nowhere. They used cloths soaked in oil spread around the decks, but you could smell the brimstone they used on them as well.'

The Friar's face expressed his surprise. 'Brimstone? They came well prepared indeed, for they were ensuring that no one on that galley survived, and yet, against the odds, here you are. What is your name?' he asked softly.

'Meddur Al Cazar,' he replied, with the first crooked smile the Friar had seen. It looked almost like a crooked sneer, as the left-hand side of the mouth would not move. The Friar wondered what the smile indicated. Only later at compline, one of the monks, Father Dominic, who spoke a little Arabic, also smiled when the Friar told them their patient's name.

'What a coincidence and how appropriate, for the word Meddur in their tongue means alive.'

A week later, the Friar joined Meddur in the garden again.

'I'm sure you would like to repay us for your care here in the infirmary, Meddur, and I think I have found a way for you to do that.'

The man shrugged. 'As you know, I have nothing, Friar, apart from the clothes you have provided and my brother's gold ring.'

'Come with me,' he insisted, and led Meddur to the scriptorium where several monks, including their archivist, were working.

'Bring it out, Father Dominic,' the Friar ordered. The monk carried a locked chest to the table and opened it; inside was a large collection of pages held together with twine. There must have been a hundred old, thin vellum sheets.

'This is one of our treasures, Meddur; it is the copied pages of the Canon of Medicine, an invaluable book. It was originally written by Avicenna, who, as you know, was not only a polymath but one of Islam's greatest philosophers and physicians. He drew together all the known knowledge of medicine in the Greek and Arab worlds. Unfortunately, almost all of it is in an Arab script, which we think may be Persian and we have not had the skills and expertise to transcribe it. You are an educated man, and we are asking if you would try and translate it for us.'

Meddur fingered one of the thin sheets of vellum. He knew he would have many long months still in this monastery if he were to survive, and at least this would give him something to sharpen his mind, so he agreed, and both the

CHAPTER SIX

Friar and Father Dominic beamed with pleasure. Each day afterwards, he spent several hours each morning reading out the translation while Father Dominic wrote it down. It was far more interesting than he expected, and before long, he was engrossed in its contents and deep in discussion with the older monk beside him.

It was only in the long nights, lying on his bed, that his thoughts turned to what had happened on the galley. He still often awoke screaming from nightmares as he relived it, and it was then that his thoughts would turn to revenge.

'I will find them and kill them for what they did,' he swore softly to himself, in the early hours, as he turned the Al Cazar family ring round and round on the finger of his right hand.

April 1100 - Marseilles

Piers had never been so happy to get off a boat as he had when he stepped foot onto the wharf at Marseilles. Taking a ship in the Mediterranean before Easter was always a risk, but needs must. It was early April, and he had to return to Chatillon sous Bagneux, for his informers told him that Henry Beauclerc was still in Paris, enjoying himself in the French court, and he needed to have a conversation with him away from prying eyes and listening ears.

He had been informed that Henry had struck up an instant friendship with the Dauphin, Prince Louis, and Chatillon did not like the sound of that, for Henry did not do anything without reason. Chatillon had his suspicions that he was building an alliance with the French King and his heir, but to what end? Was this to attack Normandy and take it from Robert, and if so, what would Henry offer the King of France in return? Would it be the Norman half of the Vexin which the King had long coveted? Or was he garnering support for his claim to the English throne, which meant that time was running out for Duke Robert's return?

Piers turned and helped a pale-faced Gabriel up the rope ladder to the wharf, where his son swayed and grabbed his father's arm.

'I thought we would die, the size of the waves as they swept over our ship. I was sure the boat would be swamped, and we would sink; the crew could not seem to bail out fast enough,' he gasped.

Gironde climbed happily up beside them. 'Don't be such a ninnyhammer, Gabriel, that was a mere squall or two. The fishermen in Genoa told me they had seen waves over four times the height of a man, and whales bigger than a house. If I was not so keen on joining the Horse Warriors, I swear I would consider becoming the captain of my own ship, sailing the seas for adventure, and fighting pirates like Father and Finian did,' he announced.

Horses were waiting for them with several of their men on the wharf, and they rode up to their estate where they would spend only a few days,—a week at the most—for Piers needed to be in Paris to see what damage was being done. He had arranged for Conn Fitz Malvais to come from Brittany and join them there, for he needed to talk to the young warrior away from his family. They would leave for the long ride up to the Chateau the day after he arrived by boat in Marseilles.

CHAPTER SIX

Gabriel felt better as they rode up to the estate above Roucas Blanc and he talked with his father.

'I tried my hardest to persuade Mother to come home; I told her about Cormac and Fergus and how much they had grown and how she would hardly recognise them. I said that Dion missed her company, that Ahmed had never really recovered from her kidnapping, and that he missed her desperately as both Gironde and I did.'

Chatillon felt saddened as he looked across at his son riding beside him. Gabriel had always felt things more deeply. His own conversation with Isabella had been brief. He told her he expected her to be back with them in the autumn, for he believed he had found the means to stop the blood feud. He told her that the Chateau was her home, and that was where Coralie should be brought up, with her family and friends.

'Do not fear, Gabriel, she will return to us; it will just take time, as she has been through a terrible ordeal for the past few years.' His son nodded in understanding as they rode on, smiling as they watched Gironde galloping ahead, and whooping as he raced through the estate gates.

A messenger was waiting for Edvard when they entered the hall; Chatillon walked over as he saw Edvard shaking his head in consternation.

'Trouble?' he asked, walking over to stand beside him.

'Alain here has found Mishnah, and she's alive but not in a good way. She has spent the last six months in a dockside inn, come whorehouse, in Medina Mayurqa. The innkeeper refuses to let her go, or sell her, as even now, she brings in a lot of money as one of the Sheikh's favourite concubines.'

Chatillon raised an eyebrow. 'Edvard, take three men and promise the innkeeper he will wake with his balls in his mouth if she's not in the boat for your return trip,' he ordered. Edvard smiled and went to pick his men.

Two days later, Conn and Georgio arrived, and they all came out onto the steps to greet them.

'How did I know you would not come alone, even though I requested it!' exclaimed Chatillon, while Georgio looked sheepish, as he realised that Chatillon was truly not pleased to see him at Conn's side.

'He is very hard to shake off, almost like a shadow, Piers; I'm sure he thinks that he may miss something,' smiled Conn.

'Or like a limpet that you cannot detach,' added Gironde, while Chatillon smiled at his eldest son developing a cutting wit.

They settled into the estate to await Edvard's return, and Chatillon and Conn strolled up the hill, in the morning sunshine, while Georgio was occupied in training the twins in hand-to-hand combat. As they sat again on the weathered bench, Chatillon did not say a word for some time as Conn sent the odd questioning glance in his direction; he assumed he had been brought here for a purpose.

'The last time I sat here, my wife told me she still loved me, but despite that, because of what she had been through, she was not coming home,' he murmured.

Conn inclined his head. 'That must have been hard for you to hear after years of searching for her, and I know how much you loved her.'

'And still do Conn. I must have had hundreds of women, but only three have touched my heart. Gabrielle de Semillon was the first to break my very young and tender heart. Bianca, I loved dearly and would have made her my wife, but she was murdered, and I blame myself for that. Finally, I seem to have lost Isabella. There's no doubt that we were meant to be together, but now barriers are holding us apart. I'm trying one by one to remove those barriers, and I need your help,' he said, looking into Conn's eyes.

'Anything you ask, Piers, for my debt to you for rescuing me and saving my life, and that of Georgio, is barely paid,' he replied.

'That slate has been wiped clean, I assure you, Conn, but this will be dangerous, and it may even result in your torture and death if we're caught, or fail in our attempt,' proclaimed Chatillon, pulling no punches and turning to face him to see the effect of his words.

Conn was intrigued and remembered the conversation he had had on this bench a year before, when he'd opened his soul to Chatillon. He presumed that Piers was now appealing to the darker side of his character that he had described to him.

'An assassination?'

Chatillon nodded. 'I will not give you any details yet because it has not been agreed upon or finalised. You will be the first to know when it has, and any information stays between you, Edvard and me. Do you understand, and more importantly, are you prepared to take this risk? To be part of what could be a perilous undertaking?'

Conn nodded, and Chatillon smiled; it seemed as if he had found an apprentice.

'Come, show me how good your archery skills are,' he said, standing and striding downhill.

'Not that good, I'm afraid; my weapons are swords, daggers and staff. I have had little time for bows and arrows,' he said, catching up with him.

'I intend to take you back to the Chateau, where you will spend a few months training with Dion, who is probably one of the best archers I have ever seen. I watched her take the eye out of a running pheasant for a wager. When she has finished with you, you will never be as good as her, but you will be the equal of one of her archers,' he announced. Conn was unsure, but he was pleased to return to the Chateau, where he would see Marietta again; she had intruded on his thoughts a lot recently.

Chapter Seven

May 1100 – Chatillon Sous Bagneux

It was mayday when they finally arrived back at the Chateau. It had taken them far longer than expected because of Mishnah's poor health and condition.

Edvard had brought her to the estate on the hills above Marseilles, but it was immediately obvious that she could not undertake a long journey for several days. She was thin, bruised and battered, with open sores on her ankle from the shackle. The innkeeper had been taking no chances with such a beauty and had chained her to the bed. He had ensured a constant stream of men went up to that room every day, determined to make back the silver he had spent on her. She was a shadow of her former self—her beauty dimmed—when Edvard found her.

The innkeeper, intimidated by Edvard, had given in immediately when he heard the name Chatillon, and he led them up to the room. Edvard had spent a reasonable time in the whorehouses of Paris—it was his one weakness—but even so, he had been shocked at what he'd found. The room was small but filled with a large bed covered in a stained and filthy sheet. Mishnah, with dull eyes, was chained and sat in a short, dirty, torn shift on the floor in the corner. She had wearily recoiled away when Edvard and his men came in, thinking they were more customers.

Instead, Edvard had knelt beside her and taken her hand. 'Mishnah, we have come to take you out of here; Piers De Chatillon sent us.'

She had blinked at him for a moment, unsure of what she was hearing. The innkeeper had appeared with an awl and hammer to remove the shackle, and she cringed away again. Edvard could see the old and new stripes and bruises from beatings on her body, and he glared at the man who had mumbled excuses.

'She's stubborn and refused to do what I ask; she even bit one man last week, down there, left teeth marks and drew blood,' he said, pointing to his groin. Mishnah had suddenly hissed and lunged at the innkeeper, getting her hands around his throat. As he crouched on his haunches, he toppled backwards, and she was on him so fast that, at first, Edvard could do nothing as her fists beat down on the innkeeper's face. Edvard heard the man's nose break, and blood spurted as he pulled her off him. Mishnah had screamed in fury and rage as she was pulled back, but Edvard had pulled her tightly into his arms and held her there, talking softly until she calmed. The innkeeper pulled himself to his feet, blood dripping from his nose.

'Get her some clothes, or I swear I will chain you to that bed and send half a dozen men to do to you what they did to her!'

The man scuttled away, and his wife appeared soon after with a worn linen shift and a plain overgown, both of which had seen better days.

CHAPTER SEVEN

When they had arrived at the estate above Marseilles, Chatillon had come out to meet them and was saddened and angry at what had been done to her. She was painfully thin, with dark circles under her haunted eyes and matted hair, but Piers could see that she had once been a beauty. When Edvard lifted her from the horse to the ground, her legs had given way, and he'd picked her up and carried her into the large manor house. The Steward's wife had been called and was equally horrified at what she saw, as they carried her to a small chamber. She called for water to be heated to wash every inch of the poor woman. She fed her, found a clean shift and put her to bed.

Mishnah had slept fitfully for two days, waking only for more food, and Edvard had checked on her constantly. Opening the door late one night, Piers had been surprised to find him sitting beside her, stroking her hand and talking quietly. Her eyes were closed, and her face was peaceful, but Piers did not think she was asleep. She had been given no kindness such as this for a long time.

On the third day, Piers had found her awake and found himself being regarded by a pair of beautiful green eyes.

'You must be Irish originally with eyes such as those Mishnah. I know a beautiful blonde Saxon lady called Merewyn de Malvais who has eyes like that. Her mother was the daughter of an Irish king.'

She had given him a weak smile. 'Thank you for coming back to find me; Isabella was right, you are a very handsome man.'

Chatillon had smiled. 'She asked that we find you. I'm sure you have been through hell for the last year, and you will have dark memories and deep scars from that time, but I promise they will fade in time, and you will be safe with us. In a few days, when you have recovered your strength, we will need to leave. I'm taking you home with us.'

Her eyes had lit up. 'To the Chateau? I believe it is surrounded by beautiful green woodland with a river. I have heard so much about it, but will Isabella be there?'

Chatillon had shaken his head, and she'd seen the sadness in his eyes. 'Not at first, for like you, she needs time to recover, and then she will return home to us.'

'She was magnificent! Like a female warrior in old tales. I watched with awe how she handled her captivity and manipulated him. It was like an act, as if the real Isabella was standing to one side watching him with disdain.'

Chatillon had raised her hand to his lips. 'I taught her to do that, but I'm sure she could never have got Coralie away from his clutches without your help, Mishnah, and you paid for that. Now it is our turn to repay you.'

Mishnah was still not well enough to ride alone, so Edvard had rigged a saddle using thick rolled blankets, for her to ride behind him. Usually taciturn with people he did not know, As they travelled north, Edvard had kept up a steady stream of conversation, describing the Chateau and all the people who lived or worked there—much to Chatillon's surprise and delight. When they finally rode through the gates of the Chateau, Mishnah felt as if she knew it inside out.

As usual, everyone came out to greet them, and Chatillon introduced Mishnah as the person who had given Isabella hope during her captivity. Mishnah had improved but was still fragile, and Edvard put her in Ahmed's hands, promising to visit her later. Ahmed had smiled despite being crestfallen; he had scanned the riders as they rode into the large courtyard.

CHAPTER SEVEN

There was one person he'd hoped to see, but she was not there. However, he knew that Gabriel would come and find him, and tell him everything that had happened in Genoa, and why Isabella was not with them.

Even though Isabella had not returned, it was a festive and joyful meal that night. Finian was very excited at the foals born from Morvan's stallion. Every mare he had been presented with had foaled, and they now had half a dozen promising youngsters. Hearing the pride and enthusiasm in Finian's voice, Chatillon promised to come to the paddocks the next morning but then turned his attention to Finian's wife.

'Dion, I have a very important task for you, and I need you to begin tomorrow if you will. I wish you to turn Conn into an archer as good as any of your men.' Georgio looked up from his trencher in surprise, as this was the first he'd heard of this, and he raised a questioning eyebrow at Conn, who just shrugged it off.

Dion looked at Conn. 'Can you even fire a bow?' she asked, with a grin.

'A little, perhaps. I can hit a target most times, but it has never held much interest for me; too slow. I like more instant results with the feel of a sword, or staff, in my hands.'

Dion gave a mock gasp of outrage. 'Slow? I could put an arrow in your throat while you still drew your sword. You do know you are falling for a Barbarian, Marietta,' she declared.

Marietta blushed; she had been delighted to see Conn arriving with the party that rode in, but was horrified that Dion would mention it. However, Conn just grinned at them both.

The next morning, Conn, with Georgio tagging along

behind as usual, went to the meadow where Dion waited with six of her archers. They had fled England with her after the battle of Rochester, as they would have lost their lives for taking part in the rebellion against William Rufus. Chatillon now paid them a retainer, as part of the large armed force he kept at the Chateau.

In only a short time, Conn was forced to eat his words. Dion had set up a target, and he could not believe the speed and accuracy of the archers as he watched open-mouthed. He was still nocking his arrow while the man beside him had already loosed six, and embedded them all in the plank leaning on the fence. Further to his embarrassment, he found that a grinning Georgio was better at it than he was; there was much laughter as Conn's arrows landed in the trees and bushes behind the wooden plank.

He spent two hours every day for a week, developing blisters on his fingers while his forearms ached as he used different muscles to draw the powerful hunting bows. Eventually, Dion took pity on him and gave him an archer's thin leather glove and forearm guard. By the end of the first week, he was hitting the plank every time, so Dion moved it further away.

Chatillon stood watching with Finian. He was pleased with Conn's progress, but Finian was curious about this sudden training for the young Horse Warrior.

'Dare I ask what you have in mind for him?' he asked Piers, watching his wife beat every one of her men in speed and accuracy.

'I have been offered a significant assignment which I may agree to take, depending on certain conditions, and which I will confirm in Paris next week. The reward for my success in this assignment will be a charter, signed by the head of the

CHAPTER SEVEN

Ibn Hud dynasty, to bring the blood feud to an end.'

It was quiet for some time, with only the twang of oiled bowstrings and the thud of arrows into the wood as Finian mulled this information over.

'How dangerous is this assignment? I presume it will mean killing someone of import?' he asked, in a low voice.

Chatillon could hear the note of concern in his friend's voice.

'Don't worry, Finian, for I will have everything planned as usual, and no blame will attach to any of us.'

'Dare I ask who you will kill if only you and Conn are involved?' he whispered.

This time it was Chatillon's turn to pause, but he trusted this man implicitly, and their friendship was almost back to what it had been, before Finian's cousin's attack on the Chateau.

'At this moment in time, only three people know of the target; I'm not even going to tell Conn who it is until we take ship.'

'Three? So that is obviously you, Edvard, and the person paying for this. He must be very influential in bringing Abu Ja'far to the table to sign this charter. I would guess that it is either Henry Beauclerc or Ranulf Flambard, and they want you to kill Duke Robert so that he can't regain Normandy.'

Chatillon laughed. 'Very good, Finian. I have taught you well, and you are almost close to the truth.'

'Surely you can't kill Robert. You have spent twenty years moulding him into the ally and pawn of the Holy See, and I know he's also your friend,' he blurted.

'Do not fear. It isn't Duke Robert whom Henry Beauclerc wants me to kill; it is his other brother, the King of England himself, William Rufus.'

Finian's face registered his shock at the audacity of such an assassination.

'The King? You cannot possibly be planning to kill the King of England,' he whispered, in a shocked voice.

'William Rufus is a divisive figure, as you know. He has scant regard for the Church and often disregards, or actively works against, the Holy See's orders, requests and criticisms. He is abetted and aided by his morally corrupt creature, Ranulf Flambard, who has now been created Prince Bishop of Durham. Yet he still manages to squeeze rich and poor alike for their every last groat.'

Finian frowned, for he was still nonplussed.

'Even if you manage to kill him undetected, Piers, what can Henry Beauclerc possibly gain from this death? Is it not Duke Robert who is King William's heir, and rightfully so? That was agreed, signed and sealed in Rouen before the Norman and English lords, and you witnessed the document for the Pope. I was there with you.'

'I leave Henry to make his moves once the King dies; I will have little involvement on purpose. Not a whisper of blame must attach to the Holy See. Henry will seize the throne once William Rufus dies; he must do this before Duke Robert returns from the Crusades. Robert now has a young wife who may already be carrying his child, which, as you know, would be the heir to the Norman and English thrones.'

Finian nodded in understanding. 'So he has to act immediately. When are you planning this for?'

'We need to be in England in July. I have business to conduct in the English court for Pope Paschal, that gives me a reason to be there.'

'Have care, Piers. This is a dangerous undertaking, and if

anything goes wrong, then you and Conn could be languishing in prison for a long time, or dangling on the end of a rope. The English seem to be uncommonly fond of hanging, and I have been there with the rope around my neck in Rochester, before I was rescued at the last moment. It is not an experience you would relish.'

Piers just smiled, slapped his friend on his shoulder in reassurance and left him to his thoughts.

However, Finian was still unsettled by the revelations as he peeled off his tunic and prepared for bed. Dion, her head propped up on one arm, could see that he was preoccupied.

'What is it, my love?' she asked, as he untied his braies, kicked them away and stood naked by the open shutters to breathe in the night air, which now carried the scent of early blossom. It was one of those warm spring evenings, and her eyes travelled hungrily over his muscled frame in the candlelight.

Eventually, he turned and gazed down at her. 'Nothing that will not keep,' he said, throwing back the cover and dropping his lips to hers as he climbed to sit astride her.

She ran her hands up his powerful thighs and then clasped his manhood, making him gasp and laugh.

'The one thing I have always enjoyed about our lovemaking, Dion, is that from the very first time, you were not shy in taking what you wanted,' he said, his breathing becoming ragged as her hand began to move. His hands stroked her breasts and squeezed her nipples before his mouth descended on them.

Her hands moved to caress his shoulders, and she gripped his hair. 'I want you deep inside me, Finian; for some reason, I have thought of nothing but you doing this to me all afternoon.'

He laughed and, spreading her legs, fulfilled her request. Moving his hands under her buttocks to lift them, he drove deep inside her, making it her turn to gasp and cry out with pleasure. Afterwards, they lay entwined on top of the cover, a light sheen of sweat on their bodies. Finian gazed down at her as his fingers lightly followed her curves. He adored his feisty, clever wife and could never imagine life without her, and somehow, after his conversation with Piers, Dion seemed more precious to him than ever.

'So are you going to tell me what is troubling you? I can see it in your face,' she whispered. And so he told her of the conversation that day and the assignment Piers was considering undertaking.

'Mother of God!' she exclaimed, sitting up.'Has he lost his wits? Has all this with Ishmael driven him mad? You can't kill a king and hope to get away undetected. They will hunt him down. Will they come here? Will this assassination implicate us? They have no love for either of us after what happened at Pevensey and Rochester,' she demanded, her concern for her family resulting in a shrillness and panic in her voice.

'No, Dion! They will not, I swear. Piers de Chatillon is a French lord in his own right. They can't touch him here in France, I promise you,' he said, pulling her close into his arms. He pulled the cover over them and whispered reassurances to her, but it was a long time until sleep came for either of them as they thought of the implications of this act.

The next morning, after putting some of his horses through their paces, Finian searched for Edvard, whom he found, as usual, helping Mishnah in the kitchen garden as they had become firm friends. Mishnah had gravitated to Ahmed as he'd looked after her so well, and treated her for various ailments she had picked up during her time in the whorehouse. Now she helped the Arab doctor to prepare simples and concoctions for the many villagers who came to the gates seeking help.

Finian stood with the plump, red-faced Madame Chambord, who was there to get some air after the hot fires of the kitchens, and to collect fresh herbs for dinner. Watching Edvard and Mishnah together, she smiled As Ahmed came to stand with them, she congratulated him for the care he had given. He inclined his head in acceptance.

'She also looks much better due to your plentiful and delicious food, but her sleep at night is often disturbed and troubled. I have given her a sleeping draught to take each evening. Only time will heal both the physical and the invisible scars,' he said.

'They seem to be healing each other, for Edvard isn't completely recovered,' she said, gesturing at the laughing pair with a knowing smile. That made Finian laugh aloud, and Edvard straightened, shading his eyes to see who was there.

'Can I have a moment of your time, Edvard?' asked Finian. The big man bid farewell to Mishnah reluctantly, handing back her trug basket, while Finian waved him to follow him to the paddocks, out of earshot of anyone. Once there, Finian shared his concerns about this assassination.

'Is this definite, Edvard? I know he plans to go to Paris next week, ostensibly to meet with King Philip on Papal business, but now I realise there's no doubt that he will meet with Henry Beauclerc as well, to accept and finalise this assassination.'

'Finian, you have known Piers De Chatillon as long as I have. He does not take unnecessary risks. If accepting Henry's proposal helps him bring Isabella back, I can't see him refusing to do it. However, Conn is to be part of this; although I know the plan is incomplete, we're waiting for other pieces to fall into place. Both you and I know the time and effort he put into finding and saving Conn's life; he would never risk it again,' declared Edvard.

Finian stared thoughtfully at Edvard's calm face for a while.

'You are right, I suppose. I just don't like him taking unnecessary risks after all we have been through together over the past few years.'

Edvard put an arm around his friend's shoulders. 'Ever since we met this man, we have spent our lives on a knife edge at his side; it is how he operates and lives, and I can't see it changing.'

Finian laughed. 'You are right; I seem to have become a worrier, God forbid. I will pray, however, and do everything I can to ensure that that knife edge does not end up cutting us all. We have watched, assisted or carried out dozens, if not a hundred assassinations, with or for him, but this is different; killing a king is not something we should ever accept with equanimity, Edvard.'

'You may be right, but you know Chatillon as well as I. Once he has made his mind up to accept, it will make no difference who it is; it will just be another throat to slit, another body to lower to the ground before walking away to disappear into the night.'

Chapter Eight

June 1100 – Paris

Conn and Georgio hadn't made it to the French court on their last visit, but now they were arriving in the Ile de Cité and were both impressed by the size and splendour of King Philip's palace, on the island in the middle of the Seine. King Philip had always enjoyed his luxury, and he'd brought the best craftsmen to Paris during his reign. The result was marble-floored halls and pillars, and every wall hung with a rich tapestry that created corridors of colour, as they walked towards the audience chambers.

As usual, the King was holding court, and Piers suddenly felt the loss of his friend Gervais, who had always briefed him first on the King's current thoughts and inclinations. His informers told him that King Philip had not yet appointed a new Seneschal to replace Gervais, although he had a few candidates in mind. It was a post of high importance, politically and socially, giving the incumbent significant power, so it would not be awarded lightly. However, Chatillon thought he knew what King Philip was about. His son Louis, the Dauphin, had disappeared from court after Philip had repudiated his mother, Queen Bertha, in 1092. The young

Louis had fled to his mother's court and had only recently been persuaded back to Paris, despite the King still openly living with his mistress, Bertrade. Having finally improved relations with his heir, King Philip decided to give Louis many of the responsibilities that had belonged to Gervais, as Seneschal.

The chamber was packed when Chatillon, in his usual striking black velvet, gold embossed papal tunic, strode in accompanied by two tall Horse Warriors, dressed in their signature laced leather doublets with crossed swords on their backs. A buzz of conversation broke out, mainly among the ladies, many of whom were Chatillon's conquests. But now he had arrived with two exceptionally handsome warriors in his train, one of whom looked very familiar.

King Philip smiled; Chatillon always liked to make an entrance, and the Papal Envoy always relieved the tedious boredom he felt at these events. His son Louis however, standing behind his father, narrowed his eyes in surprise at the effrontery of the Papal Envoy, to bring armed men into the King's presence without permission.

Chatillon stopped before the King and bowed before waving a hand at Conn.

'Sire, may I present Lord Conn Fitz Malvais.' This again caused a buzz of interest as everyone knew the Malvais name. Louis heard his father's sharp intake of breath and looked down at his father in surprise. Who was this Horse Warrior to shock his father, he wondered.

King Philip leaned forward in his chair and openly stared at Conn, who stood unperturbed, as he had been forewarned about the often blatant curiosity of the French King. Finally, Philip sat back and laughed.

'Touché Chatillon, we will speak later on this. You are welcome to my court, Conn Fitz Malvais, as I greatly admire your father, Luc de Malvais, whom I have fought against several times and rarely ever defeated.'

The King's younger brother, Hugh de Vermandois, stepped forward and slapped Conn on the shoulder in welcome.

'I must say you are the image of your father, and I will freely admit that he always terrified me in battle.' Laughter and applause broke out in the chamber at the duke's words.

'And this young man?' continued the King, waving a hand at their companion.

'This is Georgio de Milan, another knight, and both are Reconquista Warriors who have recently returned from fighting in Spain against the Berber forces. They rode alongside El Cid,' he announced to the chamber.

Again a buzz of acclamation broke out with rapturous applause for the two young men. Conn took it in his stride and bowed to the packed room while Georgio stood wide-eyed, not used to such attention for his exploits.

Chatillon stayed for a short time to arrange an audience with the King, while Conn and Georgio were surrounded by the ladies and young bucks of the court who wanted to know more.

Prince Louis watched in envy; he would have given anything to have ridden off to war in Spain. Instead, he had to satisfy himself by defending the borders of the French Vexin, although he had firm plans to take back all of that province from Norman rule.

Louis watched Chatillon and his father with interest; he knew they had been friends since their younger days. He also knew they had worked together to help Duke Robert

Curthose defeat his father, King William. The more he learnt about Piers De Chatillon, the more wary he was, but the more he wanted to know. Undoubtedly, the man was a consummate diplomat and arch-manipulator. However, Louis decided that this was a man he could learn from, and he intended to be in the private audience arranged with his father, as Gervais had usually been. For now, however, he would go and introduce himself to these Horse Warriors and arrange to take them hunting the next day.

Chatillon finally managed to extract the two young men, and they returned to his house by the river, as he had messages to send to the Pope, and to Henry Beauclerc, to inform him that he had arrived in Paris. To his surprise, his Steward awaited him on the steps outside, as they rode into the courtyard.

'Sire, you have a visitor. I have placed him in the garden. I believe it to be Count Henry of Normandy.' Chatillon raised an eyebrow at this news; so Henry was here and obviously impatient, but it was not a wise move, on his part, to be seen coming here to meet with the Papal Envoy privately.

'Come with me, Conn, and I will introduce you to Henry Beauclerc, who is, of course, your uncle, but let us not share that information with him.' he said, with a sardonic smile.

Henry did not look like either of his brothers; he was taller, and took after his mother, with fair hair to his collar and a handsome aesthetic face. He greeted them affably and was immediately taken with Conn, recalling his time spent with Morvan de Malvais and the Horse Warriors, in Caen, as a young man. Chatillon encouraged Conn and Georgio to leave as the two men had business to discuss in private, but not before Henry had promised to go hunting with them.

CHAPTER EIGHT

'Have I met him before, Chatillon? Those blue eyes look familiar, although he's very like his father, Luc.'

'No, Sire, he has recently come to the courts of Europe, but has spent many years fighting the Moors in Spain,' answered Chatillon, calling for some wine as they sat under the trees in the shade, well away from prying eyes or ears.

Henry opened a leather pouch and pulled out a vellum document. Unfolding it, he handed it to Piers, who perused its brief contents. It was a clear charter for the blood feud of the Ibn Hud dynasty to cease forthwith against Piers De Chatillon, his family and compatriots. Of significance on the left was the signature and royal seal of King Alphonse of Leon and Castile. This was the document that Pope Paschal had spoken of, and to the right was his sweeping signature and papal stamp. Beneath this, it was witnessed by Count Henry, Lord of Domfront. There was one space left for the head of the Ibn Hud dynasty to sign.

Chatillon raised his eyes to Henry.

'You have gone to a great deal of trouble on my behalf, Sire. Are you certain that Abu Ja'far will sign and honour this document?'

'I assure you he will, as too much is at stake for their family Taifa. Also, I do not have a heart of stone, Chatillon, and I know what you have suffered over the past few years. Who would not want revenge for what was done to you and your family? But I also need reparation for what my brothers have done to me. Robert betrayed me, taking the silver of my inheritance, giving me land in return but then taking it back again, so I lost everything. At the same time, William Rufus and Flambard ensured that I was cut out of the inheritance of both Normandy and England. They have left me with no choice, Piers.'

Chatillon pursed his lips and regarded Henry solemnly for some time before taking a mouthful of wine.

'Two things, Henry. Understand that if I agree to this assassination, then I will have ensured that no blame, or the slightest sniff of evidence leads to me or mine; however, the first sign of treachery from you and I swear I will have planted a trail to your door for the King's death. Let us not beat around the bush here, Henry—this is murder, pure and simple. You are advocating the murder of your brother,' he said, starkly, while watching Henry's face, which showed no emotion, not a hint of fear or uncertainty.

'I swear, Chatillon, on my sainted mother's soul, I will be true to this and to you.'

Again, Chatillon paused, as this was not a matter to be dealt with lightly, before continuing....

'The second is that in no way would I ever consider harming Robert. Leave him be, Henry; he has a new wife and possible legitimate heir on the way. Let him have and keep Normandy, for he fought long and hard for it.'

'I can swear to do that, Chatillon, but only for as long as he leaves me be, as well.'

Piers had no choice but to accept that and inclined his head in acceptance.

'I presume that you have prepared the ground and built considerable allies in England, and Normandy, who will support your claim and possible seizure of the crown.'

Henry nodded. 'I have spent years doing that, Chatillon; I have invested a considerable amount of time there recently. I made sure I was at the King's side at the inauguration of the new hall at the Palace of Westminster, and I must say it

CHAPTER EIGHT

is an impressive edifice. But I have questions. What of the Holy See? Where does Pope Paschal sit on this issue? I hear he does not have your uncle's razor-sharp mind and political acumen; I believe he's a gentler soul. Is he condoning this assassination?'

Chatillon narrowed his eyes. He was never ready to accept any criticism of the Pope he was serving unless it was well deserved, and it was early days for Paschal.

'No, he is not another Pope Urban, but he is clever and astute, and more importantly, he has me at his side, Henry, and I assure you that I will always protect the Pope and the Holy See against anyone I see as a threat.' At that point, he leaned forward, and his hard, unflinching gaze locked onto Henry's eyes. The Count lowered his eyes immediately as Chatillon sat back and continued.

'Paschal knows of our conversations, and like any Pope, he will look the other way and deny any knowledge of it, but in return for allowing me to assist you, he will expect you to support the Holy See when it comes to the Church in England. All vacant posts of Archbishop and bishops are to be resolved immediately. Flambard has been filling the King's coffers for years with the revenues from those vacant posts.'

'I swear, Chatillon, that I will take heed of these requests, and Flambard will be held accountable for robbing my country's Church and people!' exclaimed Henry forcefully.

Chatillon smiled at how Henry was already calling England his country, even though William Rufus was still on his throne in London; he seemed very sure of himself and that Chatillon would accept this assignment. He leaned forward again, his face close to that of Henry Beauclerc, and in a low whisper said, 'I will agree to plan the assassination, Henry, in exchange for this document, which I want to be signed and sealed as soon as possible. I intend to leave for England in a week or two, but I suggest you leave in the next few days, as I need you established in the English court well before the event to allay any suspicions.'

Henry nodded. 'Do you already know where and when it will happen?' he asked, with an eagerness for his brother's death that was quite chilling.

'Only when I have finalised all the arrangements will I tell you what you need to know and what part you will play. This may not be until I have been in England for several days; I will perforce keep my distance from you, Henry. It was foolish of you to come here to my house so openly. I suggest you develop a friendship with Conn Fitz Malvais over the next day or so before you leave, as he is crucial to my plan in England, and it will not seem unusual for you to seek out his company there. Also, be sure to make the acquaintance of Walter Tirel if you have not already done so. Now I bid you farewell.'

Henry stood, the uncertainty crossing his face at being so summarily dismissed, but he realised the Papal Envoy was right; he should not have come here.

The next morning, Conn and Georgio joined a hunting party of twenty to hunt in the forests to the southwest, led by Prince Louis and Henry Beauclerc. Chatillon meanwhile sent off a short coded message to Pope Paschal telling him that the business had prospered and he was leaving for England shortly. Not a whisper of what was planned would ever be written down or shared outside of the tight circle he had created.

The hunters came back triumphant with several deer and a huge boar. They called at Chatillon's house to partake of refreshments and bid farewell to Conn and Georgio. Chatillon was pleased to see the banter between the young men, and Henry, as good as his word, was loudly congratulating Conn on his prowess with a bow.

Later that afternoon, Chatillon made his way to the palace for his private audience with the King. Philip greeted him as affectionately as ever, waving him to a chair.

'So, Chatillon, Duke Robert, the conquering hero, returns in triumph from Jerusalem. Will he receive a good reception in Normandy, do we think? he asked.

'Flambard must no doubt be furious that Robert has married an exceptionally wealthy heiress; his Vifgage with William Rufus will be paid off. I assure you that we will arrange an assembly of Norman nobles and Archbishops that will leave Flambard, and William Rufus, in no doubt where Pope Paschal stands on this,' answered Chatillon.

King Philip smiled. 'I admit I will feel happier with Duke Robert back in Normandy; he tends to respect the borders we have established due to our past alliances. As will Prince Louis,' he said, waving his hand over to the window behind them.

Chatillon steeled himself not to turn and look to where the Dauphin was sitting; he was just relieved that he had not shared anything indiscreet or for the King's ears only. He purposefully crossed his booted legs and took a slow sip of wine.

'I must admit that it feels strange, Sire, to come here without Gervais stalking the corridors and keeping everyone under control; you must miss him too as a friend and advisor.'

King Philip nodded. 'His knowledge and experience of France, the court, and the politics of Europe, were second to hardly any, except yours. But Louis is learning at my side and will help me to choose his replacement.'

Chatillon glanced back at the Dauphin for the first time and inclined his head in recognition, while the King continued.

'So, Chatillon, tell me of the Horse Warrior, Conn Fitz Malvais. Is he the child we had so much speculation about? Was he the child the Warrior Monks stole as part of Pope Dauferio's devious plans?'

Chatillon narrowed his eyes in annoyance at King Philip for mentioning any of this in front of the Dauphin.

'Yes, Conn was kidnapped along with several other young boys. They tried to blackmail his father, Luc De Malvais, but that was madness, and Conn was rescued. Now Conn is developing into a powerful warrior like his father, who has asked me to take him to the courts of Europe to rub off a few of his rough edges. As you know, I was there when we rescued him, and I have always had a bond with him. Moreover, my ward Marietta has fallen in love with him.'

King Philip laughed. 'Another wealthy heiress snapped up; the court bucks will be devastated. But what of his mother? Were the rumours true of a link to King William's family?'

'Most decidedly not, Sire. Conn's mother is a local blue-eyed Breton beauty who was given a house on the edges of the Malvais lands. It took a long time for Merewyn to forgive Luc for straying.'

Philip rested his chin on his hand and looked thoughtful, and Chatillon could see that he was not totally convinced; however, to his relief, the King murmured, 'He is the image of his father, I must admit.'

Chatillon nodded and thanked God for the strong Malvais bloodline.

CHAPTER EIGHT

'So, we've agreed, Sire, that we will support Duke Robert on his return,' stated Chatillon.

King Philip inclined his head but then sat forward and lowered his voice.

'Chatillon, my friend, I have two issues you may be able to assist me with. First of all, surely it is time for the new Pope to lift the order of excommunication from my head that your uncle, Pope Urban, placed there.'

Chatillon shook his head.

'Philip, you have always been a great defender of the faith and the Church, but you will be the first to admit that your love for Bertrade de Montrade made you fall by the wayside. You kept her as your mistress openly while still married to Queen Bertha. After Bertha's sudden death, you married Bertrade, but she's still married to Fulk of Anjou; there has been no divorce or dissolution of that marriage by the Holy See. In the eyes of the Church and the rest of Europe, you are a bigamist. Paschal can't possibly lift that excommunication while you flaunt your mistress as your wife and call her Queen.'

King Philip's head dropped to his chest as he sighed, 'I can't give her up, Piers. Bertrade is my life and has borne me children!'

Chatillon did not reply but lifted his hands in exasperation and let them drop.

'And the second, Sire?'

'My brother Hugh, although his spirits appear good, has been shamed that he did not fulfil his vow to reach Jerusalem. My brother isn't a coward, Chatillon. He's a brave man who was brought low by disease in the Holy Land. Like several others, he had no choice but to return. Now, however, Pope

Paschal is threatening to excommunicate him as well, if he does not take his place on the next crusade. I feel as if the Holy See is persecuting others in my family, Chatillon, because of me.'

Piers shook his head in denial.

'Sire, there are a dozen, such as Stephen of Blois, whom the Pope has threatened unless they complete their sacred vow. I assure you this isn't personal in any way. Pope Paschal still values your support.'

The King did not look convinced, so Chatillon took his leave moments later, and Prince Louis came to sit by his dejected father.

'I thought that there may have been something of more import in this meeting than all that,' he announced, with a slight sneer.

King Philip laughed. 'You will learn in time, Louis, that those conversations were highly significant. Although Conn Fitz Malvais is the son of Luc, I think I know who his birth mother was but have no way of proving it, and now she is dead. I assure you that Piers de Chatillon knows, and somehow had a hand in it. If I'm right, then Lord Conn Fitz Malvais could indeed prove to be a very dangerous man.'

To the Prince's frustration, the King refused to say anything further as it was not a rumour he wanted to get out. Better to sit on what he thought he knew and find a way to use it in the future. However, the Dauphin's curiosity was ignited, and he determined to discover more about the matter.

A week later, Chatillon and the young warriors were back at the Chateau, and Conn had renewed his morning rides with Marietta. She had enjoyed her sojourn in the French court and had flirted outrageously with the young French nobles, but even that, and Conn's long absence, had done little to mitigate her feelings for the handsome Horse Warrior. They stopped in a wide glade near the river, and letting their horses graze, sat for a while amongst the early summer meadow flowers as Conn recounted his impression of King Philip and the Dauphin; he made Marietta laugh with his impersonation of the King.

Suddenly, conversation dried as he gazed into her expressive grey eyes, and before he could help himself, his hand had reached up and stroked her face, gently following the line of her jaw, and then his fingers lightly trailed down to her rounded breast. His hand moved down under her gown and lightly stroked her thigh.

Marietta stayed still, but her breathing became faster, and she closed her eyes to enjoy the moment. As far as she was concerned, he could have lain her down and taken her there and then, and she would not have naysayed him. Suddenly his hands held either side of her head, his lips descended on hers but gently, almost a friend's kiss rather than a lover's, and she opened her eyes again to see him rising to his feet. He held out a hand and pulled her into his arms.

'I'm sorry I shouldn't have done that; I should not make love to you, as I would be abusing Chatillon's hospitality and taking advantage of a beautiful young girl.' He led her back to her horse, while she gritted her teeth in frustration, for she wanted him to take advantage. He cupped his hands to lift her into the saddle, and his hands caressed her calf as he placed her booted foot into the stirrup.

'What if I had wanted you to make love to me, Conn? Surely that would not be so wrong, and you know that I have feelings for you.'

'I have a conscience, Marietta. I must admit it does not appear very often, but Chatillon has become my patron, and I cannot repay him by deflowering his ward.'

There was little she could say to that, and she kicked the spirited Arab mare into a canter heading back to the Chateau. Conn sighed watching her go. He had certainly been highly aroused by her and could easily have lifted her gown higher and made love to her on the grass, but he meant what he said; the only offer he should be making to Marietta was marriage, and he was not ready for that yet.

Chatillon and Edvard were strolling back from the paddocks, through the meadow to the postern gate, when Marietta went past at speed, followed several moments later by Conn. Neither had looked happy. Watching them, Chatillon shared his concerns about their relationship with Edvard, who shrugged.

'You may as well try to stop the tide coming in as stem the attraction between those two. You need to remember who Conn's parents are; Morvan and Princess Constance carried on a forbidden love affair for a year. Even though Constance was forced into a marriage with Count Alan of Brittany, she loved Morvan until the day she died. Marietta's mother, Hildebrand, gave up everything to run away with Brian Ap Gwyfd, her horse whisperer, and then she became your lover in Genoa. It is in their blood, Piers. I presume you know it is Marietta's name day this weekend. Madame Chambord is preparing a feast for her with all types of jellies, tarts and delicacies.'

Chatillon put a hand to his head. 'Of course, she is twenty-one, and I'm sad to say that my wardship will be over. I need to hand back all of her affairs.'

CHAPTER EIGHT

Edvard nodded. Part of him was also relieved as she would now employ her own factor, for Edvard had managed most of her businesses and properties—an exhausting job.

Marietta was also saddened by the end of the wardship, but she assured Piers that he would always be a father to her. She spent several hours in his business room with him and Edvard, and she was wide-eyed at what she was hearing, her head spinning.

'Marietta, you have always known you were a wealthy heiress,' exclaimed Chatillon, at her surprise.

'Yes, but I had never before realised the extent of the land, property and numerous businesses my mother had invested in.'

'I assure you that Edvard has employed a very capable Factor, in Genoa, who manages most of the mercantile side of your wealth, but I suggest you visit Genoa as soon as possible to become acquainted with him. You will also need to meet your bailiff, who runs your large estate and all of the tenancies on your land. I will send Finian, and several men, with you for protection, and I think a certain young man may want to go with you to visit his mother again.'

Marietta nodded abstractly, and he thought it was because she was somewhat overwhelmed by what she had heard. However, he soon found it was something else.

'Conn told me you will leave for England soon, and he is going with you. I know I shouldn't say this, but try not to take him into too much danger,' she pleaded.

Chatillon steepled his fingers and looked at her flushed cheeks. 'You truly love him, don't you, Marietta?'

She shyly nodded and could not meet their eyes.

'And does he reciprocate that love? I may be handing over

my wardship, but you are right—I do feel like a father to you, and if his interest is sincere, he will have to approach me for your hand.'

Again, she looked away from them for several moments before answering.

'We enjoy each other's company but have not discussed the future yet. I can't imagine being with anyone else.'

Chatillon nodded in understanding, while resolving to talk to Conn, and Edvard put a hand on her shoulder in reassurance.

'Come, I believe Gabriel has written a special song for you, so let us go down and hear it, then you can tell him that he's going with you to Genoa. I have the harder task of telling Finian he may be away from Dion and his family for several months,' he said, laughing.

Edvard held Chatillon back for a moment at the door.

'There are still several of the Sheikh's assassins out there; make it a large number of men you send with Finian, for there's no doubt that she will also be a target.'

'Do you not think I'm aware of that, Edvard? I could not live with myself if anything happened to her because of this feud,' snapped Chatillon.

'Yes, but you are so preoccupied with this new assignment, I'm reminding you of other dangers closer to home.'

Chatillon took a deep breath, put a hand on his old friend's arm, and nodded.

'We will remain vigilant, and I will reinforce this with Finian, but he knows as well as we do that they are still out there.'

Chapter Nine

July 1100 - The Chateau

Preparations were afoot in the Chateau for the two large groups leaving this week. Marietta and Gabriel, escorted by Finian and his ten men, were setting off in two days for Genoa. They would arrive at the end of July and stay there for a few months. Chatillon promised to join them there once his business was completed in England. He was determined to maintain a presence in Isabella's life; as her husband, he knew he could insist that she return, but he had no desire to do that against her will. She needed to be ready, to want to return to her home and family.

Edvard stood by the window in the business room going over any tasks that would need completing in the Papal Envoy's absence. However, Piers could see that his attention was occupied by what was happening below in the garden. Ahmed was giving Mishnah and his apprentice Raoul instructions on plant husbandry and cultivation in the apothecary's physic garden. Piers stood and came to stand beside his friend at the open window.

'Time is a great healer, Edvard; Ahmed would be the first to say that, and the memories of what she has been through will fade.'

Mishnah had cast off her Arab garb as soon as she escaped, and now she was in a fetching green gown; her long auburn hair was braided and hung down her back. At that moment, she glanced up and saw them at the window. Her face lit up, and smiling, she waved a hand.

'That was for you, not for me!' said Chatillon, laughing as Edvard coloured up. Just then, the Steward arrived clutching a leather pouch.

'This has just arrived, Sire; I have sent the messenger to the kitchens as he has ridden long and hard from Marseilles.'

Chatillon scanned the two documents and smiled before turning to Edvard.

'This is exactly what we needed, Edvard; our friend Roger Borsa, the Count of Sicily, has indeed investigated the death of Bishop Odo of Bayeux. He, apparently, also had suspicions about the Bishop's sudden death when he had appeared in good health. The physician, who attended the Bishop, has told Count Roger that he does not doubt it was poison. The second document is from Archbishop Alcherius of Palermo, who also investigated the death of such an important bishop, and friend, whilst staying in his palace. He uncovered the name of the Sicilian knight, Guido Di Messina, who arranged the poisoning. He arrested him and sent him to Roger Borsa, who imprisoned and tortured him until the knight admitted he was paid a fortune in gold to kill Bishop Odo.'

'The same gold that Walter Tirel offered you to assassinate Odo,' suggested Edvard.

Chatillon agreed. 'Di Messina gave up Tirel's name almost immediately. Borsa is having him publicly beheaded, drawn and quartered this week. He has seized the knight's land and

CHAPTER NINE

gold and now says he is once again in our debt.'

'That can only be a good thing with a man as powerful as Roger Borsa,' said Edvard, who still watched Mishnah from the window. Chatillon shook his head in amusement.

'Go down and help them. I have the plan's final details to draw together; now that this has arrived, it will pull the last pawns into place on the board.'

Edvard stopped at the door. 'One thing that occurred to me, Piers; have you asked Conn how he feels about helping to murder his uncle, a family member?' Edvard knew by the closed expression on Pier's face that it had not occurred to him.

'I have not even told him who the target is yet. I intend to do that on the ship to England, although, after Henry Beauclerc's visit in Paris, he may well have guessed,' conceded Chatillon.

'I suggest you broach it before you leave, or you might find he refuses when you get to London, and you will have lost a key player. I would also explain to him your justification for an assassination such as this. I know you never would usually think of doing that, but if you are developing Conn into your apprentice, I think you should.' So saying, he left Piers staring at the papers on his table, deep in thought.

Two days later, the party leaving for Genoa mounted up outside the Chateau. Conn, who had continued his rides with Marietta despite their slight tiff, helped her to mount, and held her hand far longer than necessary. She leant down to whisper to him.

'Be careful, Conn, for I know that what you're doing with Piers will be dangerous. Make sure you return to me, for I promise I'll wait for you as long as you wish.'

Conn raised her hand to his lips and, never one to allow

his feelings near the surface, replied, 'I'll do my best, my lady, but I truly expect you to be snatched by some rich lord or merchant in Embriaco's court in Genoa.' She slapped his hand away in frustration at him.

Meanwhile, Chatillon gave detailed instructions to Finian, while Dion stood impatiently devouring her handsome husband with her eyes. Finally, he came and pulled her tightly into his arms.

'I'll miss you, my love, but it will only be for a few months. Ensure that Cormac and Gironde go down and halter-lead the new foals daily, so they are used to being handled.'

She nodded, wrapped her arms around him, and ran her hands up his back.

'I love you, Finian Ui Neill. Don't take any stupid risks. I am with child again, and I hope it will be the daughter you hope for,' she whispered.

He gave a joyful laugh and hugged her tight. 'Possibly a Yuletide baby again; take care of yourself and our little colleen, my love. We will call her Finula, and I promise I'll be back well before Yuletide, probably at all hallows. I promise you, Dion,' he shouted, as he mounted his Destrier at the front of his men, and led the cavalcade out of the courtyard and through the gates. Dion stood for a long time, tears streaming unashamedly down her cheeks, staring after him until everyone except Ahmed returned inside. He put his arm around her shoulders and led her back inside.

The next day, Piers watched Conn training with Dion and her men. They were now working with moving targets, and one brave soul was cantering by while holding a long wooden Norman shield with a target painted on it. Dion and her men hit the target every time, while even Conn managed to hit the shield rather than the man or the horse, which was reassuring. Chatillon called him over when he had finished.

'You've come on a great deal as a bowman; let us walk and talk as I need to discuss what we will do in England.'

They walked down to the river, and once Conn was facing him, Chatillon began.

'I think it is only fair that I tell you, with some reluctance and still a few misgivings, that I have accepted this assignment, and the target is someone of significant importance.'

Conn slowly nodded. 'I had surmised that it might be Duke Robert, Flambard or even William Rufus and narrowed it down to the latter two, as we are going to England.'

'One of those two is your uncle, a blood relative. Do you feel any qualms about helping me with this?' he asked, searching Conn's face for a reaction.

Conn shook his head. 'I reasoned that it would not be Robert as he's also your friend, and is still returning from Italy. As for Flambard and the King, I have met neither but have heard no good of either of them. They will be no loss.'

Chatillon smiled at Conn's cold assessment.

'If it is any consolation, although the King will die, it will hopefully not be your arrow that kills him. You are almost like a decoy, but someone who will aim for the target if our assassin misses.'

Chatillon was pleased to see that Conn accepted that without a flicker of emotion, despite the family connection.

'Can I share any of this with Georgio? We rarely have secrets from one another,' he asked.

'The simple answer is no. I only ever share the details of an assignment with two other people, Edvard and Isabella. Doing that has kept me alive and all of us safe. I'm only taking you into my confidence as you have expressed a desire for me to involve you in this type of work; don't make me regret it. Does Georgio know anything of your interest or involvement?'

'No, it was not something I wanted to share, yet Marietta guessed,' admitted Conn.

'So you are already keeping secrets from Georgio, and most of the time, you are a closed book to people, which I like. Marietta is astute, and she's aware of my profession and what I am paid to do. However, I have to ask, do you have any intentions towards Marietta, or is she just a harmless flirtation to while away the time?'

Conn stared into the river for several moments before answering.

'I care for Marietta; it is certainly more than a flirtation. I have deep feelings for her at times that I do not understand. I have not been in love yet, but this doesn't feel like the emotion the songs, poets and skalds sing and speak of. I get a warmth when I look at her, and when I'm here, I want to be with her. But honestly, she does not fill my every waking thought. As you realise, Chatillon, I'm ambitious. I long for the excitement that we had in Spain, but I want more than that. My father, Morvan, has given me a small estate, but that isn't enough, so I have to make my way in the world and make my own luck and fortune. With all of that, I do not feel that I'm ready for more serious entanglements yet, although if I were looking for a wife in a few years, she would be the woman I would choose. She is sweet and loving but independent and feisty. I know she has fallen in love with me, but I have tried not to encourage her, for she will no doubt find someone else in Genoa, and I'll be away making my fortune.'

CHAPTER NINE

Chatillon's spirits dipped slightly as he knew how much those words would hurt Marietta. However, he liked Conn's honesty, and he agreed with him. The young warrior was only twenty-two years of age, with time ahead of him for commitments to a wife and family, which often complicated matters.

'You are right; Marietta is in love with you, and now she can't see past that to look at any other man. She will no doubt be willing to wait for you, but she is of marriageable age and has a host of suitors, many of whom are attracted by her wealth; but she's astute enough to discourage those, or if she doesn't, then I do. Just don't expect her to wait too long. I know that you and Georgio have decided to become sellswords, and I have no doubt your services will be required all over Europe. While you do that, I will call you back or send assignments your way.'

Conn inclined his head in understanding, but suddenly felt a sadness he had never experienced before at the thought of letting her go, to let another man take her, marry her, bed her. The images he brought up in his mind triggered a wave of anger. Still, he knew Chatillon was right; it was less cruel to let her go now and find love with another man.

They turned and walked back to the Chateau, entering through the postern gate, but as they separated to go their different ways, Chatillon held up a hand.

'We leave in two days; you must tell Georgio tonight that he is not coming to England and is needed here to guard Gironde and the family.'

Conn sighed. This was not a conversation he was looking forward to, but it was on his shoulders as he had chosen a pathway that Georgio could not take. He knew his friend would be devastated.

Chapter Ten

Early July 1100 - Monastere de St Benoit

Meddur spent every morning with the archivists in the Scriptorium. Four monks were silently working on various manuscripts in the large room. Some were copying full books or treatises for other houses of God, and some were working on the detailed, colourful, illuminated letters and borders of Bibles, Gospels and Psalters. The tables of the latter monks had been placed directly under the high windows to access the light they needed. Meddur liked to stand and watch the illustrators for a while as they brought beasts, vines and flowers to life on the pages. They were highly skilled; most used cured quills for their letters and script or to outline, but the illustrators also had a range of small delicate brushes to colour their designs. Although he was there with them every morning and had been for months, he was still not accepted, and he still saw the nervous glances they gave him and his frightening, scarred face and body.

Each week the anger and frustration grew inside him at the scars and injuries he carried and endured. He was still in pain every single day, but he was purposefully trying to wean himself off the opioids that Friar Francis administered each night and morning. He had been a handsome, strong, fit man, someone women desired; he knew that now they would turn their faces away as he approached. He was like a monster or walking ghoul from the old stories, and he dared not look anywhere, in water or on a pewter plate, to see his reflection. He could already see the horror and, worst of all, the pity on other people's faces.

By the beginning of July, he realised he had to start putting his plans into action, as it was approaching the time when he would have to leave the monastery. He visited Friar Francis and asked him if a letter could be sent to Abu Ja'far, the head of the Ibn Hud family in Zaragoza.

'I want them to let my wife and children in Zaragoza know that I'm alive and did not die in the conflagration at Cabrera when the ship went down, as they no doubt have been told.'

Friar Francis looked at him in surprise, as Meddur had never mentioned family before in any of their conversations, and he agreed immediately to send for Brother Tomas, who would bring him the materials he needed and arrange to have the letter sent.

An hour later, Meddur sat with an empty vellum sheet before him. He closed his eyes briefly and thanked God that his right hand had been only lightly scarred on the palms, as he had tried to beat out the flames. He made slow progress at first as he had never used a sharpened goose quill to write, and it took some getting used to, as it sprayed the ink with too much pressure. Fortunately, Brother Tomas always carried a small knife to scrape the scattered drops of ink from the vellum, and showed him the best way to use the quill at an angle, with only a small amount of pressure. Meddur explained to him that in the Arab world, they used reed pens, which did not bend so much. The monk left him, and Meddur turned the vellum sheet over and began again...

Beloved Brother,

I am sure you were saddened at the news of my demise and, therefore, will be surprised to receive this missive. As you will no doubt be aware, my ship and men were attacked and overwhelmed by the Horse Warrior forces of Piers De Chatillon. Allah was no doubt looking after me when engulfed in flames, I was pushed into the sea and later rescued by fishermen.

I am now in the infirmary of St Benedict, several leagues northeast of Marseilles. I have perforce kept my identity secret. I go by the name of Meddur Al Cazar, and I send you his crested ring to prove the veracity of this letter.

I need you to send silver and a cohort of my men to bring me back to Zaragoza, where I will return to the bosom of my family to recuperate.

Your brother,
Yusuf Ibn Hud

Brother Tomas had not gone far, and now he returned and stood quietly, watching the concentration on Meddur's face as he wrote. He was always uneasy in the man's presence but could not exactly say why. They now had a name for him, but despite his traumatic injuries, there was a ruthless bitterness about the man that Brother Tomas had seen at times. He had heard him at night pacing in his room raging against fate in his Berber tongue; it unsettled the young monk.

Realising that Meddur had finished, Tomas stepped forward to sand the ink so it would not smudge when folded or rolled.

However, Meddur took the folded paper of sand from his hands and did it himself, aware that Brother Tomas knew a spattering of Arabic. Meddur folded the vellum sheet, and as Tomas went to pick it up, Meddur put out his good hand to stop him.

'I want it sealed before it goes,' he said, picking it up so Brother Tomas could lead the way to the Friar's room, where, sealing the message, he placed it inside a thin leather pouch and tied it with a thin cord to Meddur's satisfaction.

'I assure you that the Palace of Zaragoza will reward the monk who takes this to Abu Ja'far,' he announced, with a tone of certainty and arrogance that Tomas had not seen before.

Tomas stepped back in surprise at Meddur's presumption.

'It will not be a monk from here who takes this; we merely send it down to the port to find a ship to Tarragona. Hopefully, from there, they will find a merchant or pedlar travelling to Zaragoza. It may take many weeks, but the offer of a reward may help.'

Meddur said nothing, but Tomas saw the quick blaze of anger in the man's eyes, and his lips were thin and white as he clamped them shut before he turned and left. Tomas stared after him; whoever Meddur was, it was clear that he was not used to waiting for messages to be delivered. He decided to talk to Friar Francis after he had sent the message to the port with the stable boy.

Meanwhile, Meddur walked into the herb gardens and, finding a seat in the shade, tried calming his breathing. With every week that passed, he was becoming more impatient.

Fortunately, Meddur was lucky; his message was delivered in only ten days. He was working in the scriptorium when he heard the bustling sounds of an arrival. Several monks went past him, their curiosity aroused by the increasing sounds from the entrance. Brother Dominic came running back.

'Meddur, Meddur, you must come at once. The great Emir himself, of the Taifa of Zaragoza, has come to visit you.'

Meddur paled; he had not expected his brother to make this journey, and he prayed that Abu would keep his identity a secret.

He walked slowly through the stone arches and found his brother standing in the large refectory with Friar Francis and his prior. Both seemed to be overawed by his presence, his splendour and the twenty-strong armed bodyguard he had brought with him. Meddur saw the shock register on the Emir's face before he could hide it, when he saw the creature that had been his brother, Yusuf. He put his hand to his mouth and muttered an apology.

'I'm sorry, Friar, I had not realised his injuries were so disfiguring.'

Friar Francis waved Meddur forward into the light. 'It is a miracle that he's alive; a lesser man would not have survived this ordeal. His stoicism and tenacity in clinging to life astonished us all. However, we think we have now managed to eradicate all infections. He must heal and build his strength in the next few months.'

Abu Ja'far thanked him and tried to explain away his reaction, and his intervention, in coming personally.

'Meddur is not only one of our officers; he is a friend with whom we went hawking and hunting as boys. Our families have been close for many years. However, I would like to talk to him on his own if that is permitted?'

'Yes indeed, you may go into the herb garden. The brothers there are almost finished for the day, and it will be peaceful out there. Meddur, show our guest the way.'

Meddur led his brother into the shade, and they sat on his usual bench.

'I cannot imagine the hell and pain you must have endured, Yusuf,' his brother said, his eyes unwillingly drawn to the wizened claw-like left hand, with its missing fingers and strands of tortured, twisted, scarred flesh.

'You shouldn't have come here, Abu, for despite your story, they will wonder why you undertook this visit. But that can now not be helped. I am stronger each day, and I will now begin sword practice this week with some of my men that you are leaving here. I may be healing on the outside, albeit slowly, but I tell you, I burn on the inside, Abu. I burn for revenge against the men who did this, and I intend to take my daughter back,' he exclaimed, his voice rising.

Brother Tomas had come out with a trug basket, ostensibly to pick herbs in the far corner of the large kitchen garden. Instead, he was surreptitiously watching the two men, as he wanted to see how they interacted with each other. Tomas was an astute and clever young man who knew things were not as they seemed with Meddur.

Abu stared out across the garden before he answered his brother, and then he took a deep breath.

'I cannot let you continue the blood feud, Yusuf. It needs to end. It has brought nothing but pain and disaster down on your head and will disgrace our family.'

Yusuf turned and stared at his brother in astonishment.

'You cannot let me continue? It isn't your blood feud to end, Brother,' he exclaimed, in a raised voice that again attracted the attention of Brother Tomas, who moved closer and began to pick some peas.

CHAPTER TEN

Watching the monk now not far from them in the vegetable beds, Abu dropped his voice as he continued, ignoring his brother's outburst.

'Chatillon is powerful, feared and respected in equal measure across Europe. He is the friend of kings and princes and, more importantly, Pope Paschal's Senior Papal Envoy; he has been the mouthpiece of several Popes that have gone before. He has immense influence, Yusuf; you picked on the wrong man to attack. Then, to exacerbate the feud further, you kidnapped and killed his children and stole his wife to become your concubine. Did you foolishly believe that these actions would go unnoticed and unpunished in the rest of Europe? Now these powerful friends of his have turned their attention to our Taifa, to our family. Threats have been made against us, Yusuf, that could see us being wiped out by the Almoravids, when our protection from King Alphonse is removed. So yes, I forbid you to continue the feud. In a few weeks, you will return to Zaragoza, where you will rest and heal. I will arrange to bring the remaining women from your seraglios, and you will become part of our family again. Sheikh Ishmael will remain dead and buried forever.'

Abu watched as his brother stood and paced back and forth before turning, his face contorted and even more ugly with emotion as he spat, 'Chatillon! Just let me kill Chatillon, and I will take my daughter back and end the feud, I promise.'

'That would be the worst possible thing to do! Have you heard nothing of what I have just said about this man, Piers De Chatillon? You are blinded and deafened by hatred, Yusuf. You will do as I say; you will return home shortly, and we will discuss this further. Now I will stay here tonight and avail myself of the hospitality offered by Friar Francis, while I keep up the pretence of you being Meddur Al Cazar. But once we leave here, this ends, Yusuf, do you understand? All of this ends, or I promise I will have no choice but to end it.'

Yusef reluctantly nodded, shocked by the vehemence of his brother and the threat he had just made. Silence descended, but as Yusuf looked up, he caught the direct gaze of Brother Tomas. The young monk immediately turned and carried his trug basket to the kitchens, but Yusuf's eyes followed him until he was lost to sight.

Tomas dropped the basket unceremoniously in the kitchen and almost ran to find Friar Francis in the infirmary.

'Ah, Brother Tomas, at last, I need you to change this man's dressings, please,' he said with his usual calm smile while turning to leave, but the monk put a hand on his arm to stop him.

'I need to speak to you urgently!' he hissed. The Friar saw the agitation in the young monk's face and nodded.

'Change the dressings and then come to my room; healing takes priority here, as you know, Tomas. I'll see how old Josef is doing, as I fear he will never walk on that leg again.'

Tomas gave a snort of exasperation, but it was pointless ever trying to remonstrate with Friar Francis, who was rarely anything other than calm and measured, which had a beneficial effect on patients and monks alike. Finally, he found the Friar in his room and closing the door tightly behind him, he dropped into a chair opposite.

'So what is so urgent, Tomas?' Friar Francis asked, with raised eyebrows, before sitting back and regarding the young monk. Tomas had been with him for three years; he was a bright, ambitious young man with a good heart, but his one failing was impatience.

CHAPTER TEN

'I have had my doubts for some time about Meddur. I have seen the flashes of anger when he's asked to do anything, and I put this down to the arrogance of being the Captain for the Sheikh. However, I went into the garden to collect herbs and overheard snatches of the conversation between him and the Emir. My Berber is limited, but Abu Ja'far was unhappy with Meddur and ordered him to stop doing something and come home. This angered Meddur, and he shouted the name Chatillon twice. Also, Abu Ja'far did not call him Meddur; he addressed him as Yusuf.' Brother Tomas waited for a response, but Friar Francis had closed his eyes, and the young monk stared at him in frustration and anticipation.

Finally, after what seemed an eternity to Brother Tomas, the Friar opened his eyes and took a deep, slow breath before answering.

'We have a purpose here in this life, Tomas. We have been chosen to do God's work. Sometimes, that work and our choices are difficult, and then I like to think that God is testing us. We have worked for nearly nine months to save this man's life; however, I have also had my suspicions about him, and you have just confirmed them. I now know with certainty that we have just saved the life of one of the most evil men ever to sail the Mediterranean, a cold-blooded murderer of men, women and children. However, we cannot do anything about that now, and thankfully, I believe he leaves us in a few weeks to go to his brother's palace in Zaragoza.'

'So, he is indeed Sheikh Ishmael,' whispered Tomas, with a shudder. The Friar nodded.

'It is vital now, Tomas, that you do not show in any way that you know who he is. I believe that he's hiding his identity for a reason. Don't put yourself in danger, for this man would cut your throat without a backward glance. He may be badly disfigured on one side and thankful for our nursing, but I assure you the evil is still very much within him. We will bide our time until he's out of these doors, and then we will send an urgent message to Piers De Chatillon to tell him that his enemy, his nemesis, Sheikh Ishmael, is still alive and is hungry for revenge.'

Chapter Eleven

Mid-July 1100 – London

Henry Beauclerc had been in London for three weeks and was eagerly awaiting the arrival of Piers De Chatillon. He was impatient to know the plan's details and how soon it would be put into action, as time was of the essence, with his eldest brother, Duke Robert, riding ever closer to Normandy. Meanwhile, King William Rufus had greeted him warmly enough and seemed happy to have him stay for the summer. Ranulf Flambard was a different story; he treated Henry with thinly veiled contempt and was suspicious of his reasons for being back in London once again.

'I thought you would have preferred to be in Domfront in Normandy, reinforcing your fortress, yet again, as Duke Robert is returning,' he had said with a sneer.

Henry had drawn himself up to his full height. 'Who do you think you are, Flambard, to talk to a prince of the blood in such a way? You are nothing but a jumped-up clerk who has bribed and lied his way to the top of the dung heap.' He stepped even closer, and for the first time, Flambard felt a moment of alarm as Henry lowered his head to his ear.

'I swear, Flambard, that I will see my day with you, and I

promise you that day will come much sooner than you think,' he said, before straightening up and striding off towards the group of young courtiers.

Flambard stood for a while, staring after him, and then headed up the steep, narrow staircase to his room in the tower. Henry's words resonated, and he wondered for several moments if there was something he had missed. He called his servant and made arrangements to have Henry watched, as there was no doubt his words had been laden with menace. Was Henry planning to ally himself with Robert against William Rufus? he wondered. He could not settle and went off to find the King to drop a few words of caution and warning in his ear, but he found William reluctant to believe him, accusing him of overreacting.

Chatillon and his entourage were riding along the banks of the River Thames towards Thorny Island and the Palace of Westminster. He had not been here for several years and looked forward to seeing this Great Hall that William Rufus had built. Conn, who had been companionably chatting with Daniel, cantered up alongside Piers.

'I have not been to England before; it is as green as northern France?'

Chatillon smiled and replied, 'The buildings you see rising ahead of us are those of the English Court, although, like the Holy Roman Emperor, William Rufus moves his court from one place to the next. A few months ago, he was in Winchester,

CHAPTER ELEVEN

but I'm told he will be here until the early autumn, and then he will go to York. The Thames can be cold and bleak in winter when freezing fog or mists creep off the marshes and river. Even clothes in chests can become mildewed.'

Conn looked at him in surprise. 'You talk as if he will still be alive to do that, Chatillon,' he whispered, but Chatillon laughed at him.

'And so must you, Conn Fitz Malvais. We need to ensure that no finger of blame can be pointed in our direction. So we will talk to the King, his family, and his friends about plans for this and next year. It is all part of the game, Conn; I promise it will come to you naturally before long.'

'I do not doubt you have a timeline for this assassination, Chatillon, but when do you intend to share that with me? Also, I would like a clear idea of the part I have to play. At the moment, I have a vision of us galloping away to a ship before Flambard's men catch us!' he said, in an exasperated tone.

This made Chatillon laugh out loud. 'All in good time, Conn, but do you honestly believe that I could be so clumsy as to allow that to happen? I will enlighten you and Henry at the same time when the final pieces are in place in a few days. For now, we need to mingle in the court, and we have a very important visit to pay to an old acquaintance, who once offered me a fortune in gold to kill someone.'

With that, he kicked his horse forward, and soon, they were trotting through the gates of King William's palace at Westminster.

Flambard reacted with astonishment and annoyance when he was told that the Papal Envoy had arrived at Westminster without warning. He disliked being wrong-footed at the best of times, and Chatillon always managed to do that to him.

However, more significantly, Flambard had now taken for himself the position of Prince Bishop of Durham with all its lucrative revenues and power. He now realised that this position made him subservient to the wishes and orders of the Senior Papal Envoy, who was the voice and embodiment of the Pope in this court. He also knew building bridges with the new Pope, and persuading the King to do the same, was important. Flambard was aware how close Pope Urban had been to excommunicating William Rufus; he could not afford to let that happen again. So he found himself hurrying down to welcome Chatillon, with something approaching resignation on his face.

'This is an unexpected pleasure, Chatillon,' he said, with a smile that did not reach his eyes.

Chatillon laughed. 'I did not think you ever found my presence a pleasure, Flambard, but as I intend to be here for several weeks, let us hide our mutual antipathy and work together on a compromise between King William Rufus and Pope Paschal.'

Flambard turned away to hide his irritation and waved the Steward and grooms over.

'Find beds for Chatillon's entourage. The Papal Envoy will have one of the better guest rooms in the palace, as usual.'

'May I also present Lord Conn Fitz Malvais, who has enjoyed his time in the French court and is eager to do the same in England. I believe you know his father and his uncle, Flambard?'

Ranulf Flambard looked up at the tall Horse Warrior.

'Yes, I knew both when I was at Bishop Odo's side in Caen; you are most welcome here, Malvais,' he said, inclining his head in a short bow.

CHAPTER ELEVEN

'He is friendly with Henry Beauclerc and several other young nobles, so I imagine I will not see much of him during our sojourn.'

Flambard smiled again, but an alarm bell rang at that news as another warrior in Henry's camp was not welcome.

They were both warmly welcomed by a pre-warned William Rufus, and the next few days were a blur of introductions and activities for Conn. However, before dinner on the second night, Chatillon suddenly appeared in his room, with an English Lord in tow.

'Conn, this is Richard Fitz Gilbert de Clare, one of your father's closest friends. He rode at your father's side on most of his exploits, including the defeat of King William by his son, Robert, at Gerberoi.'

Richard was a pleasant, handsome, open-faced man who held out a hand and grasped Conn's.

'I was with your father when he was forced, by his brother, Luc, to give up your mother, and it broke his heart. However, he was overwhelmed when he heard that you had been born and were taken away to safety by Chatillon and your grandmother, Queen Matilda.'

Chatillon smiled at the surprise and shock on Conn's face that this man knew of those circumstances.

'Richard is part of the small group that knows of your birth, a secret that will accompany him to his grave. I assure you he is a man who you can trust. He is about to take us to meet a man to help us, who could be key to our plan—a man we need to persuade to help us.'

'He knows what we intend to do?' Conn whispered, glancing at De Clare.

'Yes, and he supports us in our plan. Richard De Clare

also fought for Duke Robert during the rebellion and was punished for it. He still sees William Rufus as a usurper and Duke Robert as the true king. He's useful because his sister, Adeliza, married a young, ambitious knight named Walter Tirel. Unfortunately, Tirel has always been a staunch supporter of William and Flambard, so we're about to go and persuade him otherwise. He is at one of his manors in Essex, so we're riding now to corner him in his den. You are coming with us, for it will be you who has the most to do with Tirel. I intend you to be his keeper when we bring him back to court, and I want you to keep him on a short chain.'

Conn reached for his swords and buckled them on, announcing himself ready, while Richard openly stared at him. 'Has anyone ever mentioned that you....'

'...look very much like my Uncle Luc? A dozen times, at least! My grandmother Marie says that we're both the image of my grandfather,' he sighed, making them both laugh.

Two hours later, under a bright moon, they were knocking on the gates of a large manor house from which no lights showed. The gatekeeper and his family had obviously gone to bed as they took some rousing, but eventually, above the clamour of barking dogs, the shouted name of De Clare gained them entry.

'This is an ungodly hour to knock us up, my Lord De Clare. I hope it isn't bad news.'

'It may be, Jenkins. Go and tell the Steward that very important guests have arrived, and to raise my brother-in-law out of bed.'

Grumbling under his breath about heathen practices, the gate-keep headed for the house while they dismounted, and a dishevelled groom, wiping sleep from his eyes, took their horses. By the time they reached the Great Hall, Walter Tirel, bare-chested, dressed only in a pair of linen braies, was descending the stairs carrying a candle. Chatillon noticed that he had filled out since he had last seen him—in Lucca, several years before—but purposefully stayed back in the shadows, where Tirel did not immediately see him.

'God's blood, Richard. What's to do? What's so important that you arrive at this hour?' he said, reaching the bottom step and crossing the rush-strewn floor towards them. The steward lit more candles, and now Chatillon stepped into the light. Conn saw Tirel's face blanch at the sight of the Papal Envoy.

'What is this?' he mumbled.

Chatillon brought two folded vellum documents from inside his doublet.

'I have here a Papal Warrant from the Pope for your arrest, trial and execution in Rome.'

Walter Tirel tried to speak, but his mouth was suddenly bone dry, and although it opened, nothing came out.

'Is this all true, Walter? Did you truly arrange the death of Bishop Odo of Bayeux, the King's uncle?' asked Richard.

Tirel shook his head. 'It's lies, Richard, all lies,' he shouted, as his wife, Adeliza, appeared at the head of the stairs, crying out in alarm at what she had just heard.

'This can't be true, Walter; it must not be,' she cried, in a voice becoming shrill with fear.

'Unfortunately, it is true. He offered the assassination to me first, then he found others to do his bidding. We have witnesses in Sicily who have now been taken under guard to Rome. We found the Sicilian knight, Guido Di Messina, who administered the poison on Walter's orders for payment in gold; he has confessed to everything. Seize him!' he shouted to Conn.

Tirel dropped the candle and broke into a run, sprinting for the stairs, but Conn dropped him to the floor, delivering several sharp punches before pulling his arms behind his back and tightly tying them at wrist and elbow.

Tirel, white-faced, was gasping for breath as Conn pulled him roughly to his feet.

'I was only following orders, Chatillon. You know that. You know who ordered Bishop Odo's death,' he shouted.

'Yes. And I turned you down—warned you to leave it—but you went ahead regardless; the pull of the gold was too much for you, Walter. I have seen the records of the manors you have bought since you returned. Blood money, Tirel, and now Pope Paschal has decided that you must pay for this crime. You knowingly assassinated one of his senior bishops, a cleric of royal blood, the brother of King William I. Now you will be taken from here under cover of darkness to a waiting ship. You will be taken to Rome, where, after hours in the hands of the Papal Guards, you will confess.'

Tirel dropped sobbing to his knees while his wife began to scream, and several servants and small children appeared.

'Get them all back to bed, Adeliza. They should not see the beating we will give their father,' shouted Richard.

Chatillon nodded to Conn, who delivered a punishing punch to Tirel's stomach, and several to his head, as he fell forward. The stairs and gallery cleared apart from a clearly terrified Steward.

'Where is your master's business room?' asked Chatillon. The steward pointed and led the way with Richard, while Conn dragged the sobbing Tirel behind them.

CHAPTER ELEVEN

'Bring us wine and food, and then we don't want to be disturbed,' ordered Chatillon.

Conn pushed the distraught knight into a chair and waited while the other two said nothing, but stared at Tirel as the tension mounted in the room. Finally, Chatillon leaned forward, and Tirel cowered back in the chair.

'There's another course open to you, Walter, a way forward, even perhaps an escape from the pain you will endure in the dungeons of the Lateran Palace,' said Chatillon, pausing for effect. He saw, with satisfaction, a glimmer of hope on Tirel's face.

'Tirel, I know you have been loyal to William Rufus, but you need to switch that allegiance to another to save yourself, your family, and your manors, which will be confiscated, having been bought with blood money. Do you think you can do that, Tirel?'

Richard de Clare jumped in, previously agreeing to play devil's advocate for Chatillon.

'Impossible Chatillon, Walter is the King's man through and through, despite William and Flambard's crimes against the Church, the people of England and the King's questionable lifestyle. It would be better to kill him now than ask him to transfer his loyalty.'

'Oh, I'm not allowed to kill Tirel, Richard. The Pope wants to hear and see a written confession that names the perpetrators of this assassination of Odo. That will mean many days, if not a week, of pain in Rome. Paschal means to make an example of him; he will no doubt be disembowelled in front of the crowds in the Lateran Square.

Tears were streaming down Tirel's face at the thought of his fate. He knew what Chatillon was capable of, as he had watched him casually hamstring his young friend, crippling him for life and then walk away without a backward glance.

'I can change Richard! I swear I will support whosoever you tell me to,' he gasped.

Again, silence hung in the room for a long time as the three men considered those words and glanced at each other, leaving Tirel to search their faces for any chance of mercy. The Steward brought food and wine at that moment, and silence reigned until the man left.

Then Chatillon sat forward so he was only a finger span from Tirel's face.

'You will now, in this room, swear your allegiance to Count Henry Beauclerc, the King's younger brother, who may be minded to reward you and your family for such allegiance, and for the role you are about to play. What say you, Walter Tirel?'

The desperate man looked from one to the other, lit by only a small candle on the table in the room; their faces looked demonic in the shadows as he tried to answer.

'Yes! My answer is yes, but what of the Pope? He wants my confession, and he wants me punished and executed.'

'Leave the Pope to me, for he may be better pleased to keep you alive to play the role we have decided for you.'

Tirel nodded and sniffled, still anxious, his hands bound tightly behind him, the marks of Conn's beating clear on his face.

'What is it I have to do? What role do I have to play?' he asked, raising his eyes to Piers.

'Oh, something very simple. You are often one of William's boon companions on the hunt, are you not? You are a renowned huntsman and bowman?' Tirel nodded.

CHAPTER ELEVEN

'I need you to spend the next week searching the Royal Forest until you find the territory of a large stag, at least a fourteen or sixteen-pointer,' ordered Chatillon.

'There has only ever been one sixteen-pointer seen; we call him the Monarch. He is very elusive, and we may search for a month and never get a glimpse of him.'

'Ah, but this will be different, Walter, for this time, your life will depend on you finding one.'

Walter swallowed and nodded. 'Is that all I have to do?' he asked in a plaintive voice.

'No, Walter, for this is only act one of the play. In a week, you will return to court, tell the King where this great beast was spotted, and then arrange a hunting party to find and kill this great trophy. You will ensure that the King, Henry and yourself will be separated from the main group. Conn will help you do this.' Walter nodded, keen to help.

'Then the dogs will give voice that they have the stag at bay, and your group will arrive first; arrows will be loosed. Your fletched arrows will have a diamond pattern, and you will fire two at the deer and two at the King.'

Tirel blinked and stuttered, 'At the King? You want me to kill the King? No, I can't do that. They will hang, draw and quarter me here for that!'

'No, they won't; Conn will be behind you and will shoot you if you fail to do this. However, if you are successful, you will immediately be whisked away to a ship, your family will already be on board, and you will go to your lands in the Vexin in Normandy, where you will stay. William Rufus will be dead, and Henry will be crowned king. Henry will announce that it was purely a hunting accident, and then you and your family will reap the rewards.'

Tirel was an astute man, and it took him some time to think all this through.

'What of the documents that you hold? The confessions?' he asked.

'I will hold them as surety that you will carry this role out, then they will be burnt,' Chatillon said, not that he had any intention of doing that.

'Come, Tirel. You are already an assassin. You have murdered one of royal blood before and shouldn't have any conscience over another. Especially when you will keep the wealth you have gained and will be adding to it!'

Tirel wearily nodded. 'I have no choice, do I, Chatillon? Kill or be killed? I will do it. I will kill the King!'

Chapter Twelve

July 1100 - Monastere de St Benoit

Sheikh Ishmael's body may have been burnt beyond recognition in places, but there was certainly nothing wrong with his mental acuity. Over the last month, Friar Francis had slowly weaned his patient off the Theriac, which, because of the opium, could have become addictive. This had removed the fog and disorientation Ishmael had felt with the earlier larger doses. The pain was still there, but bearable.

Now, as he sat in the Scriptorium each day, he noticed the glances and wariness of Brother Tomas. It made him wonder if this was because they were overawed by the visit of his brother, the Emir of Zaragoza, or if they had now worked out who he really was. He was not ready to make his move yet, so he could not take the risk of word getting back to either Chatillon or Isabella in Genoa. He decided to go in and confront Friar Francis. He watched, and waited until the Friar was alone in his large room at the end of the infirmary. He entered the room, firmly closing the door behind him. The Friar looked up in surprise.

'Meddur, how can I be of assistance? Most of your pain should be diminishing by now.'

As he often did, his patient pulled his robe over his left hand, to hide it, as he sat opposite the Friar. There was a lot of muscle and tendon damage in that arm, and the Friar watched the man's frustration as he tried to move a lower arm that stubbornly refused to obey. Meddur looked up and met the Friar's eyes.

'I think we both know Friar Francis that Meddur is not my real name.'

He pinned the old monk with a cold, hard stare from his narrowed, dark eyes.

The Friar sat back, tucking his hands in his sleeves, as he regarded the patient he knew as Meddur.

'I have had my suspicions, but I think the speed with which Abu Ja'far responded to your message convinced me that he was probably your brother. He obviously cares a great deal about your welfare.'

'Do any of the other monks here also know my identity?' he asked.

'I don't believe so; the story of you coming from the wealthy and influential Al Cazar family was accepted, and it explained the visit of the Emir. I suggest you explain the armed men, your brother left, were part of your cohort as their captain. That should satisfy any of the curious in our community,' he suggested.

However, the next words chilled Friar Francis to the core.

'What of Brother Tomas? He seems very curious, and I feel his eyes on me everywhere I go.'

'Brother Tomas is a bright young man, but first and foremost, he is a healer, as you know. I assure you it would make no difference to him who you are. He sat beside your bed night after night, and he was delighted that you survived such

CHAPTER TWELVE

horrific wounds. He would be the first to say to try to avoid infection as they are still healing, which is why he watches you so carefully.'

The Sheikh inclined his head in what seemed to be thanks but with the arrogance of attitude that Tomas had commented on.

'I have come to tell you that I'm leaving in two days to return to the palace in Zaragoza. I thank you for the care you have given me, but I would ask you not to share with anyone outside the monastery that I was ever here.'

'We would have done the same for any of God's creatures. St Benedict's monastery is a healing centre for rich and poor alike. We repair their bodies and nurture their minds and souls to make them whole again, and I would like to think that we have done that with you.'

Meddur stood with a thin smile that unsettled the Friar, set his mind into turmoil and brought a rare feeling of anxiety.

He decided to go and find Brother Tomas, who was helping in the kitchen. Instead of going into the gardens where Meddur might see them, he told Tomas to meet him outside the front gates in a few minutes. However, when the young monk appeared, the Friar set off at a pace down the hill and into the meadow below, finally stopping in a sheltered spot, where the thin grass and meadow flowers blossomed, shaded by the small trees on the hillside. The Friar often came here for contemplation and peace after a busy time in the infirmary. He turned to face Tomas.

'You know, of course, that we have been harbouring Sheikh Ishmael?' Brother Tomas, expressing his consternation, nodded.

'He tells me he's leaving in two days, and he is adamant that his identity be kept secret. I can only presume that this is for some malicious and nefarious reason. He wants people to keep thinking he is dead; in particular, Ishmael wants his enemies to think that, while he plots his revenge against them.'

'That makes sense, Friar Francis, because his brother was remonstrating with him, shaking his head and forcefully speaking to him against doing something. Ishmael was angry and did not like what he was hearing.'

The Friar gazed across the peaceful meadow; a few goats grazed there, watching the two monks as they walked back and forth beneath the trees.

'I have had my suspicions for some time, and I have been doing some investigating, Tomas. Yesterday I received information from the Bishop in Marseilles. Apparently, there has been an ongoing blood feud between the Sheikh and our Papal Envoy, Piers De Chatillon, for years. I vaguely remember hearing something about this. Ishmael even killed one of his children and stole his wife. I do not doubt that Ishmael means to continue this feud, Tomas. I need you to go north to Chatillon's home outside Paris; you must tell Piers De Chatillon that the Sheikh is still alive and out for revenge. I dare not trust this to a missive; too often, they do not arrive, and this is crucial for Chatillon and his family as they will be unprepared for what is coming. Come back to my room with me, and I will give you silver. The journey may well take you a few weeks, but you must give this information to no one except Chatillon himself. I want you to go tomorrow morning. Take my big grey horse, he is still young, and he will cope with the many leagues ahead of you. The Sheikh is leaving, but I don't doubt that he intends to kill both you and me, so we can't share his real identity. You must escape

CHAPTER TWELVE

Tomas.'

A white-faced Tomas opened his mouth in shock. 'Then you must flee also—you cannot stay here either, Francis!'

'I can't do that, I have patients to see to this week; they need me. I promise that if I see them coming, I will tell the others to run, and I will go and hide in our cold house under the cliff edge. Once inside, I can wedge the small door closed.'

Tomas, his eyes now full of tears, grasped the Friar's hands. He loved the Friar like a father, and he pleaded with him.

'Please take care. Don't become a martyr, Francis; this monastery is nothing without you leading and guiding us.'

Friar Francis pulled the young monk into an embrace, and they turned and walked back to the monastery. As they entered the large stable yard under the arch, the first person they saw was Ishmael, who was talking to his men as they brushed their horses. He turned slowly and watched them, narrowing his eyes. Friar Francis nodded and smiled at the group as calmly as ever, but Tomas stopped in his tracks and froze. Fear was writ large on his face before he started forward.

Ishmael's eyes followed them as they entered the cool halls of the old stone monastery, and then he turned to Captain Ghilas.

'Sometimes, plans change through necessity. Meet me here, before dawn, as we need to tie up some loose ends, and then we will ride for the port to take ship a day earlier. Send one of your men ahead now to get the crew on board and make ready.'

Friar Francis was having a disturbed night; one of his patients, Josef, was in constant pain from a badly crushed and broken lower leg, and he cried out repeatedly. They would have to take it off at the knee on the morrow and the man would lose his job as a dock walloper. The Friar had just closed his eyes again when he heard the main doors being opened; they had a distinct loud creak as they swung. His sleeping cell was beside Brother Tomas, and he ran next door to his small room.

'Run Tomas, run and hide!' he yelled.

Tomas shot out of bed, pulled on his leather sandals and picked up the bag he had ready on the floor. At first, he ran to hide in the chapel as it would still be dark in there—only one large candle burned. He was slim, and he managed to slip into the narrow gap behind the wooden screen at the side of the altar. Screams began to echo down the stone halls almost immediately, and he realised that Ishmael was not taking any chances; he was slaughtering the whole community of monks. He heard the sound of running feet as several older monks ran for sanctuary in the chapel, thinking they would be safe in the house of God. Behind the wooden latticed screen, fists clenched, he watched as Ishmael's men came after them and viciously cut them down despite their pleading and prayers. Tomas put his head down and stuffed his fist into his mouth to stifle his sobs. These men had been his brothers, gentle, caring souls who had done nothing to deserve this fate.

He suddenly heard a loud voice and the man he knew as Meddur appeared under the stone arch to the chapel.

'Go back and search the bodies. I want to know that Brother Tomas is dead; he can't escape. You know who he is, the young monk, thick dark hair without a tonsure. Find him, and if he is alive, kill him!'

They ran out to obey his orders, and Ishmael stood staring at the altar. Tomas could not help himself, and he began to shake; it was as if Ishmael could see through the screen and knew he was hiding there. Tomas had never known such fear. But then, Ishmael turned and was gone. Tomas found himself gulping in huge mouthfuls of air. He had to get away, as they would surely find him here. He willed himself to think, then remembered Friar Francis and the cold store. No one here would know where that was. He slowly crept from behind the screen and, running low, entered the arch into the small inner sanctuary of the altar. He slowly opened only one of the wooden shutters, slightly, as they could be in the kitchen garden searching. He waited, holding his breath but could not hear or see anything in the breaking dawn, so opened both shutters wide. It was a small window, but he gently dropped his bag out and squeezed himself through. He then ran, clinging to the shadow of the high walls, to the small arched gateway that led down to the river; he realised that his bag would slow him down and hid it behind the bench, then he unbolted and pulled the door open.

Unfortunately, the doorway faced east, and as he pulled it open, he was silhouetted in its frame. He heard a shout behind him and saw that two of Ishmael's men had appeared from the kitchen door, at the far side of the garden—their white robes stark against the dark walls. Tomas burst through the archway and down towards the river, jumping and leaping like a hare being pursued by hounds. He did not doubt that he would be slaughtered like the others if they caught him. As he reached the river bank, he glanced back. They were emerging through the gate. Seeing him, they broke into a run across the meadow.

Tomas pushed through the shrubs and undergrowth. Jumping down, he waded chest-high across the river, heading downstream. The current was strong, and it felt as if it was taking forever as he kept glancing behind. He climbed up the steep bank opposite using the branches of a willow to pull himself up, and then he ran through the thicker trees and bushes on the far side. He could hear them crashing through the undergrowth on the far river bank behind him. He ran along a deep rocky gully, and there, hidden in the cliff amongst some juniper bushes, was a small wooden door just above waist height, which had faded to the colour of the rocks. It was old with two holes where a frayed rope handle was threaded through. He pulled on the rope handle, and nothing happened. A small rockfall of debris from above had blocked it, and he scrabbled with his hands in the scree until they bled, trying to clear it. He could hear the shouts as more men joined the chase and not far behind him were loud splashes as they jumped into the water. He was frantic as he wedged his feet on the rocks on either side and pulled the rope handle back and forth, praying it would not snap or he would be lost. Slowly, the door began to move, and gripping it, he dragged it open with both hands. He turned and pulled the juniper bushes back into place behind him. Bending double, he entered, pulling the old door behind him. He picked up a plank of wood from the fruit boxes lying on the floor, threaded it through the rope handle, twisted it round and round and wedged it closed against the rock. The wooden branch was old but felt solid, and he hoped it would hold. He began to shiver and presumed it was the cold, dank cave, but then Tomas realised it was pure, unadulterated terror, and he clasped his hands tightly together to stop them from shaking.

He waited and prayed as he had never prayed before, listening to their shouts moving closer to his hiding place.

CHAPTER TWELVE

Ishmael had no qualms over the slaughtering of a dozen monks and their servants as he finally disembarked from his brother's galley and then travelled overland to the family palace at Zaragoza. Even now, decades after his father had built it, the Aljaferia palace could instil awe and admiration in him. His father was a famous mathematician—you could see that in the design and precision of the geometric patterns that decorated the walls and ceilings. Ishmael had always felt at home here, for he had his own wing of rooms, but he was not prepared for the recoil and horror on the faces of servants, and even family relatives, when they saw him.

Abu Ja'far had seen the hurt and pain on his brother's face before he had turned away to hide it.

'They will get used to it before long and forget your disfigurement. My wife, Noori, has an idea about that and will call to see you tomorrow with your permission. Now I suggest you rest. I have summoned our physicians to tend to your needs.'

Ishmael nodded his thanks and admitted it was his first time on a horse, and he was exhausted by the journey. He had known the Arab physicians who arrived for many years, and he trusted their skill and wisdom. The elder one shook his head as he inspected the damage inflicted in the fire.

'I must admit I have no idea how you survived these burns, Sayyid; your care must have been exceptional. I don't know how they kept the infection at bay.'

Ishmael did, for he vividly remembered every agonising

moment of it.

'Daily washing with Mercury Chloride,' he muttered, and the physicians, after a glance at each other, sagely nodded.

'There's still a lot of healing to be done, and you must not exert yourself unduly, or travel far, until that is complete. I want you to flex the damaged hand and forearm daily, to stop them from shrinking and contracting further. Try lifting a small weight to build the remaining muscle.'

Ishmael nodded in understanding but knew he would leave the palace in a month because he was determined to travel to Genoa to find and take his daughter back.

Noori arrived veiled the next morning but unhooked the veil in her brother-in-law's presence, and Ishmael could see the pity in her eyes as she remembered the handsome man he had been. However, she was practical and business-like; she had ordered the palace leather maker to come, and commissioned him to make a thin, supple leather glove to hide the disfigured hand and much of the forearm. She then measured his face and head and explained that she would make him a thin linen cap to cover his burnt head and part of the lower left-hand side of his face. It would hide the scars where his ear used to be, and he could wear a light traditional Berber headdress, which would also help to cover most of it.

'How soon?' he asked.

'I will have it ready for you by tomorrow, Sayyid,' she said, and smiled at him. She had always been a beauty, and he raised her hand and kissed it in gratitude.

'Your women in the seraglio will be impatient for your return, as they have truly missed you,' she murmured.

She saw him frown and turn away, and she wondered if the fire had destroyed other things. Turning back, he saw her glance at his groin, which made him laugh for the first time.

'Do not fear, Noori, I'm still capable of satisfying a woman; if you were not my brother's wife, I would show you!' he said, his dark eyes smiling at her. Then leaning forward, he stroked her cheek.

She assumed a suitably shocked expression and reattached her veil, but her eyes sparkled; even injured and disfigured as he was, he still had the ability to excite a woman.

'I must go, but visit them tonight, Yusuf. Arrive when it is dark and douse the lamps until your linen hood is ready,' she said, leaving Ishmael to his thoughts and plans for that night.

Brother Tomas spent a full night and the next day in the cave, fearing for his life as he heard them still searching for him. He found some old sacks further back in the deep cavern, and shook them out in case there were scorpions or snakes. He wrapped them around his shoulders and eventually slept, but only fitfully, starting awake at the slightest or imagined sounds. He did not go hungry as the monastery used the deep cave as a cold store to age cheese and smoked hams. There was even a small cask of white wine, which Tomas broached to keep up his strength and spirits.

Finally, he emerged at what he thought may be late afternoon the next day. His heart beating wildly, he opened the door a handspan only and then waited for some time. Tomas could hear no sounds or voices but could not rid himself of the fear that they were patiently sitting on the river banks, waiting for him to appear like some animal they were hunting. Finally, he pushed the door open further and crawled to sit on the ground outside. Tomas waited again for some time but heard nothing to alarm him, so he continued on hands and knees to where he could see the river and the meadow beyond.

No one was in sight, and there were no alarm calls from birds; the skylarks were still in the meadow, and the swallows were swooping low undisturbed. Tomas slowly waded back across the river, constantly scanning the bushes and river banks, and then he ran low across the tall grass of the meadow so he was closer to the monastery's walls. The arched postern gate to the kitchen garden still stood wide open, but there was no sign of the marauders. As he crept along the walls, he decided that entering the gardens was too dangerous; he would instantly be seen. Instead, he thought it wiser to go all the way around to the front gates, for there was cover there, where he could hide in the trees and bushes, and if they were still here, he would hear them in the stable yard. He did not doubt for a second that they would still be looking, or waiting for him. The Sheikh could not allow him to live and escape with this information.

He stood in the bushes near the front gates for some time, listening to the stillness only punctuated by birdsong. Then he bravely emerged and put his head around the archway. One of the older grooms, a local boy, lay face down in the yard, a pool of dried blood by his head and flies buzzing. He noticed that all of the Berber horses were gone. Could they really have left, he wondered.

Clinging to the outbuildings, he moved inside and crept to the stable. The few monastery's horses were in their stalls,

CHAPTER TWELVE

stamping impatiently as they had not been fed or watered for a day. They have truly killed everyone, Tomas thought, as clinging to the walls, he headed for the heavy wooden doors into the entrance hall. They stood half open, and part of him did not want to enter, did not want to see what he knew he would find inside. However, he had been trained well, and he felt responsible for seeing if any of the monks still lived. Were there some lying injured that he could help? Or what of the half dozen patients? They would need help or water. He could not leave them.

As he slipped through the doors to the refectory, the silence within the monastery was deafening; there were usually noises from the kitchens or the infirmary or a few voices raised in psalms in the chapel. The smell of blood and emptied bowels hit him as he passed the long trestle tables. Several bodies littered the floor in the kitchen, young to old; they lay in pools of blood where they had been cut down as they ran in panic. He checked each one for life signs, but they had been stabbed and slashed repeatedly, and all had bled out quickly. He crossed to the infirmary and covered his mouth with his hand as he gaped and then retched at the horror before him. There were bodies everywhere here, and by the position of the monks, he could see that they had been trying to get the patients out to safety. He found Friar Francis bent over a bed, his hands still clutching the blood-soaked bed cover; his throat had been cut. The worst thing for Tomas was that they had killed all the patients in their beds—men and a few children he had treated and almost nursed back to health.

Tomas stood with his head down and fists clenched in anger, but then he rebuked himself, dropped to his knees, and said prayers for the repose of their souls. He knew there was nothing more he could do here, for he had to follow the Friar's instructions and find Piers de Chatillon. He went to the kitchens, filled a bag with food, picked up a small wine sack and made his way to the stable yard, where he gulped in the fresh air. Tomas went to the stalls and tacked up the Friar's large, dappled grey gelding. He hung his bags on the saddle when a hand descended on his shoulder.

Tomas spun around, his first instinct being to lash out, and he landed a blow that floored his attacker. However, he recognised the figure rolling on the ground. It was Joly, the young boy who helped around the monastery, but he was almost unrecognisable as he was covered in soot. The boy tenderly felt his jaw as Brother Tomas pulled him to his feet.

'Sorry, Joly, I'm so afraid I would have hit anyone creeping up on me. You have no doubt seen what has happened here.'

'Yes, brother Tomas, I climbed and hid in the kitchen fireplace when I heard the screams, and then everyone started running. We are the only ones left, aren't we?'

Tomas nodded. 'Yes, he has killed them all, but unfortunately, I have to go; Friar Francis gave me orders, but I need you to go water and feed the animals and then run to the nearby village. Tell them what has happened here as they will all need to be buried, and a message must be sent to the Abbot in Marseilles immediately. You can take that, as you have been there before. Use one of the quieter ponies,' he explained. However, he could see the boy was in shock, so he gave him a good swig of wine.

He mounted his horse and rode out with a wave, leaving the forlorn boy standing in the monastery yard, the house of God that Ishmael had turned into a charnel house.

Now, his only thought was to reach the road to Paris. As he

rode, he felt, in turn, clammy, cold and shivering. He was sure that was his body reacting to the shock he had experienced on seeing the slaughter, his feet slipping in the blood of his friends and brothers.

When he reached Avignon, he knew he could travel no further that day, and he found an inn, which he paid for with a piece of the silver the Friar had given him. Although exhausted, he found that sleep would not come, as the faces of the murdered monks and patients floated before him.

He was back on the road the next morning, riding towards Valence and then on to Lyon. He knew that time was of the essence, and he pushed himself and his horse to go further each day. Only one thing filled his mind now; he had to warn Chatillon that the Sheikh was alive, that Ishmael had risen from the flames with the help of the monks at St Benedict's monastery.

Of one thing Tomas was certain, this murdering Sheikh had to die for what he had done.

Chapter Thirteen

July 1100 – Palace of Westminster

Chatillon ran his fingers lightly down the naked spine of his female companion. He had been the lover of the pretty dark-haired Almodis de Mortain for over ten years; whenever they came again into each other's company, she would hungrily seek him out. She had been very young when her parents had married her to Earl Robert de Mortain, the wealthy and powerful half-brother of King William I. A much older husband meant that she had been bored and looking for excitement when he first laid eyes on her in Rouen. He had made it his mission to not only teach her about lovemaking but, being at the heart of the court, turn her into one of his best informers.

His fingers moved back and forth at the base of her spine, and she squirmed with pleasure as the first fingers of dawn penetrated the partly-open shutters. He moved astride her. Lifting her heavy dark hair, he kissed the back of her neck before gently biting it. She gasped and squirmed more as he opened her legs and knelt between them. Using his fingers to guide himself into her, he took her from behind. His hand gripped her hair tightly, and his teeth found her neck again as he plunged into her, and she squealed with pleasure.

Afterwards, he turned onto his back and stretched while Almodis raised herself on one elbow, smiling as her hand followed the dark line of hair from his chest to his groin.

'You are the only man who takes me like that. It's very exciting,' she murmured.

He laughed. 'I know,' he said, and she gurgled with laughter at his assurance.

'I have missed you, Piers, as no one makes love to me as you do.'

'I have been somewhat preoccupied of late, but I promise you, Almodis, if we are ever in the same city or court, I will always come and avail myself of your many charms. I thought you would have married again by now. It must be nearly five years since Robert's death.'

'I enjoy being a wealthy widow, Piers; you taught me how to be popular and witty at court, and I'm welcomed everywhere. I have several lovers; why do I need to marry?' she asked, swinging her legs out of bed.

'For even more influence, power and wealth, Almodis, so that you can be even more useful to me. Have I taught you nothing?'

She laughed again and lifted her clothes from the floor, where they had been quickly discarded the night before.

'I have done everything you have asked, Piers. I have entertained and bedded Walter Tirel. Now, there's a man who is boring in bed—a few thrusts, and it's over. I have ensured that he mixes with Prince Henry, who I have also bedded; Beauclerc is a very demanding young man in bed who likes to be completely in control, but he is handsome and very entertaining. What else do you require of me?' she asked, standing naked and looking very pretty with her dishevelled hair.

'I want you to sound out the older nobles, the contemporaries of your deceased husband. Find out their views on Prince Henry. Say how impressed you are, and how more like his father he is out of the three remaining sons.'

She nodded. 'You have taught me well, Chatillon, because I think I have worked out what is afoot; I will not breathe a word of it, though,' she whispered, suddenly serious.

Chatillon narrowed his eyes at her as he pulled on and tied his braies. He suddenly moved close to her, and raising his hand, he gripped her long, beautiful neck tightly.

'I will pretend for your sake that I did not hear those words; I would hate to have to snap this delicate and pretty neck. One whisper of any of my affairs from you, and I promise I would do that. You know the rules.'

He bent her backwards, tightening further, and she let out a strangled sound, but wide-eyed, she managed to nod to show she understood. He pulled her back into his arms and, holding her close, kissed her gently.

'I do care for you greatly, Almodis. I was being serious when I said you need to marry again, so you have another male protector. Perhaps somewhere out of England, away from the English court,' he suggested, in a firm voice that made her raise her eyes to him in alarm.

At that moment, there was a knock on the door and Conn strode in, stopping dead at the sight of the naked woman in Piers' arms. Piers, totally unconcerned, smiled.

'Conn, I don't think you have yet been introduced to the Countess de Mortain.'

Conn bowed, and Almodis, with no hint of modesty, turned

and inclined her head in a slight bow while her eyes ran over the handsome Horse Warrior. She reached for her gown, pulling it over her head, then picked up her soft leather boots. She made for the door, but she stopped beside Conn and put her hand on his chest.

'I look forward to meeting you again, Conn Fitz Malvais.'

Conn found himself smiling as he gazed down into her pretty face, and Chatillon laughed aloud as she closed the door behind her.

'You would enjoy Almodis, and she would certainly enjoy you. It would certainly do you no harm in the eyes of your compatriots.'

'I don't believe that would be any hardship,' said Conn, grinning back.

'So what news, Conn? If any?' he said, throwing open the shutters and standing bare-chested at the window gazing down onto the Thames.

'Walter Tirel and his men are away searching the forest for the fourteen or sixteen pointers we need. I have two of our men following them. As far as I know, he has not spoken to anyone about our tryst at his house. He has become friendly with Henry, and at times almost subservient, which worries me when people are watching Henry.'

Chatillon turned to face him while he pulled on a fine linen shirt.

'Don't worry about that, as Tirel was originally one of Flambard's minions. Tirel is also related to the royal family through his wife Adeliza, a distant cousin but still a link, so no one will wonder why he is with Prince Henry, or in the hunting party. Be seen in his company when he returns from the Royal Forest Conn, go hawking and hunting with him as he considers himself an excellent shot with a bow, and boasts of it. Organise an archery competition with Henry, but do not show off your skill; be adequate only and loudly praise the skill of Tirel in the hearing of the nobles and the King if he is present.'

Conn perfectly understood what Chatillon was about and strode off down the corridors of the palace to find Henry.

Chatillon finished dressing and went to join the party around the King, in the newly finished Westminster Hall. He felt Flambard's eyes on him the moment he arrived, and before long, had sidled over to him. Chatillon noticed the sumptuous Prince Bishop's robes he had donned, and looking him up and down, he smiled.

'Are you here for an extended stay, Chatillon? I presume you must have pressing business elsewhere,' he asked pleasantly enough.

'Anything else can wait, Flambard. Pope Paschal, and I think we have neglected the English Court for too long, so I will be here for a month or two. Paschal hopes to heal the widening rift between King William Rufus and the Holy See—with your help in your newly appointed role, of course, Flambard,' he said, indicating the Bishop's gold-decorated robes with a flourish of his hand. The King's minister had no option but to incline his head in acceptance, as Chatillon continued, raising his voice,'It has been remiss of us, Flambard, not to congratulate you sooner on your lucrative appointment. You are now the King's Treasurer, the Keeper of the Seal and a Prince Bishop of Durham. Don't get me wrong, Flambard, for I am sure these appointments and accolades are well deserved for your services to the King. I am told that you have met the King's every need economically, politically and socially

CHAPTER THIRTEEN

over the years, but now you are a bishop of the Holy See, things must be different. I suggest you back away from the role of procurer, meeting the King's demands for pleasure. The masques full of fresh young men are legendary but not something your name as Prince Bishop of Durham should now be linked with. I tell you, Flambard, in the garden this morning, I felt a change in the direction of the wind, a new fresh breeze from the west, ready to blow away the unhealthy miasma that has enveloped you here in England for some time.'

As Chatillon's last sentence was issued, he gave a slight smile, bowed his head and walked away, aware that Flambard's face was now purple with rage, and his fists were clenched.

All thoughts of gaining Chatillon's favour, or recruiting him as an ally, were now gone for Flambard. The Papal Envoy had just delivered a hard slap to his face implying, in the hearing of others, that he was no more than a pimp for the King. Flambard waved his personal chamberlain over to his side, an obsequious but cunning man, who was good at gathering information and managed a large group of Flambard's informers.

'I always want two of my men on Piers De Chatillon. I want to know where he goes, everything he does, everyone he meets. Chatillon is a storm crow, a harbinger and bringer of misfortune who never goes anywhere without leaving mayhem and death behind him, so watch him. I want to know what he is up to, even the smallest thing!'

Chatillon had walked away to join other nobles in the court, and he was pleased to see that Almodis was amongst them, dropping the hints about Henry and testing the waters as he had asked. He was surprised that Robert De Belleme was there; his father and older brother, Hugh, were recently deceased. Robert was now an even more exceptionally wealthy and powerful man as Earl of Shrewsbury. Although in the past, he had always been a staunch supporter of Duke Robert, now he was obviously back in the good graces of William Rufus as well.

Chatillon noticed that Belleme still walked with a slight limp, and he smiled at the memory of Morvan's wife, Ette, stabbing Belleme through the thigh so hard he was pinned to the ground. He had deserved it, though, as he had tried to rape her.

However, he had always had a useful relationship with Belleme, so strolling to his side, he greeted him pleasantly enough.

'It has been far too long, Robert. I was sorry to hear of your brother Hugh's death in the Welsh Marches; he was a good man.'

Robert clasped arms with the Papal Envoy, as they had worked together several times to try and enable Robert to become Duke of Normandy. However, Belleme, although a compatriot, always remained wary of Chatillon as he knew what he was capable of.

'What brings you into this pit of vipers, Chatillon? It must be something of value or great worth, for I know that you, like me, have no love for William Rufus. I will be glad to see Duke Robert back in Normandy shortly, where he belongs with his new wealthy wife.'

Chatillon knew that he had to guard his words carefully with Belleme, who was an astute and cunning man. He would not be amenable to the idea of Henry snatching the throne of England. He would want the throne to go to the rightful

CHAPTER THIRTEEN

heir, which was Robert, and he would probably be willing to take up arms to make that happen. However, that was no concern of Chatillon's, as he would arrange the assassination, and what happened next was up to Henry.

'I am here purely to build bridges between the Holy See and the King. We need Anselm, the Archbishop of Canterbury, back in England, but he is still in exile in Normandy. If I can achieve that, then my journey will have been worthwhile,' replied Chatillon.

Belleme leant close to him. 'You expect me to believe that codswallop? You bring chaos wherever you go, Chatillon. So what are you really here for?' he hissed.

They were interrupted at that moment by Conn and Prince Henry joining them. Belleme, unpleasant at the best of times, looked Conn up and down, noticing the laced leather jerkin and crossed swords on his back. 'Not another of your damned Horse Warriors, Chatillon—do you collect them?' he exclaimed.

'My Lord Earl, may I introduce Lord Conn Fitz Malvais, who spent many years fighting with El Cid in Spain against the Berbers.

Belleme inclined his head in a slight acknowledgement of such courage but then spoilt the effect with the next words.

'Fitz Malvais? So, whose bastard are you? Luc De Malvais, or his brother Morvan De Malvais, as there were interesting rumours about whom he had bedded.'

Conn kept his face rigid but clenched a fist in annoyance while Chatillon laughed it off.

'Both Malvais brothers had women throwing themselves at their feet, including your own sister, Belleme. I seem to remember that Morvan bedded her in her husband's house.

Conn, however, is the image of his father Luc, as you can see, and is almost as lethal,' he said, in a warning tone.

Belleme shrugged but kept the sneer on his face while Henry Beauclerc filled the silent pause with a loud announcement.

'We have organised an archery competition for tomorrow, and rumour has it, Chatillon, that you are to put up the prize of a purse of silver for the winner,' he proclaimed, to the crowded hall.

Belleme turned back and narrowed his eyes at Chatillon, for from years of experience, he knew that Chatillon never did anything without reason. Every move was usually calculated and planned.

'Archery?' he murmured to Chatillon, with a raised eyebrow.

Chatillon smiled. 'Only for a wager that I have with my young friend here, Belleme, a mere trifle. I look forward to it, Henry. Do you have many takers?'

Henry replied with enthusiasm.

'Over a dozen at least so far, Chatillon, enough for a few heats before the final.'

'I look forward to it, Sire,' bowed Chatillon before Belleme moved away, beckoning Chatillon to follow him.

'I see that Flambard and his men watch your every move. For that, I am grateful, as usually his eyes and his men are on me.'

Chatillon scanned the room and saw Flambard's men almost immediately, and he smiled. Had they no skill or finesse, he wondered.

'Flambard trusts no one, and honestly, given our history, I don't blame him, for without William Rufus, he is nothing. Put your mind at rest, for he is of no consequence, Belleme,' he said, before returning to Conn's side to ask softly about progress.

'Everything is going according to plan; each man knows his part. I have ordered the arrows from the fletcher; each half-dozen will have different flights or colours. Tirel's flights will have a distinctive diamond pattern, the same as the ones he will use today in the competition.'

Hearing this, Chatillon nodded in satisfaction.

'Three days after the archery contest tomorrow, Conn, the plan must be perfect to drop into place. Much will depend on you and Tirel separating our group from the main hunt; that will be the most crucial part.'

Conn nodded. He knew what was at stake and felt an odd mix of anticipation and excitement, even though they were plotting to kill the King of England in just over three days.

Chatillon bowed to the King and left; William Rufus, occupied with listening to the young musician at his side, hardly noticed.

Chatillon had reached the door when his arm was gripped, and he turned wearily expecting Flambard, who was undoubtedly unsettled by seeing him deep in conversation with Belleme. Flambard was a firm believer of once a rebel, then always a traitor, and he trusted barely any of those who rose against William Rufus in 1090. They were all marked men as far as he was concerned.

However, he was surprised to find himself looking into the face of Agness de Ribemont, Countess of Buckingham and Duke Robert's long-term mistress. She had been a pretty, buxom, lascivious girl who had wormed her way into Robert's affections. The hooks she planted were deep into his flesh, and she had held him enthralled for decades even though she married Walter Giffard, the Earl of Buckingham.

She beckoned Chatillon over into a window embrasure. He reluctantly followed, for he did not like this manipulative woman, and had hoped that Robert's marriage meant he would be well rid of her. She gave him a sly smile.

'Consorting with the enemy, Chatillon?' she quipped.

He frowned and gave her a puzzled half-smile. 'I was unaware that I have any enemies here, my lady; I am purely here on the Pope's business for a short while.'

She gave a snort of derision. 'You are never purely on the Pope's business, Chatillon. Remember, I know where the bodies are buried; Robert always tells me everything.'

'More fool him, my lady and good luck in digging up any bodies,' he said, and laughing, began to move away.

'Wait!' she said, glancing around to ensure they were not overheard.

'I presume you will be in Rouen to ensure that Duke Robert receives what is rightly his when he returns home?' she asked.

Chatillon nodded. 'I believe the dowry from his new wife will repay the loan from the King. I will be there to ensure it is above board and the vifgage on Normandy is relinquished.'

To his surprise, she gave him a sweet smile.

'I know that Robert is your friend, and I thank you for always being at his side.'

Chatillon felt his hackles rise, for this was not a woman who ever gave thanks or compliments lightly.

'I may have need of your services in a private capacity soon, Chatillon, an assignment that will be very lucrative,' she whispered.

Chatillon, every sense on alert, waited for her to elaborate...

.

'I don't believe that this new wife of his will do well in the colder air of Normandy; she's used to much warmer climes. I hope that with your help, her health will deteriorate.'

Chatillon could not prevent the expression of surprise and then incredulity on his face.

'You want me to murder the new Duchess of Normandy, who will probably already be carrying Robert's legitimate heir. Are you mad?' he asked, in a tone of disbelief.

Again, she looked over her shoulder in nervousness and then nodded.

'A death such as this is nothing to a man like you!' she protested.

'And what of Robert? Has he no say in this? He looks very happy, Agness. I was at his wedding, and he was undoubtedly in love with this young Italian beauty. Is he not allowed that happiness after many savage years on crusade?'

'He has a son, our son, William, Lord of Tortosa; he needs no other heir, and he has me. Despite what you may think, I love him, Chatillon, and I know he is only with her for her wealth. He will set her aside; if not, I will have her removed.'

His eyes narrowed at her; God save him from jealous, vindictive women who fear being scorned, for he knew how dangerous and unpredictable they could be.

'I am sorry, my lady, but I can't accept this assignment; as you say, Robert is my friend. I suggest that you wait and see what the situation is when he returns to Normandy.'

He saw the colour rise in her cheeks, and the anger in her clenched fists as she spat at him, 'I will be waiting in Rouen for them to arrive, I promise you.' Without another word, she whirled away and was gone.

Chatillon stood for a moment, and then, shrugging it off, he swore to have a private word of warning with Duke Robert when he returned to Rouen. Now, however, he had other events to fill his mind, other pieces to move into place.

'Three days after tomorrow, only three days and the English court will be plunged into chaos,' he murmured softly to himself.

He smiled at the thought, for they were right—he often brought chaos, but he thrived on the excitement and uncertainty of it.

Chapter Fourteen

End of July – London

Chatillon easily lost Flambard's men, as they were still rubbing sleep from their eyes as he doubled back across the gardens to make an unusual and risky early morning visit to Henry's chambers. He found him up early and playing with three of his children. At the last count, Piers was sure that Henry had at least half a dozen bastards by different mothers, but to give him his due, he acknowledged them all. He even set about arranging future advantageous marriages for them. The eldest, Juliana, a pretty ten-year-old, regarded Piers with a solemn distaste for taking her father away to discuss business.

'A pretty girl when she smiles,' said Henry, laughing at his daughter. I'm arranging a match for her with William of Breteuil's illegitimate son, Eustace; she will go to the family in Normandy when she is thirteen.'

Chatillon inclined his head in recognition of a good match. He was aware of Henry's prodigious sexual appetite, and he always seemed to have several mistresses on the go at the same time, while always looking for the next.

Chatillon had a firm purpose behind Henry Beauclerc

organising the archery competition, so he wanted to know how things were progressing.

'How are the arrangements for the archery contest this evening? I hear there have been many entrants.'

'Yes, word spread, and we now have so many,, we're holding the heats for the lesser ones this afternoon. I have ordered the servants to set up benches as there is much interest, and we expect many spectators. Only sixteen entrants will make it to the final event early this evening.'

'You may have to discard one of those entrants, as my informers tell me the King wants to compete. I believe your brother William is no mean shot, and more importantly, it now makes this a court event with even more spectators, which is good for us. You will have to clear a space to erect the King's pavilion,' he advised.

'Right into our hands, Chatillon, they are playing right into our hands,' he said, with a confidence that Piers did not share yet.

Chatillon bowed and left him to it. Henry was right that things were falling into place, but he knew there was many a slip between cup and lip, and Chatillon liked to deal in certainties. He went down to the butts, where he found Conn, Walter Tirel and several other hopefuls having an hour or two of practice.

'I must congratulate you both on your success, as I would wager that nearly a hundred people may come and watch the contest.' Conn smiled, but Walter looked worried.

'I hear that the King is taking part. I did not want or expect that,' he said, and Piers could hear the uncertainty in his voice.

'I'm placing a large wager on this contest, Walter, and I expect you to win. If you do, I promise I will give you half

CHAPTER FOURTEEN

of the winnings,' he said, slapping him on the shoulder but leading Conn away to one side.

'Keep his spirits up, Conn; he is a man who thrives on praise. There will be three heats this evening, sixteen, then down to eight and then the final four. I don't want you to get past the first heat.'

Conn nodded in understanding, knowing he had to play down his newly acquired skill.

'Quite honestly, Sire, some of these archers are so good that I don't believe that will be a problem, including young Beaumont over there, only seventeen years and a lethal shot.'

Chatillon narrowed his eyes at the handsome young man, obviously one of the up-and-coming cadet sons of the nobility.

'Good enough for us to hobble or take him out? Tirel must win this contest, Conn; he must be the best bowman in England.'

'I will have a word and point out that if he makes it into the final four with the King, then he must let William win.' Chatillon smiled in satisfaction and left them to continue their practice.

Chatillon arrived that evening and displayed the red leather pouch of silver to cheers from the crowds, before he took his seat in the King's open-fronted pavilion, alongside Flambard. The King was in good spirits as he had just made it into the final eight of the second round. Conn, as ordered, had ensured that he was not one of them.

The tension grew as the final eight nocked their arrows and took their positions in front of the two targets, which were white with a distinctive black bull's eye in the centre.

When the archers hit the black circle in the centre, the

crowd cheered, especially if it was one of the red-fletched arrows of the King. Henry, determined to make it a spectacle, had arranged for horns to be blown when it was down to the last four. The names were announced to more cheers, and he told Chatillon to stand and display the purse of silver again, which he did to even more cheers. The tension grew, and the courtiers sat forward in their seats, craning their heads, or at the back, they sat on friends' shoulders to get a view of the final over the heads of the crowd.

'It seems as though Tirel's incessant boasting about his prowess and skill with a bow has some truth,' Chatillon suggested to Flambard.

'He is accounted an exceptionally good huntsman by his compatriots; he is known to be able to bring down a stag or boar moving at speed every time,' agreed Flambard, defending his minion.

'It will be interesting to see if his loyalty and admiration of the King will affect his aim in this final round,' whispered Chatillon, in a stage whisper everyone heard.

Flambard sneered and replied, 'He would not be so foolish, for William Rufus would show his displeasure if Tirel misses or lets him win, and I assure you that Henry Beauclerc and Beaumont are good shots as well. There isn't much to tell between the four of them.'

'We will see. Would you like to make a small wager on who will win?' smiled Chatillon, flipping a rare gold Byzantine coin.

Flambard nodded. 'I will, of course, but on the King—his eye seems good today.'

'I will put my gold on Tirel; he seems a more consistent choice,' declared Chatillon.

CHAPTER FOURTEEN

At that moment, Robert de Belleme, seated behind them and listening to every word, leant forward.

'I will take your wager, Chatillon, but my money will be on Henry Beauclerc, despite my antipathy to him. He is less nervous, more confident of the outcome, and looks like he is hungering for the acclaim this win will bring him,' he declared.

Piers stared intently at Belleme, who was often far too astute for his own good, and he was also a well-known agitator or stirrer of the pot. If he were not careful, Piers would have no qualms about silencing him forever. A great deal of money was exchanging hands on the benches in the courtyard, and the King was emerging as the favourite, bringing a pleased smile to his lips and a flush to his already ruddy complexion.

Three targets were removed, and the remaining one was moved back, almost to the palace walls, to test the skills of the finalists at a distance.

'This will certainly sort skill from luck, although I own myself surprised to find that Henry has a place in the final. I always think of him as more of a scholar,' declared Flambard.

'That is coming on too strong, Flambard, for I have seen your spies watching him practising at the butts almost every day since he arrived at court. However, I'm somewhat curious about what he is in training for. Can you enlighten us, Chatillon? You usually seem to know what everyone is doing or thinking,' commented Belleme.

Piers smiled at the Earl's sarcasm and wit and shrugged.

'I have never had much to do with Henry; he was always too young, and quite honestly, he is inconsequential to the Holy See; a younger son with little influence or wealth. I'm aware that you are still at odds with him, Belleme, for he stole your fortress and town of Domfront from under your nose.'

Flambard laughed while Belleme sneered, but all were distracted by the cheers and applause for young Beaumont, whose blue arrow had hit the target, if on an outer edge. Henry Beauclerc followed, and his striped arrow struck close to the black bull's eye. His supporters cheered, while Walter Tirel bowed to King William Rufus, indicating that he should go next. Chatillon was concerned to see that Tirel was very pale; he could see a sheen of sweat on his brow, and his knuckles shone white from gripping his bow so tightly. Chatillon glanced at Conn and Henry in concern, but they seemed unaware of the drama in front of them. Suddenly, Tirel looked across and met Chatillon's eyes in a blatant stare, and he began to take a stumbling step forward.

'I think you are about to lose your wager, Chatillon, for your man does not look at all well. He seems to be in a trance,' declared Belleme.

'I can imagine it is nerves, shooting in the competition against the King,' murmured Flambard.

Chatillon felt his stomach knot. Tirel's stare at him was unwavering, and people would begin to notice. He did not doubt that being in such proximity to the King had unnerved him. Piers feared that Tirel was about to blurt out the plot to all and sundry, saving his own skin in the process, but handing them to William Rufus and Flambard, on a platter.

Fortunately, the King fired at that moment, and the crowd erupted into wild cheering for William Rufus, for the King's arrow was just inside the black bull's eye circle, which was a handspan wide. William Rufus was delighted, and his many acolytes lifted him shoulder-high back to his seat, as if he was already the victor. Chatillon used the distraction to stand and shout encouragement to Tirel.

CHAPTER FOURTEEN

'Come, Walter, show us of your best, you can win this, and everything is riding on you!'

Tirel had shaken himself out of his fear, and now, with a quick glare at Chatillon, he nocked his arrow and aimed at the target at the far side of the courtyard. It was rare that Chatillon prayed, but he murmured one now as he watched the arrow fly. The large crowd held their breath as the arrow thudded into the target. It had flown true and hit the black circle, not quite in the centre but closer than the King's arrow. Tirel's supporters erupted in cheers, and the other competitors came to congratulate him. He was carried, laughing, to the pavilion where the King graciously announced that the best archer in England had won, while Chatillon presented him with the purse of silver.

'Now you just need to hit that big sixteen-pointer you keep telling us about in the Royal Forest,' said Chatillon loudly, delighted his plan was coming together.

'You have truly seen the Monarch? Where was this Tirel?' asked the King, keenly sitting forward.

'We spent several days last week hunting, your majesty—half a dozen of us, not far past Cadnam. Several of us saw him. He seems to have a herd of hinds in a wide clearing there, but of course, they scattered when they heard us approach.'

'You should have split up, come at him from several directions,' added Conn, who stood beside Chatillon.

William Rufus, the excitement clear to see on his face, turned to Flambard.

'You were leaving for Winchester tomorrow, Ranulf, were you not, on treasury business?' Flambard nodded.

'Well, we will all go. Send ahead to inform them in Winchester that the court is arriving, and we will stay there for two nights. Then we will take advantage of the hospitality of Romsey Abbey and use that as a base for several days of hunting; I must find the Monarch, for I have never seen him. What a trophy that would be to hang on the walls of Westminster Hall. Send messages to the Abbess, Cristina Flambard, and tell her to make ready for our arrival.'

'And lock up or hide the young girls and novices,' Henry joked as others joined in with the laughter.

His brother frowned, not appreciating his brother's humour with the Papal Envoy present.

'Romsey is a seat of learning for the daughters of the nobility, Henry, even Matilda of Wessex is there, considering whether to take her vows.'

'I might persuade her otherwise, William, for she's the daughter of King Malcolm and Queen Margaret of Scotland. Just think what a good match that would be for our family,' he declared.

William scowled, as that match had also been suggested for him, but her aunt, the Abbess Cristina, had talked the girl out of it.

Chatillon heard Flambard hiss with annoyance behind him at such a thought; he did not want Henry making an advantageous marriage like that. Chatillon deftly turned the topic of conversation to Flambard and Belleme.

'I presume I will have the payment of the wager on the morrow, gentlemen, preferably before we leave for Winchester.' Both men looked disgruntled but inclined their heads in reluctant acceptance.

Then, realising what had been said, Flambard turned back in surprise. 'You are coming hunting with us, Chatillon?' he exclaimed.

'Yes, of course, and I'm sure we can have another wager about who brings down this great sixteen-pointer,' he said, with a grin.

'I always said you had the luck of the devil, Chatillon, in more ways than one,' spat Belleme, who was more convinced than ever that something was afoot.

Chapter Fifteen

Early August 1100 – Zaragoza

To all outward appearances, Yusuf appeared to have adopted a stoicism towards his injuries and scarring that surprised his older brother, Abu Ja'far. He did not hide away, nor did he push himself forward. Instead, he followed the advice and strictures of the physicians, spending more time than usual in prayer and meditation. He rode out with his hawks and bodyguards most mornings as he began to build up his strength. Abu noticed that his brother could walk now with barely a limp. The linen hood and Berber headdress he wore constantly helped to cover his injuries. His wife remarked that she noticed that Yusuf always sat so that the unscarred side of his face was presented.

However, anger and, at times, rage were still very much alive underneath this calm exterior. He spent an hour at swordplay each day; his left arm may be badly damaged, but he was building the muscles in his right arm and shoulder. The hours he spent each afternoon in contemplation were, in fact, for meticulously planning his next move.

His brother declared across the Taifa, and to the far corners of the Ibn Hud dynasty in North Africa, that the blood feud

CHAPTER FIFTEEN

had been resolved and all assassins were to return. Yusuf had to grip his anger and leave the room afterwards, when his brother told him he was shortly leaving to sign a charter with King Alphonse and the Pope, promising to end the feud. He had stood and explained it all to Yusuf, as if he was talking to a child, spelling out again how important was this protective alliance with King Alphonse of Castile and Leon. Yusuf, thin-lipped, his right fist clenched, had given all the right answers to his brother.

Several weeks later, returning from a morning ride, he sat with his brother in one of the cool shaded courtyard gardens; water tinkled into a fountain nearby.

'Few know that you have returned from the dead, Yusuf, and we must keep it that way, so yes, enjoy your rides, but don't go to the markets where someone may recognise you. Sheikh Ishmael is dead, Yusuf and he will not rise again. Instead, I have the brother I thought I had lost returned to the bosom of the family. We must make sure that Piers De Chatillon, or even Prince Henry, do not find out that you are alive.'

Again, Yusuf nodded in acquiescence, and his brother went away happy that he had understood. However, Yusuf had agreed only because it suited him to stay in the palace at present; he was building up his strength, and he did not want a whisper to escape that suggested he was alive. He now knew exactly what he would do, and needed the element of surprise, to carry it out. He would ride out of Zaragoza with his men in just over a week while his brother was in Leon. He knew that what he was about to do may alienate Abu and his family—there would be no coming back here—but he had no choice. He was going to take his daughter back. This child, Coralie, had a pull on him more than any of the dozens of children he had fathered; she had touched his heart, this golden child, and he would kill anyone who stood in his way of taking her.

In another part of Zaragoza, in a large merchant's house, Bernard de Bordeaux was convinced that his wife, Mariana, was moon-touched.

'I'm telling you true, Bernard, do not dare to look at me that way. A concubine in the seraglio of Abu Ja'far told me that the women of the Sheikh's seraglio are not allowed to walk freely around the palace, or even mix with them anymore, and it is because of the rumour that the Sheikh is still alive and visits them every night!' she exclaimed.

Bernard laughed at his wife, which fed her irritation at him.

'His ghost might visit them, Mariana, for he was killed at Cabrera. He was burnt to death by the Horse Warriors; they watched him and his galley go up in flames. Most likely, it is one of his sons; they must be in their twenties by now and will have inherited their father's concubines.'

Mariana shook her head in irritation. 'I tell you, Bernard, something strange is happening in that palace. The women are subdued as if they have been threatened, and Abu's wife, Nadia, barely speaks to me anymore unless it is to do with fabric.'

Mariana was always determined to have the last word, but he loved her, this feisty Spanish woman he had found. He thought no more about it, but he found a few days later the conversation kept recurring in his mind. Then he shrugged it off as impossible. He had heard the tales of the death of Ishmael; no human could have survived that.

The next day, Bernard walked to his warehouse, to supervise an important delivery from Lucca in Italy. It was a beautiful roll of silk cloth spangled with gold threads, perfect

CHAPTER FIFTEEN

for the ladies of the palace, and he would make a tidy profit as he could charge a premium price for such quality.

Returning home, he called his wife. 'Mariana, get two of the men to carry the new cloth to the palace in the next day or so, and while you are there, see what you can discover about this phantom Sheikh,' he said, with a smile and a shake of his head that said he still did not believe it.

Mariana gave him a smile of pure triumph as she tossed her head and walked away, as she knew just the woman to ask.

Bernard was away for two days in Tarragona, supervising the delivery of a valuable cargo of wines, but when he returned, he found Mariana waiting for him in the courtyard. He could see she was bursting with news, but he waved her inside, away from the listening servants.

She waited until he had pulled off his boots and made himself comfortable in his favourite chair, a glass of chilled wine in his hand. He raised his eyebrows and smiled at her.

'Well? You obviously have news!'

'Bernard, what I told you is true. I swear on my poor sainted mother's grave, Ishmael is alive. Not only that, but I caught a glimpse of him, only from behind, crossing to his quarters. They say that he is so badly burnt, as to be almost unrecognisable, and that his face is frightening, like a mask!'

Bernard shocked to his core at this, sat forward and put down his wine.

'This is the worst possible news; we thought we were rid of that murderous bastard forever, that Chatillon and his Horse Warriors had put an end to him. I must send a message to Marseille; there must be someone there who can forward my message to Morlaix. Conn is undoubtedly back there with his family, and they will break it to Chatillon that his enemy

Sheikh Ishmael did not die. He still lives.'

Early August 1100 – Genoa

Marietta and Finian had arrived in Genoa without mishap. Travelling on horseback, with pack horses, in the summer months, was always much easier than using carriages or carts on the rutted roads. They had intended to stay at Chatillon's Castello on the cliffs, but the Signori Guglielmo Embriaco would not hear of it. Marietta had been brought up in their house since the age of ten; it was still her home, and she was like another daughter to them. He had received the message from Chatillon that she had now reached her majority and was taking control of her inheritance. He had therefore facilitated several days of meetings for her, with the factors who ran her warehouses and the Genoese merchants who had been her mother's partners.

Despite being busy each day with facts and figures that made her head spin, she still made time to spend with Isabella and get to know Coralie. She found the child enchanting, but could see that Isabella was still on the back foot and defensive, so she had to clarify her position.

'I am not going to judge or question your decision, Isabella; I'm sure you have your reasons. I have stood in your stead at the Chateau and taken your place as much as possible, especially with your twin boys, but they now need you. Ahmed needs you; he is a shadow of himself without you

CHAPTER FIFTEEN

at his side. And Chatillon loves you so much. You need to return Isabella!'

All of Isabella's rehearsed arguments fell by the wayside after this speech, and she found it difficult to meet Marietta's eyes. Finian hadn't helped; Isabella had long loved him as if he were a brother, but he now treated her with a cold reserve that she found unsettling. Not so Coralie, who he dandled on his knee and played peek-a-boo games with. Finally, she could take no more, and the next day she invited him to walk in the garden with her.

'Your face says it all, Finian, for it is set into such harsh lines of disapproval whenever you look at me. Do you not have any empathy for me? Can you not see it from my side?' she pleaded, touching his arm.

He disconcerted her by moving away and sitting down, with a sigh, on the end of the nearest stone bench, where Chatillon had sat six months before.

'I understand your fear, Isabella, but we all live with fear of one sort or another. You don't seem to appreciate what we have been through while you were in captivity. Where is *your* empathy? The sadness, the downright despair, the agony of the senseless deaths of Annecy and Cecilia. Then the endless, exhausting searching for you all over the Mediterranean for years, finding dead end after dead end with Piers becoming thinner, haggard and more disillusioned by the week,' he replied, turning to look her full in the face.

She heard the break in his voice but could not find the words to comfort him, so he continued.

'He needs you, Isabella. We all need you to return to us. Dion is with child again and misses you desperately. Your friend, Mishnah, is there recovering and asking if we're bringing you back. Padraig sorely injured Edvard, and we all thought he would die; he is only just recovering from a terrible head injury. Every one of us bears the scars inside and out, but we are stronger together because we support each other like the links in a chain. But, you have broken the chain; the links are lying forlorn on the ground because of you.'

Isabella felt her eyes fill with tears. Yet again, she could think of little to say apart from, 'The blood feud—it is that constantly hanging over us, not knowing who will die next. I don't want to live like that, I can't do it any more, Finian.'

Finian snorted in disdain. 'As Edvard told me, we are not the type to die in our beds, Isabella, you know that, and you chose your path when you married Chatillon. You knew his reputation, yet he excited you, and I think he still does. I never had you down as a coward, Isabella, hiding away in corners as you are doing now. And Piers? Do you know where he is and what he is doing? Do you?'

She shook her head, and her hands clutched her robe in dismay.

'Piers is in England, risking his and Conn's lives on one of the most dangerous assignments he has ever undertaken. He is doing it for you, Isabella, because Henry Beauclerc has promised that the blood feud will be lifted, but only if the chosen target is killed!' he cried, running his hands through his hair in frustration.

Finian had to stop and draw a deep breath, and she could see the emotion on his face; his fists were clenched now on his knees as he tried to regain control of his emotions. She knew he loved Piers like a brother and would only get this worked up if there was certain danger.

'Who?' she dared to whisper. 'Who is the target?' she repeated.

Finian did not answer at first. He was angry and upset but aware enough to look around the garden, and even up at the balconies above, to ensure that no one was near them as he murmured, 'The King! Piers and Conn have gone to arrange the death of William Rufus, the King of England.'

Isabella gasped and raised a hand to her mouth in shock.

'Are they mad? This plan can never work; they can be used by Henry as scapegoats, and the blame can be firmly laid at the Pope's door,' she exclaimed.

'So many things in this plan can go wrong, and Piers knows that, but this is all for you, Isabella. He is taking risks he would never normally consider, and he is there at the heart of it. I swear that if they both swing by the neck for this, I will not hesitate to put the blame at your door!' he declared, standing and leaving her, in shock, in a sun-filled garden that suddenly felt very cold.

Finian avoided being alone with Isabella as much as possible for the next few days, so he was pleased when Marietta expressed a desire to visit and stay on her estate in the hills above Genoa for a few weeks. She wished to ride her lands, have discussions with her bailiff and looked forward to seeing the servants she had known since she was a small child. So two days later, they rode up into the hills with ten of his men.

The estate was northeast of Genoa at a place called Aggio in what her mother had called her hidden valley. Sheltered on three sides by hills, it was the perfect environment to grow acres of olives and fruit, most of which came down into the markets of Genoa. When she was still a baby, her mother had bought the estate and employed an army of men to tame the south-facing slopes, clearing the scrub and creating terraces. In the spring, when the fruit trees were in bloom, it was one of the most beautiful places in the world, and you could walk for nearly a league on carpets of apple blossom.

The estate also kept large herds of hill sheep, not so much for their meat as for their unusual fleeces, which were long and fine and prized by weavers. Finian was content to leave Marietta and a few of his men in the large, sprawling manor house and ride out with the estate workers, to begin the drive to get the sheep off the hills and mountain slopes. He was amazed how these fleet, sure-footed sheep could work their way up the steepest and narrowest gullies, where no horse could follow. They would need men on foot with dogs to get these down, so they could wait a week or so. For now, they drove seventy or so sheep down to the paddocks, and the next days would be about shearing and baling the fine wool. Much of it would also be sold to North Africa, where it was prized and sold for premium prices.

Sitting with her bailiff, learning about the fruit, olives and wool, Marietta was astounded at her mother's business acumen. Hildebrand had talked to almost every merchant that came into the port of Genoa, but she had learnt about this breed of Mariui sheep from a travelling merchant. They were a cross between the Marinid herds of the Berbers and the Castilian Merino sheep, which produced this fine fleece, and her mother had built up the herd over several years. Over two hundred and fifty animals were grazing on the hill and mountain slopes above the estate. She discovered that the profit from the wool equalled the profit from all the other acres of produce on the estate. Marietta wondered how she would ever live up to her mother's reputation as a

CHAPTER FIFTEEN

businesswoman.

Having sat in numerous meetings, Marietta was overwhelmed by how much wealth she had, and she began to appreciate just how much effort Piers and Edvard had put in to oversee it for her. Chatillon had sold her mother's large merchant house in the city, and Marietta was pleased, for her mother had been murdered there by the warrior monks, along with several servants. However, she could still feel her mother's presence here on the estate where they had spent long summers.

Marietta enjoyed Finian's company; she sat in the large shearing barns and shook with laughter as she watched him trying to learn how to shear a sheep, while the animal kicked him, butted him, squirmed and escaped several times.

At night, they sat on the old Roman terrace outside. Her mother had taken the unusual step of building window openings with shutters on the main chamber that went to the floor and opened onto the west-facing terrace. They sat there on an evening and talked for hours. Finian may be a famous Irish warrior, but he was well educated by the monks in Ireland, as the nephew of the King. He was also exceptionally well-travelled during his years in exile. He was an interesting and amusing companion, and his love for his wife Dion and their sons shone out of him.

'We both hope for a girl this time, a dark-haired beauty with her mother's eyes and temperament,' he said, laughing at the thought.

They also talked about his future plans and horse breeding programme until she finally asked, 'And what of Conn and Georgio, Finian? Once the blood feud is finished, what will they do?'

'They are sell-swords, Marietta, Horse Warriors becoming famous in their own right. They will sell their services to the nobles and princes of Europe,' he answered, while watching her face in the soft dusk light.

'You are in love with Conn Fitz Malvais, are you not?' he asked gently.

'Yes, I am, and I'm sure it's obvious; he is all I ever think about, Finian. I can't even think about being courted by any other man, and I'm prepared to wait for him, but I have no idea what he wants or thinks.'

Finian gazed out over the laden fruit trees to the mist-covered hills beyond before answering her.

'Conn is still young, but he is also physically scarred by that tattoo on his back, and by the many brutal years he spent in the hands of the Warrior Monks. I'm unsure how much you know about that time, but no young child could go through that type of treatment without it leaving its mark, as everything was about survival. Also, they were repeatedly told that their families had sold them into captivity, and that they were worthless, and not wanted. To combat that, any child would build a hard shell around themselves to survive. Piers and I openly talked to Morvan about how that experience damaged Conn. Fortunately, he was then taken to Morlaix and surrounded by the love of his Malvais family, but that hard shell is still there, and very few will ever see behind it, Marietta.'

'I understand what you are telling me, Finian. I could not have found a more complicated man to fall in love with, and my expectations of having that love returned shouldn't be too high.'

Finian sighed. 'To a certain extent, but even I have found

that Conn is remiss in some of the simplest emotions of empathy and sympathy. He may hurt you but not understand why.' Suddenly, he laughed and shook his head while she gave him a puzzled look.

'I should have realised before. Of course, this is why he gravitates towards Piers rather than to his father. They seem to spend a lot of time together away from others, deep in conversation—you must have noticed. I can now see that it is because they are both so similar. No wonder Piers thinks he has found an apprentice, as they have so much in common.'

'I see that Finian, and I know that you are warning me off, that Conn should not be for me, but sometimes you just can't help who you fall in love with,' she said, sadly.

Finian put an arm around her shoulder and pulled her into a hug.

'Give it time, Marietta, but don't close the door on other suitors, for I'm sure you will have many, and you deserve to be loved. Now I'm to bed, as we're up with the dawn again tomorrow with the sheep. Next week, we are away again on the higher slopes for several nights. Why do you not invite Isabella and Gabriel to stay with you? I think it would do Isabella good to get out from within the high walls of the Embriaco Palace.'

She nodded, said it was a good idea, and promised to send off a messenger on the morrow. However, she sat in the warm evening air for some time, thinking about what Finian had told her. Some of it she knew, but he had given her food for thought, and she knew Finian would always be truthful with her. She trusted and loved Finian like a favourite uncle. She had never met her father, but she liked to think he was like Finian. Brian was a renowned horse whisperer and warrior, tricked and murdered by the Warrior Monks as they stole Conn. It was ironic that she had fallen in love with Conn, who had been such a part of her parent's lives, but she knew she could never stop loving him despite Finian's warnings.

Chapter Sixteen

The cavalcade paused to water the horses in the River Itchen, and Conn gazed across at the impressive walled city of Winchester.

'So this was the capital of Alfred the Great; I have often wondered what it was like,' he commented as Chatillon pulled his horse alongside him, dropping his reins to let his horse drink.

'Yes, it's impressive, a Roman city originally; most of the lower walls are Roman, but Alfred fortified them. They say, however, that it's even older than that. It has always been a city of significance and became the capital of the powerful kingdom of Wessex. It's now the home of the Royal Mint and the King's Treasury, hence the number of troops stationed here.'

Conn glanced back at the King, whose laughter suddenly rang out at the antics of his young courtiers, splashing themselves and others in the river in the summer heat.

'William seems in good spirits, and I admit I found it a little unsettling when we set up camp at Alton last eve, knowing what was going to happen. The King and his brother, Henry, played and sang a song together from their youth in Normandy, smiling and laughing together, yet Henry plans to kill him in cold blood in a few days.'

Chatillon raised an eyebrow because nothing unsettled him anymore, but Conn was new to this game. Chatillon leaned towards Conn and lowered his voice.

'I have watched people smile and kiss their victims minutes before they slid their long knives beneath their ribs. It all depends on what drives them, Conn. Power, greed, influence or the more visceral emotions of jealousy, hatred and even love. They don't see the person anymore; they see an obstacle, a barrier, or even an inconvenience. You will learn to accept all of this and shrug it off.'

'How long do we stay here?' Conn asked, as they gathered their reins and pulled in behind the King, on the road leading into Winchester.

'Two nights, as the King and Flambard have business to deal with, not to mention the many petitioners to see the King, for he has not been here for nearly a twelve month. On the third day, we will go to Romsey Abbey and use that as a base for the hunt. I suggest we meet with Henry and Walter Tirel for an early morning ride tomorrow. There will be much carousing tonight, so few will be up or roused that early. Let the others know.'

Conn inclined his head and rode back to join Henry and his boon companions.

The dawn had been barely up for an hour as Conn and Chatillon rode through the meadows and along the banks of the River Itchen to meet Henry and Walter Tirel. Despite the early hour, Chatillon found they had to double back twice, and break into a strenuous gallop in the opposite direction to lose his tail. Flambard's men must be better than he thought, and he hoped Henry had not suffered similar problems. They turned into a stretch of birch trees and wended their way through, until they found a large clearing where they dismounted and hobbled the horses. Henry and Walter were already there, and the tension and apprehension were tangible.

This morning was the first time the four of them had come together—the first time Henry would admit to being the instigator of the assassination, although the other two knew that Chatillon was the architect. Chatillon could see that both Tirel and Henry were nervous; he was pleased to see that Conn was not. Chatillon took the lead....

'Thank you, gentlemen, for leaving your beds at this ungodly hour, but this is probably the only chance we will have to meet, and there are details we need to ensure before we go any further.'

Walter intervened. 'I believe I know my part; Malvais has been over it several times. I'm to lead the whole party to the area where the stag was last seen, and we will proceed in a line at first—the dogs and huntsmen moving forward ahead of us on foot, the King and courtiers, bows ready, following behind. After a short while, I say we're using Conn's suggestion to approach the denser forest from different directions. My brother-in-law will lead the first group away to the north. I will take the King's group, including the three of you, to the west, where we truly spotted a large stag. The third group will approach from the east.'

Chatillon nodded in satisfaction.

Henry butted in with a harsh laugh. 'Let's hope that this legendary stag does not appear before then, or we are all undone.'

Tirel shook his head. 'We will ensure that the other groups

make enough noise that everything will be driven west. Once the groups are separated, Conn will swear he saw a glimpse of the stag through the trees, and we all gallop after him. Then, where the undergrowth is thicker, the arrows fly.'

Chatillon turned to the other two. 'Conn, Henry; you know your parts?'

They both nodded, but Chatillon noticed how pale Tirel was at their side.

'Conn and I will leave now and gallop back,' he said, picking up the reins, but indicating to Henry that he wanted a word.

'The only way this plan will unravel and we all end on the gallows or axeman's block, is if Tirel fails, for I do not like his mien at the moment. It has the stench of fear, and we can't risk that. On the way back, I suggest you remind him how great the rewards for him and his family will be once you are king.'

Henry's eyes narrowed as he turned and glanced at Tirel. 'I will deal with him, I promise,' he replied.

The next day, they left for Romsey Abbey; it was only half a day's ride across the rolling South Downs of Wessex. The Benedictine community of women was of long-standing since the first Abbess in 907 AD. The current, powerful and influential Abbess, Cristina, was Edgar the Exile's daughter and Edgar Atheling's sister. She carried the royal blood of Wessex in her veins. She looked down her long nose with disdain at William Rufus, someone she regarded as an immoral usurper of the English throne. She knew why William had been interested in her niece, Matilda; the King had been told he needed to give his reign some legitimacy by marrying Matilda of Scotland. The Abbess had ensured that possibility was scotched, but here he was again at the

CHAPTER SIXTEEN

Abbey with his raucous and unsavoury courtiers expecting hospitality. To say the reception was chilly would be an understatement, until her eyes lit on Piers De Chatillon, and then her demeanour changed.

'You did not tell me that the Senior Papal Envoy was coming as part of your party,' she hissed at Flambard, whom she barely tolerated.

'I did not truly believe that he would come hunting, Reverend Mother,' he replied, but he received a withering glance of contempt as she turned and advanced, all smiles, to Chatillon.

'Piers, you have finally returned to our poor little community at Romsey. I cannot begin to describe how honoured and excited the sisters will be. You must address them at compline tonight, and of course, you will be full of news from Rome.'

Piers was shocked at her appearance but did not show it. *She must be approaching sixty years of age now,* he thought, but although her tall, commanding figure was still upright, she was painfully thin and pale. Leaving the arrangements for her other guests to the Steward, she led Piers away to her room, to Flambard's disgust at this lack of respect for his king.

Abbess Cristina shut the door firmly behind them and waved Piers to a chair.

'I hear the antipope, Clement, is dying,' she announced. 'I do hope that is your doing and that he is writhing in pain on a daily basis,' she whispered, before laughing mischievously.

Chatillon smiled; he had always liked this intelligent, forthright woman and had previously removed one or two troublesome individuals for her.

'I promise that Clement will be gone before the end of the summer, Reverend Mother.'

'I could see that you were shocked at my appearance, Piers, although you hid it well, but I am also not long for this world. I have a large canker inside of me that is growing by the day. My hope is that I die before Clement, and I can be standing at the gates of heaven when he approaches, so that I can deny him entrance and kick him back down to Hell where he belongs, the imposter.'

Chatillon laughed aloud; he had always enjoyed her wit, but her next words chilled him.

'I presume that William Rufus will not survive this hunting trip now that I see you are one of the party!' she said, in a loud whisper.

Chatillon made a major effort to keep his face immobile at her accurate guess.

'What on earth made you think such a thing?' he asked, with a smile, while keeping his voice calm.

It was her turn to laugh.

'You were always easy for me to read, Chatillon. Why else would you possibly be in the Royal Forest with a man we both despise? I see his younger brother is also here; how convenient for you.'

She was certainly astute, but he would not confirm or deny her accusations; that way, danger lay.

'I hope you will not spread your views abroad, Reverend Mother,' he said, smiling.

She gave him a knowing smile and ordered some refreshments for them both.

'Tell me all the news. How is Paschal coping? He is a different kettle of fish from your uncle, Pope Urban; now, there was a decisive man who took no prisoners and brooked no dissent. I miss him.'

CHAPTER SIXTEEN

Chatillon smiled, for he had first met Cristina on her way back from Rome. She was travelling with his uncle, a cardinal at the time, and he was sure that there was something more between them than friendship and mutual respect.

'So do I, Cristina; I miss his wise counsel.'

The next day, to Flambard's curiosity and annoyance, Piers declined to go on the hunt, claiming Papal business. Piers knew that the first day would be scoping the forest for the ideal spot to let loose the dogs.

On the 3rd of August, however, he joined them, but to his dismay, Flambard suddenly announced *his* intention to join the party. This was the last thing the conspirators wanted, for they knew Flambard would stick to the King's side like the leech he was. Piers approached the Abbess, who said she would see what she could do; he also approached Conn.

'Is there anything you can do to Flambard's horse that will only appear after about an hour's riding?' he asked.

Conn smiled. 'Leave it to me.'

Conn searched the ground on the way to the stables for a thin, sharp stone. Finding one, he walked along to where Flambard's large grey was munching a bag of oats, ready for a full day's hunting. A stable boy was hovering, so Conn sent him to fill a bucket of water. He nipped into the stall, and apologised to the horse, as he picked up a rear hoof and, using the handle of his dagger, hammered the small sharp stone into the softer frog area. The horse immediately whinnied and tried to kick out as Conn lowered the hoof to the ground. In no time, this would become painful, bruising would develop, and the horse would begin to limp.

Shortly afterwards, the horses were led out, and they mounted in the large courtyard of the Abbey. Suddenly, the

Abbess and her nuns appeared with trays of strongly spiced mead. These were handed around, and she personally gave the silver cup to King William, whilst joking that she would taste it first if he wished. To give him his due, he laughed as he was very aware of her antipathy to him, but because of her lineage, the King tolerated her and even smiled at her quips and digs. Chatillon watched her hand a second cup to Flambard, and he turned away to hide his smile, for he was sure there would be something unpleasant mixed in the stirrup cup.

An hour into the journey to the Royal Forest, Flambard's grey horse went lame. To Conn and Pier's annoyance, young Beaumont offered to give Flambard his horse and return the grey to the stable. So they rode on, but Chatillon dropped back beside him.

'Are you well, my Lord Bishop? You are pale and sweating. Is this due to exertion, or is the excitement too much for you?'

Flambard, a fit forty-year-old, snorted with disdain at the suggestion, but then he began to retch, and moments later, he was leaning from his horse and vomiting. Piers pulled away while waving to the squires at the back.

'Look to your master. He is unwell. I hope it is nothing serious as there were rumours of plague at Winchester. Did you mix with the lower orders at all, Flambard? I hear you like a good quality whorehouse as well as the next Bishop,' said a laughing Chatillon, as the squires backed away in alarm.

'Damn you, Chatillon, still your mouth! I have been poisoned, and it will be your doing,' he groaned.

'Don't be ridiculous, Ranulf. I have been nowhere near you, and what could I possibly gain apart from the pleasure of seeing you on your knees in the long grass, puking up your breakfast?'

At that, Chatillon turned to join the others, who were quickly disappearing into the forest ahead of him. He had a smile on his face as he cantered to catch up, but he quickly cleared his mind to focus on the important task ahead.

Yusuf Ibn Hud, once known as Sheikh Ishmael, arrived with his ten chosen men just as the sun set in Marseilles. He had used one of his brother's smaller galleys, as the ones he had remaining were too large and distinctive. His brother had left the palace at Zaragoza several days before to go and sign the charter, now in the hands of King Alphonse. He expected to be away for two weeks, which had given Yusuf time to prime his men and to arrange for the horses to be waiting in Marseilles. They would spend the night on board the ship, as no doubt even his scarred face could be recognised in Marseilles. They would go ashore to leave just before dawn, and intended to head east along the coastal route to Genoa. He knew it would take him longer than normal, for he still tired easily, but he'd learnt patience. He had discovered that his daughter, Coralie, was still there. He was also pleased that Isabella had not returned to her husband because it meant he was still causing the Papal Envoy pain.

As he rode out at the head of his men with the wind in his face, he felt exhilaration for the first time. He felt alive, for against all the odds, he had survived, and now Ishmael was riding to take back his child, and would kill anyone who got in his way.

Chapter Seventeen

August 1100 – Massy, France

Brother Tomas groaned as he put a hand to his head. He had been viciously set upon by a group of thieves and vagabonds, who had followed him from the dubious wayside inn he had stayed in at Marcoussis. He'd noticed their furtive glances and knew they were talking about him, so he'd taken to his flea-ridden pallet bed early. The next morning he had paid the innkeeper's slovenly wife and set off north, knowing that he was only half a day's ride from his destination at Chatillon sous Bagneux and praying that the Sheikh's men were not still following him. He had heard Ishmael's orders to search the roads if his body was not found at the monastery, and he had spent the last weeks travelling only at night and hiding during the day, which had slowed him down. Staying at an inn had proved to be a costly mistake.

As the road entered the dense forest, they attacked him from the trees on both sides. Tomas had tried to ride on, kicking the big grey into a canter, but two of the men on foot had grabbed the reins, jerking the horse's head violently around so that it had reared. Tomas had clung on, but then they dragged him from his horse, and he hit the ground with a sickening thump, forcing the air out of his lungs and breaking his left arm. He only remembered the first part of the beating as their boots had kicked him senseless. After several blows and punches to his face and head, Tomas finally lost consciousness. They had taken his silver, and even the large crucifix on his belt, which had a silver figure of Christ and had been a present from his proud parents.

He had come to several times but then lapsed into oblivion again from the pain. Fortunately, his big grey horse was well trained by Friar Francis, and it had galloped away into the trees, or they would have stolen him as well. Tomas finally came round as the horse had returned and was snuffling at his face. He lay on the ground groaning, his body battered, bruised and worse. He was sure several ribs were broken, and he had heard the crack of his left arm, but he now found that they had also broken his right ankle. For several moments in pure despair, he had lain there and sobbed, but then the face of Meddur came to him, and he knew he had to find the strength to move. Friar Francis had given him a task, and he feared that the robbers might decide to return and finish him off.

He had grabbed the hanging reins with his right hand and gripped them with all his strength as he used them to pull himself to his feet. He almost fainted because of the pain but was determined to get on the horse. Using his right arm and hopping to the side, Tomas made three attempts to mount the horse without success. The pain in his throbbing head was unbearable, and he was sure he passed out again, as it seemed much darker when he awoke on the ground again.

With great difficulty, he rolled onto his side and struggled to his knees. Tomas lambasted himself for his lack of courage and looked around for anything to help him. There was a log, but it was large and had fallen propped up at an angle against another tree. He hopped towards it, pulling the horse with him, and finally got himself onto it and into a kneeling position so he was able to move up it and throw his upper body onto the saddle. He knocked his broken arm on the high wooden front of the saddle and screamed in agony.

To his dismay, there was an answering howl. Wolves! It was rare that they attacked a horseman, but he hadn't managed to get on the horse yet. A second answering howl gave him the motivation to try and pull himself far enough over to get his left leg into the stirrup, enabling him to swing his damaged right ankle over. He clung to the saddle for all he was worth as his head spun, and he feared he would pass out again from the pain.

Finally, Tomas gathered the reins of the patient gelding and pushed him forward, out of the trees, and back onto the road. He dared not risk any speed, so they went along at a painful jog for the rest of the night, which jolted every inch of him, but he was determined to try and get out of the forest, while often glancing over his shoulder, still fearing pursuit from one group or the other. An hour or so after dawn, he entered the village street of Massy and slid to the ground in a gasping heap outside the local blacksmith's forge. The village dogs began to bark, and soon, several wary villages came to see what the commotion was about.

Brother Tomas, battered, bruised and dehydrated, was now running a fever and could only manage one whispered phrase repeatedly.

'Chatillon, must get to Piers De Chatillon,' before he passed out.

The blacksmith knew exactly who that was and ordered his gawping son to get the cart put to. In no time at all, Brother Tomas was in a cart heading north, his grey gelding tied behind. The blacksmith's wife had come with them in the back of the cart, dripping water into the poor monk's mouth and wiping his hot brow. The Chateau was only an hour or so away to the north, and the gatekeeper viewed this group with suspicion and dismay, as they demanded to see the master.

'Lord Chatillon isn't here; he is over the sea, in England,' he announced, reluctant to open the gates. Fortunately, Georgio and Gironde had been out early, rabbiting. They arrived just as the blacksmith's wife told the gatekeeper exactly what she thought of his parentage, in no uncertain terms and very colourful language. Gironde began to laugh, so she also vented her fury on him.

'Can you not see, young sir, that we have a dangerously injured man here, which is no laughing matter? The only word he mutters is Chatillon.'

They came and looked at the prone man in the cart, and Georgio took control.

'It is a monk, badly hurt by the look of it. Open the gate. Gironde, run and get Ahmed, for I fear there's more to this,' he ordered.

By the time the cart had pulled up at the steps, Ahmed was there waiting with Mishnah, and he ordered them to bring the monk in and lay him on one of the trestle tables in the hall, so he could assess his injuries.

'Do you recognise him?' he asked the woman from the cart, who shook her head.

'We found him on the ground outside our forge, still clinging to the reins of his horse and babbling the name

CHAPTER SEVENTEEN

Chatillon over and over. He has a right nasty cut on the back of his head, probably where they cudgelled him off his horse to rob him,' she explained.

'Do we know that is what happened?' Georgio asked him.

'The woods south of us are full of deserters and ne'er do wells looking to rob innocent folk; even a man of the cloth would not stop them.'

'He has nothing on him; even the heavy cross and beads the Benedictines wear are gone,' said Ahmed.

At that moment, Edvard appeared and listened to the tale. He slipped the monk's hand into his own and leant over him.

'Can you hear us? What is your name?' he asked gently, stroking his forehead.

'Chatillon, must get to Chatillon,' the young monk murmured.

'He needs time, Edvard, after a head injury, you know that. We will sedate him, treat his wounds and splint the breaks; tomorrow, he might tell us more,' said Ahmed, before turning to the blacksmith and his family.

'Come and sit inside, and I'll ensure that Madame Chambord brings refreshments for you.'

The woman bobbed her head in thanks, somewhat overwhelmed by this Arab physician whose fame and success were known for miles around. He was tall, thin, and bald, but intelligence and kindness shone out of his dark brown eyes as he patted her on the arm in thanks.

Mishnah had ordered warm water and bandages, and she stood patiently waiting for Ahmed's instructions on what else she needed to bring from his workroom. They worked on the young Benedictine monk for over an hour and then gently carried him upstairs to a bed. Dion, who had been suffering from her usual morning sickness, reached the gallery just as he was carried past, and she raised an eyebrow at Georgio, who was helping. 'Edvard will tell you,' he whispered.

'Anyone we know?' she asked Edvard, who ordered the servants to clear away the bloodied cloths and bowls of water.

'No, somewhat of a mystery. He repeatedly asks for Chatillon in an almost plaintive voice, but I have never seen him before.'

'We can only wait then. Are there any messages yet?' she asked hopefully.

Edvard smiled at her. Dion always bloomed when with child; her skin glowed, and her hair shone.

'No, Dion, but we're talking about Finian, who only sends a message when the world around him is in flames and he needs help. We know they arrived safely in Genoa, and he promised you, in front of witnesses, that he would be back by All Hallows.'

She stroked his cheek to thank him and went to check on her sons. Edvard watched her go, thinking how wonderful it must be to be loved by a woman in that way. She adored Finian, and it had been love at first sight for her. He had never before missed this in his life, for he had chosen a life serving Piers. But now, things were different, for Edvard had fallen in love for only the second time in his life. It was simple, for he loved Mishnah and had a wonderful friendship, but he had no idea how she felt about him. Mishnah had suffered so much at the hands of men that he told himself she would never want another, so he stayed quiet.

The young monk lapsed into a deep Theriac-induced sleep for twenty-four hours, and they took turns to sit with him throughout the night. An hour before dawn, Edvard came to

CHAPTER SEVENTEEN

relieve Mishnah, and they sat quietly together for a while.

'He looks very young and vulnerable, and at the moment he is settled, but as soon as the Theriac wears off, he becomes agitated, and he repeats Piers' name repeatedly,' she whispered.

'He has obviously been through some trauma, but was that before he was attacked? Or is it related to the attack? We will have to wait until he wakes,' murmured Edvard.

The following morning, just as Conn and Chatillon were entering the Royal Forest with King William Rufus, and Yusuf Ibn Hud was galloping towards Genoa, Brother Tomas opened his eyes and looked up into Edvard's calm face. He tried to speak, but his mouth and lips were dry, so Edvard dipped a cloth in water and squeezed the water into his mouth, while moistening his lips. The young man closed his eyes again but reached out a hand to grasp Edvard's.

'Thank you for helping me, but where am I?' he asked.

'You are at the Chateau outside the village of Chatillon sous Bagneux, and you were brought here by the blacksmith. You had collapsed, fallen off your horse outside his forge. They think you were attacked in the forest. Is that what happened?'

Tomas closed his eyes again and slowly nodded; it hurt to move his head. He tried to pull himself up but cried out in pain from his broken arm. Edvard reached over for a small cup and held it to his lips.

'This will help for the pain,' he said.

Tomas drained the cup. 'Theriac, wine and something else I don't recognise,' he whispered, while Edvard raised an eyebrow.

'Healer,' murmured the monk. 'I am Tomas, a healer, a Benedictine. I work in the infirmary, but he killed them all,' he exclaimed, his voice rising, while his head dropped back down on the pillow, as if even getting those sentences out was exhausting.

'Sleep for now; let your body repair itself. You can tell us later,' said Edvard, gently laying his hand back down as Ahmed came to check on the young man.

'He is from a Benedictine infirmary somewhere. There was killing, and people died, but Tomas escaped. We know nothing more.'

'The blacksmith and his wife say he was attacked in the forest. Was he with a group? Did they kill all of the others?' asked Ahmed.

Edvard had just reached the door when Tomas jerked on the bed and shouted, 'He slaughtered them all, even the sick and lame in their beds, all gone, all gone!'

Ahmed smoothed his hot brow with a damp cloth while reassuring him.

'You are safe here now, in the Chateau. None can hurt you here.'

'He wants to kill me as well because he knows I have worked it out!' he moaned, as he thrashed back and forth.

Ahmed held him still. Concerned that he would damage the broken bones. Edvard, however, wanted to know more.

'Who? Who is this man?' he demanded.

'He calls himself Meddur, but he is Ishmael, the murdering Sheikh,' he whispered.

Edvard and Ahmed froze at those words, and then Edvard picked up the young man's hand again.

'You have nothing to fear, Tomas; Ishmael is gone, he is dead, you are safe.'

There was a murmuring groan, but the sedative had worked, and he settled into a deep sleep.

CHAPTER SEVENTEEN

The two men sat and stared at each other for several moments, trying to work out what they had just heard; then Ahmed spoke.

'We are dealing with two incidents here, for there's no doubt that he was recently attacked in the forest.' Edvard nodded in agreement.

'However, Ishmael and his men attacked his monastery sometime in the past. The blow to his head may have brought those memories to the fore. Go and rest, as I wish to sit with him.'

Edvard went to lie on his bed, but it took a long while for sleep to come; the horror in the monk's voice, when he had shouted about the slaughter, unsettled him. It was as if he was talking about something that had happened just a few days before.

The Steward at Morlaix in Brittany went to find his mistress, Lady Merewyn. She and Ette were sorting the linen chests in one of the upper storerooms.

'A message has arrived, my lady, for young Master Conn.'

Merewyn smiled at how the servants still called a strapping Horse Warrior in his twenties the young master.

'They can't know that he is away in France with Chatillon; please leave it on the table in the business room. Luc and Morvan should be back from patrol in a day or two.

Fortunately, the two Horse Warriors arrived home late the next evening. But the message strip lay with others and was not unfurled until Luc De Malvais sat down at the table the next day. He read it in disbelief; there was no way that this could be true. He had watched Ishmael go up like a living torch, the flames before his eyes. He was the one who had thrown the lantern to smash at the Sheikh's feet; no man could have survived that. Luc pushed back his chair, and, carrying the message, he found Morvan at the paddock fence, watching his son, Gervais, schooling a promising youngster. Luc did not say a word as he handed the vellum strip to his brother.

Morvan's brow came down in a frown as he read the contents.

'This is impossible, Luc; we watched him die, his clothes and hair in flames. The galley went up so quickly that no one could have survived.'

'My thoughts entirely, although we all left the ship quickly.'

They stood silently for a few moments remembering that vivid last scene before they had all scrambled over the gunwale to escape the fast-spreading flames.

'By the time we were in the boats, the whole thing was ablaze; I remember well the heat of the flames on our faces,' exclaimed Morvan, while Luc nodded in agreement.

'We both know Bernard well, Morvan. He was one of ours, a Horse Warrior, not a fantasist by any means. He is sensible and down to earth, and his wife does have access to the seraglio. I'll send a message back immediately to try and get some more information,' said Luc, turning away.

'Get a message to the Chateau to warn Chatillon just in case this may be true; although they may still be in Paris, Edvard will pass it on,' Morvan shouted after him, not realising that Chatillon and Conn were far from Paris.

CHAPTER SEVENTEEN

Luc returned to the castle while Morvan stood in the slight summer breeze watching his son and shouting instructions. His bare arms rested on the warm wood of the top rail, but soon he was no longer seeing Gervais. Instead, Morvan weighed up the possibilities and implications if the news were true. Then he remembered that Ishmael had sworn that he would get his child back. It was a good thing Isabella was still under the protection of her father in Genoa. Undoubtedly, Ishmael would want revenge on Chatillon and possibly on them; Isabella and the child were in danger.

To his son's surprise, Morvan turned and ran up the path leading to the castle.

Chapter Eighteen

3rd August 1100 - Genoa

Yusuf Ibn Hud pulled his weary, aching body out of the saddle and dropped to the ground. He clung to the saddle leathers for a few moments and rested his forehead on their warmth. He still suffered pain from his body's burnt and injured areas; most had healed, but several were still tender and sore to the touch. The scarred skin also cracked and split in places, and each night he rubbed the unguents the physicians had given him into those areas.

He had sent some of the men ahead to find this old farmhouse, only one storey and sadly neglected, but in its day, it had been a fine house. Tiles were missing from its roof, and many fences and gates were broken or hanging. It was just as bad inside, with broken furniture, dust and dirt everywhere. He could not hire local people to clean as they needed to keep their presence quiet, even though they had discarded their Berber robes for Western dress as soon as they left Marseilles. Yusuf spread his bedroll beneath the shade of the lemon trees and told his men to clean it and repair the beds and furniture where they could. Drawing buckets from the well, they set to inside the house while Yusuf slept under the trees.

Half a day later, it was habitable, and rabbits were roasting on the spit in the kitchen. The farmhouse was outside the small village of Pegli. An hour's ride to the west of Genoa, Pegli had the best of both worlds; it overlooked the sea below and had small lakes and forested slopes around and above it, providing the inhabitants with fish and games. Yusuf was confident that no one would find them here on the slopes to the east of the village; the farm and land seemed to be long abandoned. They had brought several hawks with them, for he intended his hawkers to take down any pigeons heading from the west to Genoa. Ishmael also sent two hawkers into the city, to position themselves close to the Embriaco Palace in case any filtered through. He wanted no one in Genoa to know he was alive.

Over the following days, he sent groups of his men to scout the city. Two of them took up residence in one of the better inns as merchant traders. His informers had told him that Isabella had returned to her parent's home, and that was where his problems started. The Embriaco Palace was a veritable fortress, as were most of the great homes in the city due to previous wars and pirate attacks. The Signori himself was a tough hero who had cleared the eastern Mediterranean of pirates decades before, and still maintained his own small army. So it became a waiting and watching game.

To Ishmael, this would have been infuriating and frustrating as he had always been a man of action and instant gratification. However, the burnt and scarred Yusuf had learned patience during those long months of recovery, when he discovered that healing could not be rushed. So, now he had his men watch and learn all of the routines of the palace they could see, and eventually, they found lesser servants, stable and kitchen boys to bribe.

After a week, however, he still possessed only limited information. Yes, Isabella was there with his daughter, Coralie, and her son, Gabriel, but she never left the palace. Gabriel did, wandering with a servant and armed guard into the town to buy fripperies for his mother. Gabriel occasionally rode out with his grandfather and uncles, but Yusuf had no interest in him. So, he waited, but he knew that time was running out. He had to act soon as his brother would return to Zaragoza, and would be furious to find him gone.

Then, they finally had a breakthrough from one of the stable boys; Lady Isabella and her children were shortly travelling up into the hills, above Genoa, to stay on a large estate for a month. They were expected to leave at the end of the week. Yusuf immediately sent his men to find everything they could about this estate. Did it belong to the Signori? Would it be as well-guarded as the Embriaco Palace? Once he knew its exact whereabouts, he would send men out to scout the area. He briefly considered the possibility of snatching Coralie enroute while they were travelling, but he expected them to be well guarded, and he was right. Twelve well-armed men accompanied the cavalcade.

Yusuf had risked riding into Genoa, and his men arranged for him to position himself in the second story of a house where he could look down on them as they passed below, on their way out of the city. Gabriel was riding with the Signori's captain of the guards at the front. A tall, well-set boy, he looked much older than his years, and Yusuf could see the resemblance to his mother. There seemed to be a dozen well-

CHAPTER EIGHTEEN

trained men riding behind. Chatillon was obviously taking no chances with his family. Isabella and Coralie travelled in a well-padded carriage, with a canvas awning stretched over a wooden frame to shade them from the hot August sun.

Yusuf found that his hand was gripping the window frame as he saw the burnished golden hair of his daughter. She seemed to have grown up so much. At that moment, she looked up, and he gave a sharp intake of breath as her eyes met his. He stepped back quickly into the shade of the shutter in case her mother followed her daughter's stare. He felt shaken at first, pleased to have seen her, but then he was consumed by anger, in a way that he had not experienced since the first six months of his injuries. He clenched his right fist and, raising it to the ceiling, let out a strangled roar of rage at what had been done to him. Two of his men came running up the outer staircase in concern, but with his face still contorted with anger, he turned to face them.

'It is time for Yusuf to slink back into the shadows, for Ishmael is about to return,' he growled at them through gritted teeth.

He followed them back into the street to retrieve their horses from the livery stables. On the ride back to the farmhouse, he worked on his plan to snatch the child from the estate and get her away. It had to be foolproof. He had the advantage of surprise, for only Abu, and the trusted family members, knew he was alive and where he might be. His brother might send men after him, but he knew he had a few weeks' head start on them, which should give him enough time to take the child. The galley he brought to Marseille was now waiting offshore in Genoa; soon, he intended to be on it with his daughter and sailing for Tunis.

3rd August 1100 – The Chateau

Edvard and Mishnah returned to the bedside of Tomas, the young monk, the next morning. Ahmed stood up and stretched as they arrived.

'He has mumbled and tossed back and forth during the night but has said nothing more of import. I suggest that we lower the dose of Theriac; the swelling on his ankle is reducing, and the pain will lessen. It is a clean break; he is young, and it should heal well. Call me when he wakes,' he ordered.

Edvard only stayed for a short time as he had business to attend to. As he stood, Mishnah reached out and took his hand. He looked down at her, surprised but gladdened.

'I need to thank you, Edvard, for being a friend and for not judging me,' she whispered.

The big man laughed softly. 'Who am I to judge you, Mishnah? Expelled from my order several times for drunkenness and for far worse. Then badly injured, I see us as two travellers, friends together on the road to recovery,' he replied.

'I hope we have become more than that,' she whispered.

He brought his other hand forward and held her long, delicate hand between his, looking down into her eyes.

'I believe we have, and can become even more yet in time,' he said, and smiling, he left her, his heart bursting with joy.

An hour later, Tomas opened his eyes again. Mishnah gently lifted his head and raised a cup of buttermilk to his lips, which he gulped down. Then he dropped his head to the bolster and closed his eyes; she thought he was going back to sleep, but he began to talk in a low voice.

'There were four or five of them; they followed me from the inn and chased me through the forest. I turned into a denser area of shrubs to try and escape, but I was dragged from my horse, my foot caught in the stirrup, and they broke my ankle when they wrenched it out and began to beat me. Fortunately, my horse bolted, or I would not be here today, because he returned to me.'

He closed his eyes again, and his face was pale, as if talking was too much effort.

'I will send for our physician; he will want to check your condition now that you are awake, so don't move,' she said, standing.

He nodded. 'I need to piss as well,' he murmured apologetically, but she patted his shoulder and laughed.

'He will help you with that as well, as there's a stone jug here.' Then she was gone as Tomas lay trying to gather his thoughts. He knew he had something important to tell them, but it seemed just out of reach.

Ahmed was pleased with the young man's progress and kept the pain relief minimal. Madame Chambord brought a bowl of nourishing chicken broth, and Ahmed managed to prop him up into a sitting position, pleased to see that the food disappeared quickly.

'Can you tell us where you are from, Tomas? You mentioned an infirmary.'

The young man frowned, as if concentrating hurt his head, and then, he suddenly grasped Ahmed's hand so tightly it hurt, and the Arab physician flinched.

'He killed them all—him and his men—the patients, monks,

all dead. I am the only one left alive.'

'Was this was Sheikh Ishmael, as you shouted his name a few times?' asked Ahmed.

'Yes, and his ten men who had arrived at the monastery. I only survived because Friar Francis woke me and told me to run and hide in the cold store on the cliff. They hunted for me and came after me.'

Ahmed stroked his hand. 'You are safe here now; no one can hunt or harm you here,' he reassured him.

'You don't understand. There is something I must tell Chatillon. Before he was murdered, Friar Francis said I had to ride north to find him, to only talk to him, and tell him what had happened at the monastery. I had to warn him.'

Again, Ahmed nodded. 'Piers De Chatillon is in London; he will not return for another month, perhaps longer. However, I'll send him a message if it sets your mind at rest. Would that suffice?' The young monk nodded.

'What do you wish me to say?' he asked, his head on one side.

'Friar Francis said to make sure Chatillon knows that Sheikh Ishmael is still alive and will come looking for him, for he wants revenge!'

Ahmed blinked several times and then shook his head before saying emphatically, 'No! Ishmael is dead, Tomas; he died on the galley at Cabrera. They all watched him go up in flames.'

'I tell you he is alive; he was knocked into the seawater, which is how he survived. We have experience of burns, especially Greek Fire, in our infirmary, so he was sent to us. He was almost dead. The Friar saved his life. He was with us for nine months, but we had no idea who he was until his brother Abu Ja'far arrived with some of his men. Ishmael wants no one to know he is alive, so he killed everyone at the monastery.'

The young monk fell back exhausted onto his bolster.

Ahmed made to stand but found that he was shaking so much he had to put a hand out to the wall to steady himself.

'It cannot be true,' he whispered, as he went to the door and shouted loudly and urgently for Edvard. Ahmed pulled the door closed behind him, to try and gather his thoughts while he waited for his friend, who came striding along at once. It was rare ever to hear Ahmed raise his voice.

'What is it, my friend?' he asked, shocked at Ahmed's face and seeing his hand was shaking. He put his hands on his friend's shoulders to steady him.

'Ishmael is not dead. Somehow, he survived the fire,' he announced. Edvard looked at him in disbelief and then turned and slammed his clenched fist into the stone wall.

'God's blood! Does this never end?'

'We must warn Chatillon immediately; he has to know the danger he is in,' said Ahmed.

'The danger we are now all in once again, for that man will not rest until he has exacted his revenge,' he said, raising his hands to his head in exasperation. Then he stood stock still and met Ahmed's worried eyes.

'Isabella and Coralie! He will go to Genoa for his daughter,' whispered Edvard.

'They should be perfectly safe with the Signori; that palace is a fortress. But we must still let them know,' responded Ahmed.

'I'll code the messages immediately,' Edvard said, turning away to go to the business room, only to be met by the Steward holding out a strip of vellum.

'Urgent message from Morlaix, Sire!'

Ahmed stood beside him on the gallery as there was more light from the high windows above.

Chatillon, we have news from a reliable source that Ishmael is alive and with his brother in the palace at Zaragoza. Take care, for he will look for revenge.
Luc De Malvais

'It's true then,' said Edvard, his face pale with shock.

'What is true?' asked Gironde, joining them with Georgio.

It took Edvard a few moments to answer as he collected himself.

'Ishmael is alive,' he said.

Georgio's mouth dropped open. 'Impossible, we all watched him go up in flames.'

'Somehow, he is alive, and once again, he needs to be stopped. I will go to send the messages,' he declared, striding down the corridor to send the first message to London, while wandering how he would break it to Mishnah that Ishmael, her tormentor, was alive.

3rd August 1100 – Zaragoza

Abu Ja'far was incandescent with rage. After everything he had done for his brother, everything he had explained about the threat to the Taifa, and the danger from the Pope and the princes of Europe, he had returned to find that Yusuf was gone. He did not doubt that he had left to exact his revenge. Abu knew his brother, and had not been taken in by his insistence that he only wanted his daughter, Coralie, back. His brother was a killer, no matter what name he used, and his obsession with Chatillon and his family meant he would kill all of them if he could.

Abu knew that Isabella was the daughter of the powerful Signori Embriaco, who would not stand by if his daughter and grandchild were threatened. Moreover, he would take vengeance on the Ibn Hud Dynasty if anything happened to them. Yusuf was about to bring their house and world crashing down with his actions, so he had to be stopped.

'Send for the Portuguese, Vasquez; I need him here immediately!' he ordered.

He had to find his brother as soon as possible, and this burly, ruthless mercenary could be the one to kill him, for Abu realised now, that this was the only way to end the feud. His brother had to die.

3rd August 1100 – Royal Forest

Chatillon had drummed the plan into the heads of Henry and Tirel, so they led the King's hunting party deep into the forest to where the last alleged sighting of the 'Monarch' had been. Tirel hushed the large contingent of huntsmen and courtiers as they came to a series of glades. It was just after dawn; the dew still covered the grass, and the early sunrise dappled the trees and the undergrowth where it reached the forest floor. Conn could not resist glancing back at Chatillon, who was just behind him, and with a cynical smile, he raised an eyebrow, which made the Papal Assassin smile back; their thoughts were so often aligned. He knew what Conn was thinking. *Look at this peaceful, pastoral scene, which in no time will be covered in chaos, mayhem and blood.*

Tirel held up a hand and the hunting party halted as he gave instructions to the group that had gathered around. In a low, soft voice, he addressed the King.

'I have ensured that we're downwind, Sire. Beyond these glades, there is a stream and a larger clearing where we had a glimpse of him grazing with his hinds. Deer are creatures of habit, as you know, and I'm sure he will return there. I suggest that we split into three groups and approach from different directions. To the north, a steep cliff rises from the stream, so they can't run that way. You are in the western group with me and Prince Henry, Sire. The groups in the east and south will drive them towards you. We will take up our positions, and the huntsmen will loose the dogs on our signal.'

The King smiled and inclined his head in agreement as Prince Henry leant forward.

'Come, Brother, we have the best bowmen in this group to the west, and I'm sure the others will drive him straight onto your bow, so we need to be waiting on the far side with our arrows nocked and ready.'

William Rufus acquiesced, and they moved slowly and quietly off to the right to come around in an arc. A group of eight riders eventually took up position on a slight grassy

CHAPTER EIGHTEEN

knoll in the shadows; the King, Henry, Chatillon, Conn, Walter Tirel, his brother-in-law Richard Fitz Gilbert and two huntsmen on small, sturdy ponies with leashed dogs. They were all experienced huntsmen, so they sat silently in a line, their bows ready. Conn sat slightly further back so the King and huntsmen could not see his bow nocked with an arrow that had the diamonds of Walter Tirel on its fletching. Conn's task was to put an arrow into the heart of William Rufus if Tirel lost his courage or missed. As he sat there and waited, Conn was surprised at how calm he felt. There was no agitation or apprehension about killing the King, the man who was a blood relation, his uncle. When the dogs began to strain at their leashes and growl, he felt the first frisson of anticipation.

Chatillon was equally calm; his only concern now was the aftermath and how it would play out. He didn't doubt that William Rufus would die here today, if Henry had to cut his throat himself. He glanced over at the Prince; the only sign of nerves Henry showed was the reins passing back and forth between his fingers. Piers was still concerned about Tirel, who was pale and sweating slightly. He glanced back at Richard and indicated that he should calm his brother-in-law. Richard moved his horse silently beside Tirel's and touched his arm. Tirel jumped, but Richard smiled reassuringly at him. Just then, a hunting horn blew to the east, and their hounds were loosed and gave voice.

'By the face of Lucca, they have sighted him. Make ready, make ready,' cried the excited king.

Chatillon waved their own huntsmen forward, the huge dyerhounds straining at their leashes with excitement, as he moved his horse alongside Henry and Richard, making sure they were out of range of the arrows that were about to fly.

The sounds of men, horses and dogs grew nearer, and suddenly, a huge stag burst through the undergrowth. No one was more surprised, or pleased to see it, than Chatillon. It wasn't The Monarch, but Piers saw at once that it was a twelve or even fourteen-pointer.

'Let loose, let loose,' shouted Henry, as the stag turned to flee through the trees. A veritable storm of arrows followed as the dogs gave chase. They could hear that the stag was soon held at bay, as the other packs of dogs reached him, but the riders in the other groups were far behind them. The King, Tirel and Conn surged ahead to reach the stag.

'Shoot! For God's sake, shoot again,' shouted Henry, from behind, and suddenly, the air around Chatillon seemed full of the sounds of arrows as the other groups galloped through the trees, hallooing and excited to be in at the kill.

The great stag was now on its knees; at least three arrows had found their mark, and two dogs had the great beast by the throat. One of the nobles pointed at the King's distinctive red-fletched arrow in the stag and shouted, 'God's blood! What a shot. Well done, Sire, your arrow got the heart shot.'

However, William Rufus did not answer; he was slumped forward on his horse, and as they stared at him, concerned by what they saw, he toppled to one side and fell to the ground.

There were cries of dismay and shouts of, 'To the King! To the King! Help his majesty!' as they dismounted and gathered around him. William Rufus lay on his back, an arrow firmly embedded deep in his chest. His brother Henry was on his knees beside him, holding his hand.

'A physician, is there a physician anywhere amongst us?' he cried.

CHAPTER EIGHTEEN

Chatillon put a hand on his shoulder while glancing at the gathered courtiers.

'It is to no avail, Sire; look, the blood also comes from his mouth. He is heart and lung struck and will not last the hour, even with a physician.' Chatillon turned to Conn. 'Go and find a cart; I'm sure we passed one a short distance back.'

'Yes, the charcoal burner—he had one,' Conn said, remounting and riding back through the trees.

'Surely he will live, Chatillon,' pleaded Henry.

He turned to the crowd of shocked nobles whose eyes were on the dying king.

'How did this happen? My eldest brother, Richard, was also killed in this God-forsaken forest while I was a babe. Now I'm losing another. Whose arrow did this foul act?' he demanded, leaning forward to look. The diamond pattern was clear to all, and they turned to stare at Walter Tirel.

'This is your arrow, Tirel! God's blood! You have murdered the King,' shouted Robert de Beaumont, who had just arrived with his brother, Henry.

'Twas an accident, I swear, for I shot true at the stag. I loved William, and I was one of his most loyal supporters. You assembled here; all know that to be true,' he shouted, stepping forward and wrenching his arrow from the King's chest with both hands, which resulted in a spurt of blood that stained the King's tunic.

'No one will believe that. They will hang you and gut you for treason,' murmured Henry.

Tirel's face reflected his horror at this betrayal, from the man who had asked him to do this, the man who had promised him safety and reward. Now, it seemed as if he was betraying him and turning him into the scapegoat.

Chatillon, seeing his panic and concerned at what he might blurt out, cursed Henry for his foolish words, and pulled Walter away to one side.

'Fly, Tirel, there's a ship waiting at Pevensey; go to Normandy to your estates in the Vexin. I swear that you will not be held accountable.'

'It was a black day when I met you back in Le Puy, Piers De Chatillon; you have ruined my life,' he muttered.

'There is no time for this, Walter, for they may come and lay hands on you. Now go!' he ordered, in a low voice.

Tirel did not need further telling. He raced for his horse, mounted and, viciously pulling its head around, galloped off through the trees. The shouts of the nobles and courtiers rang through the trees behind him.

'Murderer!'

'They will find you!'

'You will pay!'

Meanwhile, Henry stood up, and Chatillon looked at his tear-stained face and saw that he was shocked now that his brother lay dying at his feet. The enormity of what he'd done had struck Henry, who was as white as a linen shroud. Chatillon put a hand on his shoulder.

'Be steady, Sire. You can do nothing here now,' Chatillon said loudly.

'Stick to your plan,' he whispered in an aside, as he turned away and beckoned the Beaumont brothers over; both were staunch supporters of Henry, who was running his hands through his long blonde hair.

'What to do now?' Henry said, turning to the nobles and opening his hands in supplication, a move Chatillon applauded in his head.

CHAPTER EIGHTEEN

'We must take the King's body to Winchester; it must be laid out in state in the cathedral as befits a King of England,' announced Richard-Fitz-Gilbert.

Henry nodded. 'Aye, we must; I'll ride ahead and tell the Bishop. Chatillon, you must come with me, for you are a witness, as were all of you gallant folk here. Your testimony will be crucial!'

Chatillon smiled behind his hand as they all nodded and indicated they would bear witness. He looked down at William Rufus, now deathly white from blood loss. There was no sign of life, but when he knelt and put his fingers on his neck, there was a faint pulse. He stood back up.

'The King is dead, and there's nothing more to do here; Richard waits with the King's body as Conn Fitz Malvais is fetching a cart to take him to Winchester. Ah, here he is now. Prince Henry is right. The rest of us must bear witness. Tirel is a renowned shot, as we all have seen, but now he has fled, a sure sign of guilt. We ride, gentlemen. We ride for Winchester to share this dreadful news.'

Chatillon walked to where Conn was dismounting and announced loudly, 'Fitz Malvais, you are responsible for bringing the King's body to Winchester. This good man, Eli Parratt the fletcher, will help the charcoal burner to lift the King's body onto the cart; Henry, use your cloak to wrap your brother's body.'

Henry unfastened his cloak and rode over to hand it to Conn. At the same time, Chatillon whispered, 'Bring him very slowly, Conn, for he is still alive.'

Henry paled even more, and then, pulling his horse into a rear, he galloped off for Winchester, with the nobles and Chatillon following at speed, leaving Conn to stare down at the dying, bleeding king lying on the ground.

Chapter Nineteen

August 1100 – The Genoese foothills

The long convoy of men and carriages bringing Isabella, Coralie and Gabriel to Marietta's estate rode through the first set of gates, at the bottom of the long, uphill drive to the manor house. Gabriel was excited and had ridden backwards and forwards on the journey, to describe to his mother what lay ahead. He had never been here, and the countryside was so different to what he was used to around Paris. His eyes ranged over the hundreds of fruit and olive trees that covered the hills surrounding the house. The estate even had its own vineyard on the lower southern slopes that produced a crisp, dry white wine.

Isabella had not been here since the day Chatillon had brought her with him, to tell a very young girl that her beloved and beautiful mother, Hildebrand, was dead. She hadn't realised then that Hildebrand had been one of Chatillon's many lovers. So although the estate certainly had a beauty about its rich verdant slopes and orchards, it also held a sad memory as she remembered the white face of Marietta, streaked with tears, and the week she spent comforting the distraught child. To Chatillon's surprise and pleasure, Isabella had announced then and there that they would bring the orphaned Marietta to live with them.

Now Marietta was fully grown—a very pretty young woman and a wealthy heiress. As they passed through the second set of gates with several guards on duty, they saw the long, low, red-tiled house ahead dominating the crest of the hill. Marietta, warned by the barking estate dogs, was waiting on the steps for them. She ran down to greet them, delighted that Isabella had decided to leave the walls of the Embriaco Palace and venture into the countryside. Coralie was wide-eyed at the novelty of the journey, the trees and the new house. She had barely been outside her grandfather's house in Genoa since they had arrived. Marietta rushed to pick her up while Anna, a faithful housekeeper since her mother's days, went to get refreshments.

'Come, Coralie, let us find you some creamy cold buttermilk to drink,' she whispered, inviting them inside. Isabella laughed as Coralie reached up her hands with a wide smile.

'You still have Anna and Josef, I see,' commented Isabella.

'They have been a part of my life since my mother bought this estate when I was three years old. This estate is their home as well. Anna is still my housekeeper, and Josef is still my Steward despite the greying hair; they are both full of life,' she explained.

Meanwhile, Finian greeted Isabella, still slightly aloof with her after their last conversation, and then he went to talk to Embriaco's men to get them settled.

'I don't envisage any trouble, but we do know that there may still be fanatical followers of the Sheikh out there who want to continue the feud and avenge his death. So, stay vigilant. I suggest you split up and join the patrols I have set up—get

CHAPTER NINETEEN

to know my men, as we're all staying here for about a month. Also, in a week or two, the fruit harvest will begin, and we will all help to gather it, which will be a change for you all after your soft city life,' he laughed.

They grinned and went to drop their saddlebags and bed rolls in the large barn. Finian watched them go and was pleased. They now had a significant cohort of men. He did not expect trouble, but after the attacks at the Chateau, he was never complacent. The assassin who breached the Chateau at Yuletide was still fresh in his mind. He was pleased that Isabella had finally left Genoa, however. That was a step forward, and he intended to ensure that her visit here went smoothly, preparing the way for her to return home.

Isabella had forgotten how charming the estate house was; originally a large Roman villa, it had been added to and improved over the years. It was now a large, sprawling manor with many rooms around a central courtyard which had several unusual features.

Instead of a great hall, it had a large stone-flagged west-facing room which was delightfully cool during the day. What Isabella loved about it was the huge square arched opening that went from ceiling to floor with great heavy folding shutters, that were moved back for most of the day but could be securely barred at night. Several long trestle tables were used for meals for all the men and staff on an evening, and the arch led onto a terrace covered in warm red terracotta tiles. The family sat out there on an evening, with a spectacular view of the hills and mountains rising behind them to the west.

Hildebrand had created a small kitchen garden here with stone-flagged pathways, and it was a riot of colour from the flowering herbs and plants. Isabella dropped gratefully into a chair with relief after the bumping and jolting of the wagon over the rutted roads. She breathed deeply as her eyes swept over the view.

'I had forgotten how thoroughly peaceful it is here; it's like another world away from the bustle of the city and the port,' she said to Marietta, who bounced Coralie on her knee.

'It was my mother's favourite place; she did enjoy the cut and thrust of her business dealings on the wharves, but here, she could be herself.'

'I never really knew her; I saw her at some of my father's dinners and events but never really spoke to her, and then she was murdered. She sounded such a strong and clever woman to raise you on your own, while building up her business empire,' commented Isabella.

'She was, and when I'm here, I can close my eyes and still see her here, sitting in your chair, her blonde hair cascading down her back, telling me about my father.'

'It is sad, Marietta, that she went far too young, but she has left such a legacy for you and your children.'

'I think Marietta would rather have her mother here to love her and spend time with her,' said Finian, walking out to join them.

'Is that another sharp barb meant for me, Finian Ui Neill?' snapped Isabella.

Finian disarmed her with one of his smiles as he sat and joined them for a while.

'We all miss you, Isabella, especially your boys, for you filled the Chateau with love. We all want you back.'

Isabella did not answer, still unsure what to say, so she watched Coralie. A small gecko had come out onto the edge of the terrace to sun itself and catch flies. Coralie was fascinated. Wriggling out of Marietta's arms, she headed towards it while her mother smiled. As Coralie reached the reptile, it fled, and the child turned with such a look of disappointment that they all laughed, which broke the ice. Gabriel joined them, and he picked his sister up.

'Come and see the puppies in the barn; they have just opened their eyes,' he said.

Finian bowed and followed the children out.

'How long are you staying with us?' asked Marietta.

'A few weeks at least, perhaps a month, but then I must return to Genoa. You will also be leaving here, are you not?'

'It all depends on your plans, Isabella; if you do not return home, I must go back there, for the boys need me.'

Isabella felt a pang of guilt at those words as Marietta continued, 'I also have another reason, as Conn Fitz Malvais will likely return with Chatillon, and I'm in love with him.'

Isabella widened her eyes in surprise and smiled at her.

'He has grown into a very handsome warrior; any woman would fall for him.'

'Is that supposed to reassure me when he is hundreds of leagues away, and surrounded by the beauties of the English court, who will try to lure him into their beds?' she asked, holding her hands up in mock horror.

Isabella laughed before asking, 'Does he return your love, Marietta?'

'I have no idea Isabella. He has kissed me, and he seeks out my company, but you've met Conn—he's like a closed book.'

Isabella put out a hand to touch her arm and reassure her.

'Who could not love you, Marietta? But you are both young. Enjoy spending time with him and see what develops.'

'Wise advice, I'm sure, but not helpful when I lie awake at night, and my stomach churns in excitement at the thought of him.'

Isabella laughed again, but not in an unkind way.

'I know how you feel, for Chatillon still has that effect on me now, and I have decided that I will return to him and my home in the autumn,' she admitted, in a whisper.

Marietta clapped her hands in delight at this news.

'We can all travel together, and what a joyful reunion that will be.'

Ishmael lay on his corded bed in the coolest room of the old farmhouse, forcing himself to rest and sleep each day. He knew he needed to eat well and build up his stamina for what lay ahead, so he sent his men to the local markets to buy fresh food and bring back any further information. He knew he had to be careful, as he could not risk a whisper that any of his men were in the city. This meant that questioning the whereabouts of an Embriaco country estate had to be subtle, but his men were meeting a dead end. Embriaco owned warehouses, a fleet of ships, and several properties but no country estates. Ishmael wracked his brain as to where Isabella was going that day, and he chastised himself for not having sent men to follow them.

The next day, he sent one of his men with a pouch of silver to question the stable boys and kitchen boys, but they had to be careful; they could not risk exposure or be seen talking to them, which meant waiting until the boys were sent out on errands. Surely, one of them knew where Isabella and his daughter had gone.

Three days later, he had a possible answer; he had forgotten all about Marietta, Chatillon's adopted ward, who was an heiress. They had been given a vague location for her estate, about a day's ride away, so he sent two of his men disguised as merchants to reconnoitre the area. When they found it, he told them to spend a few days there and watch all the movement of people in or out and assess the number of guards. Isabella had played right into his hands by leaving the city and the protection of her father's palace.

Every step of what he planned would have to be thought through and flawless if he was to carry it off, and then he would take Coralie far away to where no one would ever find her.

August 1100 – The Royal Forest

Conn told Purkiss, the charcoal burner, to back the cart as close as possible to the body, and then come and lift it into the cart. Purkiss stood wide-eyed when listening to them. He realised that this was the King, and Conn noticed that his hands began to shake. He put his hand on the man's shoulder to reassure him, and Purkiss physically jumped at the touch.

'Be not afraid. This was a hunting accident. The King is dead, and you have both been honoured by Prince Henry to help us take his body to Winchester, where he will no doubt be buried. I assure you that you will be well rewarded for this deed,' he explained.

The man was only partially reassured, as Conn wrapped the body in Henry's cloak, but he took the King's feet with Conn taking his shoulders, and they lifted him into the cart where Eli Parrat, the Fletcher, pulled him into position. The cart was filthy from years of transporting charcoal, so Richard de Clare laid his folded green cloak down, to at least keep the King's head from bouncing on the blackened boards. As they dropped the body gently into position, William Rufus let out a soft groan that Conn covered with a loud cough, and his eyes met those of Richard Fitz Gilbert, which had widened in alarm.

'Is he alive?' he hissed.

Conn shook his head and spoke loudly for the others to hear as Purkiss stood at the foot of the cart with Eli.

'It's common for a dead body to make noises such as that; it is the gut wind and trapped air in the lungs leaving the body. His spirit and soul will be long gone.'

'Dear God!' muttered Richard, shocked that William Rufus was not dead, as he tied his horse to the side of the cart and climbed up beside Purkiss on the front seat. Conn sat on the tail end, his legs dangling to ensure the body did not move. Eli Parrat mounted his horse and led Conn's behind.

It was a warm, late summer's day, and several hours later, they stopped to water the horses and rest the ageing forest pony that pulled the cart. As Conn led his horse to the stream, Richard gripped his elbow and held Conn's hand up. It was covered in blood. Conn glanced back at the cart; sure enough, blood dripped from one side of the tailgate.

CHAPTER NINETEEN

'You know as well as I that dead bodies don't bleed this long after death. The King is still alive, Malvais!'

Conn hushed him, as he had discovered that Purkiss had very keen hearing, and he didn't want to be forced to kill the two men helping them.

'He has not long to live, as he can't possibly lose that much blood and survive. Or we can finish him now if you wish, for I can hear the panic in your voice, Richard. This alarm will not stand us in good stead when we reach Winchester if you are like this, so steady yourself. Remember that Henry will remember the part you played in this plan and will reward you.'

Richard stared at the cart and sighed.

'I agree with you, but we should let God decide, for even I call a halt at regicide.'

At that point, Conn turned on him and grabbed his jerkin, even though Richard was his father's friend.

'We're all involved in this, Richard Fitz Gilbert de Clare, to a greater or lesser degree. From the moment we agreed to go to Tirel's house and threaten him, we acceded to Henry's plan to kill the King,' he hissed at him.

Richard nodded, and Conn let go of him. They were back on the cart and heading on the long road to Winchester a short time later. Conn knew instinctively to avoid Romsey, which might prove perilous with Flambard still being there. If there was any sign of life in the King, Chatillon had been sure it would be extinguished one way or another on that road.

As the dying king trundled on, the future king was riding into Winchester to share the news of the King's tragic death, and to present his own claim to the Bishop and nobles who would assemble. He knew it would not be easy, for many of them were friends and supporters of his older brother, Duke Robert of Normandy, but Henry had a plan.

Chapter Twenty

3rd August 1100 – Winchester.

Henry Beauclerc stormed up and down the small King's Chamber at Winchester Castle. At the same time, Chatillon tried to calm him as William de Breteuill, a staunch supporter of Duke Robert, had just emphatically refused to endorse Henry. He had declared to the assembled nobles in the Great Hall that Duke Robert was the next appointed heir, and they should send a messenger to expedite his return to take the throne of England.

'Nothing is to be gained by letting your emotions rule here, Henry. You must put forward a sound and balanced case for why they should make you their King. Unfortunately, the rule of patrimony will not serve you here, and not only is Robert recorded as William's heir, but you swore an oath of loyalty to that end in front of some of these nobles. However, there may be another way. I will be back shortly,' he said, leaving the frustrated prince alone.

Chatillon entered the crowded Great Hall and approached two of the Prince's powerful supporters. Henry de Beaumont, the Earl of Warwick, and his brother Robert de Beaumont, the Earl of Leicester.

'The crown is within reach of Henry's hand, and I need your voices in this hall to be loud and sustained in his favour. But first of all, come with me,' he said, while scanning the room for the man he sought. Finally, he found the noble he was looking for.

Walter Giffard, the Earl of Buckingham, was the Justiciar of England, the King's chief minister, but Chatillon knew that Giffard hated Flambard with a vengeance. Ranulph Flambard was still recovering at Romsey and, as yet, was unaware that the King, his friend, was dead. Chatillon had made sure of that by sending a message to Cristina to keep him indisposed. Chatillon also knew that although Giffard turned a blind eye to the long-running affair of his wife, Agnes, with Duke Robert, he was not happy about it; what Chatillon had in mind would give him a chance to pay Duke Robert back for years of cuckolding.

'Giffard, I need your advice. Come with us to the Prince as he needs your help.' Chatillon noticed how Giffard pulled himself to his full height, and Chatillon remembered that although he was a proud, ambitious man, he was also prone to flattery.

'We need your wise counsel,' Chatillon said, ushering him and the other two earls, into the chamber, where Henry was now calmer but still clenched his fists open and closed, as Chatillon invited the men to sit around the table near the window.

'Duke Robert is still God knows where in Europe while England is without a king, leaving you open to chaos if the Scots or Welsh attack. I can say with certainty as Papal Envoy that Pope Paschal will look with favour on the accession of Henry Beauclerc, as the Prince has already sworn an oath on sacred relics to support the Church in England, and show his loyalty to the Holy See. Something which William Rufus and Flambard did their best to destroy. We have some support among the nobles, but we need more. We need you, Giffard, to be an advocate for Henry, as you know these lords well. Is there any argument for Henry's accession to the throne that they would accept?'

Giffard said nothing at first as he stood, walked to the open window, and gazed out into the crowded bailey below, which was full of troops. Meanwhile, the four men waited in anticipation of his reply.

'The Bishopric of Winchester, one of the richest sees in the land, has been vacant since the death of Bishop Walkelin in 1098. Since his death, Flambard has appropriated the revenues from the See of Winchester. I want the position of Bishop to be given to my brother, William Giffard, and have the revenues returned to my treasury where they belong. I would also expect to keep my position of Justiciar for the new king,' he demanded, turning to face Henry and Chatillon.

Piers smiled, but it was not pleasant.

'Ambitious as ever, Giffard, but we must hear your counsel before we agree to any of these demands. Is there an argument that will sway opinion? If there is, then Henry will consider your request, and yes, you will be rewarded as the King sees fit.'

'One word, Chatillon, but a word that is rarely used. However, it does stand in law in both church and state.' He paused, and you could have heard a pin drop as they waited.

'Porphyrogeniture,' he announced.

Chatillon gave a snort of laughter at this while the other three men looked puzzled.

'What does that mean?' demanded Henry.

'It means, Sire, that you are the only son of King William and Queen Matilda who was born to a crowned reigning king and queen; your siblings were not. Therefore, this gives you an equal, if not stronger, claim to the throne as a truly royal hereditary prince,' explained Giffard.

Henry now laughed aloud as well; a laugh of relief as he stood and grasped Walter Giffard by the shoulders.

'God's blood, Giffard, not only will I give your brother Winchester but I will retain him as my Chancellor. I will need wise heads around me. Now let us go and present this argument to the assembled nobles waiting in the hall.'

The tension in the Great Hall was palpable, with a loud buzz of conversation, which quietened while Giffard declared his, and his family's, support for Henry and then put forward the argument.

There was shock at first, and tempers flared for a while as the arguments went back and forth; several still championed the rights of Duke Robert, but Giffard's position as Justiciar held weight, and the Beaumont earls made their voices heard. After some time, the dissenting voices became fewer.

Henry stood on the dais and raised his hands.

'I now claim this castle under the law of porphyrogeniture; I seize it as is my right as King Elect. Any lords who dissent may freely leave now. Beaumont, my friend, we ride at once to seize the treasury before that snake, Flambard, can appropriate it. Chatillon believes he may still be at Romsey, and I wish you to send men to detain and imprison him, for he will answer for his crimes against you all and the people of England.'

There was a cheer at that announcement as Flambard was

universally disliked.

Henry stepped down, and Chatillon put a hand on his shoulder.

'Well done, Sire, and well said, but as you know, we left your brother's body with undue haste in the forest. It would be best if you now made amends as it will arrive either later tonight or tomorrow, and you should ensure that he is buried.'

Henry nodded. 'As usual, you are right, Chatillon,' he said, before turning to Giffard and the crowded hall.

'My Lord Giffard will welcome my poor brother's body into the cathedral, where it will lie in state before being buried here, in Winchester, by the newly appointed bishop, as befits a king of England. I cannot stay for my Council, as I have no choice but to ride for London tomorrow.'

He turned away, and his eyes met Chatillon's, who inclined his head in satisfaction, but he could still not see a shred of regret or compassion for his murdered brother. Piers did not doubt that Henry would prove to be just as ruthless a ruler as his father, King William I, and possibly more difficult to control.

4th August 1100 - Romsey Abbey

Flambard found that he seemed unable to shake this ailment that prevented him from keeping food in his stomach. Anything he ate, even the thin chicken broth prepared by the nuns at Romsey, would either not rest long in his stomach or go straight through him, so he spent time in the stool closet. He was so concerned with his problems that he gave barely a thought to the fact that the hunting party had not returned. It was high summer, and he knew they had wine and victuals with them. He was again back in the stool closet when the stern voice of Abbess Cristina assailed him.

'Flambard, are you ever coming out of there? I need to have conversation with you,' she demanded.

'God's blood, Reverend Mother, can't I even empty my bowels in peace?' he asked in irritation.

'The physician has prepared a chalk and elderflower drench that he promises will line your innards. Let us hope it improves your temper as well, as I think you may want to hear this news, if you value your life!' she exclaimed, as she moved away.

Flambard, concerned at that sentence, made his way to her room where, without a word, she handed him a cup full to the brim of a thick, white, noxious-looking substance.

'So what was so important that you had to pursue me to the privy?' he demanded, after reluctantly draining the cup.

'Sit down,' she ordered, settling herself in her large carved chair behind the table.

Flambard paused momentarily at her tone and then remembered her royal lineage and the influence she seemed to wield from Romsey. Like a spider in the centre of her web, he thought, as he reluctantly sat opposite her.

'Our local woodcutter arrived with his delivery this morning, and I caught him telling what seemed to be an exaggerated tale to the servants in the kitchen. He told them there had been a hunting accident in the forest and that a body had been placed in the charcoal burner's cart and taken to Winchester.'

CHAPTER TWENTY

There was silence in the room as Flambard tried to make sense of what she was telling him. Finally, though his mouth seemed suddenly bone dry, he asked the question he dreaded her answering.

'Who? Do we know who was in that cart?' he asked, in a voice cracking with panic.

'They are saying it was the King!' she exclaimed, and for a second, he thought he saw a satisfied gleam in her eye before she turned away.

'I don't believe it, pure fantasy. The lower orders thrive on this type of make-believe and rumours. Bring him here, this woodcutter; I will flay him alive if it is a falsehood!' he demanded.

'I questioned him, Flambard; he placed his hand on the Holy Book and swore he had it directly from the huntsmen who were there. They were bringing the stag in that the King shot. I have now sent the woodcutter with two of your soldiers to find the full truth of the matter. However, if, as I believe, it is true, then you have lost your protector, Flambard, and many in that court would be happy to see you strung up.'

Flambard was astonished at her audacity in daring to say that to him, and he blustered and bluffed it out, refusing to believe that William Rufus could be dead. He pushed his chair back so hard it fell over, and he headed back to his small chamber. He suddenly found that his legs felt weak, and he sat down heavily on his wooden cot, staring at his cloak and saddlebags on the chest against the wall. *Is she right?* he wondered. Should he leave Romsey now or wait for his men to return? Surely, even if it were true, he would be safe, for he knew too much about too many of the chief nobles for them to turn on him, and most of them owed him money.

His mind went back and forth, trying to decide what to do for the best. Finally, he stood, calling for his servant to pack his belongings and take his saddlebags to the stables. He knew he had months, at least, to consolidate everything and hide his own wealth, for Duke Robert, the heir to the throne, had not even reached Normandy yet. He decided to wait for his men to return with the truth, and then if it were true, he would ride for London and summon the King's Council. He had always controlled them and would do so again.

Walking towards the main doors, he heard the sounds of arrival outside; either his men had returned quickly, or the King's hunting party was returning. He stopped at the large oak doors of the Abbey to find a much larger body of armed men. They were led by a young knight, De Perche, who Flambard recognised as one of the Earl of Warwick's contingent.

'Ranulf Flambard, you must come with us as I carry an order for your arrest and imprisonment from the Earl of Warwick, Henry de Beaumont,' he announced.

Flambard let out a guffaw of laughter.

'Don't be ridiculous; who gave him the authority to sign this, and on what possible grounds? I am a faithful servant of King William Rufus,' he shouted, as the young knight dismounted.

'By order of King Henry and the Earl of Warwick, you will be taken immediately to the Tower of London.'

Flambard found that he had to put a hand to the stone arch to steady himself. 'King Henry? There's no such king,' he whispered, as the Abbess Cristina walked out to stand beside him.

'Prince Henry appeared before the King's Council yesterday and was chosen to be our new king; he will be crowned almost immediately.'

'Impossible. What of our real king, William Rufus?' he asked, a rising note of panic in his voice, as he heard a soft laugh from the Abbess beside him.

'King William Rufus is dead, Sire; God bless his soul, he will be buried in Winchester today,' he announced.

Flambard felt his legs going as two of the armed men came and seized him. They led him to a horse where they bade him mount, tied his hands tightly in front of him, and handed the reins to the serjeant.

Abbess Cristina watched with great satisfaction as a white-faced Flambard was led out of the Abbey gates on the road to London. She allowed herself a smile as she murmured, 'Bravo, Chatillon, well played. I knew you would never fail me.'

She turned, and with a spring in her step, went to the chapel to find their priest. They needed to arrange prayers and masses for the deceased king's soul.

Chapter Twenty-one

4th August 1100 –Winchester

It was the early hours when the cart finally trundled through the gates of Winchester. It had been a long journey with an unfortunate load, and the strain showed on the faces of Conn and Richard Fitz Gilbert de Clare. Chatillon's men were waiting and directed them to the nearby cathedral where the Prior and his clergy were waiting despite the late hour. The King's body would now be treated with the respect it deserved; cleaned, anointed and placed in the waiting shroud and coffin. The King would be buried later that day after the service in the cathedral.

Having handed their responsibility to the priests in Winchester Cathedral, the two men made their way to the castle where Chatillon awaited them.

'Go and get a few hour's sleep, for we leave Winchester at dawn. Henry and his entourage are riding for London, and he has announced he intends to do it in one day. I have sent men ahead and arranged for changes of horses.

'Is he mad?' asked Richard, his face drawn with tiredness and dirt from the cart and roads.

'No. He's determined to be crowned king tomorrow in

CHAPTER TWENTY-ONE

Westminster Abbey, so we must get him to Westminster Palace and find an archbishop, or bishop, willing to carry out the ceremony. As you know, the Archbishop of Canterbury, Anselm, who should be performing the ceremony, is exiled to Normandy. I have sent messages to Thomas, the Archbishop of York, but I believe him to be in the north at Ripon, which is too far away to get here in time. So we have to get Henry to Westminster tonight so I can use all my powers of persuasion on Maurice, the Bishop of London. Unfortunately, he was one of the Chancellors and Keepers of England for William Rufus and one of his supporters. He will be suspicious of the King's death and will likely refuse to crown Henry unless I can find some leverage to talk him around,' answered Chatillon.

Richard Fitz Gilbert ran his hands over his face in frustration.

'Everything is being done with indecent haste, and if we're not careful, fingers will be pointed at us and particularly at you and your involvement, Chatillon,' he declared, in a worried voice.

Chatillon narrowed his eyes at him.

'You should know better than this, Richard. We've had dealings together for nearly twenty years, and you know that everything I do is behind closed doors with few, if no, witnesses. I only trust a few men; you are one of them, so don't fear exposure. You are tired, so I suggest you sleep well and attend the King's funeral service as would be fitting and expected. That will give a good impression, with so many of us missing. I have instructed the Prior to gather as many clergy and local lords as possible, along with a large choir. Conn and I will ride with Henry to try and resolve things in London.'

Richard looked grateful, and he went on his way while the others made for their beds and prepared for an early start.

5th August -Westminster Palace

Conn and Chatillon had often been forced to ride at speed to cover distances, but saying the breakneck ride to London was exhausting would be an understatement. Two horses and courtiers were lost on the way as the animals were blown and could go no further. When they finally reached Westminster and stiffly dismounted, Chatillon congratulated Henry on probably setting a record for the ride, as they headed for the royal chambers. The Papal Envoy lost no time summoning the Bishop of London to attend the King immediately. When he finally arrived, he was angry at being brought from his bed, to ride through the night, at this ungodly hour. The Bishop became even angrier when he discovered that only Prince Henry summoned him, not the King. At that point, Chatillon stepped out of the shadows where he had been standing quietly watching, bringing the diatribe against Henry to a sudden close, as Bishop Maurice blinked at Piers in surprise. Then he bowed in recognition of Piers as the Pope's representative.

'King William Rufus is dead. The King's Council have chosen Henry as their next king, so yes, your King summoned you, as did I.'

Bishop Maurice turned and collapsed into the nearest chair.

'What news to bring me, Chatillon? I declare I am shocked to the bone. How did the King die?'

'A hunting accident, killed by a stray arrow from one of his faithful supporters, Sir Walter Tirel. There were many

CHAPTER TWENTY-ONE

witnesses to the accident. The King has been buried at Winchester today with all honour,' answered Chatillon.

The Bishop's eyes flew to Chatillon's face as he suddenly realised why he had been brought here.

'Maurice, we can raise neither Anselm of Canterbury nor the Bishop of York, who is at Ripon, and I know that Pope Paschal's next choice would be you, as Bishop of London. You have previously held prestigious roles as King William I's Lord Chancellor and Keeper of the Seals; you are highly respected. We need you to crown Prince Henry as King of England tomorrow in Westminster Abbey.'

Maurice looked at them both as if they were mad.

'On the morrow? Impossible! The arrangements which must be made, the senior Clergy in England summoned, the oil procured for anointing the King. God's blood! It is nearly the morrow now, and the whole King's Council must be summoned. We can't possibly do this that quickly, and you do realise that Archbishop Anselm will have my innards torn out and used to strangle me if I do this behind his back.'

Seeing the panic on his face and the stubborn set of his mouth, Henry stepped forward.

'I assure you, Bishop, that your new king would be eternally grateful for your agreement to this,' he exclaimed.

'The Bishop of London is in the middle of an ambitious building programme, Sire. He is rebuilding a new St Paul's Cathedral after a fire destroyed the Saxon original. I'm sure that he would welcome additional funds and the sending of the palace masons to help him,' interjected Chatillon.

The obstinate set of the Bishop's mouth softened, and he gave a deep sigh.

'I'll do it, but I want my misgivings about this hole-in-the-corner affair noted to Anselm and Pope Paschal. I will not have this coming back on my head when the Archbishop of Canterbury finds out what we have done,' he grumbled.

Chatillon smiled, knowing they had him.

'Leave Anselm to me; just play your part as requested. Now we must leave you, Sire, to make some of these arrangements,' he said, shepherding the Bishop out.

Conn had been waiting for some time in the antechamber, and Chatillon could see his agitation as he sent the Bishop on his way. However, Maurice had not finished, and suddenly he turned and gripped the Papal Envoy's forearm.

'This haste is unseemly, Chatillon; I hope this is all legal and above board. I tell you, I feel very uneasy about all of this,' he hissed.

The last thing Chatillon needed was the Bishop to waver in his commitment now.

'I assure you, Maurice, I would not let the Pope's name be mentioned in anything that was not genuine. You must see the need for haste, as we cannot let England be without a ruler in these uncertain times. I am conscious of a whisper that the Dauphin of France, Prince Louis, has designs on not only Normandy but this throne as well,' he replied, noting with satisfaction the look of horror on the Bishop's face.

He crossed to Conn, who immediately pulled him over to a table where several candles blazed. Chatillon saw that he was holding a coded message on a thin slip of vellum.

'This has been waiting for us, but having read it, I'm in total disbelief for this can't be true, can it, Piers?' he asked.

Chatillon, his curiosity roused, took the message from him and held it to the light. Conn saw his face whiten, and his lips compressed as he read the message in a whisper,

CHAPTER TWENTY-ONE

'News has arrived here at the Chateau from two different but reliable sources that Sheikh Ishmael survived the fire on the galley at Cabrera. You would trust these sources, and so we believe this to be true. He was undoubtedly badly injured and is presently staying at his brother's palace at Zaragoza.'

It was signed, *Edvard*.

Chatillon read it silently over and over and then met Conn's eyes.

'We saw him die before us on that galley, and surely no man could have survived those flames? Could it be one of his sons masquerading as him or taking his mantle and name upon their shoulders? They must be in their twenties now,' he commented.

Conn shook his head and shrugged as he knew their supposition would get them nowhere.

'Let us accept the truth of it from Edvard, no matter how impossible and unpalatable, and find out exactly where he is, Piers. I will send messages to Bernard and his wife Maria in Zaragoza, for I have no doubt that he is one of those sources. Then we need to place men to watch him. He must be very badly injured; the flames consumed him, so surely he can't travel far, and he certainly cannot carry on the blood feud himself.'

'The blood feud that Prince Henry said would be over if I removed his brother,' murmured Chatillon, as he slammed both fists down on the table. The candles jumped and hit the ground, and the few people in the anti-chamber reacted in surprise as Chatillon suddenly turned and strode resolutely back to the King's chamber. Without ceremony or knocking, Chatillon flung open the door.

Henry was surprised at their sudden, unexpected entry, and

with a wary glance, he stood and thanked Chatillon for his intervention with the Bishop. However, Piers did not say a word. He walked over and laid the vellum strip on the table. Henry stared at it and frowned, for the words made no sense.

'What is it?' he asked, becoming alarmed at the expression on their faces.

'A message from Edvard, telling us that Sheikh Ishmael is alive and in his brother's palace in Zaragoza. I don't know how this is possible, but this will certainly be a test of you keeping your word and your promises, Henry,' said Chatillon in a cold, threatening tone.

Henry paled; he knew that Piers de Chatillon was powerful enough to thwart his coronation tomorrow, to delay it for months by denying permission for any of the Bishops to conduct it, and by then, Duke Robert may have returned, which would overturn all of his plans.

'I swear to you, Chatillon, that no one knew this and having met Abu Ja'far and knowing how crucial this alliance is to him, I would go so far as to say that he will stop his brother at any cost. He may even go so far as to kill Ishmael himself to bring this blood feud to an end. I truly believe that you have little to fear. I will message both him and King Alphonse without delay!'

Chatillon, tight-lipped with anger, said nothing but turned on his heel and left, followed by Conn, who stopped at the door.

'You do realise the implications of this, Sire. You need to act quickly, or all of our work will be undone. I have rarely seen Chatillon that angry, and if he loses Isabella because of this, you will have made a very dangerous enemy.'

Henry stood for only a few moments after the door closed

CHAPTER TWENTY-ONE

before he called for his squire and penned a message to be sent to Castile. King Alphonse, his cousin, would know what to do, for Ishmael must die as soon as possible. He sent a second message to inform him that William Rufus was dead and he was to be crowned as king; he knew that would help expedite matters.

Neither Conn nor Piers got much sleep that night as the dreadful possibility of Ishmael being alive went around in their heads. Chatillon finally gave up and was out of bed just after dawn broke.

Conn joined him in the Great Hall at Westminster to break their fast, having roused two sleepy servants.

'Do you intend to let his coronation go ahead?' asked Conn, tearing a chunk of warm crusty bread to dip in a dish of honey.

'We have worked hard to get this far, and we have influence with Henry. It would be madness to throw that away, so I need to contain my anger, for it seems as if Henry was also duped. There was genuine astonishment on his face, but I think that Abu Ja'far knew his brother was alive by the time he signed that charter,' answered Piers.

'If he is badly injured and hidden in the palace, perhaps his brother thinks he can contain and control him,' suggested Conn.

'If you were Ishmael, badly burnt and injured, probably disfigured, what would you now do, Conn?' Chatillon asked him.

Conn looked thoughtful for a few moments, choosing his words carefully before answering him.

'I would nurse my wounds and try to build up my strength again, or if I were so badly hurt that I could not, I would use others to do my bidding. I am Ishmael, the scourge of the

Mediterranean, and I am used to power, to have others obey me, so I would be frustrated at being contained or controlled,' he commented.

Chatillon considered Conn's response.

'If he is, as they say at Zaragoza, then he no doubt knows of his brother's charter with King Alphonse. It must infuriate him that these decisions have been taken behind his back. Suddenly, he is Yusuf again, dependent on his brother's will. Does Ishmael seem like someone who can be caged and domesticated to become a minor royal in the palace of the Ibn Hud Dynasty? Someone living a peaceful, secluded life to be paraded out at family events?'

Conn shook his head.

'So he has to get away. Where will he go? What does he want? He can't exact revenge on you, for the charter forbids him from carrying on the blood feud; his brother is wealthy and powerful enough to enforce that.'

They both sat absorbed in their thoughts as they finished their breakfast ale. The tables were now filling around them with soldiers, knights and lords arriving who had been summoned for the coronation of a new King. Many nodded or bowed to Chatillon; others gave him a wide berth with a wary glance.

'Coralie,' murmured Chatillon to Conn.

'Yes! Of course! That is the last thing he said on the galley—that he would get his daughter back. Thank God that Isabella and Coralie are safe in her father's palace. They are well-guarded there. However, I think it wise to warn the Signori,' declared Conn.

Chatillon did not answer but pushed the bench back and got to his feet.

CHAPTER TWENTY-ONE

"We must stay for the coronation, but then we go to Genoa. Go and send a message to Edvard; we need the fastest horses he can arrange waiting for us in Bordeaux.'

Conn frowned. 'We will need to take a cog to Bordeaux, and that will take us up to a week,' said Conn frowning, but Chatillon looked thoughtful.

'I noticed when we sailed up the Thames that there was a very large Viking galley anchored in the river. They are more involved in peaceful trading these days, but there's a large contingent of Danes and Norse who live on the banks of the Thames. Take our men, find the Captain and offer him whatever it takes to assemble a crew for the evening tide to get us to Bordeaux. If he turns us down, offer to buy the boat; if he still refuses, then we find a crew and steal it tonight. I seem to remember you are good at stealing ships,' said Chatillon with a slight smile.

Conn laughed and leapt to his feet. He wended through the trestle tables making for the stables, calling for his men as he went, but glancing back at Chatillon, who still stood with a fixed smile on his face. Conn was not deceived as he could see the worry in his mentor's eyes.

Chatillon made for the King's chamber and found Henry working with a scribe on a document he was calling the Charter of Liberties. Chatillon knew Henry was exceptionally well educated, spoke several languages, and deeply understood and loved both history and law. Henry greeted Chatillon with relief, and quietly assured him that messages had been sent. Chatillon sat and watched the document taking shape; it was crucial as all kings made a coronation statement, which included promises to the people.

Chatillon recognised the challenges Henry faced, for not all the nobles accepted him; in particular, many Norman knights were still loyal to Robert. Although Henry had given the Pope assurances, the Archbishop of Canterbury, Anselm, was still a problem that needed dealing with, for he could refuse to recognise the coronation. Also, recent history was still raw, with many of the large Anglo-Saxon population at all levels. Yet again, they were having another Norman king thrust upon them.

As Chatillon cast his eyes over the document, he realised that Henry was cleverly addressing many of these problems. Henry swore that as their King, he would no longer take or sell property or revenues from a church if a bishop died. Henry promised the nobles that their sons could now inherit their father's lands and titles, without paying the large inheritance tax that Flambard had imposed. Still, he went further by cancelling all the debts and loans the lords owed to Flambard or William Rufus. Chatillon knew this would prove very popular; in reality, Henry was buying their loyalty, and he had no doubt it would work.

Henry knew that his father, King William, had respected and used the laws of the previous Saxon king, Edward the Confessor. His father had adapted these for his use until Flambard had dismantled them and imposed far more stringent fines for any crime. Now Henry intended returning to that system, so that people would be judged fairly. He sat back and considered if anything else should be added, asking Chatillon for his advice. Chatillon leant forward and whispered one sentence.

Henry nodded, smiled and dictated it to his scribe.

'I forgive all murders committed before my coronation. However, any subsequent murders will be judged harshly.'

CHAPTER TWENTY-ONE

Henry carried the Charter of Liberties into Westminster's Great Hall, where most of the nobles were assembled, and he had the scribe read the charter to the assembled crowd. Chatillon watched their faces with interest as each point was read out. There was surprise, pleasure and downright astonishment at the cancelling of loans, and a cheer went up at that moment. However, Chatillon noticed the exchanged glances when the point about previous murders was read out; The Earl of Shrewsbury, Robert De Belleme, looked directly at Chatillon and shook his head, then gave a slight bow in admiration of the Papal Envoy's manipulation.

Henry now stepped forward.

'This Charter of Liberties shall be read out at my coronation, but it will also be read, copied and sent to every priest, bishop, and Sherriff of England to be read to my people in every town and village. I want them to know this is a new beginning, and there will be peace in my land. The abuses of William Rufus' and Ranulf Flambard's will be abolished.'

This time the hall erupted in cheers, and yet again, Chatillon was impressed by the thoroughness and charisma of Henry Beauclerc. It reinforced his earlier conviction that this was going to be a king to be reckoned with.

Later that morning, in a packed cathedral, the youngest son of King William I and Queen Matilda was crowned as Henry I of England by the Bishop of London. This would be the beginning of a new era, and Flambard was now on his way to the Tower of London to await his fate.

Hardly was the crown lowered onto Henry's head than Chatillon and Conn were out of the huge doors of Westminster Cathedral. They mounted and galloped along the north banks of the River Thames to St Bardolph's Wharf, where a large Viking longship awaited them.

Chapter Twenty-two

Mid-August 1100 –Near Genoa

Ishmael, as usual, sat in the shade looking down on the Ligurian Sea below. He was anticipating hearing a report from his captain, who, with his men, had just dismounted and led the horses out of sight into the old lean-to barn behind the large farmhouse. They had been gone for four days reconnoitring the estate and the regular patrols put in place by the Irish warrior, Finian Ui Neil, who they had seen was in charge of the men when the cavalcade of wagons left Genoa. An added complication but one that could be dealt with.

Captain Ghilas looked tired; his face and Western clothes were covered in dust from the long ride from the Aggio Valley. He bowed to the Sheikh, who indicated with a wave of his right hand that he should sit and pour himself a drink.

'What news? What have you discovered, Ghilas?' he asked, sitting forward enthusiastically. He had been patient for so long, but he knew time was running out for him, and they had to act soon.

'Sayyid, we have finally found ourselves an informer; it took so long because it soon became apparent, with only the gentlest questioning, that the estate workers are all very loyal to the family. We dared not question many more in case it aroused suspicions. However, this man is different as he only works there in the late summer months. He's a sheep shearer, but he and his family help out during the fruit and olive harvests. He is somewhat disgruntled at not being taken on permanently when positions open; instead, they took on younger men. He barely scrapes by on this seasonal work, so his eyes widened at the offer of silver for a simple sketch of the manor house. We assured him that anything he told us would never be traced back to him, and his name would never leave our lips. The next day, we followed him home and offered him more silver for a list of all the people and house servants. This was more money than he could earn in a full season. The day after, we offered him double for information on the patrols. It paid off, for he told us that Ui Neill would help round up sheep on the higher slopes next week; they would be away for two or three nights. That could be an opportunity for us, with him out of the way,' he said, laying a rough sketch down on the table.

Ishmael sat for some time in silence, looking at the sketch and thinking through what he had heard. His plan had no room for error, and there would only be one chance to carry this through and escape.

'What are your thoughts, Ghilas, having spent time on the estate and having seen the plan of the house?' he asked his captain.

'At present, there are too many guards as at least ten of Chatillon's men accompanied Ui Neill and Chatillon's ward, Marietta Di Monsi. This is her estate, where Isabella is staying with your daughter. Embriaco sent another twelve of his trained soldiers to accompany his daughter. Add to this the ten or so farm labourers and servants, then we're looking at almost three times our number. I have never been a coward, Sayyid, but to attack these numbers with a man like Ui Neill leading them would be suicide.'

Ishmael smiled, but only the unscarred half of his mouth lifted. Ghilas knew enough of his master to be worried about that grimacing smile, but to his surprise, he did not get the anger or frustration he expected.

'I appreciate your honesty, Ghilas, and I like that about you as I need men about me whom I can trust. I believe you have served me for a long time. How long?' he asked, almost surprised at himself for caring.

'Over fifteen years, Sayyid, but never until recently as part of your privileged personal guard.' The Sheikh enjoyed hearing the pride in his captain's voice, but he again stayed silent for some time.

'Ghilas is a Berber name; I remember a family of that name out in my tribal lands, horse breeders, I think.'

'Yes, Sayyid, my father and older brothers breed Arab horses for the long-distance desert races,' he answered, surprised at the Sheikh's memory and interest.

'That is good, Ghilas. As you are aware, my father married a young Bedouin beauty of royal blood. My mother was also part of Tuareg, and when she died, I inherited her tribal lands, while my brother inherited the Ibn Hud title and wealth at my father's death. Once we have found my daughter, I intend to return to those lands; I find more and more that I yearn for life back in the deserts, an uncomplicated nomadic life with my horses and hawks. I will return to my family roots, leaving this Western world with its scheming and betrayal behind me, so when I leave here, I will don the dark blue robes of my desert people. If anything should happen to me, Ghilas, I expect you to fulfil my wish and take my daughter to my mother's people. They will raise her in our world, a simpler world, but I will send a chest of my wealth with her. Do you swear to do that?'

Ghilas bowed his head. 'I swear on the Holy Book, Sayyid!'

'Good. Now I want you to send two men into the city; I wish you to find out where the Signori Embriaco buys his wine,' he said, with the same crooked smile.

The Captain looked puzzled.

'We will send it out to this estate, Ghilas, ostensibly as a present from her father; several casks of red for the guards and harvest workers and two of superior white for the family.'

Understanding dawned on the Captain's face. 'You are drugging the red wine, Sayyid.'

Ishmael laughed. 'But not for the beautiful Isabella; I want her wide awake when she feels my hand around her throat.'

Obtaining the longship had been far easier than expected, for a few of Karl's Icelandic men were crewing this boat and were overjoyed to see their saviours. The Captain took little persuading when he saw the silver Chatillon was offering for a fast trip across the channel for him and his men. Chatillon was fortunate that the weather held fair for the crossing, and with twenty oars on each side, the large longship easily cut through the calmer waters. Before long, the large square

CHAPTER TWENTY-TWO

sail was raised, and a northerly drove them south towards Bordeaux. In only three and a half days, they were pulling into the Garonne estuary with a long, steady row down to the wharves. Silver coin changed hands as the crew dropped with relief over their oars. These men would be well paid, for they were free men and not galley slaves, and they would be happily carousing in the inns and stews tonight with money in their pockets.

They climbed onto the wooden wharves and made for the stone quayside at the end, where Piers hoped to find horses waiting. They had not gone far when a shout went up, and Conn laughed aloud, for the horses were there with Georgio and half a dozen men. It was the longest the two men had been apart, and although Conn was choosing a different path, he had missed his friend; he was like a brother to him. Georgio jumped off his horse and clasped Conn in a bear hug while Chatillon waited patiently and then coughed loudly.

'Do you have any news for us, Georgio?'

'All the messages will await you at Montpellier, as Edvard presumed you would take ship to Genoa from there rather than Marseilles.'

Chatillon smiled and nodded; Edvard, as efficient as ever, sometimes knew his mind better than he did.

'We await news from Bernard in Zaragoza to let us know the Sheikh's whereabouts. But, worryingly, we have heard nothing back from Finian in Genoa yet!'

'Then let's go; I presume we have changes of horses arranged on the way, Georgio?'

'Yes, Edvard has provided them at Varaire and Rodez, as they have better quality inns. Do you truly believe that Sheikh Ishmael would go to Genoa? From what Brother Tomas told us, he was barely alive, and his left side was so damaged he could hardly use his left arm. He's in no condition to fight.'

'We can take no chances, Georgio. He is obsessed with Coralie, and although he may not be capable, he will have men who can snatch her. He may be physically damaged, but it sounds as if he's not incapacitated, and his mind will burn as brightly as ever with thoughts of revenge.'

Without further ado, they mounted and rode at speed for Montpellier.

Several days later, Conn, having ridden up the steep hill, wearily dismounted at the inn on the narrow Rue de L'ancienne Courrier in Montpellier. It was very late, but they needed to snatch a few hours of sleep here before sailing for Genoa on the morrow. Montpellier was mainly a busy fishing port, but trading cogs put in here regularly to unload or pick up cargo to move around the Mediterranean. Georgio was instructed to ride straight down to the port and wake every captain he could with the offer of silver; the cost was no object until he found a boat.

They woke a sleepy ostler who took their horses, and Conn hefted his saddlebags on his shoulder and followed Chatillon into the inn. Despite the late hour and the fact that the innkeeper had scrabbled into some crumpled clothes, the man greeted Chatillon like a long-lost friend. Conn smiled as he knew Piers had not been here for several years; the Papal Insignia on his cloak seemed to open many doors.

The innkeeper raked the still smouldering embers of the fire, added some small sticks and logs and then bustled off to fetch the messages awaiting them here. The two men sank gratefully into the settles by the fire; it was a damp, misty night out there with a chill breeze coming down from the northwest as they rode in. The innkeeper's wife, with tousled hair, bustled in carrying platters of bread, cheeses and ham as the rest of their tired, hungry men arrived. Soon, she was kept very busy serving them warm mulled ale as Chatillon unrolled the vellum strips in the leather pouch.

The first was from Morvan, who had communicated with Bernard de Bordeaux in Zaragoza; Chatillon shared the contents. The palace there was in an uproar, as Ishmael had taken advantage of his brother's absence to leave. Abu Ja'far was very angry and was said to have sent men after him to bring him back.

'King Henry was right; Ishmael's brother may find and kill him before we do!' exclaimed Conn. Chatillon's brow was furrowed.

'But where is he now, Conn? Is he on one of his former bases licking his wounds and making his plans, or has he sailed straight for Genoa to get his daughter?'

'Does he know she's there? Remember, this man has lain at death's door for half a year; surely he would expect Isabella to be back with you at the Chateau, or has he sent men there too?' asked Conn, in a concerned voice.

Georgio arrived at that moment. 'I have found us a boat; we leave on the morning tide,' he announced to the group. At another early start, a few men groaned in mock horror, but most looked forward to finding a spot on the deck of the boat to curl up in their blankets and sleep on the journey.

'Well done. Tell me, Georgio, how were things at the Chateau when you left? After all, I left you there with instructions to defend it! What happens if the Sheikh's men head there thinking they will find Coralie?' growled Chatillon at the young Horse Warrior.

Georgio looked sheepish. 'I thought I could be of more use to you here, and Edvard agreed,' he said, hopefully. Seeing no relenting in Chatillon's expression, he continued.

'Lazzo and Gironde have doubled the patrols inside and outside the Chateau. It is well defended as over twenty of your men, and your troop of archers are there. Dion may be getting bigger with child, but she's out there forcing them to practice every morning.'

Chatillon finally dropped his piercing gaze from Georgio's face as he unrolled the message from Edvard.

Everything is well here, and we are prepared for any eventuality. Our main concern is the lack of communication from either Finian or the Signori Embriaco in Genoa, despite several messages sent! Take care, Piers, and do not take too many risks. I want you and Isabella back here for my wedding in October; it will not be the same unless you are at my side.

Chatillon read the message to the two young men opposite, who both smiled at the last sentence.

'So he finally plucked up the courage to ask her!' exclaimed Conn, laughing.

'The way they look at each other and follow each other around the Chateau, everyone could see they were in love,' commented Georgio.

Suddenly, Marietta's pretty face came to Conn, and for a moment, he recalled how their eyes had met across the hall or in the paddock; how she had stroked his face in farewell. He was pulled out of this pleasant reverie by Chatillon.

'Finian Ui Neill is the worst person for communicating, but

CHAPTER TWENTY-TWO

if he or the Signori had received alarming news about Ishmael, who they presume to be dead, then I would have expected an immediate response. This is unlike either of them, and it is of concern,' murmured Chatillon, staring thoughtfully into the fire.

Conn slammed his hand on the table, getting their attention.

'He's there, Piers. Ishmael and his men are already there because the messages must have been intercepted. If you remember, Ishmael's men took out the birds arriving and leaving at the Chateau, using a hawk. He could do the same in Genoa, a simple but effective method.'

Chatillon's face was pale, his lips compressed into a thin line at the thought of Ishmael, his nemesis, yet again threatening his family. He flung the messages into the fire and watched them burn.

'It is late; let us to bed; we have an early start and must be on that boat before dawn. This time, when we find and kill him, Conn, we will ensure that Ishmael is dead, I promise you,' he said, standing and heading for the stairs.

Con and Georgio sat for a while longer, finishing their wine.

'What are our plans, Conn? Once we have yet again put an end to the Sheikh,' asked Georgio, while watching his friend's face closely. Georgio resented being left behind; he recognised and accepted the relationship Conn had built with Chatillon, but could not see why he had to be excluded, or cut out of his friend's life. He knew Conn craved more risk and exhilaration in his life, and he could see that Chatillon provided that. Edvard and Dion knew that Conn had been a part of the assassination of King William Rufus; he had heard their whispered conversations, but he also could have been useful. *Don't they trust me or think I am capable?* he wondered, as he waited for an answer from his friend.

'Chatillon wants me to stay close to King Henry; we have established a friendship, and he enjoys my company. He suggested that I set up a troop of Horse Warriors for Henry in England, the same way my father did for King William in Caen. Would you be happy to come with me to do that?' he asked.

Georgio nodded and grinned, pleased to know they would still be riding and fighting together, as that was what they had spent many years training for in Morlaix and Spain. However, he intuitively knew that Conn's role would be more than that; he did not doubt that Henry would avail himself of Chatillon's services through Conn, to remove any opposition or quell any problems. And, of course, it meant that Chatillon had a key informer in the heart of Henry's court. However, he would take what comfort he could from what was being offered—to be at his friend's side.

Conn watched the expressions flitting across Georgio's face; he had always been an open book to him. He realised that Georgio would see the formation of the Horse Warriors for what it was, but his friend did not realise that he was, in fact, protecting Georgio by keeping him away from what would be a highly dangerous side of his life. Learning to become an assassin, as skilled as Chatillon, would be his future. Georgio stood and bade him goodnight, but Conn remained for a while.

He sat back and nudged the burning log with his boot, as Marietta's face again intruded on his thoughts. He could see the large, clear grey eyes, the way her nose crinkled when she smiled, the spattering of light freckles across her cheeks. Travelling with the body of William Rufus through the forests had given Conn a lot of time to think, especially about the transient nature of life. This man had been laughing, drinking and enjoying life the day before, and now he was gone. Conn did not have any regrets over the killing—it had to be done—but it made him realise that perhaps he had to make room for Marietta in his chosen life. She loved him, and Conn suddenly realised it might be something special to be wrapped in that love.

But again, he played Devil's Advocate with himself. Was this the life Marietta deserved? Look at Isabella and what she had been put through. Could he expect Marietta to live such a life, never knowing if he would return, or if his actions would put her or their children in danger? He had to sit down and have this conversation with her after they had dealt with Ishmael.

Conn had realised that he could not imagine sharing his life with any woman but her.

Chapter Twenty-three

Late August 1100 - Aggio

Oblivious to the danger they were in, or of their saviours sailing towards them, life on the estate continued in its peaceful harmony and seasonal tasks. Coralie was left in the happy care of their housekeeper, Anna, while Isabella accompanied Marietta to walk the olive terraces to check the crop.

'I learnt so much from my estate manager and bailiff, Angelo, in my first weeks here, and he was delighted to share his knowledge as he loves this estate. They grow Taggiasco olives here in Liguria; they produce a sweeter, lighter oil with a fruitier flavour. However, because we are so high up in the hills, we harvest much earlier here than in the south. Look!' she said, pointing to the fruit. 'They are already turning from green to purple, which means we will harvest in less than a month. Most of my crop will be taken to the mills and made into a paste, which is then pressed to produce the delicious oil. Angelo tells me my workers are allowed to take large pots of it home. They love it drizzled on their fava beans,' she explained, while finding a shady spot to sit. Although it was early morning, the sun was already showing its heat on these southern slopes.

Isabella sat beside her, having checked the area under the tree for scorpions or sleeping snakes. The view over the valley and the olive tree-covered slopes, with the higher purple-covered mountains in the background, was breathtaking.

'This is a beautiful place to live, Marietta; I feel truly at peace here for the first time in a long time. Being here at this time of year reminds me of the harvests at home in Chatillon sous Bagneux, with the workers' celebrations and festivals once the crops are gathered. When I moved there with Piers from the city of Genoa, I truly loved being the Chatelaine of a huge estate, knowing most of the villagers and their families by name. I miss my old life on my estate before the Sheikh's attacks, especially as now I'm back within my father's protective, but constraining, walls again. Over the last few days, I've realised even more that I must return home as soon as possible. I have come to terms with that decision now, and I'll tell Finian and Gabriel tonight.'

Marietta clapped her hands in delight.

'That is wonderful, but you both must return and visit us again. I have decided to spend six months of every year here, although it can be very cold and bleak in the winter, when the Mistral sweeps down the valleys bringing heavy rains. We can even be cut off with snow, as we were when I was a child here. If I can win Conn, then this would be perfect for us. Only a day's ride from Genoa from where he can take a ship to most of the Mediterranean, or wherever his chosen path takes him. He will always have me and his children here at Aggio, loving and waiting for him. After all, that isn't so different from the life you chose with Chatillon.'

Isabella gazed at the earnest face of the pretty young woman beside her whom she loved as a daughter.

'Yes, you are right, although I also agreed to become Piers' accomplice, and carried out over a dozen assignments to seduce, or remove, targets he chose. He turned me into one of Europe's most desired courtesans, and I must say I unashamedly revelled in it. I longed for that excitement and danger. But you are different, Marietta. You long for love and a traditional happy family life, which I can't decry, but will it fit Conn's chosen path and the assassin he wants to become? Could you put on a tight-fitting gown and be a foil for him in the court of the Holy Roman Emperor? Could you bed any man he tells you to extract information from them? This is the life I had and the one Conn is beginning to embrace as a spy and assassin. Can you share him with dozens of other women because he uses them for his assignments? Very early in our marriage, in the first months, Chatillon taught me the difference between calculated seduction—sex as part of what he describes as his profession—and the truly deep, meaningful love we had in our lovemaking. I'm not sure you are ready for that life, Marietta. Conn is also unsure, so he keeps you at arm's length, for by the sound of it and what Finian has told me, I'm sure he also loves you.

Marietta wiped away a tear. Although she knew Isabella was being brutally honest with her, she knew she had no choice but to learn to live with that life, for she truly loved Conn and longed to see him again in the autumn when they returned to the Chateau.

They all gathered that evening in the hall for dinner, and the tables were packed, as many of the seasonal workers had arrived to harvest the early crops, and Anna, Josef and the servants were kept busy. Watching the faces of the

CHAPTER TWENTY-THREE

new workers, Marietta smiled; she could see they were overwhelmed by the unusual number of guards and warriors in the hall and out, constantly patrolling the estate. In addition, the new owner was also here, although some of the regulars had known her since she was a child. Isabella was beside her, and it had gone around the hall like wildfire that this was the beautiful daughter of the Signori of Genoa. Many admiring glances were cast at the pair of them.

As the meal finished, Isabella judged it to be time and, raising her glass, asked them to give a toast to the fact that she had decided to return to the Chateau and would travel back with them at the end of September. The joy was instant, with Finian leaping to his feet and pulling Isabella into his arms to hug her while Gabriel whooped and cheered. The crowd in the hall had no idea what was afoot, but Finian demanded music. Within minutes, Gabriel and Josef, who played a small mountain harp, had a tune going as Finian insisted on dancing Isabella around and between the long trestle tables. The men in the hall were delighted, and soon several were on their feet, claiming the serving girls and even Marietta and Anna, as they danced them all around the hall. They then had songs and more tunes and dancing until a laughing, breathless Isabella called an end to it. Finian laughed and lifting her off her feet, he swung her around while she slapped helplessly at the handsome Irish warrior. Finally, they collapsed back onto the bench.

'Can I tell them? Can I tell Dion that our sister is coming back? Ahmed will be overjoyed, as am I,' he said. She smiled and nodded, and he kissed her forehead before going off to compose a message to be sent first thing.

It was late indeed when they all went to bed in a haze

of happiness, as toast after toast had been raised. Isabella checked on Coralie, who had slept through all the noise, and then she headed for her bed, where she dropped into a deep sleep, content that she had finally decided. She was going home and back to the arms of Chatillon.

Gabriel, however, had drunk far more of the rich red wine than normal, and with all the excitement, he found it difficult to sleep. He could hear his heartbeat in his ears, and the room was spinning slightly. He remembered some men using bread to soak up the wine in their stomachs, so he wandered back to the empty hall and, picking a large crust from one of the tables, unbarred and opened one of the tall wooden shutters, going out onto the tiled terrace to get some air. He sank into one of the chairs and, dropping his head back, eyes closed, he chewed and swallowed the crust. Gabriel knew he was drunk, but he was bursting with happiness; they would finally be a family again. More importantly, his mother was returning to his father, who had never been the same since she left; there was a brittleness about him and an occasional dark sadness on his face. Now, things in the Chateau would change. It could never return to how it was, but it would be so much better; it would feel like a home again.

Gabriel realised he must have dropped off as he suddenly jerked awake and felt cold. The clouds were scudding across the half-moon in the inky black sky; a chill breeze had certainly picked up. He rubbed his eyes, yawned and then shivered. The terrace was part of the old Roman house, and they had built a small but now crumbling red brick wall, waist height, at its edge. Behind that, the wooded slope dropped gently at first, and then steeply, down to a series of deep gullies where the larger evergreen holm oaks grew in the shade below.

CHAPTER TWENTY-THREE

In the winter, these gullies gushed with mountain streams on their way down the valleys to the sea. Gabriel rubbed his arms to warm them. He could see the leaves of the silver ash trees closer to the house moving in the breeze, and then he froze. He could see a tall, dark figure. He blinked several times and then squinted, but the figure was still there, standing within the closer line of trees.

The clouds cleared the moon, and Gabriel sat forward. Was it a shadow? Was he dreaming? No! He was sure it was a man. The wall surrounding the terrace meant that he could only see the dark figure on the slope from the waist up, but from the shape and outline of the headdress against the silver birch trees, he knew the man was wearing Arab garb. Then, as Gabriel pushed himself to his feet to see more, the figure was gone, making him wonder if he had truly seen anything. He stood there unsure of what to do, staring at the now empty spot, convinced that he had seen someone. He didn't want to seem a fool by waking Finian, who would immediately know that Gabriel had drunk too much wine. Suddenly a hand descended on his shoulder, and Gabriel jumped forward in alarm, his hand going for the dagger in his belt that was not there. It was back in his room; a stupid mistake to come out unarmed and alone at night. Fortunately, as he whirled around, he realised it was only Josef, the Steward, and in relief, Gabriel released the breath he had been holding.

'Did I startle you, young master? It's time to lock up for the night—time you were in your bed,' he murmured, in admonition.

Gabriel nodded but then threw caution to the winds.

'I saw someone, Josef, a dark figure. He was standing in the trees. I'm sure it was an Arab. We should go and look for him as it could be another assassin.'

Josef stared at the trees. 'I didn't see anyone, Master Gabriel, but our patrols come across here several times a night; it could just be one of our men. However, I will take a walk and look around before barring the shutters. Now off to bed with you,' he said, in a no-nonsense voice.

Gabriel had to be content with that. Josef was in his fifties but a big, fit man. He and Anna never stopped working in the house or helping on the estate when needed; he was also sensible and calm. Marietta deeply loved both of them; they had worked for her mother and had always been in her life. He stood in the hall for a while, but as he heard nothing more, obediently went to bed and presumed that it must just have been a dream.

The next morning was busy as Finian, two of his men, and the farm shepherds were leaving for the distant higher slopes. They would be away for several nights, as Angelo, the bailiff, reckoned there were over a hundred sheep up there to bring down. They knew they would have to leave their horses a third of the way up as the terrain became too rocky and dangerous. They would continue on foot with the dogs and drive the stubborn animals down to the lower pastures. Finian firmly told Gabriel it was his duty to protect the household inside, although they all knew Captain Alfredo was in charge. Finian took his leave of Isabella and Marietta.

'Are you sure you are happy to let me do this, for you both know I'm purely indulging myself by taking part in this drive,' he admitted, with a twinkle in his eye.

'Finian, you are always on duty; you never get a rest from it, so you go and play with the sheep, enjoy the camaraderie around the campfire and bring all my sheep back to be shorn,'

CHAPTER TWENTY-THREE

said Marietta, laughing. He hugged them both, and then they were gone.

Isabella, shading her eyes, watched them ride up through the olive groves; she could see the higher peaks in the distance where they were headed. This estate was immense, far bigger than she had imagined, and Conn would have plenty to keep him occupied for some of the year if he married Marietta, she thought as they headed back to the house.

It was late afternoon when Anna came to Marietta and asked if they had seen Josef. They shook their heads, and Anna went on a search for him in the barns, where he often liked to sit and talk to the shearers. In the early evening, two carts rolled up the drive; several large wine casks were on each. The driver informed them that these were a present from the Signori for the feast, the red for the workers and a special sweet white from Rome for the ladies and household. Isabella laughed at her father's thoughtfulness, and she directed Alfredo to store them in the wine caves built into the side of the hill.

'I promise we can broach them on Friday, for Anna tells me it is the feast of St Lupicinus, the holiest Bishop of Verona, and the workers are allowed to finish a few hours early.'

Captain Alfredo, her father's man, smiled.

'I'll put a guard on the cave entrance until then, my lady, for we know how thirsty these men can be, and word of this is already out,' he said, gesturing to the men who were watching.

Isabella went to find Anna to inform her of what had arrived, for she and Josef were supposed to be preparing for the feast. She found both Marietta and Gabriel helping in the large stone-flagged kitchen, which was unusual. Marietta was expertly plucking several chickens, with a serving girl's help, while Gabriel followed Anna's shouted instructions on threading them onto a long metal spit.

'This is a hive of activity. Is there anything I can do?' asked Isabella.

'That husband of mine has taken himself off, probably lying under a tree with a jug of wine, not a care in the world, while we work our fingers to the bone,' moaned Anna.

Marietta shook her head. 'You know that isn't true, Anna; he only ever did that once, when a cart crushed his favourite hound. Josef is always very responsible. He will have gone hunting for the extra game for the feast, and I'm sure he will be back soon.'

The next morning, however, Josef had still not appeared, and Isabella could see how upset Anna was, so she called for the Captain of the Signori's guard. It may be nothing, but she felt foreboding about this unexplained absence.

'Captain, our Steward, Josef, whom you know, has not returned. This is unusual, and I'm uneasy about his sudden absence. Talk to his wife, Anna, to find his usual haunts and then search the home estate for him, please.'

At first, nothing suggested that Josef may indeed be hunting in the hills; his hounds were still here. Then Gabriel came to share with Isabella what had happened the last time he had seen Josef. His mother was understandably angry and lambasted him for not bringing this up sooner.

'I honestly believed it was just a dream. I fell asleep drunk on the terrace,' he explained, mortified that what he saw might be real.

Isabella pulled him into her arms and reassured him. Like his brother, Gabriel was such a tall, well-built boy that she sometimes forgot that he was only twelve years old, although he often reminded her that he would be thirteen in a month or so.

Later that Thursday afternoon, with the help of his hounds, they found Josef's body; he seemed to have slipped and fallen into one of the deep gullies. His neck was broken, and so it was some consolation to Anna that he would have died quickly, and not been left dying down there on his own. They brought him in and laid him in the small chapel on the hillside that the estate workers had built, as it was several leagues from the nearest church.

Distraught at first, Anna would let no one clean and lay him out except her, but soon he was laid in his best clothes on a cloth-covered table so that people could come and pay their respects. Marietta had lit large groups of candles on the altar, and in the corners, as a steady stream of people made their way in to offer a prayer and say farewell. Isabella came later when it had quietened down, and she thought Josef looked peaceful. Marietta had brought her mother's Prie-dieu from the house, for those who wanted to pray for longer, and Isabella found Anna still there on her knees, head bowed.

Isabella had liked Josef immediately the first time she had met him; Coralie would often run to him, holding up her arms. For a childless couple, they had both been wonderful with the little girl. She said a few quiet prayers, but as she turned to leave, saw something that chilled her to the bone. Josef had been placed in his best, round-necked linen tunic, and Isabella turned to his wife.

'Anna, come here.' The housekeeper, surprised at being spoken to, stood up and came to stand beside her.

'Were these marks on Josef's neck there before he fell?'

'No, my lady, they say he broke his neck in the fall.'

Isabella stood and stared at the thumb-shaped bruises on either side of Josef's neck; she had seen ones just like them once before, when Pierre had snapped Cecily's neck at the Chateau. Josef had not slipped and fallen down the gully. He had been murdered. She put a comforting arm around Anna's shoulders and then turned and left, walking briskly to the hall where Marietta was watching Gabriel playing with Coralie.

'Go and find Captain Alfredo and tell him I need him here now!' she ordered Gabriel, who looked surprised but went to do her bidding. Isabella waved Marietta over as soon as the Captain arrived.

'We need to send a message to Finian now. He must come back here as I know that Josef was murdered!'

Marietta paled. 'Surely we're safe here, as we have dozens of armed men around us.'

'Yet someone got in past those guards and patrols to murder our Steward, Marietta; I'll feel safer if we have Finian Ui Neill by our side,' she said.

She shared her misgivings with the Captain, but she could see that Alfredo was unconvinced.

'We have spent several days searching the home estate for Josef, which is a large area, and we have found no sign of any intruders, no tracks, no signs of campfires. Why would they murder a steward, an older man who would be no threat?'

'I may be chasing a false spectre, Captain, but my son Gabriel was sure he saw a dark figure behind the terrace, a figure in Arab dress. Josef went to investigate that night and never came back!'

'Why was I not told of this?' he asked, frowning at Gabriel, who explained the circumstances.

'I will send one of the regular shearers in the morning to

try and find Finian and the men, as he will know where they may be camped in the hills.'

'No, Captain, you will send that man now,' said Isabella, in a tone that brooked no discussion, and reminded the Captain of her father. Turning to Gabriel and Marietta, she could see the worry on their faces, so she decided to allay their fears.

'You heard the Captain; they have searched the estate and found nothing. For all we know, it could have just been a deserter, or robber, who got the better of Josef, and our fears are unjustified. Now we have a feast to deliver to your workers and our guards tomorrow; let us get some rest.' Not that any of them slept for some time.

The next day dawned bright and clear, and the paddocks beside the house were full of trestle tables from the hall. The local priest arrived, prayed over and anointed Josef's body, and then they had a quiet family ceremony to bury him in the orchard. Anna seemed much settled by this, and was pleased that the priest gathered the large crowd together in the paddock, spoke fittingly about Josef, and then celebrated mass, blessing the workers and the bounty they would receive on the feast of St Lupicinus. Several fat lambs and a whole cow had been turning on the spits since yesterday, and the mouth-watering smells of roast meat filled the air. Eventually, the bells rang, and the men rushed to the tables, while platters piled high with meat were served along with huge rounds of bread, to dip in the juices.

Isabella watched Marietta move amongst the tables, speaking to her workers and seasonal men. They doffed their straw hats respectfully, and she could see they appreciated her interest in them and their families. Some of the younger ones, and some not so young, flirted outrageously with her, which she took in good part, laughing and blowing them a kiss. Marietta was made for this, thought Isabella and immediately felt sad that the man she loved wanted something very different from this life.

As musical instruments of all shapes and sizes appeared, Isabella told Captain Alfredo to open the casks of red wine. This was greeted with cheers from the farm workers and off-duty guards alike. Still suffering from the surfeit a few nights before, Gabriel turned down the many cups he was offered and instead concentrated on playing his citole for several hours. As the sky darkened, Isabella and Marietta retreated to the house, leaving the crowd to their carousing, the sounds of the music echoing across the valleys.

Gabriel was surprised at how quickly the feast seemed to end. Yes, it was dark, but the fire pits still gave off a lot of light as the fat from the stripped carcasses still dripped onto the embers and hissed and flared. However, he noticed that many workers seemed to be swaying towards their pallet beds in the barns or were already rolled in their blankets under the stars. He made his way to the house, but all was quiet. To ease his mind, he walked the full perimeter of the house and met several guards who greeted him warmly; he was a popular boy and a good musician. Finally, he entered the now-empty hall and immediately checked that the bars were in place on the shutters. He told himself he was just being cautious, but he had seen the flash of fear on his mother's face. He quietly walked to her room and softly opened the door, but he could see immediately that she was fast asleep. He hoped the shepherd had found Finian, for like his mother, he felt safer with the Irish warrior close by.

Chapter Twenty-four

Early morning – The hills of Aggio

As a seasoned warrior, Finian Ui Neill always slept lightly; he would wake at the slightest sound, which had saved his life on several occasions. Dawn was only beginning to break when he heard the sound of someone brushing through the shrubs on the slopes below. It may be just an animal, as several large mountain goats up here would crop the short grass on the high slopes when they were covered in dew. However, there were also wolves, and his hand went automatically to the long dagger underneath the rolled cloak he was using as a pillow. He turned to face the direction of the sounds. Half a dozen sleeping men lay around him, rolled tightly in their blankets in the chill mountain air.

Slowly, he sat up and then moved into a crouch as he heard the tell-tale sound of moving scree under the feet of whatever would emerge from the juniper bushes. One of his men to his left also woke and met Finian's eyes, and Finian nodded, so the man stretched out a hand to wake his companion. Finian could now hear laboured breathing, and he knew it was human; he quietly drew his sword from its scabbard as his men rose to their feet, armed and ready. Some of the shepherds woke and reacted in alarm, cowering back against the rocks, thinking this was an attack by one of the roaming bands of banditi. Suddenly, a tow-headed older man came pushing through the bushes, and Finian and his men raised their swords.

'No! It is Paolo, he's one of the shearers!' yelled a shepherd who recognised him. Pale-faced with shock at what he saw in front of him, Paolo gasped for breath, bent forward, his hands on his knees. His expression became one of relief as Finian and his men sheathed their swords.

'Message!' he gasped.

Finian smiled. 'Get your breath back first; get him a mouthful of wine,' he ordered.

Paolo recovered quickly enough, and he sat on a nearby large rock.

'Sorry, I am not as young or fit as I was. You have to come back,' he told Finian.

Finian looked puzzled. 'Why? What has happened?'

'I'm not entirely sure, but the Steward, Josef, he died in a gully. They thought he slipped, but then young Master Gabriel thinks he saw the shadow of a man behind the house.'

'Did the Captain search the estate?' he asked.

'Yes, several times, and they found nothing.'

'So, why the urgency?' asked Finian, perplexed.

The man shrugged. 'It was the lady, the Signori's daughter. She insisted I ride all night to find you and bring you back. Fortunately, I knew where you would be.'

Finian stared across at the high mountain peaks now lit by the rising sun. Was Isabella being overcautious? Given what had happened in their lives, she certainly had reason to be.

'What did the Captain say?' he asked Paolo, who was taking

another grateful swig of wine.

'He seemed to think that the estate was safe and the Feast of St. Lupinicius was going ahead today. The shearers are arriving, and the fire pits are dug; I had hoped to get back for it.'

Finian weighed up what he had heard.

'Let us break our fast, and then I'll make a decision,' he announced. He sat down to think it through as the men warmed the breakfast ale on the fire, their blankets around their shoulders. He had received a direct order from Isabella to return to the estate, so he had no choice but to go back. Should he take his men or still leave them where they were needed to help herd the sheep? As he chewed on the hard biscuits and cheese, he decided that he trusted Captain Alfredo's judgement; he would leave them here.

'Come, Paolo, we have a long slope to descend to find our horses; we should make a start.' The messenger wearily pulled himself to his feet and followed Finian down through the spiny shrubs to the slopes below.

Finian watered both horses when they reached one of the many mountain brooks. However, he did not like the look of Paolo's horse; it had been badly sweated out on the dash here overnight, and now its breathing was laboured. They rested in the valley bottom for a while before they began to broach the next hill, but Finian was concerned as barely a third of the way up the slope, the horse's sides were heaving again, so they rested again. Finally, Finian had no choice but to leave the man to bring his horse back in gentle stages. This was a good quality animal, not some nag from the livery stable, and it had just been overridden; it had already cost Finian too much time.

As he topped the second hill, Finian glanced at the sun in the sky. It was almost midday, so it would be late when he arrived back, but at least he would be there. Having questioned Paolo further, he found that Josef's sudden fall in a gully worried him; the Steward had been an astute man, not one to wander over steep rocky territory at night. Also, Josef had known the estate like the back of his hand. Suddenly Finian began to regard Isabella's order with more concern. He had let Isabella and her children down once before, and Chatillon had only just forgiven him; he dared not do it again. With that thought, he shortened his reins and pushed his horse on, hoping that she was wrong to be alarmed.

Late August 1100 – Genoa

They docked in Genoa at dusk, but the sky still had a late summer glow; the sun lit the clouds from behind with a bright, luminous edge. Within moments of securing the ropes, they were off the boat and running up the streets towards the Embriaco Palace. Chatillon's emotions were conflicted; he told himself there was nowhere safer for Isabella to be than with her father. Then he tortured himself as to why Embriaco and Finian had not answered any messages from the Chateau.

They reached the high outer walls of the palace to find the huge gates standing open. This was highly unusual, and as he crossed the large courtyard, he realised that the usual handful of guards were not in position outside the entrance to the palace. With a sinking heart, Piers took the broad steps two at a time and flung himself at the heavy, closed oak doors, closely followed by Conn and his men. However, the doors were not locked, and they banged open, loudly echoing across the large marble-floored hall.

The sight that met his eyes made him draw his sword immediately, and he heard the blades scrape behind him as Conn, Georgio, and his men did the same. At the far end of the hall, an angry, glaring Embriaco stood on the dais, arms folded. Behind him were his guards, at least a dozen of them with their swords drawn. In front of Embriaco was a huge figure, his sword drawn; behind him were about ten armed Berber warriors with curved swords ready to attack. Piers noticed that a few men on both sides seemed to be slightly wounded, so there had been a skirmish before they arrived. Several of the Berber warriors now turned to face the newcomers, and he saw the worry on their faces as they realised they were sandwiched between the two groups of armed men.

At that moment, Embriaco's booming voice filled and echoed around the hall.

'Ah, Chatillon, I believe you have arrived just in time, as this brute here has tried to force his way into my palace and is now demanding answers that I'm not prepared to give.'

The Signori was an imposing figure at any time, but Piers could feel the tension in the room and see the anger in every part of Embriaco's body; he shot a concerned glance back at Conn with a raised eyebrow.

'This could easily turn into a bloodbath,' the Horse Warrior said softly.

Suddenly the leader of the Berbers turned, and Pier's eyes widened in surprise as did Conn and Georgio's, for they knew exactly who this man was.

'God's blood, Da Vasquez, why are you here? Surely you are not doing the work of Sheikh Ishmael?' exclaimed Chatillon, still holding his sword as this man could be very unpredictable.

Da Vasquez sheathed his sword and told his men to do the same, which they did reluctantly, casting nervous glances at the armed warriors. Conn suddenly noticed the dark blue edging to their robes.

'They are the elite guard from the palace in Zaragoza; they are Abu Ja'far's men, Piers,' he exclaimed.

Chatillon sheathed his sword and went forward to greet the famous Portuguese mercenary he had employed several times.

'God's wounds, I'm glad you are here, Chatillon, for this knave, this puke of piss, has no idea of how vital it is that we find the child. He refuses to believe that Yusuf is alive.'

Seeing that Embriaco was about to explode, Chatillon held up a hand to still the mercenary's diatribe, and he stepped forward and embraced Embriaco.

'We have sent you and Finian several messages but received no reply. Da Vasquez is telling the truth; Ishmael somehow survived, and we believe he's heading here to snatch Coralie. The Emir has sent Da Vasquez and his men to stop and probably kill his brother.'

The Portuguese mercenary nodded in agreement.

'We finally tracked Yusuf to an old farmhouse outside of Genoa. Some of the locals told us that he and his men had been there for several weeks, but now it is deserted. He has gone, and he could be here in the city waiting for an opportunity.'

Embriaco paled and ran his hands through his hair in alarm

CHAPTER TWENTY-FOUR

and disbelief.

'I have had no messages from you, but they are not here, Piers. Isabella and Coralie have gone to stay with Marietta for a month on her estate at Aggio. However, I ensured they were well guarded with Finian, your ten men, Captain Alfredo, and his men, at least twenty in total and all trained warriors.'

Conn listened to this with growing concern and stepped forward.

'We need to go now, Piers. He will have been here in Genoa watching and waiting with his men. He will have seen them leave and could have attacked them on the journey, or he could be sitting on the estate watching them for a chance to take the child.'

'Where is this estate? How far is it?' demanded Da Vasquez.

Chatillon met the eyes of the mercenary with a penetrating stare and raised his hand.

'Let me make one thing clear. I will be the one killing Sheikh Ishmael if we find him. He has done immense harm to me and my family, and you may have his body to take home for his brother.'

Conn watched in apprehension as the two men stared each other out, neither giving anything away with their expressions. Finally, Da Vasquez bowed his head in acceptance.

'From what I have heard, you have much right, but I swear I'll step in if you falter in any way, for that man cannot live—I have my orders. We will mount up and wait outside,' he said. He reluctantly bowed his head to the Signori, who stepped forward and anxiously clasped Piers by the shoulders.

'Go and protect them, Piers; I just hope to God you are not too late,' he exclaimed, his face a mask of concern.

Late evening – Aggio

Ishmael stood on the slopes looking down on the estate, the noise of the music echoed around the valley, and the flames of the braziers and fire pits burned bright. He was pleased with the success of his plan so far. One of his men was inside the estate, taken in by another seasonal worker. This man would signal that the drugged wine had taken effect on most guards and workers. Now his men were lying in wait to kill the patrolling men that walked the outskirts of the home estate. Then they would move in to remove the half dozen sentries outside the house as silently as possible. If his informer was correct, the only man inside the house was Gabriel De Chatillon, a mere boy.

If all went well, he would have his daughter in a few hours and be on his way down to the coast, where a boat was waiting. They would then sail to his true homeland, the deserts of his childhood. There was no one to stop him, and no one would ever find them. Gradually, the shouts and the laughter diminished from below, and the fires dimmed to a glow. Ishmael smiled as he waved his men forward into position. Soon, a flaming torch would be waved to say that it was safe for him to ride down and enter the house. As Ishmael waited, he realised that part of him wanted to see Isabella again, for he still felt the tightening in his loins when he thought of her. The other part would never forgive her for stealing his daughter, Coralie, away.

CHAPTER TWENTY-FOUR

The signal flared, and as he mounted his horse and rode down through the olive terraces, he was still undecided whether to let her live or not.

Chapter Twenty-five

Aggio Estate

The patrols and guards proved to be no problem to Ishmael's men, for it was dark, and they had the element of surprise. Not only that, they had watched the patrols for some time and knew exactly the paths they would take and the best places to attack. The paired patrols were overwhelmed by greater numbers; some fought back and struggled, but they all died. It was now the early hours of the morning, and the sentries outside the house were also not at their best. Two had lit a small brazier and were appreciating its warmth in the chill breeze when the Berber knives flashed, and their throats were cut. The two men on the terrace put up more of a fight, and they wounded one attacker, slashing his forearm from elbow to wrist before they were overwhelmed by sheer numbers.

Captain Ghilas, having checked on the drugged men and guards in the barns, joined them outside the house and ordered the signal to be given. A torch was lit and waved back and forth. They had been lucky, so far, in that most of the attacks had been carried out in silence; he had worried about the louder altercation on the terrace, but the heavy wooden shutters were closed and barred, and the skirmish

CHAPTER TWENTY-FIVE

had not roused the inhabitants of the sprawling manor house. Now they returned to the front entrance where two dead men lay sprawled on the steps; one of them was Captain Alfredo, lying in a pool of blood, his eyes staring sightlessly up at the night sky.

In no time at all, Ishmael dismounted in front of the house, and he greeted Captain Ghilas.

'All is well?' he asked softly, and Ghilas nodded in the affirmative, while telling his men to take all their horses down the track, leaving them tied under the trees for a quick departure.

They moved to the large oak doors, and Ghilas told the Sheikh to stand back. He gently knocked on the door as he knew a young servant slept just inside the entrance, in a small room in the short corridor leading to the large, tiled, open courtyard in the centre of the villa. As the door opened, the sleepy young man was yanked out, a hand clapped over his mouth, and the hilt of a sword descended on his head to send him to oblivion. Ishmael put a hand on his Captain's arm, stopping him from going further; the Captain turned in surprise as he knew the plan well.

'Ghilas, if I say to take the child, I want you to carry her to your horse and ride away down to the boats. Do not wait for me in case things don't go to plan. We know my brother's hounds are hot on our heels!'

Ghilas nodded in understanding; this had been talked of before, but he understood the Sheikh's need to remind him, for they did not know what they would face inside, or outside, the house before the night was done. Without another word, Ishmael and his men slid into the dark halls of the old manor house, heading for the rooms of the sleeping occupants.

Ishmael felt a sense of triumph as he strode through the silent stone-flagged corridors of the large manor house, lit only by the occasional guttering torch in the wall sconces. Yet again, he had outwitted them all, and Piers De Chatillon's family lay sleeping here totally unprotected. He smiled at the thought as he stepped into the Great Hall. It had been completely emptied for the feast; the trestle tables and even the top table had been taken outside. All that remained was the raised dais and one or two chairs. He went up the step and stood on the dais looking at the hall while Captain Ghilas waited.

'This will be perfect; I want them all brought in here. Light as many candles as you can find, and unbar those shutters, so we can leave quickly through there if, by chance, my brother's men arrive at the front. Now, you men know what to do, two to each room, tie their hands and bring them in here. Ghilas, bring another man. Let us go and visit my wife.'

Isabella had suffered another night of troubled sleep; she was uneasy, and she prayed the messenger had found Finian. Finally too warm, she had kicked off the light cover and dropped into an exhausted, deep sleep. She woke to the pressure of a blade at her throat and two dark figures at the side of the bed. The man holding the dagger said nothing while the second man tied her hands tightly in front of her and gagged her. She struggled and kicked out at them, receiving a blow for her trouble. It brought back horrific memories of her kidnapping from the Chateau. But then the nightmare truly began as a soft voice from the shadows addressed her.

'Don't struggle, Isabella, for they have instructions to mark and scar that pretty face if I tell them to, and that would be a shame.'

Isabella shook her head in shock, and denial, as a cloaked

and hooded figure emerged into the light of the candle that had now been lit. It was Ishmael. But that was impossible—he was dead. She gazed in horror as he came and stood beside her. He waved the Captain and the guard back and sat on the bed, the right-hand side of his face turned towards her.

'No, I am not dead despite the best efforts of Chatillon and his friends. I felt I had to come and find you and Coralie again, for after all, in Berber law, you are still my wife—still mine to do with as I please,' he said. His right hand moved to caress her breasts.

Isabella screamed into the gag, arching her back. She thrashed around, trying to move away, but he moved his hand to her throat and pinned her to the bed so that she choked.

'You will do everything I say, Isabella, if you want the rest of your family to live!'

Tears ran down her cheeks, unhindered, as he pulled her roughly to her feet and pushed her ahead of them into the hall, which was a blaze of light. Gabriel and Marietta were already there on their knees, hands tied in front of them and a rope around their necks held by a dagger-wielding guard behind. She was pushed to her knees beside them, and a noose dropped over her head and tightened. The hall now had one chair in the centre, where Ishmael sat as he regarded his captives. He said nothing for what seemed an aeon, while even more of his men entered and lined the walls.

'Do you know what it feels like to be almost burnt alive, Isabella? Can you appreciate the agony I have endured over the last year since that happened? But despite all of the pain, one flame burned bright in my breast. Can you imagine what that flame might be? If I allowed you to speak, I imagine the word revenge would be on your lips, but you would be wrong. I longed for my daughter, the light in my life, that you extinguished when you stole her from me. Ah, and here she is....' he said, as Anna emerged from behind the screen carrying the sleepy child into the hall.

Two men escorted her, one a big, dark, ugly man who positioned himself in front of the screen, glaring at the prisoners on their knees in a way that made Isabella fear for all of their lives. The other man pushed Anna towards the Sheikh.

Coralie was rubbing her eyes and blinking in the light, but was still clutching the doll Chatillon had given her in her other arm. Ishmael could not take his eyes from her, his golden child; he stood and, reaching out, took hold of the little girl's fingers and raised them to his lips, while Anna glared at him with an all-consuming hatred. Coralie's brows came together in the way that Ishmael remembered, when she was presented with something different that she was unsure of, or disliked.

'Coralie, it is I, Vava. Do you not remember your Vava?' he said, attempting a crooked smile.

However, Coralie was unsure; it was a year since she had seen her father, and she looked for her mother. Seeing her mother and her brother tied, she was scared, and began to sob. Anna stepped back, pulling the child's hand out of his. Captain Ghilas stepped forward as Ishmael hissed at the housekeeper.

'Do you not know who I am, woman? I'm her father.'

Anna gathered all the moisture in her mouth and spat at him, to the shock of everyone assembled in the hall.

'I know who you are. You are a heathen monster, who should have been consumed in flames, but I promise you that you will burn in hell fire, for you are the murdering scum who killed my poor husband Josef as well!'

Coralie, by now, was screaming in fright, but the Sheikh did not hesitate; his left side might be damaged, but he had practised relentlessly to build up his sword arm. Drawing his right arm back, he delivered a punishing punch to Anna's face, and everyone heard her nose crack as it broke and blood spurted. Ghilas grabbed the child as the woman toppled back over, and her head hit the floor with a thump, putting her out cold. Marietta, who was not gagged, screamed abuse at the Sheikh, and received a hefty blow to her head from the guard behind, making the room spin.

The Sheikh closed his eyes for a moment; he felt as if he was losing some control here, making him uneasy as Coralie kicked and screamed in the Captain's arms. He ordered him to take the child outside in the night air as it might calm her, which the Captain perfectly understood.

Gabriel was full of rage; his life had once again been almost perfect, but now Ishmael was back, bringing evil and terror back into their lives. Conscious that he was the only man there, he worked tirelessly at loosening the bonds, making his wrists bleed in the process as he worked them back and forth. Seeing the fury on his face, Isabella shook her head at him; he would be cut down in seconds if he tried anything.

Outside, Ghilas and one of his men made for the horses, which had been brought under the trees, ready for them to leave. He pulled a thin striped bed roll from another horse and wrapped it tightly around the sobbing child to tie her to his chest in a type of papoose often used by the women of the desert. He had young children of his own, and he murmured soothing sounds to her and stroked her hair until she settled. Then he mounted and pushed his horse into a trot, followed by his man behind.

He had orders to ride down the valleys towards the sea. A small boat would be waiting on the Ligurian coast for them just off Cape Belvedere, south of Genoa, with a chest of Byzantine gold to smooth their passage; this gold would also be her dowry. He knew that boat would take them to the galley waiting further offshore, and then it would return to the shore to wait for Sheikh Ishmael and his men. The galley had orders to sail if the Sheikh had not appeared before midday of the next day, for Ishmael knew the reach of Embriaco and his fleet of ships. The child was going back to her people in the far deserts where she belonged, an area Captain Ghilas knew well. But first, Ghilas had to keep to Ishmael's plan to leave an item of her clothing on the cliffs.

Finian had ridden warily onto the home estate from the northwest. He rode along the boundaries of the estate until he could ride down the tracks through the olive terraces to the barns. It worried him that he was never challenged, and he came across none of his many patrols. He dismounted in the deep shadows near the water troughs, and, leaving his horse to drink, he crept along the long side of the barn. A soft glow still came from the fire pits, and he could see at least a dozen men with their heads and arms on the trestle tables; he half expected them to be dead, but he realised they were sleeping. He walked inside the barn, and it was the same; most of their men lay in their blankets or on pallet beds, snoring. There seemed no cause for alarm, so surely all was well, and by the look of it, there had been a good feast day celebration.

He padded across the large open courtyard towards the entrance and found the first bodies; even the young serving boy lay on the steps, although Finian could see no wounds,

CHAPTER TWENTY-FIVE

and he found a pulse when he felt his neck. He went stone cold at the sight of Captain Alfredo, a seasoned and outstanding warrior, who should not have gone down without taking several with him, but there were no other bodies, no enemy he could see. Surely one or two assassins did not achieve all this, he thought, as he spotted more dead sentries against the manor house walls.

Drawing his sword, he took a deep breath, frightened at what he would find inside, for it seemed as though he was too late. He pushed the great door, but it was locked and barred inside. Had the women and Gabriel managed to keep the attackers out, he wondered, as he walked around the sprawling house. The rooms had every shutter still closed and locked on a night as he had ordered.

However, as he walked around the back of the house and the terrace, he heard footsteps. He flattened against the wall, as he watched the dark shapes of two men stride out, and make for the trees further down the track. It was dark, but he could hear the welcome whinnying of horses out there, and moments later, two horses emerged from the trees and rode off down the long track. Finian had seen the white Berber robes, so he waited a few moments in case others appeared before moving further around the building. As he followed the path to the rear of the house, he could hear a raised voice and see that light shone out of one of the large open shutters onto the terracotta tiles. He backed away from the light, stepping back over the wall into the shrubs in the dark behind, while positioning himself to see into the room.

Finian's eyes widened in shock at what he could see; a tall man in dark blue Berber robes and headdress stood in the centre of the room. He looked familiar, then the man turned his head slightly, and Finian gasped. He repeatedly blinked, unable to believe what he saw; he even rubbed his hands across his eyes, thinking it was tiredness, but no…. Ishmael was alive! He asked himself how that could possibly be, as he watched the Sheikh raising and punching the air with his right fist, as he berated his prisoners. Finian moved as far to the left as he could, and he saw Marietta, Gabriel and Isabella all bound with armed men behind them, but he could also see more men along the right wall.

He clenched his fists in fury and frustration as he watched another two men, carrying logs, enter the hall from behind the carved screen that hid the servant's kitchen entrance. There must be at least nine or ten men in there, and he was only one man; it would be suicide to try any attack on his own, which could only result in their deaths.

For one of the few times in his life, Finian Ui Neill felt lost for a solution. What he needed was a diversion, but he had no men. Suddenly, he thought of the horses; perhaps he could drive several horses into the hall. The shutters were tall and wide enough to get them in, and in the ensuing confusion, he could shorten the odds by killing several and riding out again. He mulled this momentarily, thinking of the advantages of launching a few smaller attacks that would give the impression of more men than just him outside. With this in mind, he made his way towards the Sheikh's horses under the trees; now, he just needed a miracle.

Chapter Twenty-six

Ishmael had finally stopped his rant against her, and Isabella watched, in trepidation, the men coming in from the kitchen, as they laid down their load of logs on the dais and went to get more.

'I have thought long and hard about what I wanted to do when I arrived here. My brother signed a charter, an agreement to end this blood feud. He gave his word to the Pope and to the princes of Europe, but I didn't sign anything, or give my word to them. I had no clear idea of what I would do until I saw you again, but you have brought pain and destruction into my life, Isabella. History is full of women like you who have lured men to their deaths, so I have decided on a compromise. I shall allow Chatillon's children to live, to keep my word to my brother, Abu, for what is a man if he breaks his word to his brother? But you, Isabella, you renounced your former marriage to him, in front of witnesses, with your hand on the Holy Book. You are my wife. I control your destiny and your life, and you shall die here in this hall. I shall watch you suffer as I suffered. You will feel the agony and intense pain of the flames. My men will build your funeral pyre here on this dais; you will be bound hand and foot and be placed on top of it. You will not struggle; you will go willingly, or I promise your son will join you. I'll enjoy striking the tinder and watching the flames rise before we depart, leaving your children outside so they can hear your screams, as I screamed as the flames melted my flesh.'

Marietta stared at the Sheikh in horror, while Gabriel, his mouth soundlessly working, tried to get words out to scream, 'No!' But he found that he could not speak. He pushed himself to his feet but was brutally knocked to the ground by the guard behind.

Finian had just reached the horses and was untying them when he heard the familiar sound of galloping hooves, in the distance. His first thought was that this was more of the enemy, and he backed into the trees, but standing there in the dark, he then reasoned this was unlikely. Listening to their approach, he recognised that a considerable number were coming at speed; he wondered at first if one of his men had escaped, raising the alarm, and then realised that was impossible given the distances. Friend or foe, he did not know, but he had to take the risk of stopping them, for the lives of the family were at stake. Finian drew his sword and ran down the drive as fast as he could towards them. He did not want Ishmael and his men to hear them coming, or he could slaughter all the prisoners.

Chatillon and the Horse Warriors had ridden so hard that their horses were almost blown. Da Vasquez and his men were close at their heels, determined not to be shaken off in the twists and turns of the mountain roads leading to Aggio. Piers had a tight knot of fear in his stomach that he had hoped never to feel again, as he prayed they were ahead of the Sheikh. Conn galloping beside him had no idea what they would find, but he feared the worst and dared not speak about it in case

CHAPTER TWENTY-SIX

it became a reality.

According to the timeline of Da Vasquez, the Sheikh had been here for weeks, waiting, watching and planning, but to do what? Snatch the child or exact revenge? He knew Ishmael would kill anyone who stood in his way, including Marietta. She had spirit and courage; if she got the chance, she might try to stop him from taking Coralie or from hurting Gabriel and Isabella. He tortured himself with these thoughts as they galloped towards the estate.

After what seemed a lifetime, they turned into the gates of the long track which wound up the hill towards the house, and they slowed to a canter, unsure what they would find when they reached the house. Chatillon suddenly reined in and shouted to stop. Chaos ensued behind them as horses collided, and Conn drew his sword as he saw a dark figure with a sword running towards them, until he realised the figure was waving his arms.

Finian recognised them, and he dropped to his knees on the drive in relief while gasping, 'Thank God, Piers, I thought you and Conn were in England. We must make haste, but dismount first and leave the horses here, and I'll tell you all. We need to be clever, or he will kill them all. It is Ishmael! He's here, Piers. Ishmael's alive. *Alive*, Piers!' His voice broke with the emotion and relief of it all.

Chatillon pulled him to his feet and embraced the Irish Warrior.

'We know, Finian, we came as fast as we could. We sent urgent messages to both you and Embriaco, but he must have intercepted them.'

Da Vasquez pushed his way to the front, glaring at the small group.

'What is amiss? Why have we halted?' he demanded.

'Da Vasca, this is Finian Ui Neill, who is to tell us what is happening.'

Da Vasca bowed his head, in recognition of the formidable reputation of this Irish warrior, but replied, 'Let us be quick then, for we must stop him.'

Finian explained what he had found and then led them to the scrubland on the hillside, so they could stand hidden but see the terrace and open shutters. Chatillon and Conn took in the scene at a glance, and their breath stopped in their throats as they realised the danger their loved ones faced. Piers gave a low growl, and Conn touched his arm.

'Rushing them will not help us; Finian says nine or ten of the Sheikh's men are in there, and all three prisoners have ropes around their throats and daggers above their heads.'

'The problem lies in the fact that we're all on one side of the manor; we need to somehow get men in there behind that screen,' whispered Georgio, as Chatillon gave him a glance of respect.

'I'll send my men around there; we will find a way in,' declared Da Vasquez

'Yes, but not without making enough noise to alert them; everything is barred and locked,' exclaimed Finian.

Suddenly, there was movement in the hall, and as they watched, the Sheikh sat back in the chair as his men stacked more logs on the dais.

'What are they doing?' whispered Georgio.

'Building a pyre, I would say,' suggested Da Vasquez, as Conn turned to him with a shocked expression.

'He is going to burn them! We need to go in now.'

'This is what Yusuf will see as justice for what he has

CHAPTER TWENTY-SIX

suffered, and he enjoys watching others suffer; I have dealt with him for years. I know how his mind works,' added the Portuguese mercenary with a shrug.

Finian suddenly put a hand on Chatillon's arm.

'That has given me an idea, Piers; I have thought of another way into the house. There's a chute down to a storeroom off the kitchen, used for logs and sacks of flour. I may be able to prise open the trapdoor without making too much noise as I remember it is old.'

'Go and try, Finian, but take no risks and do nothing rash,' whispered Chatillon.

'I'll send two of my men with you, Ui Neill. Meanwhile, I think we can move closer; many of the candles have burnt low, and some are guttering and about to go out. The light is not cast far from the door, and we can line up either side of those shutters, ready to go in and support the Irishman when he makes his move,' said Da Vasquez.

Chatillon agreed, and they silently crept forward, ready to line up in position. From where Piers placed himself in the deep shadows, he had an oblique view of the hall. He could see the large carved screen at the back; there were three of Ishmael's men on the left, and a woman's body was on the floor, possibly a servant, her face covered in blood. He could see Marietta clearly and half of Gabriel but not Isabella, so he moved further to the left. Now he could see the back of Ishmael in his chair and Isabella, white-faced and gagged; there were also two more guards in view on the left wall. It felt like a lifetime as he watched what was happening before him, as they finished building the pyre to almost waist height. He felt helpless and filled with impotent rage, but too many guards could kill the captives before they could reach them.

They needed Finian's distraction.

Suddenly, he saw a flicker of movement at the end of the screen behind the pyre, so it was hidden from Ishmael's view. It was Finian telling them he was there with two of Da Vasca's men, and his heart soared. This was their chance.

In fact, Finian Ui Neill was on his own; he had sent one man to quietly open the large doors into the house, to bring in more men. He had sent the other to untie the Sheikh's horses and chase them off, so they had no chance of escape. Finian watched and waited in the shadows for a chance, knowing the warriors he trusted would rush in and back him up from the open shutter when he started the diversion.

Suddenly, Ishmael stood and ordered them to pour oil onto the pyre, tie Isabella's legs and feet together and place her on top. Marietta pushed to her feet and screamed, 'No!' The guard behind her beat her to the ground, and then, grabbing her hair, he pulled her back into a kneeling position, and tightened the rope around her neck, so she was gasping for breath.

That was too much for Piers, and he felt he had no choice as he stepped forward into the hall, sword drawn.

Gabriel shouted, 'Father!' and the Sheikh whirled in surprise. Finian, seeing what was happening, ran out from behind the screen, jumped onto the dais and attacked the guard pouring oil onto the pyre, slicing off the arm that was holding the jug of oil. However, the corners of the hall were dark, and Finian had not seen the formidable, brutal-looking guard in front of the carved wooden screen; the man now quickly stepped up behind Finian and, using two hands, thrust his sword through the Irish Warrior. Conn gasped in horror as he watched the expression of surprise on Finian's

CHAPTER TWENTY-SIX

face, looking down at the blade projecting from his stomach. Finian's brown eyes met the shocked ones of Chatillon across the hall, and the Irish warrior murmured, 'Dion, take care of Dion, Piers,' before dropping his sword, which clattered off the pyre onto the dais. Then Finian fell forward onto the pyre. The towering guard put a foot on Finian's back and pulled his sword out, as Isabella let out a muffled wail of despair.

The Sheikh clapped his hands in delight, and turning, he smiled at Piers.

'It seems your warriors are not as indestructible as you thought, Chatillon,' he said, just as Conn, Georgio and several of their men came in to stand behind Piers.

'If anyone moves or raises a blade, I swear I will cut her throat.' He nodded at the guard who held the blade so tight against Isabella's neck that drops of blood appeared.

'You and your men will back out and leave,' he demanded, just as the huge mercenary, Da Vasquez, pushed his way through Chatillon and his men to glare at Ishmael.

The Sheikh's eyes widened at first, and then he laughed harshly at the sight of him.

'So, my brother has unleashed his war dog, has he? Let me guess, Vasquez; you will kill me and take my body back to be interred in the family mausoleum, as if I died of my injuries on the galley. That way, no disgrace is left on the Ibn Hud family name. But, to do that, you must decide if you are ready to sacrifice these innocents, Da Vasquez. How will my brother's signed charter look if I kill the Papal Envoy's wife and children because of your actions here? It seems as if we have reached an impasse. Instead, you will all leave this hall, and then shortly, we will negotiate my safe passage out of here, and I will release them all!' he exclaimed.

This speech was too much for Marietta, already white-faced and traumatised by Finian's death. She raised her tied hands and yanked the rope from the guard's hand behind her, rising to her feet again.

'You lying, treacherous, murdering bastard! I know what will happen. You want to burn Isabella alive. Don't trust his word, Chatillon; I would rather die than be left here being forced to watch Isabella burn,' she cried, wrenching herself further forward, while the guard reaching out, struggled to hold onto her hair as she tried to shake her head free.

'So be it!' declared the Sheikh, standing and nodding to the angry guard. Before Chatillon or Conn could move, the Berber raised his right hand and plunged the dagger into Marietta's chest. Conn let out a roar of rage as he charged across the hall to kill the guard.

Gabriel, who finally worked his bonds loose, rose and flung his elbow hard under his guard's chin as Finian had taught him to do. The man fell backwards as Gabriel grabbed Finian's fallen sword from the dais, then he turned and repeatedly stabbed down at the man on his knees. Gabriel, in a white-hot fury, turned on Ishmael, who had drawn his sword as Da Vasquez strode towards him. Before the Portuguese mercenary could get there, Gabriel had swung Finian's sword with all his might, slicing through the top of Ishmael's right arm to the bone. The Sheikh fell to his knees, and seconds later, Da Vasquez had run Sheikh Ishmael through, twisting the blade in his body as he grinned down into his face.

'The war dog always wins. You should have learnt that over the years with me, Yusuf,' he hissed.

Meanwhile, Chatillon and Georgio had raced for Isabella, but they knew they were too far away, at the end of the hall, as the guard raised the knife to stab down and fulfil his dying master's orders. Piers howled 'No!' as he ran, knowing he would not get there in time, but then suddenly, one of Da Vasca's men, who had been with Finian, appeared from behind the screen and jumped from the dais; he slammed the man's hand away and sliced his blade through his neck.

The guard's blade had scraped Isabella's shoulder and arm on the way down; she was bleeding but alive as Piers removed her gag, cut her bonds and pulled her into his arms. She clung to him, crying uncontrollably for Finian and Marietta, as if her heart would break. He held her tight, his mouth in her hair as she raised her tear-stained face to him.

'Coralie? Did you find her, Piers? She was taken outside by the Captain to stop her crying. You must find them.'

Piers shook his head. 'There was no one out there when we arrived, Isabella, but he may have been hiding if he saw us. We will send the men immediately to search the buildings and estate. Not one of his men will escape.'

Isabella was not convinced, and letting out a wail of anguish while breaking free from Piers, she stumbled over to the Sheikh who was dying. Blood ran from his scarred mouth onto the strewn rushes below his head. His Berber headdress had fallen backwards, and she saw the true horror of the burns to his face and head. But she had no sympathy for this man whom she loathed and hated with a vengeance.

Leaning close to his face, she whispered, 'Coralie. Where is she? I know you would never hurt her; you love her.'

The Sheikh ran a blood-covered tongue over his thin lips as he struggled to answer.

'You are wrong, Isabella; if the child rejected me, my captain had his orders. He would take her to the coast and fling her from the cliffs; a quick death. If I could not have her, then no one else can!'

She beat on the dying Sheikh's chest with both fists.

'No, that can't be true; she was your golden child, you loved her,' she cried, tears streaming down her face.

Ishmael coughed up even more blood, and his eyelids fluttered as he whispered, 'Dead, Isabella, she is dead, I swear it on the Holy Book.'

These were the last words he spoke as he let out a long, shuddering breath. Isabella dropped her head into her hands and screamed, raging loudly against fate while Gabriel knelt beside her and put his arms around her. Da Vasques' eyes met Chatillon's, and he raised his eyebrows and slowly shook his head, not ready to believe anything that came out of the Sheikh's mouth.

Chatillon ran his hands over his face and stared down at the body of his nemesis and his distraught wife. Even in death, Sheikh Ishmael had delivered more anguish, pain and heartbreak. His eyes travelled to the pyre, and Finian's body slumped forward over it, and from there, they travelled to Conn sitting on the floor with Marietta in his arms. Piers could see that she was still alive, but only just as the blade had delivered a heart stroke, and blood was on her lips, which now had a bluish tinge.

Leaving Isabella with Gabriel, he walked over to Finian, gently lifted him off the pyre, and laid him out on the dais. Piers folded the Irish warrior's arms on his chest when suddenly Georgio handed Finian's sword to him. He laid it on Finian's body, and wrapped his hands around the hilt, before gently closing those now dulled brown eyes, placing a hand on his forehead to push back the usual unruly lock of

CHAPTER TWENTY-SIX

dark hair, now showing occasional strands of grey, that had always flopped onto his forehead.

Piers put his head down and prayed for the soul of his dear friend; he smiled as he remembered their first meeting. He was a new Papal Envoy, travelling to Prague and full of self-importance, while Finian was a bristling, arrogant Irish warrior who thought he was the best swordsman in the world. Before long, they had found they were equally matched, had saved each other's lives and became firm friends. Suddenly he found the tears coming, and he could not stop once they started. Kneeling beside Finian's body, Piers cried himself dry for the friend he had lost, while resisting the temptation to stab Ishmael's body repeatedly with his dagger, until it was shredded.

Georgio stood back, unsure of what to do or say. Everywhere he looked, there was grief brought about by that evil man. His eyes travelled to his friend Conn, and he could see his lips moving as he comforted Marietta. Georgio dreaded to think of the impact this would have on Conn. Loss had been part of Conn's childhood, devastatingly affecting his character and emotions, and now he had lost Marietta.

Conn held Marietta tightly as if he would never let her go; she was dying, and she knew it, but was still conscious and determined to talk in a soft whisper.

'I want to be buried here, Conn, in the orchard near my mother. I dreamed that you and I would raise a family here, but it was as if I knew that could never be; it always seemed just out of reach.'

She had to pause as her breathing became noticeably more ragged. Conn saw more blood trickling from her mouth, and he wiped it away as she took a long breath.

'I love this place, Conn, and I want to be buried here. We could have found love and peace here, so I have left the estate to you. Promise me that you will come here and talk to me when you need peace. I will always be here, and I will always be listening. I hope you marry, find a woman to love and bring your family here. I want to think of your children running on these slopes.'

Conn found his tears were dripping from his face onto hers, and he gently stroked them from her cheeks.

'I was coming here to tell you that I loved you, Marietta, and that I wanted you to be part of my life.' He pulled her even closer, folding her into his arms. He stayed like that for a long time until he felt a hand on his shoulder. Piers and Isabella stood beside him.

'She's gone, Conn; you need to let her go now so that we can wash her and lay her out on her bed,' said Isabella, her voice breaking.

He pushed himself to his knees and stood with Marietta in his arms.

'I'll carry her to her room,' he said, reluctant to let her go as he followed Isabella down the corridor. He laid Marietta down on her bed and kissed her forehead before making for the door.

'She loved you so much,' said Isabella, pulling him back into an embrace, but he soon pulled away from her as if it was too painful.

'I know, Isabella, and I left it too late to tell her I reciprocated her love. I will regret that to the last days of my life,' he said, and then he was gone.

The next day, Da Vasquez clasped arms with Chatillon in farewell. Isabella and Gabriel stood on the steps, watching.

CHAPTER TWENTY-SIX

'As usual, I'm always at your service if you need me, Chatillon.'

Piers nodded and gave a thin smile, as he saw that the Sheikh's body had been tightly bound and wrapped, and was now hung over a pack horse. Da Vasquez followed his gaze.

'An ignominious end for the most feared pirate in the Mediterranean, but one he deserved. I would have dropped him in the nearest cesspit, but with the money Abu Ja'far is paying to bring the body back, I could retire, so it is worth my while. Although I assure you I'm not considering retiring for some time yet,' he said, grinning at Piers.

Brutal, unpredictable but lethal and highly effective, Piers could not help but like the man, though he treated him with wary respect.

At that moment, a Berber horseman cantered up, one of Da Vasquez's men; he dismounted and handed something to Chatillon while touching his forehead in respect.

'This was found on the cliffs, Sire, but there was no sign of a body below, and we searched thoroughly as ordered. We discovered that Captain Ghilas and one other man had a boat waiting, which took them out to a galley waiting offshore, but the boatmen say they saw no child with them.'

'I noticed that the Sheikh was wearing indigo Tuareg dress. I have never seen him wear that before; he was always in white,' said Chatillon, turning the wooden cross doll in his hands that had belonged to Coralie.

'Yes, the robes go back to the roots of the nomadic tribes that travel thousands of miles, trading horses in the huge deserts; they merged with the Bedouin and Berber people. Sometimes, these tribes travel as far west as the Western Sea of Darkness, or down to the eastern Egyptian Kush, or even Ethiopia, to graze their horses. These tribes are often impossible to find, Piers,' he said meaningfully. Piers knew what he was implying as the mercenary continued.

'You can end this here and now, Piers, accept that she is probably dead, or spend your lives once again searching for a child that might be alive, and will be almost impossible to find in the deserts,' he said, in a soft undertone that the people on the steps would not hear.

Again, Da Vasca's eyes found Piers in a long look that spoke volumes; Piers understood what he was saying. Without further ado Da Vasquez mounted, raised a hand in farewell and rode away, taking Ishmael's remains with him. Both Isabella and Gabriel felt relief at seeing the body leave the estate. He might be truly dead this time, but it was as if a malevolent force still emanated from the body. Piers watched them ride away for a while until they were a smudge of dust on the hillside while he made a decision. Then he turned, the doll in his hands and walked back to the steps.

'My love, she's truly gone, there is no doubt. They found this on the cliffs, and a child was not taken into the boat,' he said softly, folding his distraught wife in his arms and pulling Gabriel into a hug.

Later that morning, Finian's body was sent to Genoa to be embalmed for the journey back to Chatillon Sous Bagneux, to Dion and his children. Finian was going home to be buried in the family plot. Chatillon had sent a long, written missive with a messenger to Edvard. This was not news to be sent with a bird, and Chatillon did not envy him the task of breaking it to Dion and the others, as Finian was much loved and would leave a hole in all their lives.

That afternoon, they buried Marietta in the orchard close

CHAPTER TWENTY-SIX

to her mother. Conn had hardly spoken since the previous night. Now, he stood beside the grave for some time after the others had left. Then he knelt and brought a small posy of her favourite cornflowers from his doublet. Georgio stood and watched him from a distance but sadly turned away, unsure what to say or do to help his friend.

Sometime later that evening, Conn made his way to the barn and saddled his horse; instead of riding down the track, he rode north onto the hills behind the home estate, where he sat and watched the sun slowly sinking in the west for some time. Then, having made a decision, he deliberately turned east. Conn needed to be on his own, possibly for some time, and he knew if he turned west, that would never happen, for they would find him. He needed new horizons and nothing to remind him of what had happened here in Aggio. He knew his departure would hurt and disappoint several people, but he had no choice.

Chapter Twenty-seven

Late October 1100 – The Chateau

Chatillon sat in his business room, deep in thought. Two missives were sitting on his table, both of which had come from the hands of royal messengers. He had opened neither of them. Instead, he was composing his own letter to Pope Paschal informing him that he was, unfortunately, relinquishing his post as Senior Papal Envoy. He could imagine the scrabbling and backstabbing among the lower envoys, that would take place to obtain this prestigious post when they heard the news, and he smiled at the thought. He continued the letter, assuring Paschal that he would still be available for advice, but he could no longer play an active role as he needed to spend time with his family. However, he promised the Pope that he would still be available for what they called *additional services* when needed.

He halted and thought about that for a moment. Was he truly still prepared to travel the length and breadth of Europe to remove troublesome clerics, or individuals, creating problems for the Holy See? He needed Conn to reappear, to take on this work, but nothing had been heard of him since he disappeared into the night, several months

CHAPTER TWENTY-SEVEN

before.

The door opened, and Edvard entered the room, sinking into a nearby chair with a sigh; it had been a long night for them all.

'How's it going? Is there any sign?' he asked his friend.

Edvard shook his head. 'Ahmed and Isabella are there with Dion. Ahmed says it is a breach and has called Mishnah in, as she has long, slim hands which might be able to turn the babe.'

Chatillon groaned and ran his hand through his hair, which seemed to have more strands of grey since the events on the estate near Genoa.

'The last thing those children need is to lose their mother as well as their father.'

The shock of Finian's death had devastated Dion and had been responsible for pushing her into premature labour. Very few mothers survived breach births, but at least Dion had Ahmed at her side, bringing his immense set of skills.

'Are you going to open those? They arrived yesterday,' said Edvard, indicating the sealed folded missives on the table.

Chatillon assumed an expression of distaste and regarded the pile of vellum as if it were poisoned. After this summer's events, he was unsure whether he wanted to step back into any of the political turmoil of Europe's courts, hence his letter to Pope Paschal.

Edvard leant forward and picked up the nearest one, breaking the distinctive seal of Henry I, the new King of England. Unfolding the thick quality vellum, he handed it to Piers, who quickly scanned it while Edvard placed another log on the fire. It was October, and autumn had arrived with wet and blustery winds that had swirled the leaves around the garden and taken the petals from the late roses.

'So Edvard, as we thought, Henry is determined to marry into the Royal House of Wessex to give his rule some legitimacy. The King needs my help as Archbishop Anselm is refusing to agree to the match, as he thinks that Matilda has already taken her vows as a nun.'

'Did she?' asked Edvard, with a cynical smile, knowing how these things could be brushed under the rug.

'No. She did not. Her aunt at Romsey, Abbess Cristina, forced Matilda of Wessex to wear a nun's veil, to protect her from the marauding young nobles eager to marry a Saxon princess. Unfortunately, I have had news that Abbess Cristina died a few weeks ago. A great lady and a huge loss to the Abbey at Romsey. However, I'm sure we can find a senior nun at the Abbey who can corroborate this. See to it, Edvard, for King Henry tells me he wants to marry his Saxon bride and crown her before Yuletide.'

Edvard gave a low whistle of astonishment.

'He is certainly in a rush, Piers; I presume this is to do with Duke Robert's imminent return,' he said, pointing to the second missive on the table.

Chatillon inclined his head while breaking the familiar seal of Normandy on the second document. He scanned its contents, read it a second time and sat back, staring into the flames from the now-burning log with a frown.

'Robert has returned to Rouen to a hero's welcome as the saviour of Jerusalem, as we expected. He was immediately greeted with the news that William Rufus had been killed, and for the second time, he had been deprived of the throne of England by a younger brother—a brother who has broken an oath of homage taken with his hand on sacred relics. If you

CHAPTER TWENTY-SEVEN

remember, his father, King William, went to war with Harold Godwinson for the same reason: oath-breaking. History is repeating itself, Edvard, and to make matters worse, Henry's troops are still occupying the fortress of Domfront and parts of the Cotentin. Robert plans to invade England to depose Henry and claim his throne. He is asking for the Pope's support, due to the oath-breaking, and expects me to leave at once for Rouen to be at his side to advise him.'

Edvard looked perplexed. 'What happens when he discovers you were there in the forest when Rufus was killed, for he knows your trade, and Robert is astute; he will suspect you had a hand in it. Also, the Pope sanctioned the assassination, as it played into the hands of the Holy See to remove William Rufus, who was anti-Church. Surely, this request places you and Pope Paschal in an impossible situation. Having spent a fortune preparing and supporting Duke Robert in the past, you chose to back a different horse, his brother Henry, but Robert does not know this yet. This will have to be handled with great caution, Piers. Are you sure that Pope Paschal is up to anything this incendiary yet?'

Chatillon closed his eyes and did not reply for a while, as the simple answer was no. This situation would fill Paschal with anxiety and panic. He leant to the side of the table and, picking up the resignation letter he had been writing to the Pope, crumpled it in his hand and threw it into the fire. He had no choice but to continue.

'You are right, Edvard; Paschal can't handle this. He does not have the skills to play one side off against the other, and ensure that the Holy See emerges unscathed, without a whisper of blame.'

The door suddenly opened, and Isabella stood there smiling,

holding a tightly wrapped red-faced baby with a shock of Finian's dark hair.

'She has finally arrived, somewhat bruised and battered, but with God's grace, she seems a healthy babe. Dion has called her Finula, a name they both chose when they decided it had to be a girl this time.' Piers and Edvard stood and came to admire this new bundle of life in the Chateau.

'One life ends, a much-beloved person gone, and another arrives,' said Edvard, wiping away a tear for Finian, who never got to meet the daughter he so wanted.

'How is Dion?' asked Piers.

'Inconsolable, saddened, totally lost without Finian, as you would expect, but I hope this little one will give her something to concentrate on for now,' she said, her eyes filling with tears of sadness.

'Can you give her to Edvard? I need to talk to you, Isabella.'

Edvard happily took the baby, as he even had hopes of his own since he had married Mishnah earlier that month. Piers led Isabella to the seat by the fire, and sitting opposite her, took her hands in his, his forefinger gently caressing the back of each hand as he smiled into her eyes.

'You have no idea what it has meant to us all to have you come back to us here, despite everything that happened,' he said.

'I think it was because of what happened, Piers, the dreadful loss of Finian, Marietta and Coralie. I knew I did not want to lose you and the boys as well.'

He squeezed her hand and lifted her fingers to his lips, gently biting the tips as he had always done, which made her smile. It had been strange and even awkward at first, for so much had happened, but now their lovemaking was back to what it had been, perhaps even more loving, if that was possible. They needed each other.

'I have been thinking of giving everything up apart from my life on the estate, ensuring that you and my sons had my full attention. I can see us taking them to court soon and finding them wives. I will transform myself into a grand country gentleman for you, Isabella.' He paused, trying to find the next words but then heard a snort of laughter from his wife.

'Do you honestly expect me to believe that, Piers? You are not in your dotage by a long way, and you would die of boredom within months. We can still do things like that while you continue to dabble in, and manipulate, the politics of Europe.'

At first, he wore an affronted expression that her expectations of him were so low, but seeing her amused smile, he finally smiled back and conceded that she might have the right of it. He indicated the open letters on the table.

'Trouble and war are brewing again in Europe, and I feel that the Holy See will be involved; we may have to pick a side, which will be difficult and have far-reaching consequences.'

Isabella leant forward and stroked his face.

'We need you, Piers. We love you dearly, but Paschal needs you as well. I presume Duke Robert has returned, and I can imagine his rage. However, there is one thing you need to do—send out your informers to find Conn. Yes, he is grieving and needs time, but he also needs you to give him a purpose in his life. Find him, Piers. I know that Georgio has already gone to search for him, but he is young and does not have your resources and wide net of informers.'

'I promise I'll do my best, Isabella, but sometimes when someone wants to be lost, it can be difficult to find them.

Marietta left him the estate as if she knew what would happen. She left signed documents in Genoa to give the whole estate to Conn, along with a very generous stipend. The rest of her fortune she left to Gabriel.'

Isabella's eyes widened; she had not known that. Gironde, of course, as the eldest twin, would inherit the Chatillon title, a vast portfolio of property and estate, but Piers would always have made provision for Gabriel as well. Now, he did not need to, as Gabriel would be a very wealthy young man with the raft of businesses Marietta had possessed.

'Marietta always had a special bond with Gabriel; they sang songs and wrote poetry together, talking for hours. Does he know?' she asked.

'Not yet. I have only just finished finalising the documents.'

'Could we go together and tell him? I know it will make him sad, for he loved her, but I hope it will bring him some happiness as well,' she said softly, the sadness back in her eyes at such pointless deaths. Piers nodded and stood.

'I'll join you in the solar shortly. I wish to visit Finian's grave first,' he said, kissing her forehead. Piers found his feet often took him to the grass-covered mound overlooking the paddocks. Dion had wanted Finian to be near the horses he loved rather than over in the family plot. Piers stood and stared down at the stone slab he had requested from the stone mason. It had his friend's name, and the design of the Celtic pin Finian always wore to fasten his cloak underneath it, an eternal knot that represented the cycle of birth, life, death and rebirth. Chatillon bent and ran his fingers over the design, thinking how appropriate it was.

'I have no excuse now, Finian, not to reply to Duke Robert and with Paschal's permission, I will leave for Rouen. Isabella has sanctioned me to remain as the Papal Envoy. Am I pleased or disappointed? I hear you ask. Being typically Irish, you would have presented both sides of the argument, made me choose one and then argued against it no matter which one I picked. You loved a good debate.'

Chatillon sighed; he missed his friend, even though he was surrounded by others here at the Chateau, for Finian was his sounding board for ideas and problems. The Irish warrior would always prick his conscience and ask him questions others avoided. He knew Finian had been good for him, for he was rarely challenged.

'Did I do the right thing, Finian? Not sending men to discover if the child lived. If she is alive, is she happy?' he asked.

He often wondered if Coralie was truly out there in the great deserts among her father's people; he believed it to be true, for Ishmael had loved his child. The family would know who she was, and Coralie would be loved and revered by them as the golden child of the Sheikh.

He had endured months of Isabella's and Gabriel's deep sadness at her loss, nights of tears, not only for themselves, for their loss, but for the short life they thought she had, heartbroken that she had not lived to grow to womanhood. In his mind's eye, Chatillon liked to think of Coralie in ten years' time; she would be riding a blood Arab stallion across the desert, her blond hair flowing behind her, a true Bedouin of royal blood who would not remember any other life. He thought that Finian would probably tell him that time would be a great healer for his wife and son, and that he did the right thing to let the child go.

However, Isabella was right about Conn, and Finian would

have berated him for not sending men to find him sooner. As he bade Finian farewell, he decided to send birds out today. There was no trace, or word, of the distinctive young warrior, so Chatillon believed Conn had gone east; Georgio had thought the same. He would find him.

But he had something important to do first as he walked up the staircase to their bed chamber. It was a comfortable, colourful room with his mother's rich tapestries on the walls. Under the window was a chest, and on top of the chest sat the wooden cross doll that had belonged to Coralie, the one he had given her that was found on the cliffs. It was a constant, often nightly reminder of the child that Isabella had lost and an admonishment to him for his decision not to look for her.

He strode over, and without hesitation, he picked up the doll and, opening the heavy lid of the chest, placed it at the bottom beneath some of his clothes. Piers then locked it, and after doing so, he took a deep breath. He stared down at the chest, and although it was only a child doll, he liked to think he was locking away some of the legacies of his nemesis and enemy, Sheikh Ishmael. After several years, he had finally triumphed over him, but so many lives were lost at such a high cost.

He strode to the window and watched his son, Gironde, and Finian's eldest son, Cormac, train the young warhorses below. A new year was approaching, and they had the chance of a new beginning as a family. But war was coming again; he did not doubt that. He now had work to do, and he smiled to himself as he realised Isabella was right; in reality, he relished the thought of going to Rouen, for he would have to use all of his skills to keep this war from their doors and the doors of Pope Paschal. And he knew that as Papal Envoy, he was one of the few men who had the power and influence to achieve that.

Read more

My next, and third series is **The Tattooed Horse Warrior** series.

You can read the first chapter of book one, BYZANTIUM, on the next page.

The Tattooed Horse Warrior Series

BYZANTIUM

October 1100 – Constantinople

Georgio had been in the fabled city for only a few hours and had decided to take a room and leave his horse at one of the better inns near the walls. Handing his horse to an ostler, he carried his dusty, worn saddlebags into the inn. The innkeeper eyed this new arrival warily, for Georgio was in the full Horse Warrior regalia with his scarred leather-laced doublet and trademark crossed swords on his back.

'How long are you staying?' he asked the young warrior in front of him in a neither welcoming nor friendly tone.

'I am not sure, but for several nights at least; I am here searching for a friend,' he replied with a smile that had little effect on the taciturn older man.

The innkeeper grunted in reluctant acceptance but then demanded payment upfront. Georgio, reaching for his saddlebags, straightened up and raised an eyebrow in surprise.

'Do you ask that of all your guests?'

The innkeeper snorted with disdain before replying.

'No, only the foreign strangers like yourself and shifty individuals who may be up to no good that I do not trust.

We had many of those during the last crusade, leaving a lot of damage, and now they are considering starting another to go back to protect the Holy City. Madness, I tell you. Even more will die.'

Georgio stared at him in dislike, but he had little choice, so he took a silver coin from his purse, which the innkeeper dared to bite to check it was genuine. Georgio rolled his eyes in disbelief but followed the waiting serving girl up the stairs to a small room that looked out onto the city's high, dark, forbidding walls. He walked to the window; the shutters were wide open, and the odours of the midden and piss pit behind the inn floated up from below. He stepped back, wrinkling his nose and shook his head, thinking how Conn would have had the man by the throat if he had spoken to him like that. Georgio knew he had the well-deserved reputation of a fearsome warrior in battle, but he tended to be an easy-going soul unless challenged or threatened. At the same time, his friend, Conn, often revelled in and enjoyed any confrontation.

The girl was still standing inside the open door, surely not waiting for a tip, he wondered, glancing at her, but then she smiled.

'I can provide extra services if needed during your stay here. A tall, handsome soldier like you, I would even give you a discount,' she said, grinning at him.

Georgio smiled and thanked her but declined the offer. And taking her gently by the shoulders, he propelled her out of the room, closing the door firmly behind her. He sat on the bed and gratefully pulled off the high leather boots. He stood and placed them against the door as an early warning system and then lay down on the bed to rest his weary back and shoulders after a week of riding for hours every day, combined with sleeping rough most nights since his stay in Thessalonica.

He closed his eyes and tried to sleep, but his thoughts churned around as he recalled the months of searching, following a thin, cold trail and only the odd clue as to where Conn was headed. He was fortunate that Conn was distinctive. Georgio was tall, but Conn was a hand taller as well as dressed as a Horse Warrior with the unusual crossed swords on his back; he found people in the towns and villages remembered that. He found in a few places that Conn had left mayhem and anger behind him with threats to kill him if they saw him again, so Georgio made a hasty exit. It appeared that a grieving Fitz Malvais was even quicker to anger, quick to kill when threatened and quick to swive a chieftain's pretty wife while her man was out hunting with his men.

While he lay there trying to sleep, Georgio admitted to himself that he was somewhat overwhelmed by the size of the city, but he had been trained by the best, so he divided the city into four parts in his head. He would search each part in turn; if Conn were here, he would find him. The missing Horse Warrior would need a bed, so Georgio would first try all the inns in each quarter of the city.

The first day proved to be fruitless; he was searching in a better part of the city not far from his inn, but no one had seen a tall Horse Warrior. Even in October, the city was hot, as the high, thick walls tended to keep the winds sweeping off the sea and the hills to a minimum. He returned to the inn hot, dusty and tired. He ate some food, washed and ventured out again, this time heading for the less salubrious establishments near the harbour, of which there were several.

He struck lucky at the third run-down alehouse; a scar-faced barkeeper remembered Conn.

'Yes, he was here, drunk and causing trouble two nights ago, but he paid well, so we let it pass. Usually, he would have been thrown out; the lads over there enjoy a bit of roughing up.'

Georgio turned and glanced at three sullen individuals sitting near the fire, who seemed to be weighing him up, probably assessing the weight of his purse. He suddenly realised his mistake of bringing a full purse to the streets at night. Even the young pot collector, a thin, gangly lad, was shaking his head in comical dismay while watching the drama unfold. However, Georgio was not the type to be frightened off by a few ruffians.

'Do you know where he went or where he would be staying?' he asked, producing a coin. The barkeep pocketed it but then shook his head.

'No idea, never seen him before or after that night,' he grinned and nodded at the men near the fire.

Georgio grimaced in frustration as he made for the door, but at least he knew he was on the right track; Conn Fitz Malvais was here somewhere in the city.

Georgio stood on the quayside for a while, expecting to be followed, but there was no sign of them; perhaps they were deterred by the swords on his back, he thought as he turned back to stare at the dark waters behind him. Suddenly, a hand touched his shoulder. Georgio whirled around, dagger drawn, into a crouch to face his attackers. But it was the pot boy, tall with dark hair and eyes, a good-looking lad who Georgio thought was about sixteen. The boy had stepped back in alarm, but the Horse Warrior sheathed his dagger.

'A good way to get killed, lad, sneaking up on people like that!' he exclaimed.

'I am sorry, Kyrios, I did not think. I was coming out here to help but also to warn you.'

Georgio smiled at the use of the Greek word for Lord; he, alongside Conn, had been knighted by King Peter of Aragon in his service, but he rarely used the title Lord.

'This man you seek, he wears swords like this as well?' the boy asked.

'Yes. You saw him as well, in the inn? Was he fighting?' asked Georgio with a smile.

'No, I was not there that night, but I have seen him,' he declared.

'Where?' demanded Georgio, stepping forward.

'Coming out of the gate in the barracks. He is a tall, broad-shouldered, impressive warrior. Eyes are drawn to him, especially with those swords. He will be one of the mercenaries there, as our Emperor Alexios Comenius is recruiting foreigners again for the war against the Seljuk Turks. I wanted to go and join, but my mother lives alone; I am her only son, and she refused to let me become a soldier,' he said woefully.

'You would also be too young,' pointed out Georgio unhelpfully, but he flipped him a coin for his information.

'I have my name day in a few weeks, and then I will be eighteen. Surely that is old enough?' he asked.

Georgio looked at the thin young man before him; he was sure he would see every rib if he lifted the thin, dirty tunic. He changed the subject, not wanting to offend the boy.

'What was the warning?' he asked.

'Atreas and his men left by the inn's side door; they are waiting for you in the dark to take your purse. They will probably cut your throat,' he announced in a matter-of-fact voice.

Georgio laughed at him, then asked, 'Do you know where they are waiting?'

The boy nodded. 'They are getting set in their ways; they use the same doors and archways to hide in. It is the main route for people to return to the city.'

'Is there any way of getting behind them?' he asked.

'You mean to get around them? To escape?'

'No, for me to come quietly behind them,' he explained as the boy's eyes widened.

'I did say there were three of them, and these are hard thieves from the wharves; few would take them on,' he exclaimed.

Georgio shrugged, and the boy sighed at the foolishness of this warrior.

'We will have to go over the rooves. It will be dangerous,' he blurted to another snort of laughter from Georgio.

A short time later, Georgio softly dropped from a low roof into a dark, narrow, stinking alley coming up from the harbour. He flattened himself against the wall, drawing his long war dagger as the boy dropped behind him, but kept his distance as instructed. The alley curved and widened, and Georgio could see the faint moonlight on the harbour through the arch at the end. It also showed the shapes of two men whispering to each other. However, he could not see the third man, which worried him as he crept slowly forward. His boots slid on the stinking refuse beneath his feet, and he knew he would have to be careful not to slip or slide.

It was dark in the shadows, but fortunately for Georgio, the lone man standing in the doorway just ahead of him spat out into the alley. Georgio had been trained in stealth by the best warriors in the world, and he moved forward in silence. The man had craned forward to watch his two friends when Georgio slid in behind him; swiftly pulling his head back, he slit the robber's throat with only the slightest gurgle. Wide-eyed and excited, Darius slid in behind him.

'Which one is Atreas?' whispered Georgio.

'The bigger thick-set man on the left; he is telling the weasel-faced one off for moaning.'

The two men were arguing as it seemed to have taken far too long for the warrior with the full purse to appear, and the weasel wanted to return to the inn. Suddenly, there was the unmistakable sound of drawn steel close behind them, and both men reacted, reaching for their swords. Georgio slashed at the weasel's arm before his sword was out of its sheath. The man stood frozen, staring at where his hand had once been as his sword clattered to the ground and blood flowed freely from his arm. He let out a strangled yell and ran, holding his arm to his chest.

This left the leader, Atreas, who now realised they had possibly taken on more than they expected, so he tried to bluster his way out as he backed out towards the harbour. Atreas was no swordsman; he relied on surprise in dark alleyways. The Horse Warrior followed him, sword in hand, out into the wider space, where they circled each other warily.

'You have killed and injured my men. Can we not now call a truce and go our separate ways?' he suggested, his brow beaded with sweat.

'A truce suggests that we had engaged in a war, Atreas, but you set up a cowardly attack, three men onto a poor unsuspecting stranger in your city.'

Realising that talking would not help, the robber assumed

a resigned expression and then suddenly charged at the Horse Warrior, raising his sword high. Before the sword descended, Georgio had run him through, as Darius stared open-mouthed at the speed and skill of this man with the crumpled body at his feet.

Georgio cleaned his sword on the dead man's tunic and turned to face the boy.

'Tell me, Darius, do you enjoy working at the inn?'

The young man shook his head.

'Good, for I will now engage you as my servant. This post might mollify your mother as you will not exactly be fighting, well, not yet anyway.'

Darius was too overwhelmed to speak; he just nodded enthusiastically as Georgio put two further silver coins in his hand.

'Your next three months' wages. Buy a decent tunic tomorrow; I cannot have my servant looking like a ragamuffin from the streets. You can give the rest to your mother. And now for bed, for we have a busy day tomorrow. Early tomorrow morning, you will turn up at my inn beside the city walls and show me these barracks you spoke of tonight.'

Without further ado, Darius stepped over the dead body of Atreas without a backward glance. Then he trotted after the tall warrior striding ahead of him, but he could not keep the grin from his face as he clutched more money than he would see in a year to his thin chest.

Author note

Writing the last book in 'The Papal Assassin Series' was sad, as Piers De Chatillon grew into one of my favourite characters. However, as you know, the history of that turbulent Medieval period certainly does not end there.

In only a few months, King Henry had built or bought allies and consolidated himself on the throne while courting a Saxon princess. By the end of October 1100, he had married Matilda of Wessex and ensured she was crowned Queen. He was determined that as King, he would present a different image from his brother William Rufus and beget legitimate heirs with Norman and Saxon blood in their veins. Also, his Charter of Liberties and Ranulf Flambard's imprisonment proved very popular among the nobles and the common people.

There are several differing accounts of the death of William Rufus in the Royal Forest, and I have read many of them; a few are contemporary, but most were written later. They're still being pored over by historians and academics, and the story is still being rewritten today, for it was both a timely and convenient death for Henry.

One argument purports that it was purely a hunting accident which was common in these times. I consider that highly unlikely, for certain things become very clear as you bring more pieces of the puzzle together. That version does not explain why Walter Tirel fled, apparently for fear of being blamed or used as a scapegoat. Yet, there was no pursuit of him, and he was never held to account for the killing of the King. His compatriots said he was a renowned archer and was unlikely to let loose the supposedly wild shot that killed the King. In the following year, several members of Tirel's family received significant advancements and rewards from King Henry.

I also believe that it was no accident that Henry was there with his brother that day; he had certainly shown in the past how single-minded and brutal he could be when he threw Conan from the tower in Rouen. It was also convenient that, being in the forest, he could immediately make his dash to seize the treasury at Winchester while his brother's body was still warm. Or, as some accounts have it, still alive and dripping blood all the way to Winchester. Both Eli Parrat and Purkiss, the charcoal burner, were real people there in the forest at that time, with the body of William Rufus.

King William Rufus was not popular as he and Flambard stripped the people and church in England of their wealth, so very few mourned him. However, the indecent haste with which Henry was crowned only two days after his brother's death spoke of careful planning. Henry was a ruthless, astute, clever individual who left nothing to chance, and these traits would become more apparent during his reign.

AUTHOR NOTE

You have to feel for Duke Robert at this time; the conquering hero returns but has lost the throne of England again. He has no choice but to try and take it back…. But that is for another book in another series as the thwarted king strikes back.

S. J. Martin

August 2023

List of Characters

Fictional characters are in *italics, and* real characters are in **bold**.

France – Chatillon Estate at Chatillon sous Bagneux
Piers De Chatillon – Papal Envoy and Papal Assassin.
Isabella De Embriaco – his wife, poisoner & assassin.
Gironde & Gabriel – their twin sons.
Annecy – their daughter who was murdered.
Cecily- Chatillon's unknown granddaughter who was murdered.
Marietta De Monsi – Chatillon's ward and wealthy heiress.
Conn Fitz Malvais – illegitimate son of Morvan De Malvais and Constance of Normandy.
Georgio of Milan – Friend and warrior comrade of Conn.
Edvard of Silesia – Chatillon's vavasseur and friend.
Finian Ui Neil – Irish lord & mercenary.
Dion - Finian's wife.
Cormac & Fergus – their young sons.
Ahmed – Physician, apothecary and expert poisoner.
Mishnah – Concubine of Sheikh Ishmael.
Daniel – Chatillon's Captain.
Lazzo –Finian's Captain.
Madame Chambord – Housekeeper & cook.

Paris
King Philip of France.
Louis – His eldest son, the Dauphin.
Bertrade de Montford – the King's long-term mistress, still married to Fulk of Anjou.
Gervais de la Ferte –Seneschal of France.
Lord de Salvais.
Lucette de Salvais – his wife.
Chevalier de Salvais – his son.

Monastere de Saint Benoit
Friar Francis.
Tomas, the Benedictine healer.
Father Dominic – the archivist.

Rome & Brindisi
Odo de Chatillon – Piers' uncle and Pope Urban II, who died in 1099.
Cardinal Raniero – who became Pope Paschal II in 1099.
Antipope Clement.
Count Geoffrey of Conversano – wealthy Norman Lord in Brindisi.
Sibila of Conversano – his daughter and wife of Duke Robert.

Crusaders
Robert Curthose, Duke of Normandy. Eldest son of William the Conqueror.
Odo, Bishop of Bayeux, Earl of Kent, Robert's Uncle, murdered in Sicily.

London
King William Rufus. Second son of William the Conqueror.
Ranulf Flambard – Chancellor & Prince Bishop of Durham.
Henry Beauclerc – Youngest son of William the Conqueror.
Almodis de Mortain – Lover of Chatillon.
Robert De Belleme – Earl of Shrewsbury.
Walter Giffard - Earl of Buckingham and Justiciar of England.
Agness de Ribemont – Countess of Buckingham and long-term mistress of Duke Robert.
William – Lord of Tortosa, their illegitimate son.
Richard Fitz Gilbert de Clare.
Walter Tirel.

Winchester, Royal Forest & Romsey Abbey
William de Breteuill – A supporter of Duke Robert.
Robert de Beaumont – Earl of Leicester.
Henry de Beaumont – Earl of Warwick.
Eli Parratt – Fletcher.
Purkiss – Charcoal burner.
Abbess Cristina.
Matilda of Wessex.

Spain
King Alphonse of Leon & Castile.

Zaragoza
Yusuf Ibn Hud - Sheikh Ishmael, Saracen pirate.

Mishnah – his concubine.
Captain Ghilas.
Abu Ibn J'far – Head of the Ibn Hud dynasty in Zaragoza.
Bernard de Bordeaux.
Maria – his wife.
Ernesto Da Vasquez – A Portuguese mercenary employed by Abu Ja'far.

Morlaix
Luc De Malvais – Breton Lord & Horse Warrior.
Merewyn – his wife.
Marie De Malvais – his mother.

Morvan De Malvais – brother of Luc, father of Conn.
Ette De Malvais – his wife.
Gervais – his son.
Marie – his daughter.

Genoa
Signori Guglielmo Embriaco - Leader of the Genoa Republic.
Captain Alfredo – Leader of the Signori's guards.
Josef – The Steward at Aggio.
Anna – His wife and the housekeeper.
Coralie – the Sheikh's daughter.

Glossary

Bailey - A ward or courtyard in a castle, some outer baileys could be huge, encompassing grazing land, stables, blacksmiths and huts.
Basilica – An early Christian church or cathedral designated by the Pope and given the highest permanent designation. Once given, the title cannot be removed.
Bezant – Gold or silver coin minted in Byzantium.
Boon – A favour or a loyal friend.
Braies - A type of trouser often used as an undergarment, often to mid-calf and made of light or heavier linen.
Chatelaine – The lady in charge of a large establishment and holds all the keys.
Chausses – Attached by laces to the waist of the braies, these were tighter-fitting coverings for the legs.
Citole or Vielle – An early stringed instrument similar to fiddles.
Cog – A ship – Clinker-built trading ships with a single mast and a square-rigged sail. They had wide flat bottoms allowing them to load and unload in shallow harbours.
Compline – Usually held at 9 pm in monasteries, it is a service that commemorates the burial of Christ and is a time of reflection before rest.

Dais – A raised platform in a hall for a throne or tables, often for nobles.

Dauphin – The title of the eldest son of the King of France.

Doublet – A close-fitting jacket or jerkin often made from leather, with or without sleeves. Laced at the front and worn under or over, a chain mail hauberk.

Emir – A monarch or aristocrat in the Arab world.

Fealty – Sworn loyalty to a lord or patron.

Galley – low long ship with banks of oars and up to two sails, used for war or piracy and manned by slaves.

'Give No Quarter' – To give no mercy or clemency for the vanquished.

Greek Fire – An incendiary weapon going back to Roman times. A compound based on naphtha and quick lime, which would burn while floating on water.

Gunwale – The top edge or rail of a ship's hull.

Harbinger – Anything or anyone who foreshadows a future event, an omen of something bad.

Holy See – The jurisdiction of the Bishop of Rome – the Pope.

Keep/Donjon – A fortified tower, initially made of wood, then replaced by stone, built on a mound within a medieval castle.

Lateran Palace – The main papal residence in Rome.

League – A league is equivalent to approx. Three miles in modern terms.

Leman – An illicit lover or mistress.

Miasma – An oppressive or unpleasant atmosphere or unhealthy vapour.

Mien – A person's appearance or manner, especially as an indication of their character or mood.

Mozarab – A name given to Christians living under Muslim rule who adopted the Arab language and culture but did not convert to Islam.

Pallet Bed/Palliasse – A bed made of straw or hay. Close to the ground, generally covered by a linen sheet and also known as a palliasse.

Pell – A stout wooden post for sword practice.

Pell Yard – A large yard in which warriors trained using a variety of weapons.

Pottage – A staple of the medieval diet, a thick soup made from boiling grains, vegetables, and meat or fish, if available.

Prie-dieu - A kneeling bench designed for use by a person at prayer.

Refectory – A dining room in a monastery.

Saracen – Members of Arab tribes who professed the religion of Islam in the Middle Ages.

Sayyid – the Arabic word for a lord or noble person.

Seneschal – A senior position or principal administrator of the royal household in France.

Sennight – The space of seven nights and days.

Seraglio – The women's quarters in a Berber palace.

Solar – The solar was a room in many medieval castles on a top story with windows to gain sunlight and warmth. They were usually the private quarters or chambers of the family. A room of comfort and status.

Stews – Low-grade houses of ill repute, often dangerous establishments.

Taifa – A medieval independent Islamic kingdom in the Iberian Peninsula.

Theriac – A concoction or panacea of opium, rich wine and honey as a sedative and painkiller.

Tonsured – The shaving of some part of the head for religious purposes.

Vavasseur – Manservant, majordomo, a right hand man.

Vedette - An outrider or scout used by cavalry.

Vellum - Finest scraped and treated calfskin, used for writing messages.

Vifgage – A living pledge to repay a debt in return for providing security on a loan in the form of land or buildings. (Duke Robert pledged Normandy)

Maps

MAPS

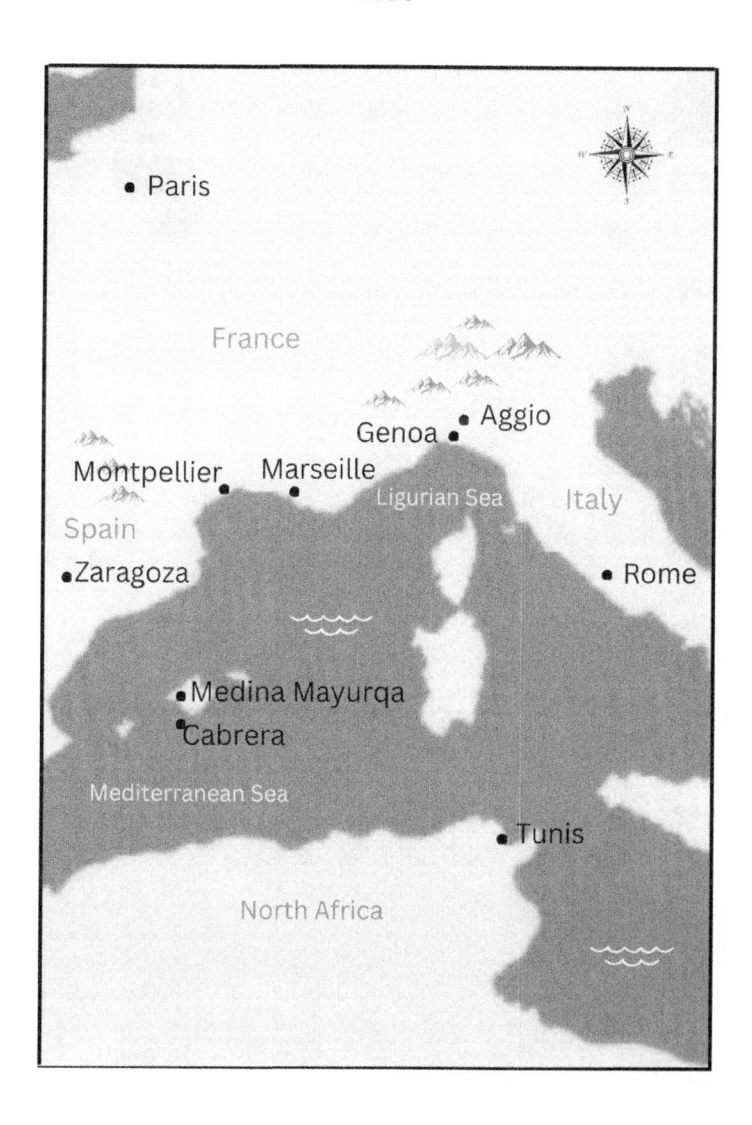

- Paris
- France
- Genoa
- Aggio
- Montpellier
- Marseille
- Ligurian Sea
- Italy
- Spain
- Zaragoza
- Rome
- Medina Mayurqa
- Cabrera
- Mediterranean Sea
- Tunis
- North Africa

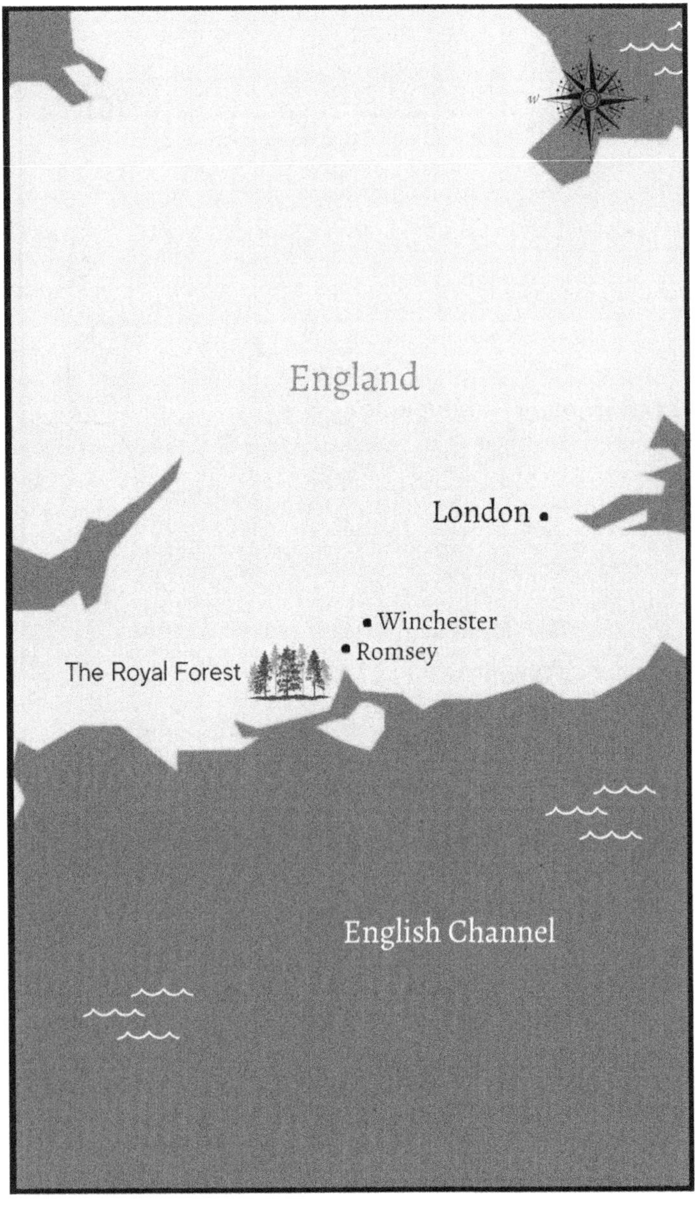
England
London
Winchester
Romsey
The Royal Forest
English Channel

MAPS

About the author

I have adored all aspects of history from an early age, but I find the lawlessness, intrigue and danger of medieval times fascinating. This interest in history influenced my choices at university and my career. I spent several years with my trowel in the interesting world of archaeology before becoming a storyteller as a history teacher. I wanted to encourage young people to find that same interest in history that had enlivened my life.

I always read historical novels from an early age and wanted to write historical fiction. The opportunity came when I left education; I then gleefully re-entered the world of engaging and fascinating historical research into the background of some of my favourite historical periods.

There are so many stories out there still waiting to be told, and my first series of books, 'The Breton Horse Warriors' proved to be one of them. The Breton lords, such as my fictional Luc De Malvais, played a significant role in the Battle of Hastings and helped to give William the Conqueror a decisive win. They were one of the most feared and exciting troops of cavalry and swordmasters in Western Europe, fighting for William the Conqueror and then for his son, Duke Robert.

My second series of novels is based on a captivating character from the first series. My readers clamoured for the ruthless Papal Envoy, Piers De Chatillon, to have his own series, and so the Papal Assassin series was born. It is amazing how an immoral, murdering, manipulative diplomat and assassin can seize the imagination as he cuts a swathe through Europe. Undoubtedly, he is an enthralling and mesmerising character; I will be sad to let him finally go.

I hope you enjoy reading my books as much as I have enjoyed writing them.

Social media links

Website moonstormbooks.com/sjmartin
Twitter X twitter.com/SJMarti40719548
Facebook www.facebook.com/SJ Martin Author
Instagram www.instagram.com/s.j.martin_author/

Also by S.J. Martin

The Breton Horse Warrior series

The Breton Horse Warriors series follows the adventures of our hero, Luc De Malvais and his brother Morvan. It begins in Saxon England, during the Norman Conquest and travels to war-torn Brittany and then Normandy. Luc De Malvais is a Breton lord, a master swordsman and leader of the famous horse warriors. He faces threatening rebellion, revenge and warfare as he fights to defeat the enemies of King William. However, his duty and loyalty to his king come at a price, as his marriage and family are torn apart. He now has to do everything he can to save his family name, the love of his life and his banished brother…but at what price?

The Duke, the Girl and the Ermine
A short story.
Following her mother's death, Cecilia Gallerani, a talented and beautiful young musician, had spent most of her life within the cloistered walls of a convent in Florence. However, at the age of sixteen, all of that was to change.

In 1489, at the court of Lorenzo Medici in Florence, whilst taking part in a performance, she came to the notice of Ludovico Sforza, the powerful Duke of Milan, who insisted that her father bring her to his court.

The Papal Assassin series
The Papal Assassin series follows the adventures, life and times of the darkly handsome swordmaster Piers De Chatillon. A wealthy French noble, the young influential Papal Envoy of several popes and a consummate diplomat, he spreads his influence, favours and threats around the courts of Europe.

He is an arch manipulator, desired by women and feared by men; he is also a lethal assassin used by kings and princes alike. His adventures take him back and forth across Europe in the turbulent seas of politics and intrigue in the 11th century.

Meanwhile, an array of enemies plots his downfall and demise. With the help of his close compatriots and friends, he manages to keep them at bay, but time is running out for Piers De Chatillon, and danger draws ever closer to his beautiful wife, Isabella and their children.

Printed in Great Britain
by Amazon